AFRAID
TO DIE

**Center Point
Large Print**

Also by Lisa Jackson and available from
Center Point Large Print:

Left to Die
Chosen To Die
Born to Die
Wicked Game
Without Mercy
Malice
Devious
Running Scared
Absolute Fear

**This Large Print Book carries the
Seal of Approval of N.A.V.H.**

AFRAID TO DIE

LISA JACKSON

CENTER POINT LARGE PRINT
THORNDIKE, MAINE

This Center Point Large Print edition is published
in the year 2012 by arrangement with
Kensington Publishing Corp.

Copyright © 2012 by Lisa Jackson LLC.

The text of this Large Print edition is unabridged.
In other aspects, this book may
vary from the original edition.
Printed in the United States of America
on permanent paper.
Set in 16-point Times New Roman type.

ISBN: 978-1-61173-495-9

Library of Congress Cataloging-in-Publication Data

Jackson, Lisa.
Afraid to die / Lisa Jackson. — Large print ed.
p. cm. — (Center Point large print edition)
ISBN 978-1-61173-495-9 (library binding : alk. paper)
1. Women detectives—Fiction. 2. Police—Fiction.
3. Women—Crimes against—Fiction. 4. Serial murders—Fiction.
5. Oregon—Fiction. 6. Large type books. 7. Psychological fiction.
I. Title.
PS3560.A223A47 2012
813'.54—dc23

2012021320

AFRAID
TO DIE

PROLOGUE

San Bernardino County
Six Years Earlier

What the hell is she doing here?

From his beat-up, unmarked car, Dylan O'Keefe squinted into the night, his eyes narrowing on a figure darting through the shadows of the empty lot across the street. Watery blue light from a single streetlamp at the corner of the street illuminated the weed-choked space where a couple of abandoned vehicles had been left to rust, and the air was thick, smells of exhaust and wood smoke heavy in the air, though no traffic was visible, no fires burning.

But there had been in this small town in the foothills of the mountains, and recently, as evidenced by the cluster of four-wheel-drive units parked near the De Maestro hideout.

Though it was December, the terrain was dusty, a hardscrabble landscape for what was essentially a ghost town, abandoned for the most part after the gold in the surrounding hills had been depleted a hundred years before. Only a handful of residents called this area home, but it was obvious someone resided in the dirty bungalow with its sagging tile roof and stained stucco walls. The porch had rotted and been repaired, and the stuff in the yard, the kids' toys and Christmas decor, was, no doubt, part of the facade, an attempt to make the house fit into the neighborhood, to look "lived in" by a family.

All a lie.

And about to come crashing down.

Except that now, in the middle of the stakeout—an effort to ensure that Alberto De Maestro was, indeed, within the dingy walls—a dark figure was slinking through the shadows, a figure he'd recognize anywhere as Detective Selena Alvarez. Everything they'd worked for, the operation that had been in play for sixteen months, was suddenly about to go sideways.

Damn it! "You see her?" he whispered to his partner.

"Mmmhmmm." Rico, forever noncommittal, was nodding slowly, his fleshy face sweating in the lamplight, his eyes focused in the direction of the empty lot.

"She *can't* be here!"

"Leave it be." But even Rico was at attention as Selena crossed the sagging fence between the two lots, now on De Maestro's property with its ramshackle bungalow, shades drawn, the yard littered with toys and Christmas decorations, most of which had lights that had burned out. Even the string wound around the base of the single palm tree outside was missing bulbs.

All part of a front anyway.

O'Keefe reached up, turned off the interior light and opened the passenger door.

"Wait! What're you doing?" Rico demanded.

O'Keefe didn't wait for recriminations or arguments. He'd already landed on the cracked cement, his service weapon drawn. He had to get to her, to call her back.

This was all wrong.

All wrong!

If De Maestro got wind that she was outside . . . Silently he crossed the street, was aware of a breeze rolling over the asphalt, kicking up dry leaves and a rustling plastic bag that skated past a few parked cars. A dog, penned in the yard, hidden in the night, started barking wildly.

Oh, God, no!

Still Alvarez moved forward.

Don't! he silently screamed, fear curdling inside him. What was she thinking? Why was she here? The dog began to howl. *Get back! This is nuts—*

Blam! A side door flew open.

"Shut up!" a man yelled from the doorway, his lean body in silhouette, a handgun visible. Alberto De Maestro. Target of the sting. Linchpin of the De Maestro drug cartel. *Jesus, God! He was* right there!

No! No! No!

O'Keefe's heart pounded in his ears.

Another man appeared in the doorway, obviously trying to talk some sense into De Maestro, to pull him inside, but the bigger man was having none of it, and as the dog quieted and somewhere in the distance a siren wailed, he turned, looking straight at Alvarez.

Oh, God.

A smile as evil as all of hell curved his lips, showing off white teeth as he raised his gun. "*Perra*," he said, aiming, his voice slurred.

Alvarez froze.

Too late.

Running now, his weapon raised, O'Keefe yelled, "Drop it! Police! *Policia*! Alberto De Maestro, drop your weapon!"

"Fuck off!" Spinning agilely, De Maestro turned his gun on O'Keefe. His malicious grin widened. The devil himself. "*Feliz Navidad, bastardo*!"

With that, he pulled the trigger.

CHAPTER 1

Her skin was tinged with blue.

Her flesh becoming stiff—which was perfect.

Her eyes, through the ice, stared upward, yet they saw nothing and, unfortunately, she couldn't appreciate how much love, affection and thought was going into this work.

No longer did her shallow breath cause the ice to melt near her nose, and her mouth, thankfully, had closed, her lips perfectly fused together, a darker blue . . . like Sleeping Beauty, he thought as he carefully poured another layer of water over her.

Ice crystals formed over her naked body, glazing the youthful flesh, sparkling in the dim lights of his cavern.

So beautiful.

So perfect.

So dead.

Humming along to Christmas music playing from his battery-operated docking station in this, his private chamber, he sculpted. Carefully. With precise attention to detail. Perfection; that was what he was striving for. And he would get it.

He kept his sculpting room at thirty degrees, just below freezing, and his breath fogged as he worked in his underground studio. Though a snowstorm was raging through this section of the Bitterroot Mountains, down here, deep in the caves, the air was calm; not a breath of the wind could be heard.

Wearing a neoprene suit, gloves, boots and ski mask, he silently wished he could strip bare, feel the bite of cold air against his flesh, feel more alive, but that would have to wait. He couldn't be rash, couldn't allow any bit of his skin or hair or even sweat to mar his work.

Besides, there was always that sticky problem of DNA once the police became involved. That would be soon, he knew, because this piece of art was nearly finished. A little more whittling here, a bit of shaving there.

"Oh, the weather outside is frightful," he sang along under his breath as the music reverberated through these linked caves that he'd claimed for his work. Hidden deep in these foothills, the caverns provided a perfect spot. A natural spring provided the water he needed, and battery-powered lights gave off a bluish glow. When he needed brighter light, he donned headlamps to illuminate the areas where he needed to work.

From deeper within his workspace he heard a pathetic mewl and he frowned. Why wouldn't *that* woman just die, already? He'd given her enough sedatives to knock out an elephant and yet she lay on the precipice between consciousness and death, lingering. And moaning. He frowned, hit his chisel with his hammer and the blade slipped, slicing through his glove and nicking his finger. "Damn!" Blood, *his* damned blood fell in a singular drop along the ice. Quickly it froze and he, rather than smear it, let it dry, all the time irritated at the delay. Once it was solid, he cut around the rivulet, giving wide berth and making certain that no hint of red disturbed his perfect piece of art.

He was sweating by the time he was finished

excavating the blood. Carefully, telling himself to be patient, he began pouring clear water from the spring over that flaw in his masterpiece. Allowing the water to freeze, he waited impatiently before pouring a little more, until there was no hint of a fissure, no blemish visible.

"Perfect," he whispered, satisfied.

He stared down at his artwork, the naked woman encased in ice, and he couldn't help but lean forward, bending close enough to lick one ice-encased nipple. His tongue tingled, the interior of his mouth so cold that a ripple of pure, icy pleasure worked its way through his bloodstream, starting out frigid, but, as his mind created scenarios where his body was rubbing up against her arctic flesh, he felt the tiniest niggle of excitement, the start of arousal.

He rolled his tongue over the ice, imagining the salty taste of her, the bud of her nipple hard in his mouth. He'd sink his teeth in, just a little, to mingle pleasure with pain. He let out a quiet moan as his fantasy emerged.

In his mind's eye, he saw another beautiful woman, her hair falling freely behind her as she ran, laughing, her voice echoing through the wintry forest. Snow had drifted against the scaly trunks of the pines, ice collecting on the long needles.

He raced through thick powder, chasing after her, watching in arousal as she tossed off her clothing, piece by piece, dropping a blouse, a skirt, a scarf into nearby snow drifts. Finally her bra was discarded and she, in only panties, continued to run.

He was closing the distance and taking off his own clothes, kicking off his boots, but his cold fingers fumbled with the buttons of his shirt, and his jeans, they were difficult to pull off and toss aside, so he couldn't catch her, had to race to catch up.

He thought of what he would do to her, how he would thrust into her, make her cold body turn molten and heat the snow that fell until it melted over her skin.

But in his hand was his knife. The one with the handle made from the antler of a four-point he'd killed three years earlier. He remembered felling the buck, with just an arrow . . .

He was closer now . . . his heart pounding, his fingers clenched over the hilt of the knife.

Only inches from her, a half step behind when she turned, her lips turning blue, her eyes bright, her cheeks crimson with the frosty winter air. A playful smile tugged at the corner of her mouth. So perfect. Like an angel's.

Then she saw the knife.

Her soft grin fell away. Shock, then horror registered on her beautiful features and she stumbled, nearly falling, throwing up more white powder as panic set in and she ran faster, not playfully, but spurred on by terror.

His nostrils flared. He sprang forward, giving chase.

Within a few strides he caught her, his free hand tangling in her mass of long hair and then . . .

A blur.

All he could remember was the slash of warm blood spraying scarlet over an icy white snow-drift . . .

No! He snapped back to the here and now. He couldn't let his mind stray from his work.

The ice was melting in his mouth. His erection was full and bulging, straining against the hot neoprene. Straightening, he felt a moment's disgust for his weakness and forced his ever-willing cock to stand down.

What had gotten into him?

He gazed down at the naked woman and noticed the place where his mouth had melted the ice and left too much of his DNA. Not smart, not smart at all. Certainly not something a person with a near genius IQ would do.

Quickly, as if in working swiftly he could erase the damage he'd done, he started chiseling out that spot where his mouth and saliva had touched and melted the ice.

The bitch in the back room let out another moan and his jaw tightened. She'd die soon enough and her perfect body would show no bruise or cut or anything that would hint at violence. Then, she, too, would be encased in ice, a perfect specimen, another work of art.

Glancing at his watch, he noted he still had enough time to finish for the day. His wife wasn't expecting him for another hour. Plenty of time.

Carefully he pumped more water from the stream and poured it over his work in progress. She wasn't quite ready, he thought as he gazed into her wide-open eyes.

But it wouldn't be long.

Thankfully, the moans from the other cave had stilled and he could concentrate again, sluicing water over her while under his breath he muttered, "Let it snow, let it snow . . ."

". . . let it—" *Click!*

Selena Alvarez slapped the snooze button on the clock radio, then, thinking twice, turned the alarm off and rolled out of bed. God, she *hated* that song. Then again she wasn't too big on anything to do with the Christmas season.

She had her reasons.

Not that she wanted to think about them now.

Maybe ever.

Though it was dark as midnight, the digital readout glowed a bright red, telling her that it was four thirty in the morning, her usual time to get up and get going. For most of the year, she tackled each day as if it were a challenge, but as autumn faded and the days of November bled into the heart of December, she felt that same old ennui that accompanied the holiday season, a definite energy sap that darkened her mood. Her usual take-the-world-head-on attitude hibernated for the winter and she had to work doubly hard to find her usual enthusiasm for life.

"Idiot," she muttered under her breath as she stretched her muscles.

She knew the cause of her change in attitude, of course, but she never discussed it, not even with her partner. Especially not her partner. Pescoli just wouldn't understand.

And Alvarez definitely wasn't going to think about it now.

Her new puppy, a mottled mix of some kind of shepherd and either a boxer or lab, roused in his crate, stretching and barking to be released while her cat, Jane Doe, who always slept on the second pillow of the bed, lifted her head and blinked.

Seeing that Alvarez was awake, the puppy made I-need-to-go-out whines that turned into excited yips. All the enthusiasm she was lacking seemed to manifest itself in the half-grown dog.

"Hey, you know better," Alvarez admonished the pup before letting him out of his kennel. Immediately he began leaping and barking at her despite her best efforts of controlling him. "No, Roscoe! Off! Down!" He streaked into the living room of her town house, running in circles around the ottoman and coffee table before wiggling with excitement at the patio door.

Alvarez glanced at the cat, who'd climbed onto a shelf over the desk and took in the scene with feline disdain. "Yeah, I know. Don't rub it in." Seconds later, she let the dog outside, where he disappeared into the darkened corners of her small yard to, no doubt, lift his leg on every tree, bush and post he could find. It was still snowing, she noted as she closed the slider against a gust of winter air so cold it cut through her flannel pajamas. Through the glass, she saw that the pots she'd left on her patio were covered with five inches of icy white fluff, the lawn, before Roscoe tore into it, blanketed in a peaceful coat of white.

Yet she found no peace or serenity with the snow.

Adopting Roscoe had been a rash decision, especially on the heels of buying this town house, but now it was a done deal and the stupid dog had burrowed a special little spot into her heart.

Despite his faults.

"Pathetic," she told herself.

Bounding back to the slab of concrete that was her patio, he started clawing at the glass of the sliding door. She cracked it open and he tried to race inside, but she caught him by the collar. "Not on your life, guy." Using the hand towel she hung on the door handle for just this purpose, she wiped each of his huge paws before allowing him inside again.

Rarely did she go to the gym now; instead, she ran with the dog, wearing him out before she showered, dressed for the day and left him in the laundry area. It wasn't an ideal set up, but as soon as she was convinced he was completely housebroken, she figured she'd install a doggy door and then could forgo hiring the neighbor woman to walk him at noon. She seldom stayed late at the station any longer, opting to bring her work home with her.

Which was probably a good thing.

But reminded her only that she was alone.

Not that she hadn't dabbled in dating in the past year. A few had been interested in her, but she hadn't returned the favor. She'd dated Kevin Miller, a pharmaceutical salesman who was a gym rat in his spare time and was always talking about his job. He'd bored her to tears. Terry Longstrom was a psychologist who worked with juveniles who'd been arrested, and he'd taken her on a couple of dates, but for all of his good points, she just didn't find him attractive, and as shallow as that sounded, she couldn't pretend to be interested in him. The worst of the lot though was Grover Pankretz, who had once worked in the local DNA lab before his job was eliminated when the company had downsized. A brilliant man but a little too possessive from the get-go. He'd wanted to get serious by the second date. So she'd ended that before it really began. Fortunately all of the men interested in her had moved on, either away from the area or onto new relationships. Terry and Grover, she'd heard, had married.

The truth was simple: She just wasn't ready to date seriously . . . as evidenced by her ridiculous fantasy for an older, unavailable man like Dan Grayson, who just happened to be her boss. Typical.

"Face it," she told herself, "you really don't want a man in your life."

She finished with her morning routine and drove to the sheriff's office on Boxer Bluff. Traffic was snarled in the usual places and backed up where a single car had slid sideways just before the railroad tracks. All the while the snow kept falling and her wipers worked double-time to slap the flakes away.

God, she hated this time of year.

It seemed that here, in Grizzly Falls, the Christmas season brought its own share of disaster with it. Despite the holiday wreaths on the doors, the trees decorated and glowing festively in the windows, and the twenty-four-seven deluge of Christmas carols from the local radio stations, trouble lurked in the shadows of all the radiant joy. Not only did domestic violence cases escalate during the holiday season, but, in the past few years, some homicidal maniacs had terrorized the locals.

Not exactly a season of peace and joy.

The road was slick in spots, but her ten-year-old Subaru gripped the road and churned up the frozen, icy streets without any trouble. The Outback was another change in her life, though of course she knew that all the new cars and town houses wouldn't fill the hole inside her. The pets were a step in the right direction, she thought as she pulled into the parking lot of the station. She'd inherited the cat on a case last year, as its owner had been the victim of a vicious murder and she'd felt a connection to the animal, but the puppy had been an intentional, if irrational decision.

What had she been thinking?

Obviously *not* about pee on the carpet, chewed furniture or vet bills; nope, she'd seen something warm and cuddly, with bright eyes, a wet nose and a tail that wouldn't stop wagging when she'd visited the shelter.

"Stupid," she told herself as she drove toward the station, but she couldn't help but smile. She'd thought Roscoe would be some kind of protection, keep burglars at bay.

Yeah? Then why did you feel as if someone had been in your house last week, huh? Remember that premonition that something you couldn't describe had been changed at the town house? Where was Roscoe the guard dog then?

Of course, it had probably been nothing, just her case of nerves after interviewing Neil Freeman, yet another sicko who had let his eyes run all over her while she questioned him about his dead mother. Turned out the mother died of natural causes . . . but his demeanor, his salacious turning of every answer into something sexual and the way he touched the tip of his tongue to his lips as he stared at her had really gotten to her. Which was probably just his intention. Twisted creep!

She told herself again that Freeman had *not* been in her house and that Roscoe would have let her know it if he had.

And how would he do that? Face it, Alvarez, you're becoming one of those *kinds of pet owners.* Inwardly, she cringed.

Damn it, she loved that dog and maybe, just maybe, Roscoe was just what she needed. She knew only that no matter what, she wasn't going to give him up.

Wheeling into the parking lot, she turned her thoughts to the weeks ahead. There was the Christmas party for the office, of course, and Joelle Fisher, the receptionist cum Christmas elf, had already decorated the department and started talking about the Secret Santa exchange that she always organized. Alvarez wasn't interested; she just knew that she'd pile on a lot of extra hours over the holidays. *That* was her Christmas tradition; let the people with families stay home.

It was just easier.

She locked the car, then half jogged through the falling snow to the back door of the building.

Stomping the melting white fluff from her boots, she paused in the lunch room, frowned when she saw the coffee hadn't been made and reluctantly started a pot. Then found her favorite cup, heated water in the microwave and located the last bag of orange pekoe.

A pink box lay open on the table, a few picked-over cookies visible, but she ignored them for now. At this time of year, with Joelle in charge, there were certain to be fresh goodies arriving on the hour.

Unwrapping her scarf, she made her way to her desk, deposited her purse and sidearm, hung her jacket on a hook and started through her e-mail and messages, making sure all the reports were filed on one case, getting ready for a deposition on another and seeing if the autopsy report had come in on Len Bradshaw, a local farmer who died in a hunting accident. His friend, Martin Zwolski, had been with him, and while going through a barbed-wired fence, his weapon had gone off, shooting Len in the back and killing him dead.

Accident or premeditated?

Alvarez was buying the accident scenario. Martin had been distraught to the point of tears and beleaguered by Len's friends and family. It all seemed to be an accident, but Alvarez wasn't totally convinced, not until the investigation was buttoned up. There were three loose ends that kept her from totally buying Martin's story.

First, the two men were poaching on private property, neither one with deer tags, and second, Martin and Len had been in a business together that had gone bankrupt two years earlier, largely due to the fact that Len had "loaned" himself a good portion of the company profits. Also, another little tidbit that had come to light was that Len had once been involved with Martin's wife. Martin and Ezzie had been separated at the time, but still . . . It was all just a little too messy for Alvarez.

She checked her e-mail.

No autopsy report yet.

Maybe later today. Flipping over to the missing persons information, she checked to see if Lissa Parsons had been found.

Lissa was an acquaintance, a woman Alvarez knew from a couple of classes she took at the gym. Twenty-six and single, with short black hair and a killer body, she worked as a receptionist for a local law firm and had been reported missing a week earlier. When the detectives started asking questions, they'd deduced that Lissa had actually been missing for over a week. Her boyfriend and she had been through a rough patch and he was "giving her some space," and her roommate had been out of town for a couple of weeks, an extended trip to Florida, only to come home to an empty apartment where the organic produce in the refrigerator was beginning to rot. Lissa's purse, cell phone, car and laptop were all missing with her, but her closet was untouched, her wardrobe neatly folded or hanging, a hamper in her bedroom filled with dirty workout clothes.

The roommate, boyfriend and an ex-boyfriend had rock-solid alibis. No sign of forced entry or a struggle at the apartment. It was as if Lissa had just left for the day, intended to return and hadn't bothered. Her cell phone and credit card activity showed no use after the day she went missing.

Alvarez didn't like it. Especially the fact that she'd been missing for nearly two weeks. Not good. Not good at all.

And it seemed from the most updated information that she was still missing.

No body.

No crime scene.

No damned crime.

Yet.

All of the nearby hospitals had been checked and she hadn't been admitted, nor had there been any Jane Does brought in. Nor, of course, had Lissa been arrested by any local agency.

Just . . . gone.

"Where the hell are you?" Alvarez wondered aloud as she sipped her tepid tea. She didn't expect to see her partner for another hour or so, but Pescoli showed up before her usual time with a cup of coffee from one of the local shops in hand, snow melting in her burnished hair, her face flushed.

"What're you doing here at this hour?" Alvarez asked, spinning her chair around as her partner stood in the doorway. "Somebody die?"

"Bad joke this early in the morning." She took a sip from her cup. "I had to drop Bianca off at school early for dance practice." Bianca was Pescoli's teenage daughter, a junior now and as headstrong as she was beautiful. A dangerous combination and it didn't help that the girl was smart enough to play each of her divorced parents against the other. It worked every time. Though Pescoli and her ex had been divorced for years, there was still a lot of animosity between them, especially when it came to their kids. Bianca and her older brother, Jeremy, an off-again college student who lived with Pescoli in between his attempts at "moving out," worked them both.

"I thought the dance team practiced after school."

"Limited gym space." Pescoli glanced to the window. "Basketball, wrestling, cheerleading, dance team . . . whatever, they all juggle times, though right now, basketball has priority, I think. So for the next two weeks, Bianca has to be at school at six forty-five, that means she's got to get up around six, and believe me, it's killing her." Pescoli's lips twisted into a thin smile at the thought of her teenager struggling with the early-morning routine. "And this is just day one. It's damned hard to be a princess when you have to be up and at 'em in the friggin' dark. What did she call it? Oh, yeah, 'the middle of the night when no one with *any* brains would get out of bed.' " Pescoli was shaking her head. "I'm tellin' ya, we're raising a generation of vampires!"

"Vampires are in."

"Go figure." She turned serious, pointed a finger toward the computer screen on Alvarez's desk where a picture of Lissa Parsons was visible. "The autopsy report come in on Bradshaw?"

"Not yet."

Little lines grooved deep between Pescoli's eyebrows. "You know I'd really like to believe Zwolski—that it was an accident—but I just can't."

"I know."

"Something just doesn't quite fit. What about the Parsons missing persons case?" Pescoli asked.

"Not yet."

"Hell." Pescoli took a sip from her coffee. "Hard to say what's going on there," she thought aloud. "Just a flighty girl who got a wild hair and took off for a while, or something else?" Obviously not liking that idea, she frowned even deeper. "Still nothing on her car?"

"Don't think so. I was going to walk down to Missing Persons and talk to Taj, see what she has to say."

"Let me know." Pescoli patted the doorway and started to leave when the familiar *click, click, click* of high heels caught her attention.

"Toot, toot! Coming through!" Joelle warned in her little-girl voice as Alvarez caught a glimpse of the tiny receptionist, her beehive of platinum hair sprayed with red and green glitter, her snowman earrings catching in the fluorescent light as she hauled several stacked plastic tubs toward the lunchroom.

"Breakfast," Pescoli said. "Come on, I'll buy you a cup of coffee."

Together they followed the bustling dynamo who never seemed happy until every square inch of the station was decorated for the holidays. Paper snowflakes sprayed with silver glitter hung from the ceiling, garlands of fake greenery swagged through the hallways, a revolving Christmas tree was twirling in the reception area and even the copy machine had a red pseudo-velvet bow with a sprig of mistletoe taped to the wall behind it. Like, sure—someone would try to steal a kiss while making copies of arrest reports. *Nothing more romantic than a smooch over the hum and click of office machinery,* Alvarez thought cynically.

"Here we go!" Joelle dropped the plastic tubs onto one round table and paused only to unwrap a plaid scarf of green and red before opening the first tub. *"Voila!"*

Inside were cupcakes lined up neatly, each decorated with Santa faces or snowmen faces or even reindeer faces. "I picked these up at the bakery," she announced as if it were a sin, "but I did bake my famous Christmas macaroons and Russian tea cakes." Another bin was opened to display the cookies. "And the pièce de résistance," she teased, while opening the third bin, "Grandma Maxie's divinity! Mmm." She hurried to the cupboard where she'd stashed several trays earlier in the week, and satisfied that they were still sparkling clean, started arranging her favorite delicacies.

"I'm getting a sugar high just looking at these," Pescoli said.

Pleased, Joelle let out a little-girl giggle. Though she was over sixty, she looked a good ten years younger than her age and her energy seemed boundless—at least at this time of the year. "Well, help yourselves!" Once the trays were perfect, she scooped up the bins and hurried down the hallway to her desk at the front of the station house. "And remember, the drawing for the Secret Santa is at four!" she called over her shoulder. "Detective Pescoli, I expect you to participate!"

Pescoli had already bitten into a cookie and almost moaned in ecstasy. Under her breath she said to Alvarez, "The woman drives me nuts with all this holiday stuff, but I gotta say, she does bake a mean macaroon!"

CHAPTER 2

Detective Taj Nayak didn't have any good news. "It's a mystery," she said as Alvarez cruised by her office later in the day. "It's like the woman just disappeared into thin air. She left work at her usual time, a little after five, and just never made it home.

"We know she stopped by the gas station, where she bought a full tank, a pack of cigarettes— Marlboro menthols if that means anything—a sixteen-ounce Diet Coke and a Twix bar, all put on her debit card. Here, you can view it yourself." Taj typed into her keyboard and pulled up a black-and-white film, which began to play on her computer monitor. "So here you go. See— " She pointed at the screen where a woman who looked like Lissa was at the counter of the convenience mart. "So here she is paying for the items, then walking back to her car." The screen flipped from the image of the cash register and attendant to the canopied area where up to eight cars could pull into the pumps. "It's hard to make out too much," Taj said, "other than that she takes off out of the gas station and heads north when her apartment is south." Sure enough, on the screen, just visible in the upper corner, Lissa's little Chevy Impala turned right. The film continued to roll. "Here's the SUV that followed her out of the station, but we checked; it was driven by a teenager on her way to basketball practice. Two other girls in the car, all confirmed; a Toyota 4Runner, owned by an insurance sales-man in town. It's his daughter's car, and when we talked to the daughter and her friends, none of them even remember following Lissa's Impala." The tape stopped suddenly. "Search parties have found nothing. So either she disappeared because she wanted to, somehow ditched her credit and debit cards and we'll locate her car, or . . ."

". . . She's dead."

Taj nodded as her phone rang and she reached for it. "Then she'll be your problem, I guess."

"Hope not." Alvarez meant it. However, the woman had been missing for nearly two weeks. What were the chances that she was still alive?

If she'd been in a bad mood in the morning, the news that Lissa Parsons was still missing only brought her down even further. It didn't help that on the way back to her desk she ran into the sheriff.

A tall, rangy cowboy type, Dan Grayson was one of the best lawmen in the state and had been sheriff for years. Divorced, he'd invited her over to Thanksgiving last year and she'd made a fool of herself by showing up to his place for what turned out to be a family Thanksgiving, complete with Hattie, his very single ex-sister-in-law or some such thing, and her adorable twin girls. She'd come expecting a romantic evening that hadn't developed, and until the moment that she'd met Hattie, Alvarez had actually harbored some ridiculous fantasies about the man, despite their age differences—fantasies that, no doubt, Grayson and his ex-sister-in-law had witnessed. It probably wasn't as big a deal as she'd made it in her mind, but since then, she'd backed off and reminded herself that he was her boss. Nothing more. *NOTHING* more.

"Mornin'," the sheriff drawled as he met her, his eyes kind, his smile sincere. If he'd felt any awkwardness about the situation last year, he'd been man enough not to show it, and over the months her humiliation had dissipated. He'd even invited her over to Thanksgiving again this year, but she'd worked the holiday instead, preferring to avoid any new, embarrassing scenes.

"Morning. Hey, Sturgis," she said to his dog, a black lab who followed him everywhere and wagged his tail at the sight of her. She patted his broad head and he yawned, showing off his long teeth and spotted tongue.

"Joelle brought cookies and cupcakes and God only knows what else."

"Already sampled; got my sugar rush for the morning."

His lips twisted beneath his moustache. "If

she had her way, everyone here would be hopped up for the entire month of December."

"And twenty pounds heavier." She made the joke, noticed that his eyes twinkled in that sexy way that always got to her, then made her way back to her desk without veering off to the lunch room.

She had plenty of work to do and didn't need to think about Dan Grayson.

Around noon, she drove home and took a crazed Roscoe out for a jog. The walking trails through a nearby park had their paths cleared of snow for the most part, so she walked him into the entrance of the park on Boxer Bluff, then started jogging, urging him to follow on the leash. The air was crisp and cold, burning a little in her lungs as she started breathing harder, but the trail was scenic, winding through the trees on the cliffs high over the river. She hadn't bothered with her iPod or iPhone, and instead of listening to music, heard her own breathing, the slap of her running shoes on the asphalt and the rush of the Grizzly River pouring over the falls for which the town was named. The park was serene, the thick blanket of snow covering the winter grass and clinging to the boughs of the evergreen trees.

She met a few other walkers, bundled in heavy jackets and wool hats and gloves, their breath fogging in the air.

"On your left," she heard as a tall, athletic runner passed her as if she were standing still, then nearly tangled in Roscoe's leash as the rambunctious pup lunged playfully at him.

"Hey!" the runner said angrily, his pace thrown off.

And merry Christmas to you, too.

Alvarez watched him disappear as snow began to fall again. The dog slowed on mile two, and by the third and final mile, Roscoe's tongue was hanging out and he was panting. "Feel good?" Alvarez asked as they walked back to her town house and she let him inside.

Three miles, come hell or high water, and the dog was good for the day. So tired, he spent the rest of the day in his bed until she returned at night.

As she heated soup in the microwave, she walked through the shower and threw on her clothes. With one eye on the television news, she ate quickly while Jane Doe curled on her lap and the dog eyed her every bite. "Mine," she reminded him when he belly-swamped across the kitchen linoleum to her and looked up with pitiful dark eyes. "You'll get dinner when I return."

He thumped his tail but didn't stop staring at her. "I'm not buying it." After finishing her soup, she placed her dish and spoon in the dishwasher, then, as both her pets settled in for their afternoon naps, she bundled up and headed out again.

• • •

At four o'clock on the nose, Joelle let her assistant handle the front desk and marched into the lunch room with her red Santa's hat with the well-worn fake white fur. Inside it, Pescoli knew were the names of everyone in the department. "Come in for the drawing!" Joelle yelled. "Secret Santa time!"

"I thought we just did this," she muttered under her breath to no one in particular. She'd returned to the station only minutes before and now wished her interview of the Bradshaw family had taken longer.

"Come on, come on! You, too, Detective," Joelle said at the doorway to Pescoli's office.

"This can't be mandatory. Isn't it violating my workplace rights or religious rights in some way?"

"Oh, pooh!" Joelle was having none of it. "Don't be a grinch!" She stood on a little stool in the middle of the lunchroom and seemed oblivious to the fact that other people had serious work to do. Waggling the ridiculous hat, she motioned anyone in the lunch room closer and the assault wouldn't stop there, Pescoli knew from experience. If someone didn't partake, that employee was hunted down to his or her desk to draw from the hat. If that didn't work, then a name was drawn at random and left in an envelope at the declining employee's work area. It was an unwritten law that everyone,

35

regardless of religious background, partake.

"Santa Claus is nondemoninational!" Joelle had proclaimed one year when Pescoli had played the religion card.

"You mean denominational," Cort Brewster, the undersheriff, had corrected.

Joelle had winked at him and wrinkled her nose, as if she were being cute—the bimbo. "Of course that's what I meant."

Now, as her iPod played her Christmas carol rotation that seemed to include only Bing Crosby's "White Christmas," Brenda Lee's "Rockin' Around the Christmas Tree" and Burl Ives's "A Holly Jolly Christmas," the sheriff himself sauntered into the lunch room; Pescoli rolled her eyes and whispered, "Do something."

"I will." To her dismay, Grayson was the first one to draw a name. "Your turn," he said out of the side of his mouth as he checked the name on his tiny scrap of paper.

Nigel Timmons, the dork from the lab, was up next. His thinning hair was sculpted into a faux hawk, and he'd recently given up glasses for contacts that seemed to bother him and give him a wide-eyed stare. His skin was sallow, his frame slight and he was a genius when it came to anything to do with chemistry or computers. As irritating as he was, the twenty-six-year-old was invaluable to the department and he knew it. Smirking to himself—while once again, Bing was crooning, "I'm dreaming of a . . ."—Timmons withdrew a piece of paper from the hat, looked it over and read the name upon it, then, being the goof he was, placed it in his mouth, chewed and swallowed. "Top-secret stuff," he explained and Alvarez looked pained.

"We're not in sixth grade," she said.

"Speak for yourself." Timmons flashed her a grin and started perusing the remainder of the day's baked goods before snagging a cookie that he held in his mouth while he picked over the fudge and cupcakes.

"I think Timmons had graduated from Yale by the sixth grade," Pescoli whispered and Alvarez's pained expression grew more intense.

"Don't remind me that he's freakin' brilliant, okay?"

Everyone took their turn, then walked back to their desks, and Pescoli, rather than suffer Joelle's ridicule for the second year in a row, plucked a name from the hat. *Anyone but Cort Brewster,* she thought, as she'd had to deal with him last year and their relationship was anything but smooth, as her son, Jeremy, and his daughter, Heidi, couldn't quite break up. Each parent blamed the other for the kids getting into trouble. She opened the scrap of paper, and damn if it didn't have the undersheriff's name on it. "Sorry, it's my own," she said hastily, returning the label to Joelle's hat before the receptionist could protest.

Brenda Lee was rockin' away. Quickly, Pescoli swiped another scrap and this time saw Joelle's name on the paper. God, that was worse, but she was stuck. As it was, Joelle eyed her suspiciously, so she walked quickly back to her desk and wondered what the hell would she get a grandmother who looked like Barbie and was stuck in the sixties. God, that was half a century before.

Pescoli didn't have time for this nonsense. If she were going to fret about Christmas gifts, it damned well better be for her kids or Santana. Good Lord, what was she going to get *him* this year?

"How about nothing?" he'd suggested when she asked him what he wanted for Christmas. "Then after I unwrap the box, you could put it on."

"Not funny," she'd said but had to swallow back a smile.

"And you're a liar." They'd been alone at his cabin and he'd advanced on her then, kissed her and carried her into the bedroom.

That had been a new and heart-racing experience. She'd never been petite and, though not fat, wasn't small. Santana hadn't seemed to notice as he'd hauled her over the threshold and tumbled with her onto the bed, then made love to her as if she were the only woman in the universe.

Now, her blood pumped hot just to think of it.

Which she wouldn't. Not at work. Nor would she examine all her motives for not moving in with him. The invitation had been open for over a year, make that close to two, but she'd resisted, preferring to play it safe. Neither of her previous marriages had been perfect, so she wasn't interested in falling head over heels in love again.

Too late, her mind told her, but she sat down in her desk chair and turned her attention to her work. Secret Santa be damned; she needed to find out if Martin Zwolski was the most unlucky person on the planet, or if he was a cold-blooded murderer who was about to slip through the cracks.

The steeple bell was just striking the half hour as Brenda Sutherland hurried across the icy parking lot of the church. So it was eight thirty and Lorraine Mullins, the preacher's wife, had *promised* that it wouldn't run past eight. *Promised.*

But then she hadn't counted on Mildred Peeples going on and on about the costs of the new church. Mildred was ninety if she was a day, sharp as a whip and opinionated to the nth. She wasn't about to keep on track with the Bible study meeting about the giving tree they were establishing this year and had preferred to go over, line by line, the "ridiculous" and "outrageous" costs of constructing the new church. "This is the Lord's house," she'd insisted, "and everyone in town, every single parishioner should give their time, money and labor into its construction. Lorraine?"

she'd asked the preacher's wife. "Did you see the estimate for the plumbing? Did you?" Her face had flushed beneath her thick powder and she'd wagged a finger at Dorie Oestergard, wife of the unfortunate contractor assigned to the job. Though it was well known that he'd cut his usual fee by 25 percent for the church, Mildred was certain he'd "padded the bills" and she'd been vocal about it. "Your husband should be ashamed of himself, Dorie. It's highway robbery! Can't he read his own bills?"

That comment had elicited a gasp from Dorie, but Mildred was on a roll and didn't stop. "If you ask me," she'd said, "the devil's behind this. He's always there, y'know, Satan, he's just over your shoulder, waiting to pounce." Her lips had pursed for a second, and before she could rant on, another person on the committee, Jenny Kropft, had asked Mildred if she would be so kind as to give her blackberry crumb cake recipe to the cookbook the group was assembling. Mildred had been too smart not to see that she was being diverted, but had been pleased just the same.

"Save me," Brenda whispered now, her breath fogging in the night air as she crossed the near-empty lot and unlocked her car. This, the old church, was located high on the bluff in the hills overlooking the city. The church and parsonage had been built in the late 1880s, and though modernized over the years with indoor plumbing, electricity, forced-air heat and insulation, the buildings were still as drafty as they were charming, and the congregation was growing each year. As it was, on Sunday morning, the old choir loft was filled with parishioners, and on Easter and Christmas, there had to be an additional two services added for the once- and twice-a-year members of the flock. In the harsh Montana winters, the old buildings suffered, as did everyone inside.

The new church was a great idea in Brenda's mind, as was Preacher Mullins's introduction of rock renditions of traditional songs by a couple of young musicians in the flock. Though traditionalists like Mildred might balk at the changes, if they could bring new, young blood into the church, Brenda was all for it. Maybe eventually she could convince her two teenaged boys to get up and attend services again, though she doubted it, especially with Ray, her ex-husband, setting such a stellar example of being a hedonistic, self-indulgent jerk!

At the thought of the boys' father, she scowled, sent up a little prayer for humility and a way to find forgiveness in her heart, then caught the anger simmering in her eyes in the reflection of her rearview mirror. "Please, give me strength," she whispered as she shoved her old Ford Escape into gear, backed up and headed out of the church lot. The boys were with Ray tonight and she had to accept the fact that *she* was the one who had decided Ray Sutherland was the perfect man to father her kids. "The follies of youth," she said under her breath and tried not to dwell on Ray and his failings as a husband and dad.

She'd hoped to pick up a few odds and ends Christmas presents at the local pharmacy and gift shop, so she drove across the bluff to the strip mall, where she sneaked in, just before the store was to close, and grabbed a stuffed reindeer for her nephew and some plastic Christmas-themed blocks for her niece. She'd been eyeing them both for a couple of weeks, and with the coupon she'd clipped in the Sunday paper, she got two for the price of one.

Feeling better, she paid for her purchases and thought about treating herself to a hot chocolate at the coffee shop, then thought better of it. Her job at Wild Will's restaurant downtown didn't cover the expenses of raising two kids on her own, so she kept her "going out" money to a minimum and partook of the fancy coffee drinks she confined to her account at the restaurant, where she got a twenty percent discount. Sandi, the owner of Wild Will's, was generous with her employees and she'd given Brenda the job as a waitress when Ray had walked out five years earlier.

Already the car's interior had cooled, so she cranked up the heat and the radio that played

"Christmas, all day, every day," and hummed along as she drove toward her house. Snowflakes caught in the beams of her headlights, seeming to pirouette and dance as they fell. Through neighborhoods with plastic Santas, wicker reindeer, fresh garlands and colored lights strung on eaves and foliage, she drove as the heater finally kicked in. Her house was located close to September Creek, a few miles out of town. A little two-bedroom cabin she and Ray had bought three years into their marriage, it was beginning to show signs of age. In the divorce, she was granted ownership of the house, though she was still making payments to Ray each month and he was supposed to reciprocate with child support . . . Oh, yeah, that worked. Fine on paper. She'd considered stopping the payments to him but didn't want to deal with a lien. Though she'd hated to do it, she'd contacted a lawyer and intended, after the first of the year, to take the son of a bitch to court.

Stop it! It's Christmas! Again she caught her gaze in the rearview mirror and again she saw the anger that seemed to be forever lurking just beneath the surface of her gaze. It was something she was working on. A Christian woman, she believed fervently in forgiveness. She just couldn't find it in her heart when it came to Ray.

Someday it might happen, she thought, once she found another man to fix the sagging porch, replace the old pipes under the sink and hold her long into the night. Oh, what she wouldn't do to find a real Prince Charming the second time around. At forty-two she wasn't ready to give up on love.

Well, at least not yet.

The residential houses gave way to countryside, where snow covered the surrounding fields and drifted against the fence posts. Even the skeletal brambles and berry vines took on an unlikely serenity with the snowfall.

As she turned off the main road, she noticed a car parked at the side of the road. Its hood was lifted, a man peering at the engine. She slowed, the beams of her headlights catching him in their glare. He waved, flagging her down, and she told herself to be careful, then she recognized him as a regular customer at the restaurant and as a member of the church.

Slowing, she rolled down her window as he scurried through the piling snow to the driver's side.

"Hey," she said. "You got a problem?"

"Darned thing just died on me," he said "and I left my cell phone at home. Can't call my wife."

"I could call her."

"That would be great." He flashed the smile she'd always found endearing. "Or maybe I should?"

"Sure." Turning, she reached into her bag, found her cell and said, "I know it's about out of battery life, but it should work . . ." As she straightened again, she was making certain the phone was on when she felt something cold against her neck. "Wha—" A second later, pain scorched through her body. She screamed and twitched losing all control as he pressed the trigger on his stun gun. *Dear Lord, help me,* she thought, jerking and trying to scream. Her phone slipped from her palsied fingers, and horrified, she watched helplessly, unable to fight as he unlocked her door, bumping his head on the frame and losing his hat for a second, before he hauled her into the cold weather. She tried to fight, to punch and kick and bite, but all her efforts were futile as her mind could not control her twitching, useless body.

No, no, no! This can't be happening.

She trusted this man, knew him from church, and yet he was coldly throwing her into the backseat of his sedan and locking the door. She was helpless to do anything to save herself. The world was spinning, her body flopping on the vinyl of his backseat, and for a few minutes he left her alone in the frigid car only to show up, get behind the wheel and drive in the same direction she'd been heading.

Why? Her mind screamed but she had no control of her tongue, couldn't say a word, and listened feebly as he snapped on the radio and an instrumental version of "Silent Night" filled the interior.

Oddly, he didn't bother with the heater, and as the miles rolled under the car's tires, Brenda wondered where he was taking her and, oh, God, what he planned to do to her.

He's a Christian man. This is just a prank, she tried to convince herself, but she knew, deep in her heart, that whatever was in store for her tonight, it wouldn't be good. Over the strains of the Christmas carol, Mildred's theory echoed through her mind, haunting in its precise prediction:

The devil's behind this!

He's always there, y'know, Satan, he's just over your shoulder, waiting to pounce . . .

CHAPTER 3

"I can't," Pescoli said into her cell phone as she eased her Jeep down the long, snow-covered drive to her house. The wheels of the Jeep cut fresh paths in the snow as she drove through the trees and across a small bridge that spanned the iced-over creek running through her few acres in the foothills outside of Grizzly Falls. When the trees parted, her headlights flashed against the front of the house. Not a single light was glowing from within. "I have a feeling both of my kids are MIA. And that would be A-G-A-I-N." The bad feeling that had been with her most of the day, while trying to sort out what happened to Len Bradshaw, still lingered.

"I won't say it," Santana said and for that she was grateful. She knew how he felt about both of her teenagers needing a serious father figure in their lives.

"Good. Don't. Then I won't have to unleash my inner bitch."

"God knows we don't want that."

"No, we don't." She clicked on the remote to open her garage and watched the snow fall in front of her headlights. What she wouldn't do to drive over to Santana's place right now, take him up on his offer of drinks and dinner, then spend the night with him, but responsibility called. Responsibility in the form of her children, wherever the hell they were. "I'll call you later."

"Do that." She was about to hang up when he said, "Regan?"

"Yeah."

"You deserve a life, too."

"That I do." She couldn't agree more. And he wasn't wrong about her kids. She just wasn't ready to admit it. Yet. "Later." She clicked off and pulled into the garage, her headlights flashing on the back wall that still held bins of Joe's tools. Her heart tore a little bit when she thought of her first husband, who, like her, had been a cop. Joe Strand hadn't been a perfect man, far from it, but she'd loved him and he'd given her Jeremy, who had all of his father's good looks and none of his sense of responsibility. Joe had been killed in the line of duty during the worst of their marital rough spots. "I think I failed, Joe," she said as the engine ticked and the headlights died, leaving the garage in total darkness. The wind rattled the window casings and she realized it had been a long time since she'd talked to her deceased husband, something that had been her regular practice in the weeks, months and years after his unexpected death.

Since Nate Santana had come into her life, Joe's image had begun to fade. Finally.

It hadn't happened when she'd been married to Luke "Lucky" Pescoli. In retrospect, Luke should have been a fling. Instead, desperate not to raise a child alone or some other such garbage, Regan had ended up marrying the loser. Lucky became husband number two and father to Bianca. A truck driver, Lucky was sexy and handsome in that bad-boy way she found so fascinating. He, of course, hadn't had a faithful bone in his body. The marriage had been a mistake from the get-go.

Not that she could do anything about it now. And she did get Bianca out of the deal.

After her divorce, Pescoli vowed never to get involved again, and then she'd met Nate Santana and all of her willpower had dissolved with one flash of his sexy, cowboy smile and flicker of naughtiness that she recognized in his eyes. They'd sparked from the first time they'd laid eyes on each other, a chemistry that was as undeniable as it was unfathomable.

Trouble was, he'd gotten serious and she was trying not to be rash. She'd told herself over and over again that *this time* she was going to take it slow, let her head rule her heart for once, rather than the other way around. But Nate Santana was making it difficult. Damned difficult.

Dragging her briefcase and laptop from the car, she headed inside and was immediately greeted with excited yips and scurrying feet as Cisco raced across the linoleum. A terrier of indeterminate mix, the dog wasn't as spry as he had been. At twelve, Cisco was definitely slowing down, but he never failed to give an enthusiastic and heartfelt greeting each and every time she walked through the door.

"Jer?" she called, snapping on the lights, though she knew her son wasn't around due to the lack of his truck being parked in its usual spot at the front of the house. "Bianca?" she yelled a little louder as she dropped her laptop and briefcase onto the counter, but aside from Cisco's frenetic dance at her feet, she heard nothing.

"Great." She let the dog out and checked her phone for voice messages or texts.

Nada.

"Some things never change." While Cisco took

care of business outside, she noted that there was a pizza box on the counter with several bits of crusts and a couple of globs of cheese still within. "More good news." At least half a dozen cups were situated near the sink, not rinsed and placed in the dishwasher, but at least not scattered all over the living room. As for the dishwasher, it was full, clean dishes ready to be put into waiting cupboards, if only anyone had noticed. She tried to be patient, she really did; after all, she was the one who had encouraged her son to go back to college and he had, if taking six hours really counted as being a student. "I'm workin' my way into it," Jeremy had said.

"God forbid you take any time away from playing video games. Come on, Jer. There's more to life than annihilating fake soldiers on the flat screen."

"But I'm playing with other people, from all over." He pushed a button and Pescoli heard rapid machine-gun fire before another victim died a bloody death in a burned-out bunker on the television screen. "I'm part of a team."

"Yeah, you are. And it's called Team Strand-Pescoli. And lately, soldier, you haven't exactly been carrying your weight."

"Oh, Mom."

"I mean it!"

"This is more than just a video game!"

"Seriously?" she'd countered. "You think?"

"I know. *Call of Duty* isn't just a video game," he'd told her, controls in his hand as he stared at the television.

"Sure it is. Watch this." She'd walked over and turned off the television.

"Mom!"

"Yeah?"

Seeing she meant business, he'd had the brains not to argue. Pescoli considered the bitten tongue a baby step, but a step in the right direction, though, of course, he still needed some sincere attitude adjustments.

Now as Pescoli unzipped her jacket and tossed it over the back of a chair, Cisco raced into the house and took up residence near his bowl, barking loudly until she found his kibbles in the pantry and measured out half a cup. He danced on his back legs and spun in tight little circles as she poured the scoop into his dish. "Oh, come on, it's not *that* late," she said. "It's not as if you're starving." However, he wolfed down his food as if he hadn't eaten in a week rather than in a mere twelve hours.

Pescoli tried each of her kids on their cells. Neither picked up. She left quick voice mails asking them to phone her back but knew they wouldn't bother listening to her message. They never did, so she texted each of them.

Where R U? Call ASAP!

She thought about pouring herself a beer or a

glass of wine but thought she'd wait until she found her kids.

I'm an adult now, I can do what I want. You have no say over me.

Jeremy's proclamations rang in her ears. His "adulthood" had been a serious bone of contention between them. She figured as long as she was supporting him, he wasn't anywhere near mature enough to be considered an adult and he should report in. He didn't see it that way, of course, and his room, located in the basement, didn't look any more organized or adult than it had when he was twelve. As for Bianca she was as headstrong as both her parents and of the age where she was testing her bounds, pushing the limits on her freedom.

Her phone dinged, indicating she'd gotten a text, so she checked the screen. From Bianca: With Michelle. Xmas shopping. Home soon. Xoxo.

Okay, she couldn't complain about that one, she supposed, though she'd like to. Michelle was technically the kids' stepmother, though Pescoli hated to think of the twenty-odd-year-old as anything close to a parent of her children. She was Lucky's current wife, had long blond hair, a killer figure, and despite her innocent look was a cunning woman who had, for reasons indiscernible to Pescoli, zeroed in on Luke and married him soon after college. Michelle played the part of the bimbo to a T, but there was more to her than met the eye. Grudgingly, Pescoli had to admit she took care of the "girly" things with Bianca. They got their pedicures and manicures done together, went out to lunch or coffee and shopped 'til they dropped, seeming to delight in every sale that came along.

At least Pescoli didn't have to do those things that made her uncomfortable. She'd work with Bianca on her homework and had signed her up for every sport from soccer to tennis to horseback riding and would gladly have coached, but Bianca, from the get-go, liked all the things that Pescoli detested about being feminine.

You know, Mom, there's something wrong with YOU, not Michelle, Bianca had once accused. *What is it with you? It's almost as if you have to prove you're more of a man than a woman and it's gross!*

"Bingo," she said now, and texted back, **K**. Bianca's one letter response meaning, "okay."

Jer, of course, being the "adult" he was, didn't bother to text.

She should have taken Santana up on his offer! Instead, she tackled the dishes, turned on the dishwasher, then took the overflowing garbage and empty pizza box out to the exterior can, where snow had piled four inches, covering the lid. The night was quiet, snow falling.

Her cell phone jangled as she walked into the

house and she smiled when she saw Bianca's face and number fill the small screen.

"Hey," she said as she walked into the living room, where the Christmas tree, without an ornament or light, stood in the corner.

"Hi, Mom!" Bianca was breathless.

"Where are you?"

"Still at the mall. Michelle and I just had dinner and I still have tons of shopping to do. So I was thinking it would just be easier for Michelle if we . . . um, finished and I stayed over at Dad's."

"For the night?"

"Yeah. Michelle said she'd get me to school in the morning."

Pescoli tried to ignore the pain in her heart. "You've got your homework."

"What do you think?" Bianca said, copping an attitude for a second before adding quickly, "Of course I do. I'm finished with my report for English and I just have a little more algebra."

"Spanish?"

"Finished."

She wanted to say no, and "get your behind home," but that was just selfish and territorial on her part and wouldn't help with Bianca's attitude or her being involved in her father's life. "Okay, then." Ignoring a little hole in her heart, she added, "I'll see you . . . when? Hey, wait, is Michelle going to get you to school early? For dance team?"

"Yeah. She *wouldn't* let me miss that. It's important, she thinks. You know she was captain of her cheerleading squad when she was in high school."

And that was about two years ago, Pescoli wanted to say but bit her tongue, even though the fact that Luke's current wife was still in her twenties bugged the hell out of her. "Okay, then let's have dinner tomorrow. Seven. Good?"

"Good."

"Maybe we'll get lucky and Jeremy will deign to join us."

"Yeah, right."

"I'm serious."

"What're the chances of you and Jer both being home for dinner? Or me, either. Jeremy and I do have lives, y'know. And face it, Mom, you're *always* working."

That stung as it was the same accusation she'd heard from Santana on more than one occasion.

"Point taken. But let's try. Tomorrow. Get our Christmas plans straight."

"Fine. Whatever." Sounding put-upon, Bianca hung up quickly and was off to do whatever was so important with Michelle, the pseudo-bimbo who seemed to be in the running for Stepmom of the Year. "Great," Pescoli said to the dog, then decided to get over it. She rustled up leftover spaghetti, a spinach salad that had seen better days and half a glass of merlot.

"Cheers," she told herself as she pulled out a bar stool, sat down and, while reading what she'd missed in the paper this morning, dug in. She thought of Santana again and realized he was right: She couldn't live the rest of her life for her kids. Not that they would ever think so. And maybe she did work long hours, but her work mattered, damn it, and was for the good of the community. Besides, she loved it. Pronging a meatball as if her life depended on it, she turned her attention to the paper, then decided that soon, come hell or high water, her family was going to trim the tree. Together. Even if it killed them.

She spent the next few hours dragging the Christmas decorations out of the attic, sorting through them, checking to see that strands of lights that worked last year still glowed brightly when they were plugged in. Once she'd separated the yuletide wheat from the chaff, she left the good ornaments and lights near the tree, threw away everything broken, and filled half a garbage bag with items to donate. She thought about baking cookies, decided it was too much work, then decided to either skim off some of Joelle's goodies the next day at work or stop at the grocery store on her way home from work, where she could grab Chinese food from the deli and cookies and candy from the bakery, if Joelle's stash failed her.

Both kids would be home and they'd have a bit

of "normal" home life, if there was such a thing.

Satisfied that she was making a step in the right direction, she started into the bedroom when her cell phone rang. Finally. Jeremy decided to check in. But she was wrong. The number that appeared on her screen was unfamiliar.

"Pescoli," she answered automatically.

"Oh, Detective. Hi. It's Sandi. Down at the restaurant." Sandi Aldridge was the owner and manager of Wild Will's, an establishment that had been a landmark in Grizzly Falls for years. Tall and lanky, Sandi was a shrewd woman who wore enough makeup to make a runway model wince and always kept one of those over-shadowed eyes firmly focused on the restaurant's receipts for the day. "I didn't want to bother you, but I really don't know what else to do." That didn't sound like Sandi, an opinionated woman who knew her own mind and didn't mind telling you just how to run your life and anyone else's as well.

"It's fine." Glancing at the clock on the microwave, Pescoli noted it was after ten. "What's up?" She was getting a bad feeling, her cop senses heightened since never before had Sandi called her.

"It's one of my waitresses. You know Brenda Sutherland, right?"

"Tall, blond, quick smile." In her mind's eye, Pescoli saw the woman, a friendly sort. Pretty. Always handy with a refill of coffee. Pescoli thought Brenda Sutherland had a kid around Bianca's age. "Sure."

"Well, she didn't come in today. Was scheduled for the lunch shift and to work through dinner. Never showed. Never called. I phoned her cell and her house and got no answer."

"This is unusual?"

"Completely out of character. Brenda has never called in sick since she started with me. Never missed a day of work, unless one of her kids was down with the flu or something, and then she always called in and made sure her shift was covered. Most responsible waitress I've ever hired and I've had myself a few."

That she had. Sandi had been managing the restaurant for years, long before she split with her husband. She'd ended up with Wild Will's in the divorce and had turned a mediocre restaurant into one of the most popular establishments in town.

"I don't think anyone's filled out a missing persons report," Sandi was saying. "Her boys are with their dad tonight; something to do with their custody arrangement and the holidays, I believe. I remember her saying that, so she would be alone. But I drove up to her house—it's a cabin near September Creek on Elkridge Drive—and it was dark. No one there. Worse yet, I drove by her car parked on the side of the road just past the turnoff from the county road. It looks abandoned, a couple of inches of snow on it; I thought about calling nine-one-one but decided it might be smarter to phone you first, being as you know Brenda and all."

Pescoli's heart sank. The abandoned car didn't sound good. "Was her car disabled? Flat tire?"

"Don't know. Didn't really look. I just went up to her house and knocked on the door, called her and heard the phone ringing inside. No answer. As I said, it's just not like Brenda." Sandi sounded worried and Pescoli didn't blame her.

"I'll take a run up there," she said, "and I'll get back to you. In the meantime, if you could find her ex-husband's name and phone number, maybe his address and any friends or relatives who might know where she is, that could help. Could be she broke down and had someone come get her. What direction was the car going when it was left?"

"North. Toward her house."

That, too, wasn't good. It sounded as if she had been heading home. "She was at work yesterday?"

"Yes. And she mentioned she had a church meeting last night. First Christian. You know, they're the ones who are building a new church outside of town on some acreage Brady Long left them."

Pescoli was nodding, though, of course, Sandi couldn't know that.

"I did call Mildred Peeples. She's on every committee that the church has and a busybody to boot. Knows everybody's business and she said Brenda was at the meeting, kind of antsy, like she had to be somewhere. At least that was Mildred's take. She said the meeting broke up half an hour late, around eight thirty. As far as I know, no one's seen her since."

Not a good sign.

"Did you call the ex?"

"Ray? No way. He's a sick son of a bitch though. He's probably behind this; I wouldn't put it past him."

"Does he live in Grizzly Falls?"

"In an apartment. I don't know exactly where."

"Okay, got it. I'll check it all out."

"Thanks, Detective."

"No problem." Pescoli hung up and started for her bedroom to change out of her robe and pajamas.

The bad feeling that had been with her just got a whole lot worse.

CHAPTER 4

"Okay, so go over it again. What's going on?" Alvarez asked as she climbed into Pescoli's Jeep. She'd taken the call from her partner fifteen minutes earlier. Pescoli, obviously driving, had said, "We need to check something out up near September Creek. Brenda Sutherland, the waitress at Wild Will's, didn't show up today and the boss, Sandi, can't find her. Her car's abandoned not far from her house, so I'm going up there. You in?"

Of course she was and now they were headed out of town, Pescoli behind the wheel, the scent of cigarette smoke tingeing the air. Though Pescoli had quit years ago, she was known to sneak a smoke whenever she got stressed.

The holidays tended to do that to people.

Pescoli explained about the phone call from Sandi Aldridge as her Jeep climbed the hills outside of town. The snow, thankfully, had stopped falling and the countryside seemed deceptively serene. "But there's no body," Pescoli said. "No report of violence. No missing persons report."

She turned her vehicle down Elkridge Drive, and not two hundred yards in, she noticed the abandoned vehicle.

"Why wasn't this called in?" Alvarez asked as Pescoli passed the snow-covered car and parked on the side of the road, fifteen yards ahead of it.

"Deputies stretched thin. Wrecks, electrical outages, fires from space heaters, you name it and this isn't a major road, so it's not patrolled often."

"What about the neighbors?"

"That's the problem," Pescoli said. "Not many up here. Not year-round at least."

That much was true, Alvarez thought. This area in the mountains was spattered with a few summer homes, all closer to the lake. They climbed out of the Jeep, breaths fogging in the subfreezing temperatures, careful as they approached the car. Over four inches of snow covered the roof. "Been here a while," Pescoli thought aloud and brushed the snow from the icy driver's side window to shine the beam of her flashlight inside. "Nothing."

Alvarez looked through the frosty pane as well. The car appeared empty except for a plastic sack from which peeked a glassy-eyed stuffed animal. Looked like a reindeer.

"Christmas gifts?" Pescoli muttered.

"Maybe."

"Why leave them?"

"Why leave at all?"

"Good question."

Pescoli called the abandoned vehicle in, then, to cover their bases, Pescoli secured a search warrant not only for the car but also Brenda Sutherland's house as well. After waiting for the tow truck and a deputy to stay with the vehicle, Pescoli drove onward, taking a sharp right and following a twisting, snow-covered lane through stands of icy hemlock and pine that opened to a small clearing and the missing woman's home, a two-bedroom cottage tucked far from the road.

Pescoli parked.

Alvarez yanked her gloves a little higher on her wrists. "No lights except for the Christmas strand." She nodded toward the house.

"It's late."

"Yeah, but . . ." She looked at the house.

The front porch seemed to sag a bit, but a string of Christmas lights had been strung over the eaves. Alvarez checked her sidearm as she climbed out of the Jeep. Clicking on her flashlight, she surveyed the area and noted the path to the front door was covered in snow, one set of footprints softened with the falling snow approaching and encircling the house before leaving again.

"Sandi Aldridge said she knocked on the door and poked around the house, trying to see inside to check on Brenda Sutherland," Pescoli explained as she ran her flashlight's beam over the tracks.

"The only set." She made her way up the front steps and shined the beam of her flashlight over the exterior. Though the downspouts showed rust and wear, the little cabin, set between thickets of trees, appeared homey. A bike had been left on the porch near a pair of boots that had been kicked off randomly. Several pots held dying plants and the welcome mat was worn thin.

Aside from a breath of wind, the night was silent. Pescoli knocked on the door and rang the bell. Chimes echoed inside the house, but no footsteps approached.

"Mrs. Sutherland?" Pescoli called through the solid oak panels. "Brenda?"

Nothing. Just the sigh of the wind and creak of frozen branches.

"She could have taken advantage of the no-kid thing and taken off," Pescoli thought aloud. "But it doesn't seem likely. One of the boys, his name is Dave or Darren or Don or . . . no, it's Drew, that's right. He's in Bianca's class, or she has some classes with him; I've heard the name before and I think the mom was pretty devoted. Besides, as a single mom, she probably wouldn't have ditched the job."

"Or the car."

"Good point."

They walked around the house, investigated the empty garage where clutter abounded and a dark stain on the cement floor suggested that Brenda Sutherland's car might be leaking some kind of fluid.

The yard was empty, thick with snow, and they climbed the back steps to another wide porch, this one complete with retractable clothes line and empty hornets' nests tucked in the roof.

Pescoli pounded on the back door until it rattled, then checked. Unlocked.

"Got lucky," she said and pushed it open.

No snarling guard dog bolted from the interior, so they stepped cautiously inside, walking quickly through a small kitchen, where the faucet dripped over a sink of dirty dishes and the smell of tomato sauce hung heavy in the air.

Moving quickly through a small dining cove with a red laminated table circa 1960 where two milk glasses and cereal bowls had been left, they entered the living area, which was much tidier, the worn furniture with straightened pillows and a rag rug coiled over scratched hardwood floors. A woodstove stood on one wall, cold to the touch, ashes piled within. The two bedrooms were empty, one with a set of bunk beds and clothes scattered everywhere, the other with a neat double bed, Bible on the nightstand, flannel nightgown and matching robe hung on a hook on the backside of the door. Her closet had a meager, if functional, set of clothes and the bathroom was small, cluttered and well used.

No upstairs.

No basement.

No Brenda Sutherland.

"Definitely missing," Pescoli said, stating the obvious to the empty rooms. "Guess we'd better have a chat with the ex."

"I can't help thinking this is a lot like Lissa Parsons."

"Don't even go there," Pescoli warned, but Alvarez could tell from her tone of voice and the worry in the lines of her forehead that she'd already come to the same conclusion that the two missing women were somehow linked.

The next day, things definitely started out on the wrong foot. For some reason Alvarez's alarm didn't go off, probably because she'd slapped the clock silly the day before, and she realized, belatedly, after letting Roscoe out the door, that she'd missed her session with her martial arts instructor. He hadn't called but left a text and she responded, apologizing and feeling out of sorts.

What was wrong with her?

She *never* was late. *Never* missed an appointment. *Never* bought anyone else's excuses about being flaky. Sure she'd had a bad night's sleep with Jane Doe up half the night and thoughts of the missing women running in circles through her brain, but still, she shouldn't be so off-kilter. "Pull it together," she told herself, feeling a headache coming on as she stepped into the shower. Cold needles of water pounded her bare skin for just an instant before she jumped out of the tiled enclosure. Wrapping a towel quickly around her shivering body with one hand, she checked the temperature of the shower spray with the other, wiggled the handle and discovered not a drop of hot water anywhere.

"Great," she muttered, wondering what else could go wrong. The answer, of course, was plenty. And it did. She threw on her clothes and realized the puppy wasn't tagging after her. Nor did she hear him. With the dread that comes only with the experience of being a mother or pet owner, she hurried downstairs and found Roscoe, pillow in his mouth, stuffing flying through the air like snow in a snow globe. "Stop! Drop it!"

she ordered and he, thinking it was a game, ran around the coffee table and bounded through the kitchen. "I don't have time for this," she warned, nearly catching him only to have him streak by, tail between his legs, ears flopping. "You are in *so* much trouble!"

When she finally cornered him in the powder room, she was breathing hard and her temper had cooled a bit. "Oh, come on." She didn't have time to clean up the feathers and stuffing littering her living area, but she put him in his pen, grabbed her purse, wallet, sidearm and badge and left him standing behind the wire mesh managing to look as miserable as any dog on earth. "You'll be fine," she said feeling ridiculously guilty before locking the door behind her and heading for the garage.

Though it wasn't yet eight in the morning, she called the maintenance man for the building and asked him to check on her water heater. He was a lazy twenty-six-year-old who preferred spending nights as the bass player for his band rather than his days fixing up the property, but he was cheap and, if given enough time, was handy enough. He'd done some side jobs for Alvarez in the past and she was certain he could determine what the hell was wrong with her hot water tank. She only hoped she wouldn't have to replace the damned thing.

At the office, she found a cup of blistering-hot coffee and tried to shake herself out of her bad mood by munching on a reindeer cupcake, eating first the sugar-coated antlers and then its whole damned head. It didn't help.

Twenty minutes later, she was just answering some e-mail when Pescoli dropped by her desk. "Want some bad news?" she asked.

Alvarez glanced up. "You mean some *more* bad news?" she asked. "It hasn't exactly been a stellar morning and so, the answer is no."

"Yeah, well, I think you'd better hear this. Your buddy J. R. has just been released from prison. A technicality and his lawyer screamed loudly enough that it looks like there might be a whole new trial."

"Crap." The headache that had started early this morning and had been exacerbated by the couch pillow evisceration was really beginning to pound inside her skull. J. R. "Junior" Green, the creep of all creeps, was an ex-pro football lineman who had turned coach and pedophile. Alvarez had been instrumental in sending him up the river and he'd sworn that he'd return the favor by ruining her life. "He's guilty!"

"As sin. We just have to prove it all over again."

Her headache throbbed, and as Pescoli walked off, Alvarez's cell phone rang. She checked the number, saw that it was Terry Longstrom and didn't pick up. She couldn't deal with him right now, at least not personally. If he needed to talk to her about business, he could leave a message; then she might call him back. Maybe.

She reached into the top drawer of her desk, found a bottle of Excedrin she used only if her periods were severe. Those times she washed the pain killers down with some kind of herbal tea. Today she popped two into her palm, tossed them into her mouth and swallowed them dry.

It wasn't yet nine in the morning, and so far, the day was turning into a nightmare.

A couple of hours later, while Pescoli was checking with several members of the Bible study group at Brenda Sutherland's church, the members of which were some of the people who'd last seen Brenda alive, Alvarez headed over to Missing Persons, where she made some inquiries, asking Taj about other women who may have been reported missing.

"Let me see," Taj said, typing into her keyboard and studying her monitor.

Alvarez was antsy. She'd been waiting for hours to talk to Taj, as all night she'd tossed and turned, wondering what connection, if any, there was between Lissa Parsons and Brenda Sutherland.

She wasn't one to believe in coincidences, and if the past few winters had taught her anything, it was to be wary. For a small town, Grizzly Falls had its share of nuts. There were the harmless ones, like Ivor Hicks, who, pushing eighty, still swore that he'd been abducted by aliens years before on Mesa Rock. He'd been brought to the mother ship and was experimented upon by a reptilian race headed by a particularly nasty general named Crytor. He'd sworn that his experience with the aliens had *not* been due to his intimate relationship with Jack Daniel's. Alvarez wasn't convinced. Then there was Grace Perchant, a woman who lived alone with not one, but now two wolf-dogs, her older female named Sheena and a newer addition, a big male that she called Bane. So now, in Alvarez's opinion, Grace had a bona fide pack. Great. Convinced she spoke with ghosts, Grace was always making weird predictions that strangely came to be. Again, she was, at least to Alvarez's way of thinking, for the most part, benign.

However, on the other side of the coin, Grizzly Falls had seen more than its fair share of sadistic killers recently, psychos who had terrorized this area for three years running. As Pescoli had said often enough, "It's the cold around here; the sub-zero temperature brings out the crazies."

Alvarez, a woman of science, couldn't put her finger on what was the cause of the horrid phenomenon; she just didn't like it. And now, with two women missing, she felt that little tingle at the base of her skull that warned her of bad news.

"We have quite a few missing people," Taj said, scrolling down on her computer screen. "An elderly man wandered out of an elder facility and he's still not been located; two potential teenaged runaways, a set of twins, probably abducted by their own father; and a baby taken out of the hospital."

"I'm looking for another woman, somewhere between nineteen and forty, probably, but not necessarily."

"Well, there's Lara Sue Gilfry," she said, her eyebrows pushing together. "She went missing about a month ago . . . let's see. Okay, here we are." A serious picture of a redheaded woman with wide blue eyes and tight, pale lips appeared. "She's twenty-eight and is pretty transient. Moves around a lot. Last seen on November sixth at the Bull and Bear bed-and-breakfast, where she worked as a maid. Said to have a significant scar on her right leg, just above the knee, after a motorcycle accident when she was in her teens, and a tattoo of a butterfly on her left ankle." Taj tilted her monitor so that Alvarez could get a better look at the missing woman. "She's estranged from her family; her mother died when she was two, father when she was a teenager, and the stepmother has been through a series of relationships. Lara Sue kind of fell through the cracks. Been on her own since she was sixteen."

Alvarez felt a cold drip of apprehension trickle down her spine. "What about boyfriends? Or cousins? Girlfriends?"

Taj was reading. "No serious boyfriend and she

was kind of a loner, kept to herself. The owner of the Bull and Bear let her stay in an attic room as part of her compensation."

"Did she leave with her belongings?"

"Yeah. So that's why the case is iffy. She could be one of those people who just float from town to town."

"What about money? Checking account? Bank card?"

Taj shook her head. "According to her employer, he'd pay her, then go to the bank with her so she could cash her check. She paid for everything with cash."

"Great. What about a computer, a Facebook or Twitter account?"

"So far, none found."

"All young people do the social-networking thing."

"If she had one, we couldn't find it." Taj stared up at her. "And we looked."

"Okay. So maybe she just took off."

"Probably."

"Can you forward what you've got on her to me?"

Taj was nodding. "You got it."

"Thanks."

Alvarez left the Missing Persons department with a bad feeling she just couldn't shake.

No bodies.

No crime scenes.

But now three missing women.

Where the hell were they?

Calvin Mullins had never liked the police. No matter what shape or size, cops made him nervous, even Cort Brewster, one of the deacons in the church and an undersheriff with the county sheriff's department. A pious man, stalwart in his faith, devoted husband and loving father of breathtakingly beautiful daughters, Brewster was, nonetheless, a cop and that bothered the preacher.

Today in the church office, he was faced with another member of the Pinewood County Sheriff's Department. This one, Detective Regan Pescoli, was causing him to sweat beneath his crisp shirt and sharkskin jacket. He was seated at his desk, his sermon printed out as he just went over it in highlighter, hoping to beef up some of the more salient points, when Pescoli, a brash, arrogant woman if he'd ever seen one, had knocked and stepped inside.

"Your wife said you'd be here," she'd said before introducing herself and taking a chair without him inviting her inside. Just then Lorraine had texted, and his cell phone, on vibrate, had nearly skittered across his desk, as the warning, "Police detective on her way to see you," appeared a little too late on the screen. That was the trouble: Lorraine had never learned to text properly and quickly.

High tech, Lorraine was not, but she was a faithful and forgiving wife, mother of his three daughters.

Pescoli was beautiful, in that hard-edged, woman-in-control way that he found a little bit of a turn-on. A few inches shy of six feet, she stood tall, and what he could see of her hair reddish brown-blonde, and a little unkempt. Intelligent eyes assessed him.

He pasted a smile onto his face and hoped it appeared beatific. "What can I do for you?" he said, standing as he shook her hand.

His office was small but neat, decorated with hardbound books on philosophy and religions of the world, given just the right amount of color with pictures on the wall of the Lord and beautiful spots on earth, as well as his framed degrees and awards. Though he believed that pride was a sin, accomplishments were certainly proof of piety, struggle and self-improvement: all good qualities.

A small basket of poinsettias sat on one corner of his desk. Lorraine always made certain that flowers in season, "God's handiwork," graced his office.

"I'd like to talk to you about Brenda Sutherland."

"Has she been found?" he asked hopefully. He truly admired Brenda and her faith, her difficulty in raising two stubborn boys alone.

"Not yet."

"Oh, dear. I pray she comes home safely," he said and meant it.

"You saw her recently?"

"Yes. Of course. I pop my head into the study groups when I can, and Brenda was with my wife's group the other night. They were discussing our giving tree." He folded his hands over his sermon, left over right, showing off his wedding ring.

But, as the cop asked a few more questions, he felt his tie tightening and beads of sweat dotting his back. He gave a short history of his ministry, neglecting to mention that he was originally from Bad Luck, Texas, though, from the degrees on the wall, it was obvious that he'd graduated from Southern Methodist University. That's where he met and married Lorraine.

"So how did you end up here, in Grizzly Falls?"

He spread his hands. "I go where the church needs me," he said and it really wasn't a lie. After spending a decade basking in the warm Arizona sun at a parish in Tucson, there had been a problem, a minor indiscretion with an eighteen-year-old daughter of Cecil Whitcomb, one of the church deacons. Peri had come to him for guidance and he hadn't been able to ignore her lips, always glossy and full, her tongue, how it flicked against her teeth so seductively, or the pull of her T-shirts across breasts that could fill a man's hands and then some.

Peri had needed comforting during the time of her parents' separation.

He'd obliged.

And things had heated up, with this young, perfect woman willing to do things in the bedroom that Lorraine considered "vile" and "animal." Even now, when he remembered mounting Peri from behind, her smooth rump pressing hard into his abdomen, those glorious breasts hanging into his willing hands, his teeth and lips pressing hard into the back of her neck, just to nip, mind you . . . oh, dear Lord. It had been ecstasy, sinful joyous ecstasy. And when Peri's luscious warm mouth and tongue had worked her magic on him . . . he'd been transported to an erotic state of pure heaven . . .

"Preacher Mullins? Did you hear the question?" the cop asked and he jerked back to the present, grateful for the desk that separated them so that she couldn't witness the bulge at his crotch. What had he been thinking, letting his mind wander so. "Do you know Brenda Sutherland's ex?"

"No . . . uh, I knew she was divorced, of course," he added, trying to appear concerned, "that there were some . . . issues . . . because of their sons, but, no, Ray Sutherland isn't a member of the church and I've never even seen him."

She asked a few more questions, nothing all that worrisome, at least concerning him, but he wondered if she'd be back. No doubt she'd start digging into his past and then his little indiscretion would come to light.

He couldn't imagine Lorraine standing at his side again, holding his hand, lifting her tiny chin proudly in a show of solidarity and support for her unfaithful fallen husband once more.

Dear Father, why now? When things were going so well? She would leave him if all the old demons were brought to light; he knew it. He'd be further disgraced and now she was with child again, possibly the son he'd been praying for. His daughters were a joy, oh, yes, three delightful girls, eight, six and four, all with near-white hair and pale blue eyes. But this time, he was so hoping for a boy. A big, loud, strapping son who looked less ghostlike than the girls, who were carbon copies of their mother.

Lorraine was a good woman, but it would help him if she could ever just come close to having an orgasm. If so, then she might understand that all the carnal pleasures of the flesh, at least between a man and his wife, were not repulsive.

He walked to the window and stared through the frosty panes to the crèche decorating the side yard of the church. Mary, Joseph, the shepherds, all cloaked in a new mantle of snow, the angled floodlight showing off the backdrop of the stable.

Preacher Mullins had thought being banished to this godforsaken tundra had been the worst punishment possible after his problems in

Arizona, but now, if what had happened in Tucson was discovered by the police and the press, he might be sent somewhere else. Just when his flock was coming together and his wife finally, at least on the surface, seemed to have forgiven him.

He bowed his head. "Father, be with me. Give me strength. Let me never fall into temptation again. Please, Father of all, lead me. Give me strength. I pray for this and all things in Jesus's name. Amen." Letting out a long, shuddering sigh, he hoped for divine intervention.

Today, it didn't reach him.

The music took him away.

Soft. Melodic. Instrumental versions of traditional Christmas carols and those classical pieces associated with Christmas. Nothing frothy, light or the least bit irreverent today. He needed to *feel* the piety resounding in the notes that filled this cavern and resounded in his heart.

Thankfully, his new subject had quieted down. He couldn't afford the distraction of her moans. She was past pleading with him now, nearly succumbing to her fate, so he was able to concentrate.

As he slathered the woman in water, watching in fascination as ice formed over her naked body, he felt that supreme satisfaction that comes with a job well done. She was in the perfect position, her legs bent so that she appeared to be kneeling, her head bowed, her hands folded in prayer. That had been tricky.

Moving unwilling body parts into precise position took strength, patience and a practiced eye. He'd been careful to nudge toes, fingers and vertebrae into the correct position. Now, as the water sluiced over the body, firming up, he glanced to the desk he'd fashioned out of a crude work-bench, and lining it, pinned to the cork board he'd installed, were dozens of photographs of kneeling women. He'd enlarged five diagrams that showed a praying body from different angles and was able with the freezing temperatures to ensure that his creation was in the exact position he needed.

Oh, yes.

As he surveyed her, he grinned. Her expression was perfect, serene and pensive, absolutely pious, nearly enraptured. Yes . . . oh, she was ready, though there were hours of work to be done, layers of ice to enwrap her, painstaking sculpting to finish the job, but when he was done, she would be a masterpiece and so different from his first.

Of course he was talented, to deny it would be obscene, but his gift was not only special but vast. Though his work would bear his signature, no two statues would be alike. He took the time to marvel at his first piece, so near completion. It was a bit whimsical, the frozen woman, who'd been lying down as he'd molded the ice around her, now standing, her arms raised, her hands curved toward the coved ceiling of this cave.

Her expression was joyous, a wide grin visible through the ice, her eyes open wide.

She was ready for display.

He felt a little sizzle of excitement at the prospect. He knew just where to place her.

With his first sculpture, he'd gone for the frivolous, happy aspect of the holidays and she'd turned out perfectly. But he couldn't sit on his laurels, oh, no. Never. His time was limited to the frigid days of winter so he couldn't slack off.

And he had to show his diversity. Of course. So while Number One was light spirited, with this newest piece, Number Two for lack of a better name right now, he'd taken a more serious approach, trying to create a sense of reverence. Of piety. Of pure devotion.

He doubted anyone would understand his need for perfection, the subtleties involved, but as long as he knew the depths of his dedication and talent, then the rest wasn't important.

Humming along to the notes of the "Dance of the Sugar Plum Fairy," he felt inspiration well deep in his soul as he worked with excruciating precision. He only had a few hours, so he couldn't afford any mistakes.

He smiled at that ridiculous worry.

He didn't make mistakes.

Of course he didn't.

That was just one of the things he and God had in common.

CHAPTER 5

"You're such a liar," Alvarez accused Pescoli as they drove down the steep hill that separated the older section of town from the new. Near the river, the buildings had been built near the turn of the previous century, some, like the courthouse, built in the late 1800s. There were newer buildings interspersed with the old, but this section of town definitely had an Old West feel to it and the town fathers made a point of keeping it looking as if the "Old Grizzly Falls" could be used as the set for a western movie or television series.

Up the hill, past a few old mansions that had been built by copper and timber barons, the newer part of town spread along the cliff face and into the surrounding countryside. While on the waterfront brick-and-mortar buildings stood tall, above, on Boxer Bluff, a few strip malls, fast food restaurants, the new school and hospital became part of what townsfolk laughingly called Grizzly Falls's attempt at "urban sprawl."

"A liar?" Pescoli eased her Jeep past the courthouse, where the Christmas tree was already adorned with hundreds of white, twinkling lights that sparkled twenty-four-seven. "Why is that?"

81

She found a parking spot one block up from Wild Will's and eased into it.

"The Secret Santa drawing. You didn't get your own name the first time you picked a name from Joelle's Santa hat."

Pescoli cut the engine. "I did, too."

"Nope. Big lie." Alvarez climbed out of the seat and slammed the door shut behind her.

"How would you know? Oh, don't tell me. You drew my name! Oh, great. I'll probably end up with boxes of herbal tea or some such crap from you."

"I thought you hated the game."

"I do."

"Then why worry about what you'll get?" Alvarez picked her way over the crusted, dirty snow that had been pushed against the curb by snow plows. "And, no, I didn't end up with you; I could just tell. My powerful skills of detection."

"Yeah, right."

"Admit it, Pescoli, you cheated."

Pescoli scowled as they crossed the street. "Okay, so you caught me. Big deal." She was really agitated. "I just couldn't deal with trying to find cutesy little gifts for Brewster twice in two years. Trust me, that's my own personal version of hell. It's bad enough I have to deal with him as my damned boss. I refuse to play games with the man!"

"Jeremy and Heidi ever break up?"

"From your lips to God's ears," Pescoli grumbled as she walked through the doors of Wild Will's, where as soon as they were inside, they were greeted by Grizz, the stuffed grizzly bear standing guard at the door. Over seven feet tall, his lips pulled into a permanent snarl, long teeth gleaming, razor-sharp claws extended, he was always in costume, a regular ursine fashionista who was dressed with the season. Today he was wearing elf attire, complete with a silly little hat decorated with a jingle bell, a red and green coat and huge striped stockings around his hind legs.

"Is it Grizz or Will Ferrell?" Alvarez joked, though she wasn't in a jovial mood. The holidays always brought her down and the three missing women were bothering her. It didn't help that the hot water situation at her home hadn't been alleviated. Jon, the sometimes repairman, had been ducking her and she'd been reduced to heating water on the stove or taking a shower at the gym. Jon had left her a message on her phone earlier: "Hey, uh, this is Jon. Got your message about the hot water. I'll get to it ASAP." What a joke, the guy had no idea what ASAP or STAT meant. It was irritating. Damn irritating, but she wasn't going to focus on it now.

It was around one o'clock and the restaurant was busy, all of the booths and most of the tables occupied. Conversation buzzed through the high-ceilinged room and a fryer in the kitchen sizzled, competing with the strains of Christmas music filtering from hidden speakers.

A hostess led them to a table in the center of the large dining area, where, upon the rough-hewn walls, heads of animals stared down at them. Alvarez had always thought the decor bordered on the macabre and never felt completely comfortable with the glassy eyes of deer, elk, a moose and even a cougar glaring down at the patrons.

They had settled in and ordered before Sandi swept by. She put on the brakes when she spied Pescoli. "Don't suppose there's any news?" The lines in her face seemed deeper than usual, her eye shadow a sparkling metallic green, probably in homage to the season.

"Not yet."

"Damn!" She shook her head and her eyes narrowed suspiciously, green eyelids even more noticeable. "You'd better check out Ray, the ex. Brenda and he have been in a battle royal for those boys. He wants full custody and so does she. There's always something going on there, with the courts. He's even had the gall to call your damned department and report her if he can't get through to his kids, and he's been on the phone to human services, sending them out to Brenda's house, trying to prove she's unfit or some such nonsense!" Sandi snorted at the insanity of it all. "A mean one, he is." Nodding as if agreeing with her own theory, she pointed a red-tipped nail at

Pescoli and jabbed the air in front of Pescoli's nose. "If you ask me, she was way too good for him, and he knew it! I never did like him. A real loser."

"Aren't they all? Exes, I mean?" Pescoli asked and Alvarez guessed she was thinking of her own.

"Well, yeah, most of 'em! And you can sure throw mine in there." Her red lips pursed thoughtfully. "Although Connie Leonetti gets along with hers. She even bakes him *and* his mother cookies for the holidays. And I'm not talking about the arsenic or Ex-Lax-laced kind. If you ask me, that's just an abomination of nature." She didn't crack a smile at her attempt at humor. "I just hope you find Brenda. And it's not because I've had to pull double-duty without her. She's really a sweet, sweet woman and when I think of those boys of hers . . . Oh, man, she adores them." Sandi's lower lip quivered a bit and Alvarez wished there was something that could be said, some platitude that would soothe her. There wasn't.

Clearing her throat and squaring her shoulders, Sandi said, "If you ask me, Ray Sutherland is behind this. He didn't want the divorce and wasn't happy with the custody arrangement. If I were you, I'd be lookin' at him hard. *Real* hard." With that, she saw a table that needed to be cleared and took off, her quick steps wending her expertly through the tightly packed tables. Closing in on a lackadaisical busboy, she snapped her fingers to

85

gain his attention. Obviously the pudgy teenager wasn't quick enough with his dishpan and towel to suit Sandi.

Probably no one was.

As far as Ray Sutherland went, they'd already talked to him, this morning, early enough that the trucker had obviously just rolled out of bed at the pounding on his apartment door. He lived on the second floor of an L-shaped stucco building. A surly sort with the beginning of a pot belly and in serious need of a razor, he'd seemed genuinely surprised when they'd told him about his ex-wife.

Had he been nervous?

Maybe.

Alvarez had noted that he ran a hand through his dull brown hair, all of which was sticking up at odd bed-head angles.

"Of course I have no idea where she is," he'd said, perturbed. "Why?"

"Because she didn't show up for work, she's not at home and her car is abandoned at the side of the road."

That made him blink, some of his just-woken-up outrage fading. "Jesus. What happened?"

"That's what we're trying to find out," Pescoli had said. "Mind if we come in?"

Grumpily, he'd allowed them into a mess of an apartment, throwing some newspapers and jackets and a wadded blanket out of the way so that Alvarez could sit on the grimy cushions of a beat-up couch while Pescoli stood near the door. The shades were drawn and Sutherland, cinching the belt of his striped robe around his belly, settled into a fake leather recliner that had seen better days.

He'd answered their questions while yelling at his boys to get ready for school. When he'd gotten no response when he'd craned his neck back to the bedroom wing of the small apartment and called to them, he'd gotten up for a few minutes, trod down a short hallway, opened a door and given some muffled orders before reappearing and taking up residence in his chair, positioned in front of a flat screen that seemed to be six feet if it were an inch.

When asked, he'd offered up an alibi for the night his ex had disappeared. Though he didn't seem sorry to hear Brenda was missing, he did appear shocked.

"She should be more careful," he'd muttered, reaching into the top drawer of the small table positioned near his chair. He withdrew a pack of cigarettes, found it empty and, swearing under his breath, crumpled it. "I tell her all the time."

"Why?" Alvarez asked.

"Because she's the damned mother of my kids, that's why!" At the mention of his offspring, he'd glanced down the hallway, scowled, then said to Alvarez, "Are we done here? I've got to get my boys off to school."

"We may have more questions later."

"Yeah, yeah. Fine." He'd gotten to his feet and began lumbering toward the bedrooms again while Alvarez and Pescoli had taken their leave.

But maybe Sandi was right, Alvarez thought now. Ray Sutherland, a trucker, might have given an Oscar-worthy performance this morning. But she doubted it.

While Pescoli dug into her burger and fries, Alvarez picked at her salad of field greens and her cup of shrimp bisque, all the while tossing the case over in her mind.

"Don't see how you live on that crap," Pescoli said, pointing a French fry at Alvarez's meal before dredging the crispy potato strip through a puddle of ketchup on her platter.

"Ditto."

"I don't think Ray Sutherland's our guy." She plopped the fry into her mouth.

"If there is a guy."

"Right. If there is a guy. Could be three women just took hikes, y'know. It happens."

"You don't believe that."

"Nope. I don't. Just don't like the other possibilities." She thought for a few minutes as she took a final bite of her burger before tossing the remains onto her plate.

They split the bill and Alvarez was shrugging into her coat when she saw Pescoli's gaze narrow. "Uh-oh," she whispered.

"What?" She turned and from the corner of her eye saw Grace Perchant approaching.

"Here comes the nutcase," Pescoli said under her breath, her words barely audible.

If Grace heard Pescoli's remarks, she didn't react. Thin and pale, dressed in a long white coat that seemed to billow around her, Grace walked slowly and steadily toward their table. Her pale green eyes were fixed on Alvarez with the intensity of someone incredibly determined.

"Detective Alvarez," she said, her voice low.

"Yes."

Almost as if in a trance, Grace grabbed Alvarez's hand, and from the corner of her eye, Alvarez noticed Pescoli reach for her sidearm. With a slight shake of her head, Alvarez silently told her partner to stand down. She wasn't in danger.

"What is it, Grace?" she asked.

"Your son needs you."

"What? I don't have a son."

Grace's fingers tightened. "He's in grave danger."

"Who are you talking about? I don't have a son." Her gaze locked with that of the kook's.

"He needs you," Grace repeated, and then, as if suddenly realizing how awkward the situation was, that people in the surrounding tables had stopped eating to stare, Grace released Alvarez's hand as quickly as she'd gathered it.

Then, looking straight ahead, she walked out of the restaurant.

Pescoli snorted. "I told you, nutcase with a capital N."

"Yeah." Alvarez flashed a bit of a smile as she pulled on her gloves.

Sandi scurried over. "Geez, I'm sorry about that," she said. "Grace is a bit off, I know, but she usually keeps to herself."

"Don't worry about it," Alvarez said and was already on her way to the door. "It's no big deal." Which, of course, was a lie. Another one. Inside she was shaking, the old familiar pain taking hold of her, but she wouldn't think about it, not now.

You have to someday; you can't just shove this into a dark corner forever.

Okay, fine. Just not today. And though Grace was a bona fide oddball who thought she could talk with ghosts, Alvarez couldn't just shake off her warning. Even though Alvarez didn't believe in all that psychic nonsense Grace tried to peddle, it was true that the strange woman had helped the department in the past. Several times. If nothing else, she brought a calmness, an equanimity to some of the most brutal and barbaric cases. It was weird. And bothered Alvarez.

Still she couldn't brush off the woman's concerns out of hand and Grace's dire warning chased after her for most of the afternoon, drifting into her brain while she was trying to concentrate on something—make that anything—else.

Even when she discovered that Ray Sutherland had taken out a life insurance policy for two hundred thousand dollars on his ex-wife only six months earlier. Long after the divorce. Alvarez hung up from the insurance company and leaned back in her chair. What the hell was that all about? Alibi or not, the man had serious motive to have his ex-wife killed. The insurance proceeds coupled with gaining full custody of the kids was more than enough motive.

Except you're not sure she's dead yet. Don't jump the gun.

Even now, while her mind was occupied with the mystery of Brenda Sutherland's disappearance, Grace's chilling words reverberated through her mind:

Your son needs you. He's in grave danger . . .

Oh. Dear. God.

CHAPTER 6

"Oh, no, you don't," Dylan O'Keefe muttered as he took off after the punk kid in jeans, jacket, watch cap and boots. A backpack swung from one thin shoulder as the boy sprinted easily through the drifting snow. Running down side streets, cutting through alleys and across yards, ducking around corners, climbing fences and creating a zigzag path toward a residential section of Grizzly Falls, Gabriel Reeve ran.

Where the hell was he going?

A bad feeling stole over O'Keefe as he rounded a corner and heard a dog barking frantically from somewhere in the darkness. He dashed across a deserted street. Barely eight in the evening, and this part of town was quiet as hell. Despite the earlier plowing, the snow was collecting again, his boots sinking into three inches of accumulation, snow falling past the street lamps to pile on a handful of cars parked near the curb.

He followed the fresh tracks across a side yard, and thankfully the dog he'd heard didn't come bounding across the snow, so O'Keefe kept running, squinting through the curtain of snow. Icy air slapped him in the face and chilled a path to his lungs as he zeroed in on his quarry again, a punk of about sixteen, tough as nails and wanted for armed robbery.

Trouble was, Gabriel Reeve, the JD in question, just happened to be his cousin's kid. Aggie had begged him to look for Gabe and O'Keefe had reluctantly agreed, even taken money to start his investigation. Now, he was in it deep. All in all, a bad situation.

Too bad! Like it or not, he'd ended up in Grizzly frickin' Falls, and so far, he thought, the boy didn't realize that he was being tailed. But that was about to change. Now that he was this close, O'Keefe wasn't going to let the kid slip through his fingers again.

Down an alley and along a path, the boy ran, with O'Keefe, hopefully, just out of view. But he didn't like it; Reeve was just too damned close to Selena Alvarez's home, and she was one woman on this planet he meant to avoid at all costs.

Just damned luck the kid had led him here.

Right?

He didn't have time to think about it. The kid vaulted yet another fence and took off on the other side. O'Keefe, less than ten seconds later, did the same, landing hard. He found himself smack dab in the side yard of a group of town houses; the complex that Selena Alvarez now called home.

He knew where she lived, of course.

Had kept track of her and realized she lived in Grizzly Falls and worked for the sheriff's department, but he hadn't known her street address until he'd checked with DMV before driving into the city limits.

Great. Just . . . frickin' great. What were the chances? he wondered as he watched the kid slink past a hedgerow of arborvitae, a few branches bending under the weight of the snow. The boy flattened himself against the side of a garage, glanced over his shoulder, then crept quickly around the corner of the end row house.

Alvarez's unit.

"Son of a bitch," O'Keefe muttered under his breath. He hadn't crossed the damned state of Montana, chasing Gabriel Reeve to Grizzly Falls, only to lose him. No way! It was time to snag the kid, haul him back to Helena and make Reeve face the music *before* O'Keefe had to deal with Alvarez.

He unbuckled his sidearm from its holster but left the safety engaged. He wasn't going to use the Glock. No. It was only insurance. He just wanted to scare the kid and get him out of the area quickly. Besides, he figured Reeve was armed and didn't want to round a corner only to end up on the business end of a pistol without his own weapon ready.

A fresh blast of arctic wind swept through the buildings, slapping his face and cutting through his jacket with a bite as sharp as all of December.

You should call the cops; let them handle this —just tell them where the kid is.

But he didn't and he had his reasons, even if they were flimsy as tissue paper. For one thing, the kid was a relative, his cousin's boy; for another, he wanted answers himself before the cops got to the boy.

He followed Reeve around the corner and found himself at the garage side of the town house just as twin beams cut through the night and the sound of an engine reached his ears. A small SUV turned onto the street running past the town house, and somewhere nearby—from inside the condo—a dog barked wildly. O'Keefe stopped dead in his tracks, hoping the driver of the car wouldn't notice him as the Subaru passed.

No such luck!

Instead, a grinding noise filled the night as the garage door began rolling upward. The Outback, sending snow flying beneath its tires, zipped into the driveway, the beams of its headlights splashing up against the building and, no doubt, throwing his silhouette into relief.

Great.

In the drive, the Subaru skidded to a stop and Selena Alvarez, all fire and ice, flew out of the driver's side. Her service weapon was drawn and her dark eyes, glittering with suspicion, zeroed in on him. "Police! Freeze!" she ordered, two hands on her pistol. "Drop it!"

He let go of his gun and it fell into the snow.

"Hands over your head!" she ordered, moving around the open door as the car dinged in protest. But the dog had stopped its frantic barking . . . "Wait! What? Dylan O'Keefe?" she whispered in disbelief, and some of the starch in her spine seemed to leave her. Confusion clouded her features. Damn, she was beautiful. Still. In that intriguing, intelligent way that he'd found so damned fascinating and nearly deadly. "What the hell are you doing here?" she demanded.

"Chasing a suspect." He tamped down the cold

blue fury that burned in his gut by just staring at her, and for a few seconds, he was thrown back to another place and time. The San Bernardino stakeout that had changed his life forever.

"But . . . wait . . . you're chasing a suspect *here?*"

"That's right. And he's gonna get away if I don't nail his ass. No time to explain." Not that he could. What were the chances that he'd end up here? What the hell was *that* all about? *Coincidence? Or just bad luck?*

"For the love of God." She was shaking her head, her hair as black and shiny as a raven's wing and in stark contrast to the whiteness of the snow falling around them. He'd hoped he'd never see her again. But here he was. What was it his old grandma had said? *If wishes were horses . . .* and so on and so forth.

Now that she recognized him, she slowly lowered her weapon. "Dylan effin' O'Keefe."

"Stay here," he said, "and call for backup."

In one swift motion, he pulled his Glock out of the snow and started rounding her building, wiping the barrel on his jeans as he followed the broken trail Gabriel Reeve had left.

"Wait! I don't understand."

He glanced over his shoulder. "Get back in the car!"

"No way! This is my house!" She was already slowly closing the door of the Subaru.

96

"And my collar."

"Fine. But I'm coming with you since you are chasing someone breaking into my house. I'm involved."

He repeated, "Just stay out of the way, Alvarez, and call for backup."

"You haven't?"

"Shhh!" He lowered his voice. "No. Stay here and make that damned call."

"Who is it?" she demanded.

"What?"

"The guy inside? Who is it?"

"A kid. Gabriel Reeve."

"A kid?"

"Sixteen."

"Who's he?" Her voice was a whisper.

"Trouble. One of those computer hackers who live for anarchy. Now he's wanted for armed robbery. He's moved to the big time."

"And he's in *my* house?"

"Go figure." Did Reeve know he was breaking into the home of a cop? Probably not. Otherwise the kid had more balls than O'Keefe gave him credit for. "Just dumb luck."

He was at the back corner of the house, she a step behind. Another damned fence! And the trail of footprints had ended at the unpainted boards and a spot of snow about three feet up where the kid's boots had hit before he'd hauled himself over the top.

Alvarez hadn't paid a lick of attention to him. She was at his side, her damned weapon drawn, as sexy and hard edged as he remembered, not that he had time to think about it.

"There's a gate. Just around the corner." She motioned with the nose of her gun. "I'll take the front door."

"No! Call for—oh, hell!"

Too late. She was already backtracking. This was all wrong. Going sideways. Just like before. In a moment of déjà vu, he was transported to another chase, another frantic night and the blinding pain of betrayal . . .

No time to think of it now. He circumvented the fence, ending up at the back of the property where the ground sloped downward to a frozen creek. Carefully reaching over the top of the gate, he lifted the latch and gently pushed the gate open before slipping into the yard. Snow fell silently. No lights glowed from within and the back door, a slider, was open, a curtain billowing through the darkened open space. The enclosed yard with its small patio and a few scattered pots was covered in a soft white blanket and empty. No one hiding in the shadows. He heard his own heart beating in his ears and nothing else, not even any street noise. Tense, his fingers tight over his Glock, his gaze still scouring the yard, he moved along the fence line through the falling snow.

Eyes trained on the doorway, ready to

lunge, he expected the kid to burst from the house.

But nothing happened.

He heard Alvarez open the front door. God, he wished she hadn't shown up. "Police!" Her voice echoed through the open door. "Gabriel Reeve, show yourself!"

O'Keefe waited, ready to spring, certain Reeve would run.

Still nothing.

Not a sound.

Interior lights snapped on, illumination pouring through the windows to reflect on the unbroken snow.

"Gabriel Reeve, drop your weapon and come out, hands over your head!" Alvarez yelled again and O'Keefe stepped into the dining area of the town house. Inside, Alvarez, sidearm clutched in her hand, was mounting the stairs.

She didn't so much as glance in O'Keefe's direction as he crossed the dining area, nearly knocking over a pet's dish. A step behind, he followed her to the second floor, where she opened the door to an office/guest room, then the bath, and finally her own bedroom, all of which was very neat. The beds he'd seen were made to military precision, pillows placed perfectly over matching quilts, a desk without so much as a stray paperclip on its smooth surface.

She shoved open the closet doors and found no one.

"He's not here," she finally said. "And neither is my dog."

"You have a dog?"

"A puppy, yeah. And a cat."

"Is the cat missing, too?"

"No. She's downstairs. I saw her hiding under the couch," she said automatically and walked to an alcove in her bedroom where a dormer window was wide open. "Escape route."

"Son of a bitch." He stood beside her and looked outside, where the dormer was attached to the roof. Sure enough the snow had been scraped away where, obviously, someone had slid to the edge, then probably swung from the branch of a nearby tree to land on the ground. Footsteps broke through the snow, then disappeared into the night and the tracks in the road.

O'Keefe didn't wait. In three steps, he was out of the bedroom and flying down the stairs. He wasn't about to give up the chase yet. Selena Alvarez or not. Through the open front door, he raced along the short drive to the street, where he hesitated under the street lamp. A pickup rolled past, a dog visible in the foggy window. He hailed the driver, who stopped on the ice and rolled down his window. Smoke from a dangling cigarette wedged into the corner of the driver's mouth curled out the window. From beneath the brim of a crumpled hat, the driver asked, "What can I do for ya?"

"You see a kid run by, a kid with a puppy?" O'Keefe glanced across the seat to the spot where the dog, a springer spaniel sat, head turned toward his master and the open window, its dark eyes assessing. Old dog. Not a pup.

"Nope." Three days of silvery beard shadow covered a jaw that was somewhere north of sixty. "You a cop?"

"Was," O'Keefe said.

"Well, I ain't seen anyone tonight. Whole damned town seems to have rolled up and called it a night."

That much was true. At least for this street, which was pretty much deserted.

"Thanks." He stepped away from the truck, but he did take a cursory glance at the bed, which was empty aside from a toolbox bolted behind the cab and a couple of shovels. The truck rolled away and he searched the street, looking down alleys and in the bushes that lined the yards of several homes along the street. Colored lights and garlands of cedar decorated doorways and eaves while, at one house, a snowman—missing an eye and covered in a fresh layer of frosting—stood guard near a walkway.

He didn't pay much attention, just checked all of the yards and fresh snow, looking for tracks only to come up empty. Down one side of the street and up the other, he searched, swearing under his breath, disbelieving that after three days, he'd actually lost the kid.

And it would be damned hard to find him with no phone with GPS, no car with plates, no credit cards, no friends in this town that he knew of, not one damned way to trace the kid here in Grizzly Falls. But he'd have to have money and find shelter and eat. Probably fast food.

He was jogging back to Alvarez's town house when he noticed a Jeep round the corner of the street and red and blue lights strobed the area.

Backup.

Finally.

About damned time.

CHAPTER 7

Alvarez finally let out her breath. She hoped she'd seemed cool and in command when deep down she'd been scared to death, sweating bullets. She'd nearly jumped out of her skin at the sight of a dark figure lurking by her garage; O'Keefe was lucky she hadn't shot him.

What the hell was he doing chasing some punk to her house? She'd called Pescoli, located Jane Doe and tried to piece together why some criminal would break into her house and steal her dog. For a few seconds she'd thought of the men she'd put away who had threatened her, insisted that they, when they got out of prison, would come back and haunt her.

"You made a big mistake, cunt," Junior Green had charged, pointing a thick finger at her, his near-bald head shiny with sweat and reflecting the lights of the courthouse after his conviction. "You hear me. I'm comin' back for you, just you wait!" She'd dismissed his threat as empty at the time, but when she'd thought of someone breaking into her place, he'd come to mind, no matter that O'Keefe had mentioned a kid named Reeve.

This was her home, damn it, she thought as she eyed the interior of the town house where a cold wind was blowing, and she dragged the slider door to the backyard closed. Why would the kid take her dog?

He didn't. Somehow Roscoe must've escaped in all of the hubbub, maybe even gone out the same upstairs window . . . except there were no paw prints in the snow on the roof and he would have been trapped in the backyard if he'd gone out the sliding door in the dining area . . .

"Okay, let me get this straight," Pescoli said to O'Keefe. She'd arrived after Alvarez had phoned her and Pescoli, along with O'Keefe, had returned to the house, where they now stood in the living room, not far from the front door. "You were chasing an underage armed robber who just happened to end up here and steal my partner's dog."

O'Keefe asked Pescoli, "You're her new partner?"

"Not so new," Pescoli said and shot Alvarez a questioning look.

"I don't know that he took the dog," O'Keefe replied, "but, yeah, the rest of it's essentially true. And what's worse, I lost the suspect. We need more officers to find the kid!"

"We'll see." Pescoli was obviously still trying to get a handle on what went down. "Why don't you start at the beginning? Who is this Reeve kid?" She was skewering him with green blue eyes that said more loudly than words, *And don't try to sell me any BS cuz I ain't buyin'.*

"Gabe is my cousin's son, but I don't know the kid all that well, have only met him a couple of times."

"But he's a criminal?" Pescoli pressed. "Or just a psycho dog snatcher?"

"He got in with a bad crowd. My cousin, Aggie, was worried sick, same with her husband. There was a robbery in Helena and the gun used in the crime was found in Gabe's backpack."

"How?" Alvarez asked, not following. "How did the police find it?"

"They didn't. David, Aggie's husband and Gabe's father, he found it and called the cops after he talked to his son. No one got all that excited until the cops realized that the gun was used in a robbery. No one was hurt, but a shot was fired and

104

lodged in the door frame. Turns out it was from the gun that Gabe had. Not registered. Probably bought on the street. Gabe had told his father he was keeping it for a friend."

Pescoli snorted.

"Yeah, that was bull, and after the cops left, Gabe snuck out and has been on the run ever since."

"Cops are looking for him?" Pescoli asked.

"Yeah."

"But you took it on yourself to chase him down."

"I wanted to talk to him first."

"He's not only an ex-cop and a PI, but he's got a law degree," Alvarez supplied.

"So whose side are you on?" Pescoli demanded.

"I want Gabe to turn himself in. With a lawyer."

"Meaning you?"

"Right. Doesn't mean I don't want to shake some sense into him."

"So," Pescoli said, "you're not a cop?"

"Working with someone in Helena."

"Who?" Pescoli's eyes narrowed.

"Detective Trey Williams."

"I can call him and confirm?" she asked.

"Yeah. Do that."

"I will," she said. "You haven't been deputized?"

"Officially? By the sheriff? No."

Apparently she didn't like his response. "A little loosey-goosey, isn't it?"

"I said I was working with the city."

"Strange how they do things over there, but we'll see. Now," she said, changing the subject again, "so what's the deal with Gabriel Reeve. You're his uncle . . . no wait. Your cousin's boy, right?"

"Yeah," O'Keefe said. "He's a pistol. The kid's always been trouble. Ever since they adopted him."

"He's not your cousin's?"

"Of course he is. That's not what I meant. All three of Aggie and Dave's kids are adopted. And, yeah, they are all definitely theirs. It's not a matter of blood. It's just that from the time they brought Gabe home, he was difficult. Harder than the other two. More strong willed."

"Yeah, I know about that," Pescoli said, obviously thinking about her own two kids. Pescoli's son, Jeremy, had already had several run-ins with the law.

"So you're involved because your cousin asked you to be and, oh, yeah, you wanted to help the boy out of a jam or something. Be his advocate or attorney or whatever, but—" Pescoli said, wagging a finger back and forth between Alvarez and O'Keefe. "You two know each other?"

"Worked together in San Bernardino," Alvarez said quickly. "Before I moved here."

One of Pescoli's eyebrows arched. "You were with the San Bernardino Sheriff's Department?" she asked O'Keefe.

106

"Yeah, I worked for the county." He gave a curt nod and his jaw tightened a bit. "A while back."

"That's right," Alvarez cut in and forced a smile she didn't feel while sending O'Keefe a quick, warning glance, cautioning him to keep his mouth shut. What had happened in California was a long time ago, a blemish on her career and the ruination of his. The fewer people who knew about it, the better.

"You don't look like a lawyer," Pescoli said and his mouth twitched.

"Left my three-piece suit in the truck." When she didn't crack a smile, he added, "Corporate law slash criminal law, didn't really take with me. I'm not the behind-a-desk kind of guy."

"Lots of money and lots of years in school to finally figure it out," she observed as her cell phone jangled. Frowning, she read the small screen, then her face lost some of its hard edges as she picked up. "Hey," she said into the phone, her voice a little softer than usual, indicating that Nate Santana or one of her kids was on the other end of the line. ". . . Yeah . . . No. At my partner's house. No. Just wrapping up something here. Mmm . . . about half an hour." She glanced up at Alvarez, who gave her a quick wave, silently advising her to leave. There was nothing more for Pescoli to do except dig a little deeper into Alvarez's private life and that was something Alvarez would prefer to avoid.

As she hung up, Alvarez said, "There's nothing more to do here, I guess."

And Pescoli, glancing around, nodded. "Nothing taken but the dog?"

"Nothing of value, except maybe around twenty bucks that I had in a top drawer by my bed. My computer, TV are all in place, I had my laptop and cell phone with me and I don't have any jewelry or silver that's worth much, though I can't find a hoop earring . . . one with a fake ruby in it. One my grandmother gave me years ago. I could have lost it, I suppose, and misplaced the cash, but I don't think so. Maybe a couple of other things are missing. I can't find my locket, one I had since high school but never wear, and a ring or two; stuff I haven't looked at in years. And a week or so ago, I noticed one of my silver stud earrings wasn't with the other one. I looked around, couldn't find it, but didn't think much about it. All of the stuff that I can't find, if you add it all together, isn't worth a hundred dollars, maybe not even fifty."

"Weird." Frowning, Pescoli gave O'Keefe the once-over, and asked, "So what's your story? I take it you're not on the force any longer."

"No story."

"You're a PI now."

"Uh-huh."

Her eyes narrowed. "As an ex-cop, you should know better. Leave chasing down suspects to the police." To Alvarez, she added, "I'll call the Helena PD. See what's up and let them know their suspect's been spotted here, chased down by a relative with a law degree, someone not in uniform. They're gonna love that."

"No doubt," he said as she zipped up her coat and headed outside, a blast of cold air in her wake, the front door nearly slamming behind her.

"Sweet, isn't she?" he observed.

"Cuddly as a porcupine."

"You two get along?"

"Yeah."

"Figures." He glanced around the living room with its smooth hardwood floors, muted rug and sleek modern furniture. Everything in white, black and tan. Only a splash of color in the art or throw pillows, one of which was deflated after suffering Roscoe's fury the morning before, all of the stuffing, batting and feathers long vacuumed away. She thought of Roscoe with his big, lolling tongue, bright eyes and enthusiasm for life. Damn, she already missed that miserable pup.

O'Keefe glanced at the stairway where wet tracks were visible on the carpet. "Why do you think Reeve ended up here?"

"Don't know. Dumb luck?" Jane Doe, who had been perched on one of the dinette chairs, plopped down and, with a dismissive glance at O'Keefe, trotted over to Alvarez, where she began walking in figure eights and rubbing against Alvarez's ankles.

"Maybe." He rubbed a hand over his jaw, his five o'clock shadow scraping beneath his fingers. "But he seemed to beeline here. From the pizza parlor on Grand."

"That's half a mile away."

"I know," he said. "I chased him. Reeve didn't hesitate for a second." O'Keefe walked to the sliding door and eyed it. "No forced entry."

"I must've forgotten to lock it when I let the dog out earlier," she said as she picked up the cat and held her close. Jane began to purr as Alvarez petted her soft head. "I usually double-check all the doors and windows before I leave, but I was in a hurry."

"Aren't you always?" he thought aloud and shook his head.

"I came back twice; once midday and then again after four because I knew I'd be working late, so I let him out, walked him around the complex, fed him and left. I guess . . . I guess I missed the latch."

Which was odd; but she had been out of sync all day.

O'Keefe said, "It seemed as if he were on some kind of mission, that he knew where he was going. He hitchhiked here from Helena. Why not keep going? Spokane? Or even farther west to Seattle, or down to Boise, some place bigger where he could get lost. If that's what he really wanted to do." His thick eyebrows pulled together as he worked it out. "Instead he runs directly to this complex, this damned unit." He pointed a finger at her floor. "Then he finds his way in?"

"And takes my dog."

"Possibly, but the dog could have gotten out." His jaw moved to one side as he thought. "It doesn't make a helluva lot of sense." He leaned down, eyeing the floor as if hoping for a boot print or some other evidence, and she tried not to notice how his jacket rode up, exposing a strip of skin over the waistband of a beat-up pair of Levi's. Then his gaze moved over the interior, as if he were the suspect and had just run inside, and all the while Alvarez's mind was turning over the information she'd just learned: runaway boy of about sixteen. Adopted. Who had run straight here.

Once more, Grace Perchant's weird warning sifted through her mind: *Your son needs you. He's in grave danger . . .*

She swallowed hard, petted the cat without thinking. Was it possible? Could the boy be hers? She knew nothing about the son she'd given up for adoption a lifetime ago. His age was right. And he had landed here.

Was it possible?

"I need to know more about Reeve," she heard herself saying as Jane scrambled from her hands and landed with a soft thud on the carpet.

"His rap sheet? There isn't much of one. He's still a juvenile."

"Yeah, but also, I need to know more about him personally. You said he was adopted. How?"

He lifted a shoulder. "Private adoption. Through an attorney that handles that kind of thing."

"Where?"

"Where did they find the attorney? Don't know. Probably Helena. Or . . . no. Wait!" He snapped his fingers. "They lived in Denver for a while, about the time they got Gabe and then the younger one, too." He straightened and his eyes, a flinty gray, bored into hers. "Why?"

"Just curious. You have a picture of him?" She wasn't going to confide in him about the baby she gave up; she could be wrong. Just because a woman who purportedly talked to ghosts warned her that her son was in danger, there was no reason to go off the deep end and divulge all of her secrets.

"Yeah." He flipped open his phone, hit a couple of buttons, then showed her the first of several shots of a boy with dark hair and eyes, his skin tanned, his features Hispanic. In several of the pictures, he was smiling, his teeth white and straight, but his eyes definitely suspicious. "Good-lookin' kid," he added, then showed her a picture of the family. Mom and dad, and three kids, two boys and a girl, stepping stones with Gabriel squarely in the middle.

Alvarez's heart beat a little faster, pounding in her ears. Could it be? There was some resemblance, right? Or was she imagining that the boy had a nose that was as straight as hers, that his eyes were as round . . . "Could you e-mail these to me?" she asked, her voice a little raspier than usual. She cleared her throat. "It might help."

"Sure."

She rattled off her e-mail address and he typed it in.

"Done," he said, then looked up. "You're white as a sheet."

"Am I?" She shrugged it off. "It's . . . it's been a long day." *And it's not over yet.* Glancing around the apartment, the images of the boy indelibly burned in her mind, she tried to change the subject. "There's nothing more here. I'm going to start looking for my dog. Just in case he escaped rather than was dognapped."

"I'll come with."

She wasn't certain that being around O'Keefe was a good idea, but she needed help finding Roscoe.

Together they scoured the neighborhood but found no sign of the dog. They knocked on doors and walked down alleys, eyeing carports and garbage cans, and located a raccoon on his nightly mission, his beady eyes daring Alvarez to come near the small pond where he'd broken a hole in the ice. Baring his teeth in warning, the raccoon stood his ground as she approached. Alvarez left the masked animal to its fishing and continued searching, to no avail.

They gave up an hour later and she put a call in to animal control and left a message with the local vets.

"Gabe's got him," O'Keefe said finally as she hung up. Once again they were standing in the front hallway at the base of the stairs, snow melting from their jackets to drip onto the tile floor. She unwound her scarf and hung it, along with her jacket, on the coat tree. "You want some coffee or something?" The last person she wanted to sit down and share a cup of joe with was Dylan O'Keefe, but the guy had just spent over an hour searching for her dog and, quite possibly, was on the trail of her runaway son, a boy she had tried for sixteen years not to think about.

He was about to decline, then thought better of it and yanked off his gloves. "Beer?"

She shook her head. "I only have coffee because it came in a Christmas basket. No wine either. And come to think of it, I'm fresh out of hot water, but I can heat some in the microwave."

Still surveying her living area, he said, "Coffee's fine," then asked, "You a teetotaler?"

She lifted a shoulder. "Just not interested."

"Into fitness," he observed, motioning to the free weights stacked in her bookcase along with police procedural manuals, medical texts and criminology books.

"Most of the time."

She walked into the kitchen and glanced at the empty pen where her dog had spent so many hours. Her heart ached and it wasn't just for Roscoe; no, that old painful hole in her heart, the one for her lost child, a rupture that had never completely scarred over, ripped a little more. Her hands shook a little as she found cups and the prepackaged holiday blend, then somehow managed to brew the coffee. "It's flavored," she said as she poured them each a cup. "My aunt thinks that makes it Christmasy. I don't have any creamer."

"I drink it black anyway." He'd pulled out a chair at the small glass table and she noticed that he'd aged in the past few years, but the lines around his eyes and the tiniest bit of silver in his coffee-colored hair made him seem only a little more interesting, adding to his rugged appeal.

Geez, she had to quit thinking that way.

"I'm going to have to file a report, along with Pescoli, so tell me more about the suspect."

"Not much to tell. I'm not close to him, nor really, my cousin. Aggie's a few years older than I am, her husband, Dave, is an accountant. They live outside of Helena. Aggie couldn't have kids so they adopted. The oldest, Leo, he's like a dream kid. Athlete, straight A's, already talking about

Stanford, and the youngest, Josie, she seems to be on the straight and narrow, too. But Gabe, square in the middle, he's been difficult from the get-go. A fussy baby. Colicky, I guess. In grade school he was an out-there kind of kid, a little rough around the edges with this chip on his shoulder. He got into some trouble in junior high, started running with the wrong crowd and had all the earmarks of a JD in the making. Just last year, in an effort to break him up from his friends, they forced him to go to a private school. I guess it backfired because he and his friends tried to rob a house, get this, of a judge, no less. The judge's daughter just happened to go to the same private school with Gabe. He, it appears, was the link to set up the crime."

"The mastermind?"

"Trust me, it was anything but masterful. Gabe's lucky he didn't get shot." He blew across his cup, took a sip and pulled a face. "Wow. Your aunt can really pick 'em."

"I warned you."

"I should have held out for a beer."

"You would've been holding out for a while."

"Not the first time," he said, his eyes finding hers before shifting away and an awkward silence ensued. "So, what's with your hot water?"

"I don't have any. I haven't been able to figure it out and the complex's handyman is MIA. Not unusual for Jon, let me tell you."

"Let me take a look."

She wasn't sure this was a good idea but was sick of being without hot water, so she led him first to the half bath downstairs, where he tested the water, and then did the same upstairs.

Alvarez felt her stomach tighten as he stepped into her bathroom and turned on the shower, feeling the spray, reminding her of another time and place that she had locked away in a forbidden part of her mind. She felt it then, that he, too, remembered that night, and the air in the small bathroom seemed suddenly heavy.

"Okay. Where's the tank?"

"Under the stairs." They made their way to the first floor, where he walked to the closet tucked beneath the staircase and snapped on the overhead light.

As she stood in the hallway behind him, he eyed the settings, then frowned and shook his head. He checked switches and gauges and finally shrugged. "You're right, you need a hot-water guy."

"So much for your plumbing skills," she said.

"Yeah," he admitted with a chuckle. "They're pretty limited."

O'Keefe stepped out of the closet, his hair slightly mussed, and she remembered what it had been like to lie in his bed, to hold him close, to fantasize. She'd thought, with him, she could finally let go.

She'd been wrong.

Almost fatally so.

She found him staring at her, as if he could read her mind. Which was ridiculous. Of course.

Back in the kitchen, she cleared her throat and removed the cups from the table, dropping them into the sink. "Look, I want you to know that I'm sorry about what happened in San Bernardino. My mistake."

"Forget it." He was already zipping his jacket. "Water under the bridge." But his features had hardened once more and she only hoped she wouldn't have to deal with him again. Theirs had been a complicated and hard-edged relationship, filled with raw emotion, denied sexual chemistry and a battle of wills. Neither had been able to give an inch and it had blown up in their faces.

She didn't mind that he was leaving.

In fact, she was glad.

But when the door closed hard behind him, she actually second-guessed herself.

And she hated that.

CHAPTER 8

Dylan O'Keefe, here, in Grizzly Falls?

What were the chances?

Alvarez had thought that when she'd left the force in San Bernardino County, she'd never lay eyes upon him or hear his name again. At least that's what she'd hoped. It was surreal that he'd shown up here, searching for a runaway delinquent who could be the son she'd given up as a teenager herself.

Now as she rinsed out their coffee cups and tried not to notice how empty the house felt without Roscoe, she wouldn't allow herself to dwell on O'Keefe. But she did open the e-mail O'Keefe had sent her and print out the pictures of the boy who could be her own flesh and blood. Again, she studied his features in minute detail, searching for any telltale hint of resemblance to her or anyone in her family. "Who are you?" she whispered, her heart heavy, old pain suddenly raw. Determined to stay as clearheaded as possible, she reined in her galloping emotions and attempted to think logically. She wasn't going to allow herself the luxury of falling into a million pieces. No way would she allow her personal involvement to cloud her judgment. She e-mailed a detective she knew with the Helena PD and asked about Gabriel Reeve and the crime for which he was sought.

Now that she'd been dragged into this mess, she couldn't just turn her back on it, no matter how painful the truth might be. Nor could she avoid O'Keefe, even though she wanted to avoid him. Big time. Things between them had never been good and now . . . Well, she wouldn't even go there. *You'll have to see him again. Like it or not. And Gabe, now that you know he could be your son, you'll have to find out.*

A part of her cracked inside. For so long, she'd stuffed down all her emotions about the child, the infant who had been the innocent in the horror that had been a part of her life when she'd been a teenager herself. "God help me," she whispered, though her faith in a higher being had been destroyed years before. A woman of science, she had denied her Catholic upbringing, refused to enter a church, never sought counsel with a priest, but all of that might be about to change.

Upset, she grabbed her jacket, badge, keys and cell phone and decided to look again for her dog. She'd walk along the jogging path they always took, hoping that he'd strayed onto a familiar trail, but as she half jogged through the night, feeling the depth of the cold in her soul, she knew she wouldn't find him, just as surely as she knew her life, tonight, had been changed forever.

Pescoli hated decorating the Christmas tree. Well, at least she hated decorating it alone. She mentally kicked herself from one side of the state to the other for not going over to Santana's place tonight. Instead, she was here, with Cisco, looking at some of the ornaments she'd decided to save and wondering what had possessed her.

From the looks of it, mice or rats or God knew what else had gotten into some of her favorite ornaments, so the snowflake Bianca had constructed in the fourth grade had frayed and the already-painted, cracked eggshell with Jeremy's first-grade picture had been crushed to dust. "Time to move on," she told herself and considered phoning Santana, asking him over, then discarded the idea. For now. She looked at the faded ornament that said, "Baby's first Christmas," painted with teddy bears wearing Santa's hat and inscribed with Jeremy's name and the year of his birth. Remembering how she and Joe together had placed the ornament on a low branch and taken a picture of their cuddly baby boy dressed in red beneath the tree caused her throat to clog. Jeremy had gazed up at the shiny ornaments and winking lights with wonder.

Where had the time gone?

Now, it was all she could do to keep him in college, working and out of trouble. Tall and strapping, Jeremy was the spitting image of his father. And tonight, she had no idea where he was, but she was giving him his space, because he was over eighteen, even if he was still living under her roof.

As for Bianca, she was out Christmas shopping with friends and wasn't expected to return for another hour.

"Just you and me, huh?" she asked the dog.

Her thoughts strayed to Jeremy's father, Joe Strand, a decorated cop, and a halfhearted husband. No matter what fantasies Jeremy and she had concocted, the truth was that had Joe lived, he and Regan would probably have divorced. They'd been heading down that slippery slope before a bullet had put an end to his life and any chance that they'd find the elusive and perhaps nonexistent happy ending.

Clearing her throat, she hung the silly little ornament on the tree and again told herself to get a life. The kids were nearly grown.

But not quite.

She wasn't usually a nostalgic person, but the holidays always brought out the worst in her.

As if sensing she needed to be cheered up, the dog barked sharply, front feet lifting off the floor in his enthusiasm. "Yeah, I know. Stupid, huh? Hey, look what I've got." Tail wagging frantically, he trotted after her to an overstuffed pantry, where on the top shelf she found a nearly empty box of doggie biscuits for Cisco. With an excited yip, he danced for the treat and Pescoli felt better.

"Good boy," she said and wondered where the little elf suit Bianca had bought him had ended up just as her cell phone jangled from somewhere nearby. On the second muted ring, she found the phone in the pocket of the jacket she'd slung over the back of one of the kitchen chairs.

Glancing at the screen as she answered, she recognized the number of the station. "Pescoli," she said but was already pushing an arm through the sleeve of her jacket. If someone from the sheriff's department was calling after nine at night, it just wasn't going to be good news.

Noni in dispatch was on the line. "Got a call from Trilby," she said when Pescoli answered. Trilby Van Droz was one of the department's road deputies. "She received a call for an abandoned vehicle found by the driver of a snow plow for Long Logging. Up on a logging spur off East Juniper Lake Road. Van Droz checked to make sure no one was inside and scraped off the plates to run them. The 1995 Toyota Camry is registered to Lara Sue Gilfry. Van Droz thought you'd be interested."

"I am," Pescoli said, all of her melancholy for Christmas temporarily shelved as she found her boots. "And I don't want the car moved. Yet. Not until I get up there."

"I'll let her know."

Adrenaline firing her blood, Pescoli laced her boots, then jammed her hands into gloves, grabbed her sidearm and headed for the garage. She'd call Alvarez on the way.

"So what do you know?" Alvarez asked as she climbed into Pescoli's Jeep and strapped in. Pescoli was already backing out of the driveway, snow spraying from under the tires.

"Not much. I did talk to Trilby, she was first on

the scene and she says there's no sign of foul play, but then there's nearly a foot of snow on the vehicle. Until it's towed to the garage and the crime scene guys go over it, who knows?"

Ramming the car into drive on the street, she added, "Car's definitely registered to Lara Gilfry and she's not around. Trilby popped the trunk, thinking she might find a dead body, but nothing back there but the spare, some tools and a case of old CDs."

"What about her purse? Cell phone?"

"Nothing personal found in the car."

"Not good," Alvarez said.

"You got that right. Hey, you find your dog?"

"Not yet."

Pescoli frowned into the night, squinting against a few headlights shining their way. "So what's with you and O'Keefe? You two have a thing when you were with San Bernardino?"

"What?" Alvarez said, then realized she reacted too quickly. "Just the opposite. We didn't get along."

"He's hot as hell."

"If you like that whole rugged-around-the-edges thing."

"Who doesn't?"

"Me."

"I think he's interested in you."

"Shows you what kind of detective you are," Alvarez said, glancing out the window as they passed a convenience store, windows painted with holiday reindeer while signs for cigarettes and beer glowed on the same panes. A couple of teenagers were outside, sipping from big drinks, smoking cigarettes and clutching skateboards that couldn't possibly work with all the snow and ice, at least not in Alvarez's estimation.

"I'm tellin' ya, the man likes you."

"So what're you now? An authority on romance?"

"Me?" She snorted. "Not hardly. But I recognize the signs when a man is into you."

"Oh, save me."

"Seriously."

Alvarez didn't respond.

"Now who's the liar?" Pescoli threw back at her as Alvarez glared out the window.

"Just drive."

The town, with its neon lights reflecting on the snow, disappeared behind them as Pescoli drove through the outskirts, the beams of her headlights cutting through the night as the houses thinned. No longer was snow falling, but darkness seemed held at bay, with the blanket of white that covered the surrounding fields and drifted against fence posts. Traffic was light, only a few cars meeting them as they turned onto the county road that wound into the foothills.

"Just tell me Ivor Hicks didn't find the car."

"Not this time." Chuckling, Pescoli eased the Jeep through an open gate and onto a private road owned by the Long Logging Company. The road had been plowed here, a hedge of scraped snow lining the edges of the road, a fresh, thinner layer of snow covering the gravel. "And, thankfully, Grace Perchant isn't wandering through the woods with her damned wolf-dogs tonight. Or at least I didn't hear about either of them."

"Good." Alvarez didn't want to think about Grace and her uncanny prediction. In a way, she was relieved to have her attention turned to this case and away from Dylan O'Keefe and Gabriel Reeve. For one of the few times in her adult life, Alvarez was at a loss. She'd always known that, once her son reached the age of eighteen or older, she might get a knock on the door, a phone call or even an e-mail or text from a stranger introducing himself as her long-lost son. She was even prepared for a PI coming to her door, but she never expected her house to be ravaged, her dog to be stolen, her life thrown out of kilter before the boy had reached his eighteenth birthday.

She'd been a fool.

And now her son was in trouble. Serious trouble.

Hold on there, okay? You're not even sure this boy is yours.

Alvarez wasn't a betting woman, didn't play the odds, but even she could see that Gabriel Reeve breaking into her house wasn't pure coincidence.

And now O'Keefe was involved. God, what a

mess. Who would have thought that she, a boy suspected to be her son and Dylan O'Keefe would be wound together with the same old emotionally fraying cord?

"Here we go!" Pescoli said as pulsing blue and red lights came into view. Bright beams from Van Droz's county vehicle cut through the thickets of trees, adding an eerie, otherworldly effect to the already disturbing night. A huge snow plow was at rest nearby, idling so that the driver in the machine's cab didn't freeze. Nearby was the car in question, scraped free of snow along the windows and trunk.

They parked, took the driver's statement, then shined their flashlights into the car, disturbing nothing, hoping that once the vehicle was towed to the garage, the crime scene techs would find some trace evidence to help them determine what had happened to Lara Gilfry.

Pescoli's cell phone hummed and she picked up, reading a quick text and fuming. "No," she said as she typed the short word, then turned the phone off. "Bianca wants to spend the night with Amber tomorrow night." She looked into the abandoned car one last time. "I don't think so. There is school tomorrow. Kids!" Turning her attention back to the car, she said, "Gone without a trace. What the hell is going on?"

"I guess we'll have to figure that out." Alvarez didn't like it. In the past three years, the peaceful little town of Grizzly Falls had been rocked by sick predators, all of whom had emerged with the snowfall to terrorize the citizens.

Could it possibly be happening again?

Or could the missing women have their own individual reasons for abandoning their vehicles and disappearing into thin air?

Lara Sue Gilfry.

Lissa Parsons.

Brenda Sutherland.

What were the chances that they all just up and took off without a word to anyone, without a trace, to disappear?

Not likely.

Even with the stress of the holidays.

In Alvarez's heart of hearts, she knew: Grizzly Falls was being terrorized again, a new monster emerging.

But if so, where the hell were the victims?

"You have to let me go," Brenda begged of the maniac who held her in this . . . this freezing cave located God only knew where; probably in the foothills surrounding Grizzly Falls, but she wasn't certain. She heard the sound of water dripping over some piped-in music and the area smelled wet. She was in a cage of sorts, with a cot and a sleeping bag and a bucket she was to use as a latrine and iron bars holding her in. The cave had sheer rock walls and an uneven stone floor and was lit by battery-powered lanterns, some mounted high, others placed along the floor. Partitions had been constructed, making individual "rooms," and she had the feeling she and the monster weren't alone, that he had either other victims, or, worse yet, a silent accomplice.

Ray?

No, Ray wouldn't get his hands dirty, but he knew enough lowlifes that he might have been able to connect with a psycho and offer him a deal.

Oh, dear Lord.

All she knew was that her chances of getting out of here alive were slim. She thought of her boys and her heart curdled. Where were they? Did they think she was dead already? Were they with Ray? Cameron was already talking about joining the navy when he graduated and Ray was fine with that, though Brenda had a few reservations, and Drew . . . he was so young, anticipating getting his driver's license and struggling in school. He needed her. They *both* needed her!

And Ray wasn't a good replacement.

He'd been a lousy husband and not a much better father. Sure, he'd shown the boys how to shoot a rifle, hunt and gut a deer and keep meticulous care of his tools, but that's about as far as his daddy skills went. He'd feed them crappy fast food and would have trouble getting them to school on time. Their clothes would be unwashed, and when he was gone, long-haul trucking, where would they land? At his druggie sister's house or left alone to their own teenaged devices?

The more she considered it, the more convinced she was he was behind her abduction.

She hated to think so little of him, a man she'd once purported to love, that he would do anything so vile, but Ray was known for his temper and holding grudges. She'd seen firsthand how cruel he could be, felt not only the slice of his sharp tongue but the pain of the back of his hand a time or two.

He could certainly have paid to have her removed, though she didn't give him credit for orchestrating the abduction; that took an organized, cold calculation, brains Ray didn't have.

But he would have done anything to best her.

This time, she shivered from the inside out as she stared up at her abductor.

"I . . . I'll do anything, pay anything, you just, please, have to let me go," she said through chattering teeth as the monster eyed her casually and kept on humming some inane Christmas carol that she couldn't, for the life of her, name right now. She knew she'd been drugged somehow, and from the way she was groggy or dozing all the time, she figured it was a sleeping aid of some kind. Mostly she was grateful for the mind-numbing fogginess and slumber because it kept the biting cold at bay, but in the few lucid moments she had, the brief minutes she was awake, the fear for her life collided with her concern for her sons and she was wired, jangled, shivering and crying and begging for mercy.

There was none.

He would come again.

Force her to drink the disgusting-tasting tea and she would slip into that dreamlike state between wakefulness and slumber and be grateful for the relief.

On her knees, her eyes closed, she began to pray. *Dear Father, save me . . . Have mercy on me . . .*

But in this semidark tomb with the whisper of "Winter Wonderland" slipping through these caverns, she knew that she was alone and she feared that God couldn't hear her prayers.

Of course he can. He's omnipresent. Have faith.

Her grandmother's words echoed through her mind and she remembered learning the twenty-third Psalm as Nana had read it from the old family Bible.

Out loud, she whispered, "The Lord is my shepherd . . ."

Why had she trusted the man at the side of the road?

Why did she believe that his car was stranded, that she was playing the part of the Good Samaritan?

Why did she trust him to reach into her car to use her cell phone?

The attack, the minute she rolled down the window and turned to reach for the phone, extracting it from her purse, had happened swiftly. Viciously. One second she was holding the phone, the next she was experiencing the jolting pain of a stun gun.

It had all happened so fast and so close to her house.

Now, thinking about it, tears ran down her face as she mumbled the words her Nana had insisted she memorize.

"I shall not want . . ."

The words rattled through her mind and she tried to find her faith, but deep in her heart, she knew she was doomed.

CHAPTER 9

O'Keefe threw his keys on the scarred night table situated between the two beds at the dive of a motel he'd called home for the past twenty-four hours. After kicking off his boots, he placed his Glock into the drawer, the butt nuzzling up against Gideon's Bible, made certain the door was locked and bolted, then stripped and headed for the bathroom, which was small enough that he could touch both walls. The tub/shower was clean enough, aside from a rust stain near the drain that looked as if it had been with the unit since before the Berlin Wall came down.

He didn't care, was just thankful for the harsh spray of hot water against his skin. He was still reeling from coming across Selena Alvarez again. Then there was the fact that she wasn't telling everything she knew about Gabriel Reeve; O'Keefe sensed it.

He doused his head under the spray, lathered up and tried not to think about another shower in another time and place. God, that had turned out to be a mess. He and Alvarez were wedged into his tight stall, wet tiles at his back, her warm tongue in his mouth, water cascading over both their naked, slick bodies. Her waist had been tiny, her abdomen flat, her mouth suggesting the deepest of erotic pleasures. They'd gone to dinner to discuss the case that was about to break, had a couple of drinks and one thing had led to another, so they'd ended up there, their clothes strung through the adjoining bedroom.

His blood had been pounding through his head. Hot. Hungry. The ache within him huge as he'd sudsed her smooth skin. Her breasts had been full and large, with big, dark nipples against bronzed skin with only the hint of a tan line showing where she'd once worn a bikini bra in the sun.

He'd suckled one of those incredible breasts,

then the other, feeling her spine arch against his splayed fingers as he'd held her close, taking more of her into his mouth, the heat throbbing between them.

She'd moaned in sheer ecstasy, her fingernails digging into his hair, one smooth slim leg coiling around his. It had been the singular most erotic moment of his life, and when her mouth—wet, luscious, lips a deep coral, white teeth flashing—had moved against his, he couldn't help pressing his erection hard against her.

Never had he wanted a woman so desperately; he, who had always been in charge, who had held back when he'd wanted to, had felt, with this woman, as if he'd had no will. Still kissing her, the steam of the shower billowing around him, he'd lifted her up, his hands cupping her buttocks, his intent to settle her onto his engorged cock, but she'd snapped. As quickly as if he'd poured a bucket of cold water over her, she'd lifted her head, looked deep into his eyes and said, "No! I—I can't do this. I'm sorry. Oh, God, I'm so, so sorry!" and she'd slipped away from him, scrambling out of the stall, pushing the glass door so hard it had banged against the surrounding tiles. Snagging a towel from the bar, she'd raced into his bedroom, leaving a puddling trail of water behind her.

"Selena? Wait!"

"I can't . . . I just can't," she was still saying as

he walked into the bedroom and she was struggling into a pair of jeans.

"Don't go."

"Why? So we can 'talk' about this?" she'd flung back at him, pausing to make air quotes with her fingers. "There's . . . nothing to say. I just can't do this, okay?" She'd pulled on her yellow T-shirt, her nipples hard against the thin fabric. Tears had been filling her dark eyes, and he noticed, oddly, that one of her hoop earrings had caught the light from a bedside lamp, glittering seductively from within the black, wet strands of her hair. "I'm . . ." She looked at him, one tear tracking, and said, ". . . really sorry." Then she'd angrily swiped the tear away, zipped up her jeans and, carrying her shoes, bra and panties, ran out of the bedroom, her bare feet slapping on the tiled stairs.

He'd been standing in the bedroom, so he crossed to the arched window with its small deck overlooking the parking area. Just after he heard the front door slam, she appeared, racing to her car, not so much as casting a glance up at him before climbing into the Honda and screeching out of the lot. He'd watched as her taillights disappeared into the stream of traffic of the main road cutting through this section of San Bernardino and then, speechless, he'd walked into the bathroom again, stepped into the still-running shower and turned the temperature dial far to the right, intent on taking the coldest shower of his life.

Now, under the needle-sharp spray of the dive of a motel, he realized just thinking about that night and Selena Alvarez had again caused an erection.

"Oh, hell," he muttered and, bracing himself, turned the water mixer from warm to cold.

Pescoli was right, Alvarez thought as she stepped through her front door, she *was* a liar. Not only to her partner, but to herself.

Alvarez *had* been involved with O'Keefe, though not as sexually as Pescoli was intimating. And then all hell had broken loose. God, what a mess.

She remembered not being able to eat or sleep, her emotions strung like tight barbed wire, prickly and tense, and then the mistake, stepping in the line of fire, hearing her name at the last minute before a trigger was pulled and lives were changed forever.

It's your fault. The same old accusation, one she'd tried to bury for years, rang through her mind. If only she hadn't been so emotionally strung out, if only she'd thought before she'd reacted, if only she'd stayed in control, like she'd taught herself, maybe things would be different.

Too late! Now, her involvement with O'Keefe and the resulting debacle was going to all replay again and blow up in her face! She could feel it in her bones. Which only made a difficult situation worse. She yanked the door shut behind her and latched it. It seemed as if her entire, well-organized life was splintering into a million sharp pieces, each one determined to slice her emotions.

"Pull yourself together!" As she snapped on the hall light and shrugged out of her jacket, Jane Doe appeared, trotting to greet her, white whiskers almost comical against her black coat. "Hey, girl," Alvarez said, picking up the cat, whose bones seemed to melt as she lifted the small furry body. "You miss Roscoe?" Scratching the cat behind its ears, she listened to Jane's motor start to run in a deep purr. "Yeah, me, too. Silly, isn't it?" She'd had the exuberant puppy only a few months and yet he'd managed to burrow his way into her heart.

She checked her phone for the twentieth time, half expecting that she'd hear from someone who had found her dog and located her number on his tag, or even from O'Keefe with more information on Gabriel Reeve, but there were no messages and the rooms seemed cold and empty, even though she hit the switch for the gas fireplace and snapped on several lights.

Roscoe's empty pen seemed to mock her and it was all she could do to pick up his water bowl, discard whatever liquid was inside and rinse it out.

He'll be back.

She hoped.

And what about Gabriel Reeve? Her heart twisted; she'd have to find anything she could about him. Could he be her son? If so, why had he run here? If not, what kind of coincidence was it that he'd broken into her home?

There had to be some kind of connection and she was damned sure she was going to find out what it was. She spent the next hour on the Internet, reading about crimes in Helena, finding one where a home had been broken into, a firearm used, one of the assailants who was underage having escaped.

It had to be Reeve.

She checked, found no other incidents and made a mental note to recheck with Helena PD in the morning.

And when you find out the truth, what then? What if Gabe is your son?

The thought of meeting the boy she'd given up, of dealing with his birth and the circumstances of his conception, caused her insides to twist, her head to pound. Old memories assailed her and she fought them back, as she had for nearly seventeen years. She couldn't go there, wouldn't. Not until she found out if Gabriel Reeve was really her own flesh and blood.

And what about Dylan O'Keefe?

Another wrench to her guts and she made her

way to the bathroom, where she stopped at the sink and threw cold water—the only temperature she had—onto her face. "Pull yourself together," she told the woman staring back at her, the woman whose face was pale and whose eyes were haunted by demons from her youth. "You can't fall apart. That's not you!" But the woman in the reflection didn't seem convinced. "You need to be in control." And that was it, the problem in a nutshell; Alvarez liked things neat and tidy, everything in its place, and the mess that had been her youth had no place in her life right now.

No place.

She had too much to do.

For starters, she had a case to solve. Make that three cases, because she was ninety-nine percent certain that Lara Sue Gilfry, Lissa Parsons and Brenda Sutherland had met with the same dire fate.

As she got ready for bed, yanking off her clothes and tossing them into the hamper, Alvarez forced her thoughts away from her own problems, at least for now, and thought about the women who were missing. What the hell had happened to them?

She'd concentrate on those three tonight; only later, when the moon was high in the Montana sky, would she dare let her mind wander to that dark place she'd promised herself she'd never visit again.

Despite it all, as she closed her eyes, she knew that her life was unraveling, emotional stitch by stitch.

Calvin Mullins couldn't sleep.

The readout on Lorraine's digital clock shined a bright hellfire three forty-seven. Too early, for even his standards. Though he prided himself on rising early, on spending an hour in prayer and another twenty minutes with his journal before finally spending another forty minutes on the elliptical machine one of the parishioners had donated to the parsonage, he tried to always stay in bed until four thirty. But in these wee morning hours, when so much was happening within his parish, he threw off the covers, slid into the slippers he kept at his bedside and walked quietly down the hallway. He'd been disturbed ever since the interview with Detective Pescoli and hadn't been able to shake the feeling that things were going to get worse for him. Perhaps he could talk to the detective, impress upon her how his private life had to remain so . . .

He'd spent hours in prayer and searching his soul, but the fear of exposure was a pawn of Lucifer, and recently, with all this trouble about Brenda Sutherland, he couldn't find strength or serenity in his talks with God.

Perhaps today would be better. He changed out of his pajamas and into his exercise gear. He'd stretch, climb on the elliptical machine so that he could work out the kinks in Sunday's sermon as he worked out the knots in his muscles. Perfect! The preacher never felt better than when he was multitasking, especially when part of the tasks were God's work.

First, he'd walk to the office to pick up the pages he'd already printed and edited carefully by hand, then cleanse his mind and soul in prayer and contemplation before hopping on the machine and cranking up the resistance. Some martyrs went in for flogging or self-mutilation; Preacher Mullins figured exercise machines, if used properly, would suffice in sacrificing his flesh for the Lord. The elliptical training machine, paired with intense prayer and maybe fasting for good measure could, in these modern times, be considered a way to "sweat it out" for God, or something. He might have to do a little tongue-in-cheek sermon about what one could do in the service of the Lord; it would be a joke, of course, that could carry into the heavier text of the message.

Still mulling his new idea over, he threw on his jacket, gloves and stocking cap on his way out the back door. Outside, the night was still, aside from a slight breeze. No snow fell for the first time in hours and a silvery disc of a moon was surrounded by crystal stars flung into the dark night sky.

These predawn hours were much like, he supposed, the clarity and calm of the night of

Christ's birth. He even searched the sky for the star of Bethlehem that the Magi followed.

Mullins's heart opened a little and his fears abated as he contemplated the magic and mystery of the Christ child's birth. Here, in God's showcase, alone in the outdoors, he found his true spirit, his communion with the Father.

From the breezeway connecting the parsonage with the church, he glanced at the crèche and then stood in awe of the snow-shrouded figures.

Carefully placed lamps illuminated the snow-covered nativity scene where the Christ child lay in the manger Mullins himself had fashioned years ago. Mary and Joseph leaned over their precious newborn. An ox's and donkey's head were visible over stall doors positioned behind the manger.

It truly was a work of art.

Something was off though. He broke a trail in the fresh snow to adjust the spotlight on Mary to make certain that her poignant smile was visible from the road. Then he looked again at the scene to make sure everything was perfect. It seemed so; the shepherd carrying a lamb hadn't fallen and the three kings, wise men seeking to give the savior gifts, approached, all covered in snow, all piously . . . wait a second.

Why were there *four* kings?

He blinked. Looked again. Counted softly, his breath clouding: "Gaspar . . . Balthasar . . .

Melchior . . . and a *fourth?*" One without draping robes or a crown or a gift held in extended hands. No, the fourth figure, covered in snow, seemed more like a modern-day Frosty the Snowman.

Probably some kid's idea of a prank.

"Great," he muttered, trudging through the snow, disturbing the perfection of the scene. And, yes, he saw impressions where someone else had been here, though the tracks were softened with a three-inch layer of snow. So whoever committed this sacrilege had done it hours before.

Wait a second. The figure, partially obscured with a frosting of snow, was definitely female. Seriously? And he could see ice beneath the snow. A sculpture. Blasphemy! That's what this marring of the nativity scene was. Was the sculpture of a woman intended to be some kind of political statement, some ultraliberal nonbeliever's way of pointing out that the only woman in the crèche was the blessed Virgin Mary? Or was it, perhaps, something worse?

At least he found it before morning light, or rush hour, if that's what you could call it here in Grizzly Falls. At least school buses wouldn't stop at the corner where the children inside looking out the windows might see the obvious mistake.

Or perhaps this was something much worse. Could it be that someone knew what had happened in Tucson and was sending him a personal and humiliating message? Someone who wanted to embarrass him? Cecil Whitcomb, Peri's father? He'd never been satisfied with Mullins's slap on the wrist. Could he have traveled all the way north to Grizzly Falls for retribution? Cecil had wanted, no, make that demanded, Calvin's resignation from the clergy and, as furious as he was, Cecil wouldn't have been satisfied with a public flogging.

Nonetheless, he couldn't afford a breath of scandal to whisper through this parish, so he had to get rid of the offensive statue or whatever it was. Using his gloved hand, he tried to dismantle the thing, but it was rock solid. Heavy. "Come on, come on," he whispered, brushing the snow from the thing's "head" with his gloved hand. Sure enough, it was an ice sculpture, the features definitely feminine, but in the darkness, it was difficult to see.

Taking the time to adjust one of the spotlights so it was easier to work, Preacher Mullins returned to the crèche and the offensive piece of "art." Something was very off about this . . . It was more than a prank. With mounting dread, his innards tightening with a dark, new fear, he carefully brushed more snow away to stare deeper into the face of the sculpture and his own heart turned to ice.

Inside the thick ice, he stared into the wide blue eyes of a very dead and frozen woman.

CHAPTER 10

Pescoli's jaw hardened as she shined her flashlight into the face of the dead woman, a face distorted by an inch or so of ice. "What the hell is this?" she whispered, wondering at who would place a dead woman, naked and encased in ice, in the middle of a nativity scene at a church. Her red hair fell to her shoulders, her skin so white as to be translucent. All trapped in a thick, molded layer of ice.

The entire area was roped off with crime scene tape, and the techs were going over the churchyard, looking for trace evidence in the snow. Preacher Mullins, who'd made the 911 call, was huddled under the overhang of a breezeway linking the parsonage with the church, and his wife, white-faced and shaken, stood at his side. Police vehicles were parked on the street and the road had been blocked, traffic diverted.

From an upstairs window of the two-storied Victorian parsonage, the silhouettes of three girls and another woman, someone from the church no doubt, were staring at the activity. Every once in a while, Lorraine Mullins glanced over her shoulder and shook her head, indicating her children were to be spared this horror, but as often as the children were shooed away from the window, they returned, fascinated.

Alvarez exhaled a pent up breath as she checked in with the officer in charge. A news van had rumbled up and parked near the road block at the end of the street. Traffic slowed to a standstill as it passed and bystanders were collecting in groups.

"I think we just found Lara Sue Gilfry."

"Really?" Alvarez studied the ice-encased woman. "Who would do this?"

"Don't know, but I'd think the case is ours, as the church is just outside the city limits."

Lips tight, Alvarez stared at the weird sculpture and Pescoli filled her in on the details, how the preacher getting ready for his early-morning regimen had stumbled upon an anomaly in the crèche that he'd personally built and obviously took pride in setting up year after year. Neither he nor his wife, nor, they were certain, any of their children had heard the noise that had to have surrounded the placement of the ice sculpture.

"Looks like it was dragged here," Pescoli said, showing the trough in the snow that wound from the church's lot to the front of the crèche. They were hoping for a footprint that would show the tread of a boot or shoe, or a tire track but so far hadn't found anything.

Alvarez shined her own flashlight over the single track that was covered in snow. Shaking her head, she said, "I don't get it."

"Who does?"

"What does the preacher say?"

" 'Hide that blasphemy! Get it out of here! It's a slap in the face of the church! The good citizens of Grizzly Falls don't need to see anything so vile! Not here in God's house!' Or something close."

"Seems like you were quoting him."

"Paraphrasing. But he's not happy."

"Who would be?"

Pescoli glanced from the weird ice sculpture to Mullins's worried face and said more calmly, "Yeah, I know, but I think there's more to it than that."

"Like what?"

"Don't know. Yet." Her eyes narrowed a fraction. "But I intend to find out."

Together they interviewed Mullins. He was angry, ranting and railing about the audacity of the act, while his wife, Lorraine, appeared shell-shocked as they sat on benches in the vestibule of the church. Though warmer than outside, the foyer of the old church was still chilly. Mullins, calming slightly, said that he'd had trouble sleeping, had decided to work out and tweak his sermon. On the way to his office he'd discovered the body. He'd been pretty clear on the time, four in the morning, give or take a minute or two.

It was now after seven and, through a tracery window, Pescoli noticed that it was still dark as midnight.

Neither the preacher nor his wife knew of anyone who would do such a horrid thing; none of the parishioners were disgruntled, that they knew of, nor did the church have any enemies.

They seemed sincere, and yet, there was something about the way the wife kept her head lowered and had trouble meeting Pescoli's gaze. Could it be that the preacher beat his wife? Or was that just too obvious?

"You'll be taking that poor woman away soon," Mullins said, and it sounded more like a demand than a request.

"As soon as we figure out how to do it." They wanted to move the ice intact so as not to lose any bit of evidence that might have been trapped in the frozen water. Melting was an issue.

"It's grotesque," Lorraine finally said. Seated next to her husband, bundled in jacket, gloves, ski pants and boots, she shuddered. "Who would do such a thing? And why?"

"That's what we're trying to find out. What can you tell us?" Alvarez asked.

"I heard nothing. I was in bed all night, and I looked out our bedroom window a little after ten, I think." She glanced at her husband for confirmation. "Just after we prayed together."

"Ten fifteen, maybe ten thirty. I remember turning out the light after reading and seeing the clock at ten fifty."

"Okay," Lorraine agreed. "And I remember

looking at the crèche. It's something we take pride in. Calvin did most of the construction himself. I don't recall seeing anything out of the ordinary, no extra figure. It was snowing, of course, but the lights were focused on the scene and it was as it should be. Calming. Serene. Something I love." Her throat caught.

"And you fell asleep right after you looked out the window?"

"I have three daughters," Lorraine said, as if that explained it.

"And she's expecting," her husband chimed in proudly.

Maybe that explained the dark circles under Lorraine's eyes, but Pescoli wasn't completely convinced. Something was off here in this cold church foyer with its dimmed lights and feeling of hidden secrets.

The preacher offered, "I was asleep before my head hit the pillow."

They reaffirmed that they'd heard nothing all night long. "I even, uh, went to the bathroom," Lorraine admitted. "I don't know what time it was, but I didn't hear anything or look out the window. I, um, I kind of don't even really wake up." Lines creased her smooth forehead. "Who is the woman—the victim?"

"No positive ID yet," Pescoli said. "But we think she may have been one of three women who've disappeared lately. Possibly a woman named Lara Sue Gilfry. Did you know her?"

"Gilfry? No." Lorraine was shaking her head slowly, as was her husband.

"No," he said certainly as he grabbed his wife's gloved hand and laced his fingers through hers. "Never."

"She worked over at the Bull and Bear. It's a bed-and-breakfast in town."

"Never heard of it," Lorraine said as she stared at the floor, watching a spider as it scurried quickly beneath the bench.

"No. I'm . . . I'm sure I never met her." The preacher removed his stocking cap with his free hand, his dishwater blond hair spiking up. Without thinking, almost frantically, he smoothed it.

"So she wasn't a member of your church?" Alvarez asked.

Mullins and his wife shook their heads. "No."

"We haven't informed Gilfry's next of kin yet, so this isn't for public knowledge," Pescoli warned. "We're just looking for information."

"Okay . . ." Lorraine said, then, "You know . . . Brenda Sutherland, she's a member." Lorraine blinked hard as she lifted her head. Her lips folded in on themselves, and the cords of her neck were visible, as if she was straining hard not to break down completely. "Could this . . ." Waggling a hand to indicate everything happening, she cleared her throat. "Could this have happened to her?"

"Oh, honey, that's really getting the cart before the horse," her husband cut in, his grip on her hand visibly tightening. "We don't know what happened to Brenda. She may be fine."

"No . . . no, she's not!" Lorraine was blinking hard, her neck arching as she lifted her head defiantly. "She would never have left her boys willingly." Turning her head, she faced her husband. "You know it. I know it."

The preacher nodded slightly. The hand holding his wife's relaxed. "That's true," he admitted. "Brenda Sutherland is a devoted mother."

"Very devoted." Lorraine, pale as a ghost, met Pescoli's gaze with her own. "You have to find her. You have to!"

"And the madman who did this," Mullins asserted. "I'm telling you, this is Satan's doing. Whoever froze that woman and carved the ice around her is working for Lucifer himself!"

It was a good morning.

The sun was up, sparkling on the new-fallen snow, and a bit of a breeze was kicking up the freshly fallen powder. He trudged to the box to retrieve the paper and, walking back to the house, opened up the thin pages. There was nothing about his art inside, of course. The paper would have been to press far before his sculpture was discovered. And he'd been there, too. In the crowd held back by police wire. So he knew his picture had probably been taken by the police and there was a chance he would show up on a news camera's footage, though he doubted it. But no one would question his reasons for being in the neighborhood if he were to be asked.

He'd avoided any contact with the police as he'd stood in a group, staring at the crèche, where the police had tried to figure out a way to take out the perfect ice statue. He could have told them. A simple winch and a pickup or van, but, oh, how they'd fussed, uniformed officers, detectives, crime technicians . . .

Idiots!

It had been wonderful watching them so befuddled. Now, as he had much earlier at the church, he hummed the refrain that ran through his head. *We three kings of Orient are . . .*

Christmas was definitely his favorite time of year, though it hadn't always been so. Some of the memories from Christmases past weren't kind ones and they had the tendency to spread through his brain like corrosive acid, eating away at the gray matter, reminding him that pain and pleasure were lovers, one was not as intense without the other. He'd watched the police from the shadows. They'd flailed and stewed, talking and frowning while the stupid preacher looked on and wrung his oh-so-pious hands. Fortunately that holy moron had done his best to destroy the crime scene, hypocrite that he was. The uniforms, crime scene investigators and detectives had invaded the crèche. The disturbing thing was that he'd witnessed one of the detectives, the dark-haired one with the intense brown eyes, searching for him in the crowd, trying to identify him. Seriously, she'd eyed the bystanders, hoping that she would catch him.

Bearing gifts, we traverse afar . . .

Catch him? She didn't have a prayer. Of course he would come out the victor in this game. She just didn't know it yet. But she would. And soon.

He felt a niggle of anticipation at that, a drip of adrenaline at the thought, and he reached into his pocket and played with his hidden treasure. Oh, she'd know all right. This was about to get personal for Detective Selena Alvarez . . .

Of course, not to throw suspicion on himself, he'd left the church early while more curious neighbors and drivers stopped and stared. He'd returned home though he'd longed to stay and witness the cops' frustration, the preacher's distress.

Later, he reminded himself now as he walked around to the back of his house, stepping carefully in the tracks he'd already made through the pristine snow, and on the back porch, he slowly removed his boots, then walked into the mudroom of the old farmhouse in his stocking feet. Through the cold kitchen, past the woodstove, where his great grandmother had made her incredible biscuits, to the front of the house and the den he'd created from the old parlor.

He was certain that the "big" news story in Grizzly Falls was generating interest all over this part of the country, possibly beyond. Fortunately, he'd had the wherewithal to record every local station because he knew he would want to play the recordings over and over again. Then there was his computer; he was already reading the first bits of news as they'd started streaming on the Web. Too wired to sleep, he intended to keep watching the reports as they rolled in.

There was a thud overhead as his wife's feet hit the floor as she climbed out of bed. Mentally, he counted her footsteps, just six. Always just six. Less than a minute later the toilet flushed. Three footsteps and the plumbing creaked again as she turned on the water over the bathroom basin. Then, within three minutes of waking, she was on the stairs, her slippers quietly gliding on the old wooden steps. He waited, already irritated, 'til she poked her head into his office. "Busy?"

As if there were any question.

"Hmm." He barely looked up. God, she was beginning to get under his skin. He thought of what he would do to her . . . when the time was right. For her, there would be blood. Like the first one.

"I'll get coffee going. You were already out?"

"Yes." He had his pat answer. "Research. New article I'm writing."

"Of course." She yawned and stretched and he noted she wasn't interested in anything he did anymore. Not really. Hadn't even asked about his work. Just didn't damned care. It was as if he were invisible, as he had been all his life. Half listening, he heard her shuffle toward the back of the house, the bitch who held the purse strings, who wouldn't so much as sign on a loan he'd wanted a year ago.

She'd probably forgotten all about that.

He hadn't.

Yes, it would feel spectacular to actually place a blade to her throat, probably her favorite little paring knife, and watch her blood spurt into the ice water. For her, things would be different. Special.

While she was bustling in the kitchen making breakfast, unaware of his ultimate plans for her, and the aroma of coffee was seeping through the house, he watched every bit of information he could find online. He kept the volume low, of course.

"Oh, my God," she said. "Did you see this?"

"What?" He tried to sound bored.

"On the news! Some woman found dead in a block of ice! At the church! Our church!"

"Oh, yes." Calmly he got up from his desk and found her standing, empty coffeepot in hand, water running into the drain as she stared at the small screen of the TV she'd placed on an old microwave stand in the corner near the table. "I was there," he said, turning off the water and hearing the old pipes creak as he turned his attention to the small screen, where a reporter stood in front of the church and explained that the frozen body of an unidentified woman had been found in the nativity scene at the Presbyterian church just outside of town.

She was young and beautiful, holding her microphone to her glossy lips, wide eyes staring into the camera.

"You . . . you were there?" his wife said.

"Driving by. Stopped to see what the commotion was all about. No one knew anything, of course."

"I'm surprised you stopped."

"Well, there was a road block, I was detoured so I thought I'd check it out." *Now* she was interested in what he did. Of course.

"Preacher Mullins and Lorraine? The girls? They're okay."

"You heard what she said. The body they found was unidentified."

"It's awful," she whispered and reached for the faucet again, then filled the glass pot. Carefully, not spilling a drop, she poured the cold water into the coffeemaker's reservoir. "I don't know why this keeps happening here. It's as if Grizzly Falls is jinxed or something. Like there's some curse cast over the town."

"Why what keeps happening?"

"Murders! Someone killed this poor woman! And just last Christmas and the one before . . . you remember. Horrible!"

"This seems a little different to me," he said, tamping down his anger. "More planned out."

"Because the body was left at the church?" She shuddered. "That's worse. The church should be a place of comfort and solace, a haven. Whoever did this made a mockery of everything I hold sacred."

His blood began to race in his veins and he knew arguing further would serve no purpose and she, a woman with an IQ so much lower than his, might suspect something. "That might not have been the intention," he said as the screen flickered to an advertisement. He reminded her, "Breakfast?"

Turning, she looked up at him and some of her indignation fled as their gazes met. He saw that tiny widening of her pupil, an indication of fear. Good. She knew her place but sometimes needed to be reminded. He placed a loving hand on her shoulder, feeling her flesh through the thin bathrobe and lacy nightgown beneath. Then he squeezed. Not too hard. Just enough to gain her attention.

She wanted to yelp. He felt her muscle tense. But she didn't cry out. "Of course," she whispered, lowering her gaze. *Good girl.* She knew better than to draw away.

"Perfect." He rained a smile upon her and

patted her shoulder, then playfully wagged a finger under her nose. "Don't dally."

"No, no . . . of course not." Blinking rapidly, she turned back to the cupboard, where she pulled down another tin of coffee. Her fingers shook a bit, but she didn't spill so much as one bit of grounds as she measured out the scoops.

His world righted again, he returned to the den and checked several news Web sites as the aroma of brewing coffee mingled with the smell of wood smoke. Minutes later the sizzle of pancake batter hitting the griddle. The cakes themselves would be perfect four-inch discs, all smooth and golden. The syrup would be warming, homemade, in a jar his grandmother had used for just that purpose. The woodstove would still be burning, warming the old kitchen and smelling of a nostalgic past . . . his youth, with his grandmother and her mother, perfect . . . unmarred by the other one, the bitch who had borne him.

He wouldn't think of her now, pushed her far away, to a corner of his mind reserved for the darkness and the pain. Once again, he forced his attention to the streaming newscast.

His stomach rumbled, but he kept his eyes on the computer screen. The clock built into his computer reminded him that he still had two minutes until breakfast, so he ignored the hunger pangs as he watched yet another short clip.

He wasn't completely satisfied with the

coverage of his work. Most disappointing was that, so far, there was no footage of the sculpture itself. None! All his painstaking work, his meticulous attention to detail, his perfection . . . and not a glimpse.

So far . . .

But he knew how to deal with that.

He would have to be careful.

At the precise time, he walked into the kitchen, where the aroma of maple syrup mingled with the coffee and wood smoke.

And his pancakes, waiting on a warmed platter, were perfect and golden. Three. Just three. No more. No less. The syrup was warming, too.

Yes, his wife had done well this morning.

He would have to reward her.

Everything was as it should be . . . then he heard the music; the radio turned to a station other than that which played Christmas tunes twenty-four-seven, and he felt his old rage resurface.

She *knew* that during this time, only Christmas music was allowed; it was all part of the season. Anger flooded through his veins to pulse in his ears, thundering in his brain at her defiance.

He walked, stocking footed, to the living room, where the Christmas tree sparkled, adorned to his precise specifications, and the mantle was graced with the same spun glass as it had been for nearly a century, the tiny cardboard town with its perfect little lights stretched out over the old oak plank his great-grandfather had hand planed.

As if she'd heard him back in the room, the radio music changed and "Hark! The Herald Angels Sing," halfway through the first chorus, again played through the hidden speakers.

He was furious but calmed himself by running his fingers over the smooth wood of the mantle, though he was careful not to disturb the "snow."

She wasn't perfect.

Of course.

But he expected her to obey him.

He'd been very specific about that from the get-go and they'd even had the old vows inserted in their private marriage ceremony.

He'd remind her.

Tonight.

"You don't think we have another one, do you?" Alvarez asked once she and Pescoli had driven their separate vehicles to the office and had met in the lunch room, where, already, Joelle's booty of the day had been picked over.

"Another one?" Pescoli asked.

"Psycho homicidal maniac."

"Oh, I'd bet on it."

It was now after ten, the ice-entombed body had finally been removed, taken to a giant freezer in the crime lab, and neighbors who lived close to the church had been or were being questioned. So far, no one had heard or seen anything, which was frustrating as hell. One of the closest neighbors, Jordan Eagle, a local vet, had been up with an emergency. She'd driven to her veterinary office just after midnight, and home again around three, but she hadn't noticed anything unusual.

"Then, I was really tired," she'd admitted. "Just concentrating on getting home as the snow was really coming down and, to tell you the truth, I probably wouldn't have noticed anything unless it was right in the middle of the road."

So they were back to square one. As soon as the ice surrounding the body had melted and any trace evidence collected, they would positively ID the body, but Alvarez agreed with Pescoli: The victim was likely Lara Sue Gilfry. Even through the distortion of the ice, she was recognizable, and the scar on her leg and tattoo over her ankle sealed the deal. Staring into the dead woman's eyes through a thick obviously sculpted sheet of ice had been a shock. A lot of killers hid their victims, though there were always those who put their handiwork on display. Never, to her knowledge, in a crèche at a church.

"You think we have a serial?"

"Make that a bizarre serial killer and, yeah." Pescoli was nodding, eyeing the leftover cookies on a silver snowflake platter. "I think we might." Frowning, she selected a reindeer-face cupcake with only one pretzel antler still attached. "So what's with this place? Why is Grizzly Falls suddenly the meeting ground for all the homicidal nutcases in the area?"

"You tell me. You've been here longer than I have."

"That's right." She found a cup and poured herself some coffee from a glass carafe warming on the coffeemaker's hotplate. "You came here from San Bernardino, right?" The coffee poured in a thin, dark stream and Alvarez mentally kicked herself for letting the conversation wander even the slightest bit toward her past.

"Yeah. Has anyone contacted the person who made the missing persons report on Lara Sue Gilfry?" Alvarez was already heading down the hallway toward her office.

"It's being handled and don't duck the issue: you and O'Keefe. Want to fill me in?"

"No."

"I read the report."

Great. Alvarez felt her stomach drop. Worse yet, she nearly ran right into the sheriff as Dan Grayson rounded the corner from his office. Luckily she wasn't carrying a cup of hot tea as she did a double step around him.

"Let me grab a cup," he said in that drawl she'd always found fascinating. "Meet me in my office and bring me up to speed on this ice-mummy case. That's what the press is already calling it, you know."

Pescoli said, "Probably better than human Popsicle."

"Just barely. And don't mention that to Manny Douglas," he warned, referring to a particularly nosy and irritating reporter for the *Mountain Reporter*, a local newspaper. "He's gonna have a heyday with this one." One of Grayson's bushy eyebrows lifted and he cocked his head toward his office. "I'll be right in."

"Ice mummy?" Pescoli repeated as she followed Alvarez through the door of Grayson's office and dropped into one of the desk chairs. "Not all that clever. So are you going to tell me about San Bernardino and Dylan O'Keefe, or am I going to have to make a call to my friend who works there?"

"Is it really that important?"

"Maybe not. But since a kid wanted in an armed robbery broke into your place with O'Keefe hot on his tail, yeah, maybe it is."

There was just no getting around this. "Later," Alvarez said, not wanting Grayson to hear more than he needed to.

"I'll hold you to it."

From his dog bed in the corner, Sturgis lifted his head and thumped his tail.

Alvarez's heart twisted a little when she thought of her own dog and wondered where Roscoe could be. "Good boy," she said automatically. Again Sturgis wagged his tail, before yawning widely, showing a pink mouth and gleaming teeth, then hearing Grayson's boot steps in the hallway, actually standing and greeting the sheriff at the door. Grayson balanced a coffee cup in one hand and leaned over to scratch the dog's ears with the other.

Alvarez saw that the action was automatic; Grayson probably didn't even realize he'd given the dog attention. Just as he'd never realized how close she'd come to falling in love with him, which, in retrospect, had been foolish, a fantasy. Yes, he was an attractive man, but he was more mentor than he could ever be lover.

She glanced away then, surprised at her thoughts. Worse yet, she understood that her change in attitude had less to do with Dan Grayson and could be attributed to the fact that she'd seen Dylan O'Keefe again.

Which was just plain ludicrous. As well as disturbing. She couldn't afford to think about either man in any kind of romantic fantasy.

From the corner of her eye, Alvarez caught Pescoli staring at her, so she forced her face to remain placid. Even so, her partner had an uncanny ability to guess what was on Alvarez's mind. Today, *that* wasn't going to happen! She'd make certain of it.

"Okay," Grayson said as he settled into his creaking desk chair. "Give it to me, straight. Blow by blow. What the hell's going on at the Presbyterian church?"

164

CHAPTER 11

By five o'clock that afternoon, Alvarez didn't know much more about the ice-mummy case than she had in the predawn hours when the body had been discovered. Nor had she spent any free time with Pescoli, so she'd managed not to have to delve into the reasons she'd left California and landed here. That would change soon, because Pescoli was like a damned terrier whenever she wanted to know something; she'd ask questions until she was satisfied with the answers.

Alvarez wasn't sure she was ready to give any.

At least, not yet.

She was still reeling from seeing O'Keefe again.

Dead tired, her nerves jangled, impatience coloring her judgment, she decided it was time for a break. She rolled her chair away from her workstation and stood, then stretched, reaching her hands high over her head and hearing her spine pop. A cold cup of tea sat on the edge of her desk, her computer screen had pictures of the victim in ice and, later, after the block was slowly melted, of her dead body, which was now on its way to be autopsied.

As her family had yet to be located, the owner of the Bull and Bear identified the dead woman as Lara Sue Gilfry and a search was under way to find anyone close to her.

The media was all over the story, and despite repeated responses from the department that the public information officer would give an interview at five thirty, stations from all over the state and as far away as Seattle and Boise had been calling.

Many times the victim of a homicide was killed by a family member or someone close. However, in this case, the killer or his accomplice had gone to so much trouble to display the body, and in a public place, obviously for attention or to make some kind of statement. Going out on a limb, Alvarez thought Lara had been attacked by someone who had either come across her path and decided she would suit his needs, or had been stalking her, waiting for the right moment to strike, so that he could kidnap her and then go about his regimen of killing her, working with the ice, then exhibiting her. The sheriff's department had people looking into her acquaintances, members and neighbors of the church, enemies of Reverend Mullins and his family or the Presbyterian church, as well as local artists, especially those who sculpted and worked in ice. They'd contacted catering companies and hotels in the area, looking for a name of someone who could create art out of ice.

"Deranged psycho," she said under her breath

and stretched both of her arms behind her head, pulling on the shoulder joint, releasing the tension of the day. Some killers tried to hide their victims, maybe even kept them close to where the killer lived so he could revisit the act, but others, the show-offs, the deranged madmen who somehow thought they had to prove to the world how smart they were, loved to taunt and tease the police while terrorizing the public. This nut job, the one who put a dead body in ice, clearly fell into the latter category. *Sick, sick, sick!*

Worse yet, she'd *felt* the creep's presence, though, of course, she didn't believe in anything like "feelings" or "hunches," but there had been a fleeting moment, early this morning, before dawn, when she'd sensed an evil presence staring at her, almost known that the malicious whacko who'd killed a woman and encased her in ice had been nearby.

Ridiculous. She was, after all, a woman of science and proof. And yet . . .

Pescoli, bundled in her jacket and hat, poked her head into Alvarez's office. "I'm heading home for a while. Gotta check on my rogue children."

"You coming back in?"

"Tonight?" Pescoli asked. "Maybe. Depends on the situation at home. Bianca and I have been two ships passing in the night and that's not good."

"And Jeremy?"

"MIA for the most part. I'm trying to give him

his 'space,' " she added, making sarcastic quote marks with her fingers, "but I'm kind of sick of it. His 'space' really means for me to butt my nose out of his business even though he's living at home and not really contributing. I'm thinking it's time for an attitude adjustment talk and some changes. It'll be a new year soon." She wound her scarf around her neck and tried to tie it. "Kids," she muttered under her breath before looking up sharply. "Oh, by the way, our buddy, Preacher Mullins?"

"Mmm?"

"Not so lily white." Frustrated with the scarf, she let it hang unknotted. "Got himself into a little trouble down in Arizona, got caught in bed with one of the parishioners, who just happened to be eighteen at the time. Her father screamed bloody murder, but Mullins, because the girl was legal, was just sent packing to a new flock."

"And that would be here," Alvarez guessed.

"Mmm-hmmm." She fiddled with the scarf a little more and finally secured it in a basic square knot. "I guess Calvin shouldn't be the first one to throw stones. Glass houses, and all that."

"You think the dad in Arizona would come up here and kill someone, set them in a block of ice, just to get back at Mullins?"

"Nope. But it does give me pause. What other trouble do you think the good preacher has gotten himself into? Then there's that winter festival in Missoula next week. Guess what one of the displays is going to be?" Before Alvarez could answer, she said, "Ice sculpture. Think that's a coincidence? Think we should check out the 'artists.' " She grimaced and a moment later her cell phone buzzed. Plucking it from her pocket, she glanced at the screen. "Aaah. The prodigal daughter, wanting, yet again, to go over to a friend's." After sketching out a quick text response, she added, "Not happenin'. Not with another storm predicted. Besides, tonight is family dinner night and we're all going to be there, at the house, together. Even if it kills us!"

Dylan O'Keefe was waiting for her.

As Alvarez was walking toward her Outback parked on the street, O'Keefe emerged from his vehicle.

Great. Just what she needed after a long, exhausting day of getting nowhere. "You're making a habit of this," she pointed out.

"Guilty as charged."

"Anything I can do for you?"

"Yeah." His boots crunched in the frozen snow as he approached her car.

"You find my dog?"

"Not yet." His nose was red with the cold.

"What about Reeve?"

"Gone to ground." He looked disturbed. "You talked to the Helena PD?"

"Yeah." She was nodding as she found her keys in her purse. God, it was cold and Pescoli was right. Another storm had been predicted for this part of the state, with talk of another foot of snow. Just what they needed! "I confirmed everything you told me and tried to get more information from them, told them the sheriff's department here would work with them."

"And?"

"And they were glad; maybe not so high on your input, being as you're a private citizen and all."

"I found him, didn't I?"

"But you lost him." She unlocked the car and waited, hoping she would learn something more about the boy, if not her dog.

"I was thinking you might have an idea where he might turn."

"Me? Why?"

"Because it seems as if he targeted your house." He was staring at her in the darkness and she wanted to lie to him, to tell him that she had no idea why the boy might have chosen her place to break into, but that might not help things. Aside from her, Gabriel Reeve had a family who was worried sick about him.

"Look, it's freezing out here, but we need to talk," she said.

"There's a bar down the street."

"Uh . . . no." She thought of some of the off-duty deputies who hung out there. In fact, none of the surrounding restaurants could provide her with the sense of privacy she needed. The same could be said of a lot of places in town. Because of the recent homicides in Grizzly Falls, and her part in solving the crimes, she'd been interviewed on television and photographed for the local paper. She was a recognizable face. "Look. Why don't you come to my place?" she suggested with difficulty.

One of his dark eyebrows lifted. "Any particular reason?"

"There's something I want to tell you and it would be best done in private."

"Fine," he said, stepping away from her SUV. "I'll follow you."

Sliding behind the wheel of the Subaru, she wondered if she'd made a vast mistake. However, it was too late to change her mind. As she fired up the engine, she glanced in the side-view mirror before pulling away from the curb and she caught a glimpse of O'Keefe climbing into the old Ford that had been parked down the street.

She knew that being with him was a mistake, but she didn't feel she had any choice. She did want to find out about Gabriel Reeve, locate the boy and determine if he was her son. And she wanted her dog back.

Nosing the Subaru away from the curb, she hit the gas and pulled a quick U-turn, passing

O'Keefe and a news van that had rolled to the station and was idling near the parking lot. In her rearview, she caught the Explorer turning around with a little more difficulty, then its headlights bore down on her as she slowed for a red light.

Feeling more than a little bit of apprehension at confiding in O'Keefe, Alvarez switched on the radio and noticed that snow was beginning to fall again, the storm that had been promised rolling across the Bitterroots.

Why, she wondered, did she feel as if it were an omen?

"This is sooo lame!" Jeremy was trying to unwind last year's exterior lights in the living room and wasn't happy about it. The strand was strung out over the couch and part of the recliner before kinking its way across the carpet while the television was tuned in to some pregame basketball talk show.

"What's lame about it?" Pescoli asked from the kitchen, where Cisco was dancing around her feet, hoping for a scrap. Not that she cared why Jer was complaining. She was used to it. Leaning over the stove and one of the two working burners, she tasted the spaghetti pie sauce, a recipe that Joelle had passed out, via e-mail, earlier in the month. Pescoli had seen it while cleaning out her in-box and printed it out as it looked like something everyone in the family would eat.

Even Bianca, who was currently off her vegetarian diet, a regimen she imposed upon herself and the family every time she saw some show on television on the conditions of animals raised for feed, or some show about healthy eating. Either way, Pescoli didn't care, as long as she knew ahead of time, before she made a pot of beef stew or roasted a chicken. Today, she thought, she was safe.

"Why do we even put up lights on the house?" Jeremy complained. Lying on the floor, desperately in need of a haircut and a shave, his jeans almost falling off his butt, he plugged in the strand and thankfully, all of the bulbs glowed, casting tiny pools of eerie-colored light onto the furniture and carpeting.

" 'Tis the season. Hey, we always put up lights. And, come on, we have to have some traditions around here." She poured the sauce over the pasta and cheese pie, sprinkled a little more mozzarella over the top and shoved the heavy pie plate into the warming oven. Cooking wasn't really her thing, and if she were being honest with herself, she'd have to admit that the case was on her mind. She hadn't been able to shake the image of Lara Sue Gilfry enshrouded in ice all day and there was still Len Bradshaw's "accidental" death while hunting that hadn't been solved, not to

173

mention whatever the hell was going on with Alvarez, Dylan O'Keefe and the runaway kid wanted for armed robbery. Nonetheless, Pescoli couldn't work twenty-four-seven. Besides, her kids needed her. There had to be a balance in her life. She was going to have family time, damn it, no matter if her kids hated her for it.

And what about Nate Santana? Where does he fit into all this? He'd been patient. A saint with a demon's wicked smile. But even he wouldn't wait forever; she needed to decide what to do about him.

"Maybe it's time for new ones," Bianca offered up from the kitchen table, where she was supposed to be signing Christmas cards but was spending most of her time with her phone, texting.

Pescoli said, "New traditions?" as she'd lost the thread of the conversation while testing the sauce and musing about her complicated life.

"Mmm. Michelle's even going to change the color of her tree this year." Bianca, fingers still flying, glanced up and Pescoli was caught off guard, taken by how much her daughter looked like Luke. That was the way of it; both her kids resembled their fathers much more than they did her, which wasn't a bad thing. Joe had been rugged, a real he-man, and Luke, damn him, was almost Hollywood handsome with a bad-boy, slightly off-center smile that could melt even the coldest heart. As evidenced by the fact that he'd convinced Regan Strand to marry him.

"No more pink-flocked tree?" Pescoli asked, trying to hide the sarcasm in her voice. Why Luke's current wife bugged her, she didn't know. Yes, Michelle was younger and prettier and made herself up like a Barbie doll, but she wasn't as dumb as she acted and Pescoli certainly didn't want her cheating ex back. Never. Luke was just no damned good. At least not for her. Handsome? Yes. Narcissistic? You betcha. And he and Michelle seemed to somehow get along.

Good.

Truth to tell, it was the whole stepmom thing that got to Pescoli. Michelle, barely a decade older than Bianca, was into pampering and fluff and fake fingernails and hair extensions, platform heels and the damned Kardashians and *Jersey Shore*, for God's sake. All things Pescoli avoided like the plague. So the fact that she was influencing Bianca really got under Pescoli's skin.

"Michelle is thinking of going retro with one of those aluminum trees with spinning, colored lights on it." Bianca, as always, seemed in awe of the woman's inspiration.

"Why doesn't she really go retro and cut her own in the woods, you know a real tree with real needles and real pitch, one that smells of fir or pine and maybe isn't perfectly shaped?"

Bianca rolled her eyes. "Because she's not into

that, Mom. What she's planning to do with the house this year? It's really kinda cool."

Of course it is. "And your dad is okay with this? The retro thing?"

"He doesn't care," she said with a lift of her slim shoulder. "As long as it doesn't block his view of his new TV."

"Another one?" Oh, God why did she even bring Luke up?

"Yeah, it's *super* thin. Three-D."

"Cool!" Jeremy said and Pescoli's skin crawled. She didn't need to be reminded that there wasn't yet one flat-screen television in her home. It just wasn't a big priority and she didn't have a lot of extra money to go throwing around on electronics. She needed to change the subject. "Those cards about done?" she asked Bianca.

"Almost."

"Then it'll be your turn, Jer."

"Why? That's so—"

"Lame, I know. But, again, it's tradition and your aunts would like to hear from you." She laid on the guilt a little thick as it had been a while since she'd even talked with any of her three sisters. "You know the ones who send you all those gifts you like?"

"Fine!" he grumbled as he yanked on the lights to straighten the cord and the plug-in fell out of the socket. All the lights immediately dimmed. "Fu—"

"It's Christmas!" she cut in.

"Not yet!" he snapped, seeming to be angry at the world these days.

Pescoli was having none of his bad mood. "We don't swear anyway."

"What? Mom, you're such a hypocrite. 'We' "— he mockingly swept a hand toward her—"*all* swear." His gaze centered on his sister, defying her to pull her goodie-two-shoes routine, one that Pescoli had quit buying once Bianca had turned ten or eleven and Pescoli had caught her trying to smoke. "They're Carrie's!" Bianca had cried when Pescoli had confiscated the Marlboro Lights and then dramatically flushed perfectly good cigarettes down the toilet when she'd really wanted to stuff the half-empty pack into her glove box for one of "those" days. She hadn't. Her point was more effective watching the cigarettes deteriorate, bits of tobacco floating in a swirling pattern as the toilet flushed.

As far as she knew, the dramatic demonstration had been effective; Bianca, it seemed, was smoke free. With Jeremy she hadn't been so lucky. Not only did he chew, he didn't bother to hide it any longer. "I'm eighteen, it's legal!" But he also, she knew, dabbled in marijuana. "Weed isn't a problem. There's *nothing* wrong with it." Her arguments that marijuana wasn't legal had fallen on deaf ears.

"Okay, I'm as guilty as anyone, but let's all try to watch our tongues, shall we?"

No one answered, Bianca was still texting, her pile of signed cards not increasing, and Jeremy, still working with the lights, was watching the latest sports scores flash on the television.

Pescoli figured this was as good a family tradition as she was going to get.

Which was just kind of pathetic when you thought about it.

Chapter 12

Big mistake!

What were you thinking, asking O'Keefe over to your place? That's only asking, no, make that begging, for trouble.

"He's going to find out sooner or later," she said aloud as she walked into her town house and tossed her keys onto a nearby table. She couldn't keep her son's birth a secret forever.

He may not be your son—

"Yeah, I know!" That argument had been playing in her head over and over again, but she figured it was just denial. Unwinding her scarf and hooking it over a curved arm of the hall tree, she told herself it would be better if O'Keefe heard the truth from her, if she owned her past.

It was important, if she wanted to find the boy, and she did.

And then what? He goes before a judge for his crime?

"Of course," she said and realized she was talking to herself. She believed in the justice system, trusted in it. Even if it seemed to have backfired in the case of Junior Green.

She had to find Gabriel Reeve and turn him in; let the system do its thing, but make damned sure he had a good lawyer.

Are you going to find him one? Is that before or after you have that mother-son talk and explain why you gave him up for adoption?

"Oh, hell," she whispered as Jane Doe trotted down the stairs and became a puddle of fur in her hands when she lifted the cat off her white toes. "Life's complicated," she whispered and Jane rubbed the back of her head under Alvarez's chin.

As she carried the cat into the kitchen, she walked through the living area, picked up the remote and clicked on the news. As expected, the station was running a clip of the recent statement to the press by the public information officer. The footage had been taken less than an hour before and Alvarez watched as Dan Grayson stood, ramrod straight, next to the woman at the mic. A handsome man, very cowboy-esque with his Stetson, boots and lean, long frame. She could

179

envision him on the cattle trail, upon a horse, spending hours in the blistering sun. Rangy and tough, Grayson was a lawman with all the right morals and instincts, the first she'd been able to trust in a long, long time. Her throat constricted a little at the fantasy she'd wrapped around him, her boss.

The television picture switched to the Presbyterian church and the nativity scene. Behind the reporter, police were working, and as the camera panned over what had once been a pristine crèche, Alvarez was transported back in time to her own childhood and the nativity scenes of her youth while growing up in Woodburn, Oregon. She remembered the Christmas traditions, the gaiety, the sense of fun and breathless anticipation of her childhood. The house had been filled with the noise of her siblings, the rapid-fire Spanish of her grandmother and the scent of cinnamon for the traditional Mexican cookies that took days to prepare. There were garlands and lights, and on Christmas Eve, Grandma Rosarita's homemade tamales steamed in corn husks lent a savory aroma to the big kitchen.

Later that night, all of the extended family had piled into cars and gone to the cathedral in the nearby town of Mount Angel for midnight mass. On the way, from the window of the old station wagon, Alvarez had viewed rolling fields and farm houses decorated with colorful lights, cedar garlands and fir boughs. The old Ford had passed many nativity scenes as well, each elaborately displayed and always offering a sense of peace and serenity, reminding her of the story of the Christ child's birth.

She'd always been in awe of the manmade recreations of that holy night. Never, in her life, even as a somewhat jaded adult, would she have associated them with something as ugly and vile as murder.

Now, however, she felt as if everything good in the world was slammed right up against the bad. Black and white, no room for a slice of gray in between.

She raced to her bedroom and changed her clothes, all the time wondering what was keeping O'Keefe. He'd been following her as she'd pulled away from the station, but she'd lost him in the traffic and hadn't worried about it.

Nor should she be concerned now. He knew his way here. In the bathroom, she turned on the tap and found that, gratefully, hot water had been restored. "There is a God," she whispered, then grabbed her brush and swept her hair away from her face, snapped a rubber band in place and braided the strands. She'd just finished tying off the end with a second band when the doorbell rang.

"About time." Hurrying down the stairs, she nearly tripped on Jane, who scurried up the steps to hide in the shadows of the upper landing.

At the door, she took a deep breath, and before she worried too much about how she was going to break the news that she was very possibly Gabriel Reeve's birth mother, she checked the peephole, assured herself the man on the other side was O'Keefe, then pulled it open.

It's now or never, she thought, determined to confide in him.

"I come bearing gifts." O'Keefe stood under the lamp on her doorstep, a pizza box extended in front of him. "Figured you might be hungry."

Not really; not with what we have to discuss. The last thing she wanted was food. "You figured right," she said. "It's been a long day."

"I bet. Couldn't help but hear about the body found in the church crèche. Figured you haven't had much to eat today."

"Unless you count day-old Christmas cookies," she said, opening the door wider and standing aside, allowing him to enter. Though she hated to admit it, she was so nervous the pepperoni pizza he brandished and set on the table didn't look the least bit appealing. Her stomach was already in knots and she didn't see how tons of spicy tomato sauce, stringy cheese and greasy rounds of pepperoni would help the situation.

"And look. I brought my own." He reached into his pocket and withdrew a can of beer. "Got one for you, too." He pulled a second can from his other jacket pocket.

"Thanks, but I think I'll pass," she said as she fished into one of her kitchen drawers and finally came up with a pizza slicer she'd had since college. "Let's cut those pieces smaller." She tossed him the slicer and tried not to notice how familiar this all felt. She took down a couple of small plates from the cupboard, found some sparkling water and, feeling a little bit like a nun for not accepting the beer, scraped her chair back and sat at the small table on the opposite side from him.

"You said you had something you wanted to talk about," he said as he sliced the pizza and drew a piece away from the pie, long tendrils of mozzarella refusing to let go. After swiping them with the cutter, he dropped the piece onto her plate, then went after another for himself. "So what is it?"

Oh, God.

Now or never, Selena. Go for it.

"There's a chance . . . well, probably a good chance, that Gabriel Reeve is my son," she said, forcing the words over her tongue and ignoring the buzzing in her head. "I, uh, I'm not certain, of course—I haven't kept up with him—but I did have a baby boy about the same time as your cousin adopted Gabriel. The records are sealed, of course, until he's eighteen or something, I'm not really sure, but, at the time I gave him up, I asked that neither he nor his adoptive parents try to contact me or even find me. It was a closed adoption and that's the way I wanted it."

She swallowed hard and the weight of sixteen years of not knowing seemed heavy upon her shoulders.

"There hasn't been a day that's gone by that I haven't thought of him, but . . ." Shaking her head, staring down at the rapidly cooling slice of pizza, she fought a rash of tears that she'd bottled up forever. "I always wondered what happened to him, how his life was, what he looked like . . ." Clearing her throat, she glanced away and went to that mental place she'd found a lifetime ago, a haven that allowed her to push the pain into a corner of her mind that she kept locked.

She felt her chin start to wobble, then set her jaw. This was not the time for regret or recriminations and she refused to break down. *Refused.*

For a second the silence stretched between them and the house seemed empty aside from the soft rumble of the furnace. She felt unburdened, and yet, stupidly ashamed. Forcing her chin up, she met the questions in his eyes.

If she expected to see recriminations or silent accusations, she was disappointed. "You were just a kid," he said softly.

"About his age now."

"Jesus, Selena, why didn't you tell me?"

"Why didn't I tell anyone?" She sniffed loudly and refused to let the tears in her eyes fall. "Because I didn't want anyone to know. I . . . I still don't. But it looks like I don't have much of a choice."

Frowning, his jaw jutting a bit, he looked away, then said, "It's gonna be okay."

"Don't patronize me, okay? It's not going to be okay. It never has been and it never will be, but somehow, we'll just deal with it. *I'll* deal with it." She was in control of her ragged emotions again, the tears no longer threatening, her emotions turned from regret to determination.

O'Keefe said, "Okay. Then time for the hard question: You think Reeve knows that you're his mother and that's why he ended up here?" Clearly, O'Keefe was skeptical.

"I don't know. It seems unlikely and I don't know how he would find me. But all this"—she gestured to the empty dog pen and swept her hand to include O'Keefe—"being just a big coincidence seems really unlikely."

She felt the weight of O'Keefe's gaze and noticed that he, too, hadn't taken so much as a bite of his slice of pizza.

"What's on your mind?" she asked.

"That you never mentioned him," he finally said and she knew that he meant in the short time they were together.

"That's right. I thought I just explained that: I

never mention him. To anyone. Not even to myself, if I can avoid it. I am only confiding in you because you're looking for him, the boy I assume is he. I would appreciate as much confidentiality as possible." With as much weight as she could muster, she leveled her gaze at him. "It's a very private thing for me."

"What about the boy's father?"

"Out of the picture." She should have expected that question, but still it surprised her. Stung a bit.

"Would the father contact Gabe?"

"No."

"You sure?" he asked.

She shook her head and glared at the man across the table. "He doesn't know I had a child, okay? And that's the way I want to keep it."

"There is such a thing as paternal rights."

"Not as far as I'm concerned. I gave my son up, I refused to list a father on the birth certificate and that's the way it's gonna stand."

She saw the confusion in his gaze, but, thankfully, she couldn't find a hint of disapproval. Good.

"Look," he finally said as she plucked a piece of pepperoni from the top of her piece of pizza. "It doesn't really matter to me if this kid's your son or not; I just want to find him."

"Me, too."

"And your dog."

She glanced at the empty pen and nodded as

186

she chewed on the pepperoni. "Yeah. I miss him." Leaning back in her chair, she watched as O'Keefe finally opened his beer, a hissing sound escaping the aluminum can. "And I did double check. As I said, I'm missing some jewelry, nothing valuable, mainly has sentimental value, and the cash. I looked around and couldn't find any of it."

"Twenty bucks won't get him far."

"Hardly out of town."

"If that," he thought aloud before taking a long swallow from his beer and motioning to her uneaten slice. "Eat. We'll figure this out. One way or another."

She wasn't convinced and her stomach was still in knots, but she tried the pizza and eyed his beer. Not even looking up, he slid the second can across the table. "Live a little, would ya? You're wound tighter than my granddad's pocket watch."

Reminded of another time and place, of cool drinks on a warm verandah and palm trees catching the midnight breezes of Southern California, she thought better of accepting the beer.

This was all business.

They'd had their shot at intimacy and it had backfired. Literally. She caught the shadow in his gaze and knew he, too, had thought of their brief, but passionate time together.

"I think I'll pass," she said, her voice a little raspier than usual. Dear God, what was wrong with her? "I've got a lot of work and . . ." She shook her head. "It just wouldn't be a good idea."

"No?"

"No."

His gaze drilled into hers. "What're you afraid of, Selena?" he asked and the sound of her name off his lips did strange things to her. The answers were simple:

Of the truth.

Of the lies.

Of what we'll find.

Of what we won't.

That Gabriel Reeve is my son.

That he isn't.

And, most of all, I'm afraid of you, O'Keefe, and the way you twist me up inside.

"Nothing," she said with a confidence she didn't feel, and to prove it, she took his lousy beer, pulled the tab and took a long, deep swallow. "Let's find the boy and my damned dog!"

Unsatisfactory.

That's what all the media attention was, he thought as he walked through the barn with its smells of warm cattle and dusty feed. The animals had been fed, so he ignored their lowing and the smell, which reminded him that he would have to do the dirty work of mucking out the feeding area. Fortunately he was down to two cows, just

188

enough to keep his wife from wondering why he spent so much time in the barn. His half-finished project of shoring up the hay loft was also an excuse to spend more time away from the house.

Fortunately his wife was a city woman, with allergies to hay and animals, and never set foot in the barn. It was his domain. What she didn't understand was that the cattle were merely props, an excuse to keep this rattletrap of a barn his great-great-grandfather had bought. He'd found the secret room as a boy, and his mother, in one of her calm periods, had explained that it had been built during Prohibition when Great-great-granddaddy had supplied the locals with bootleg booze. Hence the plumbing already in the cavernlike rooms.

Now, he shoved a couple of heavy barrels to one side and found the trap door. Opening it, he flipped a switch that started the generator he'd installed himself, and then he descended the hundred-year-old spiral staircase into the natural caverns below.

He landed in the first cavern, then, hunched over, made his way along the narrow opening to the larger underground caves in these foothills. It was a ten-minute hike, but worth it because, hidden in the woods above, on the outer edge of his property, was an opening much more accessible, where he could park his truck, hook up his winch and run a cable down here. The sloping access made moving his statues easier. All he had to do was hook the winch to a pair of huge ice picks he'd fashioned, like pointed tongs that gripped the ice, then positioning the blocks on a rolling cart, he winched them up to the surface and into his truck. Seconds later, with the canopy in place, he could drive unnoticed into town, his precious cargo securely hidden and ready to be displayed.

He reached the larger caverns.

His darlings were all here.

Waiting.

Ready to be enshrined in a frozen mantel and then carved before being put on display.

No one seemed to understand the importance of his art, the pain he'd endured, the excruciating time he'd spent meticulously locating his subjects, then plotting their abductions and then the problems with holding them until they were ready, and finally, of course, the actual sculpting. The police hadn't so much as mentioned that he was an artist or that there was anything the least bit unique about his work.

All they were concerned with was "catching the killer." Nothing more.

Sheriff Dan Grayson had stood next to the public information officer on the short steps of the Pinewood County Sheriff's Department, though he hadn't said a word and had let the tough-looking middle-aged woman make a short statement, then without fielding any questions whatsoever, left the steps.

It's because they don't know up from sideways. You've got them scared and worried. They don't know what to do but they have to say something, so they give out a little information, ask for the public's help and end it. It's a good thing. It means you're in control.

The reporters weren't much better. One had even said, "The victim was discovered in a block of ice." There had been no mention of the detail in the exquisite molds, in the craftsmanship and of the artistry involved.

Idiots!

Cretins!

His fist clenched and he had to mentally count to ten before allowing his calmer interior voice to speak to him.

What did you expect? You'll have to show them. Make a bigger statement. Maybe abduct someone more well known, a person all of the community would recognize. The reporter who had stood in front of the crèche would be a good candidate. She'd been perky and talked fast, with flawless skin and . . . *No!* That woman was just another pretty face, but there was another one whom the community had embraced, who had proven herself to be clever and had outwitted several others before him.

He smiled inwardly as he thought of Selena

Alvarez. Beautiful. Smart. Quoted in the papers. Seen on the television. A local heroine of sorts.

She would be perfect to elevate his work . . .

A moan whispered through the caverns and he was brought back to the present. He had work to do! He couldn't spend any time fantasizing about his next step.

First things, first.

He found the radio and snapped it on.

Music boomed through the speakers.

He let out his breath slowly as he recognized the notes of "Silver Bells."

"Ring a ling . . . hear them sing."

Caught up in the melody, he let his anger go. He couldn't let the cretins of the sheriff's department or the imbeciles who worked for the media deter him.

He had work to do.

Work, he'd make certain, Detective Selena Alvarez would surely appreciate!

CHAPTER 13

The next morning Alvarez drove her Subaru across the railroad tracks and up the winding road climbing Boxer Bluff. With a sheer rock wall on one side and a steep cliff on the other, the road ascended the hill, splitting midway up, and then continuing to higher ground and the newer part of Grizzly Falls.

Nearing eight o'clock, the traffic was thick, and snow was once again falling heavily. Her car was handling the steep terrain, but the pickup in front of her was sliding a bit, so she hung back, giving the driver space, even though she was eager to get to work.

She'd woken up with a headache and it hadn't gotten a whole lot better despite a quick jog and a cup of tea. She'd slept poorly, tossing and turning most of the night, and woke up missing the dog and confused about O'Keefe.

Her dreams, when she had dozed, had been peppered with images of Lara Sue Gilfry's frozen body, Grace Perchant walking above the snow, her two wolf-dogs in tow, and Junior Green jabbing a fleshy finger into her face. That finger turned into the nose of an old revolver and he'd suddenly been wearing a fedora and trench coat. With a twisted smile contorting his huge, laughing face, he'd pulled the trigger.

Blam!

The scene had changed and she was running through an empty lot in San Bernardino. It was hot, she was sweating, breathing hard, searching for her missing baby in the rusted-out cars and rambling vines and litter covering the empty space. Across a wire fence, she noticed a glowing, plastic Santa with a leer, rocking on the cracked front walk of a ramshackle bungalow that she recognized as Alberto De Maestro's hideout.

No, she thought. *My son can't be with that monster.*

And yet, over the sough of the wind, she heard the distinctive cry of a frightened baby. The wails came from within the house. She tried to run faster, but her legs were leaden as the cries became ever more plaintive.

I'm coming! Oh, baby, I'm coming . . .

Frantic, she reached the wire fence and attempted to clamber over the sharp barbs, only to prick her skin and scrape her knees as she fell. She'd nearly reached the other side when the door was flung open. *Bang!* The door hit the wall and the lights within shined outward.

Alvarez's heart was in her throat.

In silhouette, Alberto De Maestro appeared, a wicked grin becoming a slice of white on his dark face, a spreading stain of red blooming on his bare, sweaty chest. "You will pay for this, *perra!*" he snarled, and over the sound of faint Christmas music, she heard the baby crying. Louder.

"Let me have him. Please."

De Maestro laughed.

"But he needs me."

"You gave him away," De Maestro reminded her cruelly. "He is no longer yours!"

She saw red. No way was this pathetic excuse

for a human being keeping her from her boy. "Get out of my way, *bastardo*!" She took a step toward the run-down house and heard her name.

"Selena! No!" O'Keefe cried as De Maestro turned and leveled his gun, not at her, but directly at the man she loved.

"Nooo!" she screamed and had woken up, her heart pounding, sitting bolt upright. Jane Doe, who had been sleeping on the pillow next to her, shot to her feet, hissing and arching her back as she tiptoed sideways across the bed, away from her crazy mistress, only to drop onto the floor and hide somewhere in the dark.

Alvarez had clutched the covers, willing her thudding heart to slow, reminding herself it was only a nightmare, nothing more.

"Get over it," she told herself now as the pickup stopped for a red light and she gave him enough room to back slide as he hit the gas. All of last night's dreams, those distorted little bits of her life that didn't fit together, were nothing more than anxiety. And she hadn't loved O'Keefe. Not really. What she'd felt for him was a mixture of lust and respect.

She had to remind herself of that one little fact, because after last night, it looked as if they would be working together trying to find Gabriel Reeve. They'd sat at the table, over the cooling pizza, discussing where the kid could have gone and the details of the charges against him.

Though the armed robbery in which Gabriel Reeve had allegedly taken part wasn't her case, nor even in the jurisdiction of the Pinewood Sheriff's Department, she'd ended up agreeing to work the case "from the inside," using the department's resources. She was pushing the envelope a little and she was uncomfortable with it as she usually played strictly by the rules, but this time, considering that her biological son was a suspect, she decided to bend the rules a bit. What could it hurt?

Just as long as you're not doing this out of guilt for what happened to O'Keefe. Keep your head on straight!

Though nothing had been said about the past or their relationship, it had been there, between them, the proverbial elephant in the living room, or in this case, on the dining room table.

When he'd left, she'd walked him to the door, keeping her distance, and then closed it quickly as he'd stepped outside. What had happened between them in San Bernardino was long over.

She had to keep reminding herself of that fact.

The light turned green, the pickup's driver gunned it and slipped back, then a little sideways before he managed to get his truck under control again and, tires spinning, inch up the hill.

Twenty minutes later, Alvarez pulled into the station's lot. Though the parking area had been recently plowed, half an inch of new snow was covering the icy potholes and cracked pavement. She cut the engine and grabbed her computer, then caught her reflection in the rearview mirror. Dark circles were visible under her eyes from her lack of sleep, much of which she attributed to O'Keefe.

The truth of the matter was that the man upset not only her emotional equilibrium, but her life as well. Somehow, she had to pull herself together.

Grabbing her computer case, she climbed out of the Outback, locked it and headed inside where, of course, Joelle had added even more lights and a silver and gold banner that spelled out "Ho, Ho, Ho!" in block letters that were punctuated by stars, then repeated, again, down the length of the hallway.

"You need to do something about this," Pescoli was saying to the sheriff as they stood in the corridor outside of Grayson's office. Pescoli had shed her jacket and was carrying a coffee cup already sporting lipstick stains, indicating she'd been here a while, but Grayson looked as if he'd just stepped inside the building before being ambushed by the detective. Bits of snow clung to the toes of his boots while flakes melted on the shoulders of his ski jacket.

"It's a sickness," Pescoli continued, pointing at the new decorations as the sheriff's dog sat near the door to his office. "This is a public place . . . I can't bring my prisoners down this way with that on the wall. What am I gonna do, Mirandize them like Santa Claus?" She was beside herself. "You have the right to remain silent. Ho, ho, ho! Anything you say will be used against you in a court of law. Ho, ho, ho!"

"Enough! I get it." Grayson held up a hand. Clearly he was annoyed at someone. Pescoli? Joelle? "Look, I just hate to kill her enthusiasm."

"This is the workplace. She can be enthusiastic somewhere else! At her house. Or her church. Or when she volunteers down at the dog rescue center or wherever else the spirit moves her. But not here!" She rotated her hand, finger pointed, to indicate the entire complex. "I mean, I appreciate the effort to be cheery and all, trying to get everyone to feel a little holiday love or whatever you want to call it," she said though Alvarez didn't believe it, "but, you know, it's kinda hard to get into the Christmas spirit when every year we get a new set of arctic storms, lose power and somehow unleash a new, gruesome psycho who thinks Grizzly Falls is his own personal play-room!"

"Oh, poo!" Joelle, hearing the tail end of the conversation, breezed in wearing high-heeled boots and a red and green plaid cape. Today tiny little cardinals were placed strategically in her platinum hair and she was carrying several Tupperware bins holding, no doubt, yet more Christmas goodies. "Detective, this isn't hurting anyone. All that nonsense about keeping

Christmas out of the schools and public places is hooey. As for the other religions, they can celebrate their holidays, too! Bring out the menorah for Hanukkah, for pity's sake! And . . . and . . . whatever the Buddhists or Hindus do, they can do it as well. Of course they can. The whole point is to celebrate. Whatever God you believe in. I just happen to be a major fan of Jesus Christ, but we can be nondenominational. Sure!" She pointed a finger at Pescoli and jabbed it at the taller woman's nose. "A few decorations, some Christmas cookies, and a little music never hurt anyone. And don't get me started on your aversion to the Secret Santa game! If you ask me, there's something wrong with *you!* What is it you have against a little fun? You of all people should understand the need to bring a little cheer into the holidays!"

Before Pescoli could answer, Joelle stormed off, red heels clicking furiously down the hallway, a cloud of steam nearly visible in her wake, the hem of her cape billowing as she hurried to the lunchroom, where, no doubt, officers were waiting.

"Guess she told you," Grayson said, his eyes twinkling despite the fact that he was obviously trying to hide his amusement. Even Joelle's reference to Pescoli's personal terrorization by a madman a couple of years earlier hadn't dissuaded him from smiling a bit.

"But I'm still right. This over-the-top Christmas

stuff has got to stop. Or at least slow down."

"Okay, I'll take it under advisement, but Joelle does have a point. You might try lightening up a bit."

"Oh, I will. As soon as our latest sicko is firmly behind bars!" She cocked her head to make her point, then turned and headed to her office without the dramatic storm out that Joelle preferred.

Grayson let out his breath slowly. "Sometimes," he drawled, as he made his way to his office, his dog following, "I think this place is more like a zoo than a police station."

Pescoli had been in a bad mood since her bare feet had hit the bedroom floor around five in the morning, much earlier than she usually arose. But it had been a bad night. Around ten fifteen, after all of the family obligations had been covered, Jeremy had announced that he was going to an eleven o'clock showing of a new action film that was being released for the holidays. "You've got to be kidding," she said. "It's eleven! You have school tomorrow."

"Friday. No big deal." He shrugged into his jacket and pulled on a stocking cap. "One class."

"At eight in the morning."

"So?"

"It's already ten fifteen."

"It's college, Mom. I don't get marked down for not showing up."

"But, isn't it finals week?"

"I've got it handled. Just chill!"

He'd been unimpressed by her arguments, zipped his jacket, scooped up his keys and left, his truck rumbling and kicking up snow, taillights fading with the snowfall. Pescoli had been left standing in the archway to the kitchen, and Bianca, sprawled on the couch while watching TV, her ever-present phone in one hand, had rolled her eyes. "He *is* an adult."

"Not by my standards."

"Uh. But he is by the country's. He can even vote."

"Frightening."

Bianca had sent a glance toward the kitchen as Cisco had hopped onto the couch near her. "So maybe you should change your standards and we could have some peace around here!"

"Nice, Bianca."

"It's just that you're always on his case and I mean *always*. I don't know why he wants to live here."

"Because he can't afford to live on his own."

"Well, that's just lame. If I were *him,* I'd move out anyway and if I were *you,* I'd *pay* him to move out!" She turned her attention back to some important text while the *Real Housewives of God Knew Where* cavorted on the screen in minidresses, high heels and hair extensions.

"I guess I'm out of it," Pescoli admitted.

"Uh—yeah!"

"You weren't supposed to hear that."

"Then don't say it."

Yeah, the evening had gone swimmingly. At least the tree was completely decorated and the lights strung the length of the eaves were twinkling brightly.

Joelle would have been so proud.

"Merry Christmas," she'd told herself early this morning as she'd finally poured herself the first blissful and oh-so-necessary cup of coffee.

She'd woken up tired after a restless night of being haunted by thoughts of the new case, not just Lara Sue Gilfry, but the other women who'd gone missing. Were they already dead? Kidnapped and killed by the same nut job who'd murdered the first victim, or had they met some other fate?

Her mind still trying to make some sense of Lara Sue Gilfry's fate, she'd checked the refrigerator, found a bread sack without so much as one heel of bread in it and tossed the bag in the garbage. Frustrated by the fact that no one seemed to let her know when they needed groceries, she'd yelled at her son, reminding him to get up, then made her way to the bathroom for a quick shower. When she'd stepped out of the bathroom, Jeremy still hadn't appeared and her temper had begun to seethe. She'd known he'd oversleep. She yelled again before heading to her bedroom, where she quickly dressed.

Still no noise from the sleeping giant.

"Perfect," she'd muttered, cinching her belt, then walking down the stairs to his bedroom, where she pushed open the door despite the pile of clothes on the other side.

"Rise and shine," she'd said, snapping on the light. In a heartbeat she realized that the room was empty, his unmade bed wrinkled, the duvet tossed to the floor. "Jer?" she said, but she was alone. Had he left while she was in the bathroom? No way. They only had one toilet, and though she'd caught him peeing off the railing to the backyard a couple of times, it wasn't his usual morning routine. No, he'd have pounded on the bathroom door, yelling about his full bladder. It appeared as if he hadn't returned the night before. His textbooks and laptop were shoved into the corner of the room, by the scarred table that held his lava lamp, untouched from when he'd dropped them yesterday. She'd seen them in that exact space.

"Fabulous," she'd muttered and reached for her cell phone just as Cisco started sending up a ruckus and the front door opened. As she rounded the corner of the stairs, she nearly ran into her son trying to sneak down to his room.

"Oh!" he said, obviously startled. "Geez, Mom, you scared me."

"Ditto." She smelled cigarette smoke on him, and beer.

"Where have you been?" she demanded.

"Out."

"From last night?"

"Yeah." His guilt was morphing into defensiveness.

"The movie had to be over hours ago."

"I crashed over at Rory's."

"I don't know who he is."

"Just a friend. I worked with him at the gas station for a while. Anyway, I really gotta go."

"To class. You'll never make it in time."

"I meant to bed."

"And skip class? Jer—"

He spread his big hands wide as he towered above her on the narrow stairs. "Look, Mom. I've got it handled. Trust me."

"How? When you've been out smoking and drinking on a school night, then lying to me about it. Hmmm. How can I trust you?"

"Then don't." He changed his tack and shrugged his shoulders. "Don't trust me. I don't care."

"And that's the problem. You don't care about anything. We're talking about your future here. Yours! Not mine!"

"Again. We're talking about it again. I'm sick of it."

"And I'm sick of you just rolling through life, letting it carry you along without any direction."

"Is this the part of the speech where you tell me what you were doing at my age? How you were playing college ball and engaged to Dad and having a goal of becoming a super-detective?" he asked.

Bristling a little, she said, "You know, I was just getting to that part, but I see it's sunken in. Good!"

"Can I go now?"

"You're asking? You the 'adult'?"

"I'm just trying to show some respect."

"Well, show some for yourself, would you? This is your life we're talking about."

"Then let me handle it my way."

Give me strength, she silently thought and realized the argument was going nowhere and fast. "Listen, I have to get to work. I've got a job," she'd said, "a pretty important one, but this conversation is not finished."

"I know," he'd grumbled as he passed her and made his way down the rest of the stairs, "it never is."

And for the first time in what seemed like forever, she'd actually agreed with him. "You got that right." She'd hurried up the stairs and wondered what had happened to the little boy who had walked down the lane carrying his lunch box, his backpack firmly on his shoulders, a smile usually on his face. God, she missed that kid and she only hoped when Jeremy ever came out of the chrysalis of his teen years, he would emerge as the smart, strong, clever man that kid had promised to be.

That'll only happen if you stick to your guns and be the mother he needs even while he's pushing you away. It was moments like this that she really missed Joe. And therein lay part of the problem: They both did. Jeremy was screaming for his father and the one she'd given him in Lucky Pescoli hadn't begun to fill Joe's fatherly shoes.

But Santana could. If you gave him the chance.

Inwardly she'd cringed at that thought because she'd always silently sworn that she could be both mother and father to her kids. Turns out, their attitudes had shrieked that she'd been dead wrong. Arrogant and wrong.

The rest of the morning hadn't gone much better.

Now, at the station, after having unloaded on an unsuspecting Joelle, she buried herself in her work. She'd deal with her kids tonight and somehow make things right with the receptionist. Joelle was Joelle: irritating, but, for the most part, benign. And besides, silver and gold Santa sayings or not, she could whip up one helluva Christmas crumb cake!

CHAPTER 14

"It was a closed adoption," O'Keefe's cousin Aggie was saying from the other end of the wireless connection. "And when I say 'closed,' I mean shut tight, locked and embedded with an indecipherable code. That was the way the mother wanted it and Dave and I agreed. Gabe was ours. Alone. We didn't want his biological mother coming back into our lives, making demands or causing trouble or wanting him back."

"Do you know if he was trying to find his birth parents? Had he checked any of the Web sites, attempted to contact them?"

"What? Gabe? No! None of my kids are interested in contacting their biological parents. I mean, I suppose they might change their minds, but not now. And Gabe, he never even mentioned the adoption even though he knew about it, of course. We've told the kids the truth from the beginning . . . Why?"

Sitting on the foot of the bed in his motel room, O'Keefe hated that he had to break the news to Aggie, especially when it wasn't yet confirmed. Then again, they were running out of time and he had to use every avenue possible when trying to locate the kid. He wished he had the kid's cell phone or computer or, at the very least, records of Gabe's activity, but the police in Helena had confiscated all of his property. "It could be that Gabe's biological mother is in Grizzly Falls."

"What? Oh my God! That's why you're there? Holy shit!" She, who rarely swore, was obviously flustered. Beyond flustered. Maybe closing in on panicking. "I don't understand. Our attorney said the mother had been living in some little obscure town in the Pacific Northwest. I figured he was talking about a suburb or rural area around Seattle somewhere, but, like I said, I didn't want to know."

"People move."

"Closer to their long-lost kids to reconnect!" she said, on the verge of hyperventilating.

"Slow down, it's not like that."

"Then what is it like, Dylan?"

"I'm not sure; still trying to sort it out. This could be a mistake, so just calm down, okay."

"That's pretty damned hard, considering."

"I know, I know, but the important thing is that I locate Gabe."

"Is he with this woman? This mother who gave him up and hasn't seen him in sixteen years?" she demanded, her voice still trembling, as if she were close to hysteria. "Oh, God, and the father, is he involved, too? This is terrible. Oh, my God, Dylan, what the hell is going on?"

"No. It's not like that. No one's involved in

anything that I know of. I was close to Gabe, he eluded me, and he broke into a house, then took off."

"So that was Gabe. What the hell is he thinking? Dave and I, we saw something about this on the news, but the reporter didn't have a name, of course, as he's underage. For the love of God, why is he running?"

"Because he's scared. Look, if you can find out any more information about the adoption, his biological parents, the dad as well, it might help. Then again, it could all be nothing."

"I just want my son back," Aggie whispered, calmer now.

"That's what I'm trying to do. Find him and bring him home."

"Please," she whispered, her voice cracking. "Gabe's a good kid. Really. This . . . this is all a horrible mistake." She sniffed loudly and then said something unintelligible.

"Dylan?" Dave said, his voice booming through the phone. "We'll do whatever we can on this end, okay? Just keep us informed."

"Will do." O'Keefe hung up and felt like crap. The kid had been within his grasp and now had disappeared. Every day he wasn't found, it was more likely he wouldn't be.

He considered calling Alvarez, but waited. Surely she would let him know if she found out anything. Or would she? The fact that she might be the runaway's mother complicated things.

Oh, hell, who was he kidding? *Anything* having to do with Alvarez complicated things. At least as far as he was concerned. To say his feelings were conflicted when he thought of her might just be the understatement of the decade.

Disturbed, his thoughts swirling with images of the woman who inspired way too much passion in him, he shrugged into his jacket and dropped the phone into a pocket, then grabbed his pistol from the drawer of the night table.

He had work to do. And, yes, it involved dealing with Selena Alvarez, whether he liked it or not.

And he didn't.

Or, he thought cynically as he locked the door of his motel room behind him and turned his collar against the bitter cold, maybe he'd been lying to himself all along.

"What in the Sam Hill's name is going on? Why weren't we told about this?" Grayson demanded. Flanked by Alvarez and Pescoli, he stood in front of the television mounted on the wall of the conference room.

On the screen, Ray Sutherland was standing in the parking lot of his apartment complex. His kids were with him and he'd placed an arm around each of his half-grown sons. The boys were somber, even shell-shocked, looking as if they would rather be anywhere than on camera. Snow was collecting on the bills of their baseball caps and the shoulders of their oversized jackets, and neither boy would look directly into the camera's eye. Unlike their father. Ray stared straight into the lens. Behind him, through a curtain of falling snow, were several parked cars, each covered in three inches of fluff, and the front of the apartment building where he resided.

"No one knew it was happening," Pescoli said.

"Why the hell not?"

"Don't know," Alvarez said.

Pescoli said, "No one at KMJC News thought about giving us a heads-up. I'm betting Ray Sutherland did this on his own."

"Idiot." Grayson was irritated, obviously felt as if he and the department had been blindsided.

"All we want is for Brenda to come home," Ray was saying, his voice catching a bit. He stared directly into the camera's lens. "Honey, if you're out there, please, call, and if . . . if someone else knows where she is, we want them to please let us know she's all right."

"What is this?" Grayson said. "We're not sure she was kidnapped. The FBI hasn't even jumped in."

"Yet," Pescoli thought aloud and watched the sadness in the two boys' faces as their father begged for his ex-wife's safe return. He seemed genuinely upset, but, Pescoli noted, no tears tracked down his face. "He's the beneficiary on

211

her life insurance policy," Pescoli said. "Just got the confirmation from the insurance company about an hour ago. Get this: two hundred thousand big ones, and he increased it about three months ago. The benefit was originally fifty grand."

"Lots of money," Alvarez said.

Grayson nodded and rubbed the edge of his moustache. "For an ex."

Pescoli thought the whole scene looked staged. "He made it pretty clear when we interviewed him that he wasn't all that fond of her."

"And here he is crying on TV," Grayson said.

"Not quite crying. No tears. Just a big show, dragging his kids out in the snow." Pescoli wasn't buying it.

"This is live, right?" Alvarez said.

Grayson scowled. "Don't know. Could've been taped."

"We would have heard about it and it looks like it's evening. I think I'll head over there now. See what's up. It's not that far from here."

"I'll come with." Pescoli was already walking through the door and into the hallway.

"Report back," Grayson yelled after them. "If I'm not here, call my cell."

Alvarez was right. Even with the evening traffic, they reached the apartment complex where Ray Sutherland had held court in less than fifteen minutes. The interview was over, the reporter, Nia Del Ray, packing up her gear into the KMJC van that was parked in the lot, a driver already waiting and smoking a cigarette that he held near a cracked window while the big rig idled.

"Hey," Pescoli said to the reporter, who was about to climb into the waiting van. She didn't bother flashing her badge or introducing herself as they'd worked with Nia before. "How about a heads-up on something like this?"

Nia, reaching for the handle of the door, paused. "Mr. Sutherland's request. No cops."

"Why?" Alvarez asked.

"Don't know." Nia's dark hair didn't so much as move as she shook her head. "I did mention it and he didn't really answer, just said something about doing it 'his way.' " Nia grabbed the door and opened it. "He called the station and I was sent out here. End of story."

With that, she climbed into the van and the driver put it into gear, then pulled out, big engine rumbling, satellite dish tucked in.

"Pisses me off," Pescoli said as she headed for Ray Sutherland's apartment.

"Everything pisses you off."

"Okay, well this guy *really* pisses me off. Wants to do it his way, like he's damned Sinatra or something." They'd reached Sutherland's unit and Pescoli pounded on the door.

It opened a crack, Brenda's younger son look-ing up at them, the chain still in place. His eyes were round and distrustful, a hank of coffee brown hair falling across his forehead.

"I'm Detective Pescoli and this is my partner, Detective Alvarez. We'd like to talk to your father."

They showed their badges and the kid looked over his shoulder and yelled, "Dad! The police want to talk to you!"

"Tell 'em I'm not interested!" the man yelled back.

"Mr. Sutherland," Pescoli shouted. "We can talk here or down at the station. Your choice."

"What? No! Oh, hell!" Obviously Sutherland wasn't happy. Heavy footsteps could be heard and the boy disappeared from the door, only to be replaced by a red-faced Ray. "What do you want?"

"We heard your interview and plea on television and our department, probably along with the FBI, would like to be involved. If this is a kidnapping case, you need our resources."

"No!" He glanced over his shoulder, scowled, then slipped outside, closing the door behind him. "Look, I only did the thing with the news people for my kids, okay? They're upset and I don't know what to tell them. I really think their mother took off, found herself a boyfriend and just made it look like she was abducted or something. She'll probably show up in a week or two. She just needed a break."

Unlikely, Pescoli thought. They'd gone through Brenda Sutherland's phone and computer records.

If she had a boyfriend, the guy was buried deep; they must've communicated through hand signals or telepathy. Yeah, right.

"And you know this . . . how?" Alvarez asked.

"I don't 'know' it for sure, of course. But it seems damned lucky that it happened while I had the kids. No one was hurt right? No sign of a struggle, no blood in the car. She just took off after going to some church meeting. If you ask me, she had a thing for that preacher, what the hell was his name? Mullins, yeah. She thought he was . . . What did she say? Oh, 'understanding' and 'caring,' and oh, yeah, 'a hunk.' Really? That pious jerk! If you ask me the guy's a phony with a capital F."

Alvarez said, "Suppose your wife was kidnapped; you'd need us to help you get her back."

"Ex-wife," he reminded them, glancing from Alvarez back to Pescoli. "There's no love lost between me and Brenda, okay? I just did this cuz my kids wanted me to." He glanced at the front door, which was now firmly shut, then the window to the living room where the blinds moved a bit. His lips tightened in impatience. "Look, we're done here. I said all I had to say and I'm not going to freeze my ass off arguing with you. Brenda will come home when she's ready or, if she really was abducted, then maybe someone will call."

"We'd like to help; monitor your phone and e-mail and—"

"Forget it." His eyes were dark and cruel. "It would be a waste of time for all of us." He hitched up his jeans by the belt and made his way back to the front door, then disappeared inside.

"Gee, I wonder why they're still not married?" Pescoli said sarcastically, then let out a long breath as she considered how her last marriage had turned sour. "I feel sorry for their kids."

"Let's hope he's right, that Brenda's taking a break or having a fling or whatever, but that she comes back, and soon."

"I don't think it's gonna happen," Pescoli said as they hiked across the snowy parking lot to Alvarez's car.

"Me, neither."

She hated to admit it, but after the discovery of Lara Sue Gilfry's body, Pescoli was convinced that whoever had killed her wouldn't be satisfied with just one victim. The scene had been too staged, the effort to display her body too involved for the creep to stop at just one event.

Nope. Pescoli was willing to bet a week's pay that the killer was poised to strike again. She knew it. Felt that cold certainty deep in her bones.

Sick as it was, Pescoli feared the next body they found would be Brenda Sutherland's.

Before heading home that day, Alvarez put in another call to the dog control center at the county as well as the local vet. But neither the officers in charge of the kennels for the county nor Jordan Eagle had any news on Roscoe. Like Gabriel Reeve, the dog appeared to have vanished. She'd checked with road deputies as well, fearing her dog may have been hit and killed in the streets, but there had been no reports of any injured or dead dogs fitting her puppy's description.

As for Reeve, she'd checked with all the local shelters and deputies on patrol in the parks and near schools, the juvenile detention center, even the hospitals, and anywhere she could think the boy might have shown up, searching for any sign of the runaway, but she'd come up empty-handed.

O'Keefe hadn't called her either, and she'd expected that he would, if he found the kid.

She rotated the kinks from her neck and reminded herself that the boy could be out of the area, long gone. All he had to have done was hitch a ride with a long-haul trucker. For all she knew, Gabriel Reeve might be in San Francisco or Albuquerque or Chicago or anywhere. Possibly Canada. Any damned where. There had been enough time for Reeve to have left the snows of Grizzly Falls and Montana far behind.

Funny that. The kid she'd tried so hard to forget. The one she'd thought of nearly daily, but just fleetingly, now, because he had come crashing back to her world, had become so much more real and tangible, and the old wounds in her heart, the ones she'd so carefully tried to heal, had reopened and oh, so painfully. Now, it had become her mission to find the kid.

Is that before or after you locate your killer? Hmmm?

She grabbed her coat, sidearm and laptop before heading through the lunchroom, where Joelle was packing up the few remaining cookies and brownies into a single plastic container, then swiping out the insides of the empty bins.

"Hey, get this!" Pescoli was heading through the room as well.

Joelle managed to throw her a dirty look and Pescoli caught it. "Hey, I'm sorry, okay?" she said. "I was in a bad mood and I took it out on your decorations. It was wrong."

"Sometimes, Detective, you should think before you speak. And as for your 'bad mood'? That seems to be a typical state for you. I think you bring your problems at home to work and it wouldn't surprise me if you take your work home with you and dump it on your family." Her shiny pink lips pursed a bit. "There should be room for joy, Regan. Even in this place where we deal with criminals, killers and rapists and thieves. That shouldn't make us so jaded and hard that we don't look for the good in the world." She tucked the tubs under her arms and marched out of the lunchroom.

"I said I was sorry," Pescoli said as they walked through the back door and heard it slam and lock behind them as a gust of bitter wind hit Alvarez full force. Man, it was cold. But clear. The snow had stopped for the time being, and above the humming street lamps, a few stars had already appeared.

"Sometimes an apology isn't good enough. At least not for someone like Joelle."

"Oh, God, don't tell me I have to write a letter or get her some little velvety poinsettia or cute little stuffed animal to place on her desk with a sad emoticon face on a card, cuz I'm not doing it."

"No one expects that. In fact, if you did, Grayson would probably order you in for a psych evaluation." Their boots crunched as they crossed the parking lot. "Just give her a break."

"Fair enough." Pescoli nodded as if agreeing with herself. "I've been checking the entrants in that ice sculpture contest in Missoula," she added. "Twenty-four of 'em."

"Seriously?"

"A quick look says that four have records, one was a DUI, another forgery, but two were violent. Domestic abuse in one case, assault in another. I'm checking those boys out."

"Need help?"

"Not yet. Oh"—she snapped her gloved fingers —"by the way, got a call from Ezzie Zwolski." They'd reached Alvarez's Outback. "Seems she wants to come in and talk to me about her boyfriend's death."

"I've always thought she'd been holding back." Ezzie Zwolski had been reticent about discussing Len Bradshaw's death, but Pescoli had been pressuring her, hoping as Bradshaw's lover and Martin Zwolski's wife, she might know more than she was saying.

"She's coming in with an attorney," Pescoli said.

"Uh-oh."

"Tomorrow, at eleven. Thought you might want to be there."

"It's Saturday."

"Go figure. She couldn't come in today, or wouldn't, and I didn't want to wait until Monday, just in case she changed her mind. So she wrangled her lawyer into spending a couple of hours on Saturday with me."

"Yeah, I'll want to be a part of it, but Ezzie wasn't there when Bradshaw was killed." That fact had already been established. She'd been at work, verified by her boss at the grocery store, her time sheet and footage from the store's security cameras.

"I know, but Ezzie has the unique position of having been intimate with both men. And she did the books for the company when Len made off with all the cash. I'm thinking she could give us some insight as to motive and how close the partners were, maybe even how long her ex might hold a grudge . . . Couldn't hurt."

"Suppose not. You know, it might be just as Martin insists. An accident."

"Maybe we'll find out tomorrow." She seemed about to head to her Jeep, then hesitated. "You know, I'm still waiting."

"For what? Ezzie to come clean?"

"Not Ezzie. You. I thought maybe you'd tell me what's really going on with you, O'Keefe and the runaway kid wanted for armed robbery."

"Yeah, I know." She glanced up the street to the coffee shop she and Pescoli often frequented. That wouldn't do. Too many people she knew might be frequenting the cozy little space. She definitely needed more privacy for what she was about to confide. "Look, how about I buy you a drink?"

"Does it come with a shot of the truth?"

"Oh. Yeah." Alvarez opened the door of her Subaru and added, "In fact, it's two-for-one night."

CHAPTER 15

"So the kid in the armed robbery in Helena *could* be your son?" Pescoli said, trying not to sound as stunned as she felt as she stared at her partner across a stained table in a private booth in the Elbow Room tavern, a hole-in-the-wall on the outskirts of town. Here, it was dark, the neon of beer signs shining in bright colors, the smell of beer pervasive, and the patrons played pool, watched sports on the televisions mounted over the bar and shucked free peanuts onto the old concrete floor.

Pescoli had been a witness to a lot of shocking things in her life as a cop. The killers who'd haunted the woods around Grizzly Falls had been cruel and bizarre. However, Alvarez's confession that she was the mother of a kid she'd given up for adoption set Pescoli on her heels. She'd thought she'd had her partner pegged and would never have guessed that the by-the-book cop with a master's degree in psychology and a diet and exercise regimen that would make a professional trainer envious would have such a dark secret that apparently had eaten her up inside. "You could have told me you had a kid," Pescoli said with a lift of a shoulder. "It's not a big deal."

"It is . . . was . . . to me." Alvarez took a sip of her wine, another shocker as she usually stuck to water and green tea and all things healthy.

"So when Grace Perchant wandered up and said your kid was in danger, you knew it was Reeve?"

"I don't believe anything Grace Perchant says. For the love of God, she thinks she talks to ghosts!" Alvarez snapped, irritated.

"Ouch! Sorry. Hell, I've been saying that a lot lately. Everyone tells me I'm insensitive or always pissed off or out of line, and I end up apologizing. Doesn't seem right." She took a long swallow from her frosted glass. "Go on."

Alvarez stared into her glass as if she could see the future in six ounces of merlot. "I didn't even know his name." She was shaking her head. "I had no contact. None. That's the way I thought I'd wanted it."

"And now?"

"Now I just want to find him." Her dark eyes were troubled and she twisted the stem of the glass between her fingers.

"What about your son's father?"

"Out of the picture. Actually, never in it," she said darkly. "Didn't even know I was pregnant."

"High school boyfriend? Something like that?"

Alvarez hesitated, then said, "Something. Not part of the equation, okay?"

Obviously a subject that was off-limits. "Okay. So what about O'Keefe? He's tracking the kid, too."

"Yeah."

Pescoli took a long swallow from her beer as the pool balls clicked from the table around the corner. "I did check on him, y'know. With that Helena detective, Trey Williams. He said the guy was legit, kind of a deputy, but not official."

"O'Keefe doesn't always play by the rules."

"So I gathered."

"But he's effective."

"That's what Williams said. So far I haven't seen much evidence of that. The kid's his cousin?"

"Gabe's adoptive mother, Aggie Reeve, is O'Keefe's cousin."

"Okay, . . . like a second cousin, or something. This just keeps getting more and more fun."

Alvarez's head snapped up and she shot a look at her partner that was hard as steel. "Definitely *not* fun."

"Bad choice of words. But you were involved with O'Keefe, right?" Before Alvarez could answer, Pescoli held up a palm. "Don't go into the whole denial thing, okay? I'm not an ace detective for nothing. I get paid to figure out this crap."

"Fine." Alvarez's jaw tightened a little. "We were involved."

Pescoli raised an eyebrow.

"Not like that. Well, not really." Alvarez looked down and swore under her breath. "We were close. I mean, the act is just a technicality, I guess. I thought . . . fleetingly that I was in love with him, that he might be 'the one,' "—her mouth twisted with remembered bitterness—"if you believe in all that garbage, which, by the way, I don't. But before things got too complicated, I backed out. Well, at least I thought I did. Turns out I was wrong." She twisted the stem more violently, watching, as if in fascination, as the bloodlike liquid sloshed against the bowl of the glass.

"And that's when everything went down in San Bernardino."

"Yeah. The upshot is that I left the department and so did O'Keefe. His actions were under review, and though technically he was cleared of any criminal charges when Alberto De Maestro was shot, De Maestro, who survived, sued everyone associated with the shooting."

"Including the department?"

"Oh, yeah. *Especially* the department. Got a lot of press out of that."

"So O'Keefe quit."

"You read about it?"

"What I could. The facts. What I didn't get was the emotional story."

"So now you've got that."

"And you're still in love with him, aren't you?"

"With O'Keefe?" Alvarez shook her head but didn't meet Pescoli's eyes. "Nah. It was a fling, make that *almost* a fling."

"And you're a liar, Alvarez." Pescoli was tired of the BS and Alvarez trying to convince everyone, herself included, what a badass she was. "You were in love with him then and you still are. So don't tell me any differently." She checked her watch and signaled their waitress. "You said two-for-one. I think I need another beer."

He'd run out of ideas.

O'Keefe sat in his hotel room, propped against the pillows of the bed, laptop balanced on his legs, an open bottle of beer on the nightstand next to a half-eaten bag of chips, dinner compliments of the minimart down the street. The television on the dresser at the foot of the bed was turned on, the volume low and casting flickering images from a local news program. He'd caught the weather from an earlier newscast and it wasn't good, more snow predicted, a blizzard blowing in from Canada.

Which wouldn't help him in trying to find the kid.

"Hell," he muttered and took another swig, draining his bottle.

With the help of Trey Williams in Helena, he'd checked Gabriel Reeve's cell phone records, but the phone hadn't been used and so far hadn't been located. The GPS system in it had been disabled. O'Keefe had checked the bus station and local hangouts where a kid could get lost, but Gabe had either not shown up or was like a ghost. He'd gone through Gabe's Facebook account and any other social media he could find, but Gabe's page was dark, hadn't been updated since before the robbery had taken place. No help; even the posts leading up to that day hadn't offered the hint of a clue as to what the kid had been thinking.

He'd been in contact with the Helena PD, who had been working the case and had been closemouthed about it, of course. However, O'Keefe's one contact, Trey Williams, had been a little more forthcoming and had reported that none of Gabe's friends were copping to hearing from him.

O'Keefe knew for a fact that Gabe's family hadn't had any contact with him.

It was as if the kid had just disappeared.

And that was worrisome. Had O'Keefe spooked him and Gabe had left the area? He could have stolen a car or hitchhiked, or God knew what else. But the boy had zeroed in on Selena Alvarez's apartment; that couldn't have been a random act. Really—what were the odds?

Uh-uh. Not a coincidence. Gabe had come here. To Grizzly frickin' Falls rather than a larger city where he could have more easily blended in and gotten lost. Also, he'd broken into Selena Alvarez's home. Not a neighbor's. Not one down the street. He'd beelined for her town house. Weird that. It was as if the kid knew she could be his mother.

O'Keefe had a call in to the attorney who had set up the original adoption, wanted to find out if Gabe had contacted the firm, but so far, O'Keefe hadn't heard back.

The kid was smart. Near genius IQ. A computer wizard. But he was still only sixteen. How could he disappear so easily?

Because you screwed it up. You almost had him!

Pushing aside all of his recriminations, O'Keefe glanced at the television again as he noticed that footage of the crime scene at the church was being played again, the camera panning over the snow-covered crèche where the body had been found. Alvarez would be up to her eyeballs in that one.

Selena Alvarez!

His jaw tightened.

Was it bad luck or fate that had brought him face-to-face with her again?

He considered another beer tucked away in the minifridge that he'd stocked earlier, then decided against it.

On the news, he caught an image of a man standing in a snowy parking lot with two boys at his side. He turned up the volume and heard the guy's pleas for his wife to come home. The boys, teenagers, looked miserable and everywhere but at the camera, but the man stared straight into the camera's lens and asked his wife to come home.

It was obvious he feared the fate that had happened to the woman found in the block of ice could have happened to his wife. Or actually, as the news reporter clarified, his ex-wife. Nonetheless, he seemed worried sick.

Poor bastard.

And the kids . . . Jesus.

He clicked off the set, grabbed his sidearm and decided to talk to Selena Alvarez again. Like it or not, she was the one connection he had to Gabe.

Telling Pescoli about the baby was probably a mistake, but Alvarez felt cornered, that the truth was bound to come out soon anyway. Gabriel Reeve had seen to that. As she drove home, she thought about the boy and wondered what she'd say to him once he was found.

"Why did you run into my house?"

"Do you know who I am?"

"Were you looking for me?"

"Do you know that giving you up was the hardest decision of my life?"

Her throat closed as she thought of seeing him face-to-face.

"Don't go there," she warned herself as she turned down the street near her condo complex and recognized O'Keefe's old Explorer parked near her driveway.

Her fingers tightened over the steering wheel and she felt her pulse elevate. Did he know anything about Gabe? Her anxiety level ratcheted up a notch. As she pulled into the drive, the door to his SUV opened and he stepped into the street.

"Any news?" she asked as she climbed out of the Outback and slammed the door shut.

"Just what I was going to ask you."

"Great. I was hoping you'd found my son."

"And I was hoping you'd have a lead."

"Been busy," she said. "If you haven't noticed."

"I did." He reached for her computer case, but she ignored his outstretched hand and walked to the front door of her condo. She didn't want to be around him; it was just too difficult, but now, because of Gabe, she didn't have much of a choice.

As she unlocked the door of her town house, she reminded herself that she had to keep this investigation professional, no matter how personal it seemed. Regardless if he was her son or not, Gabriel Reeve had an adoptive mother and father, a real family complete with siblings. She couldn't mess with that.

As for O'Keefe, he was definitely off-limits. She wasn't going to get involved with him again. Not that he'd shown any outward interest in rekindling their romance, but there was an undeniable chemistry with him, a passion she was determined to keep under wraps.

Once inside the foyer, she tossed her keys on a side table and slid out of her jacket and boots. O'Keefe, though not actually invited in, did the same as she called for the cat. When Jane Doe appeared on the stairs, poking her face through the rails, O'Keefe actually laughed. "She's a clown," he said and the cat, as if she knew he was talking about her, hurried down the remaining stairs and rubbed up against his leg.

"No, she's a traitor, from the looks of it." But Alvarez felt a smile tug at the corners of her lips. "She was an orphan, her owner killed, and since I was investigating the case and no one seemed to want her, I adopted her."

"And the dog?"

"Impulse decision." She glanced at the kennel in the corner of the living room. "I thought I'd find him by now." She felt a little tug on her heart. "I miss him. Don't get me wrong, Roscoe could be a real pain in the backside, but still . . . I guess he got under my skin."

"That can happen," O'Keefe said, and when she looked up at him, she found him staring at her. Hard. "When you least expect it."

Her throat tightened. The room seemed to shrink. She knew he was talking about their brief time together, that white-hot summer in California. It would take so little to rekindle that flame . . . so damned little. And that would be a big mistake. "I know," she said, her voice a little deeper than she'd intended, "but then when it's over, you have to let it go."

"*If* it's over," he clarified. "Not when."

She was staring at him, her gaze lost in his, and she forced herself to look away, to clear her head, to push away the thoughts of the time they shared, the kisses under the palm trees, the stolen moments in the shadows of the buildings, the night they'd been in the shower together. She remembered all too clearly the feel of his hands against her wet skin. Oh, damn. "It's the only sane thing to do," she whispered.

"Sometimes sanity doesn't enter into the equation."

"It always should," she insisted. *"Always."*

To her dismay, he reached forward and touched the crook of her arm. "Selena?" he whispered and something around her heart, that hard shell she tried so desperately to protect, started to crack. The long week, the loss of her dog, the knowledge that her son was out there, in the freezing cold, so near, yet so far, and Dylan O'Keefe, here in her apartment . . . She didn't resist when he folded her into his arms though she told herself she was every kind of fool. He placed a finger under her chin, lifted her face and kissed her. Hard. With a passion she remembered all too well.

Hot tears burned the back of her eyelids as his mouth moved over hers and she felt the roughness of his beard shadow against her skin.

A dozen memories flooded her brain. In that swift moment, she remembered laughing with him in a sudden rain shower and dashing to his pickup. Her blouse was so wet, it clung to her skin, becoming see-through, her bra visible. Inside the truck, they continued kissing and touching, the blood rushing in Alvarez's brain, her body trembling with desire. The windows of his old truck steamed on the inside while rain drizzled down the windshield and lightning sizzled across the sky. As thunder had rolled through empty streets, she'd flashed back to another time, another place, another car and the smell of cigarettes and beer, the rough fumbling hands of her cousin Emilio, the hard plastic seat of the El Camino.

"Don't," she'd said, meaning it as he'd thrown himself upon her. "Get off me!"

But he, fueled by alcohol and a need to dominate, hadn't listened. She'd screamed. She'd fought. She'd pulled the knife from his back pocket and threatened him with it, to no avail. The slice she'd made in his shoulder had only enraged him and made him more determined than ever.

No amount of kicking or screaming or spitting or crying could stop him, and there, in his father's El Camino, he'd raped her, taken her virginity and impregnated her, all in ten minutes of brutal, soul-destroying hell.

She'd never been able to make love since.

Not in the pickup in the middle of a rainstorm in San Bernardino.

Not in O'Keefe's shower.

And not, she expected, now, in her town house.

She lifted her head and stared into his eyes. "I . . . I don't think this is a good idea." Her voice was a whisper and she extracted herself from his embrace.

"You're right." Shoving a hand through his hair, he stepped away from her. "I was out of line."

"No more than I was." She let out her breath slowly. "Look, we just have a lot of work to do and anything else might blur the lines, change the focus. Right now, we have to find Gabe."

The brackets around his mouth tightened and she felt her muscles tense as if she might have to battle him. His stare was intense, but she saw something shift in his gaze. "Agreed," he finally said. "But let's grab something to eat first and then get to it." She opened her mouth to protest and he held up a hand. "For the record, this is *not* a date. Okay?" He hesitated and added, "But I'm starved and I think we need a break, now that we've established the ground rules."

"Not a date."

"Definitely not," he said.

"Then how about we just order a pizza?"

"Again?"

"Chinese doesn't deliver in this neighborhood," she said. "Besides we both like it. And we can have it here. Then we can get to work. Dino's delivers. In any kind of weather."

"Like the U.S. post office?"

"Oh, yeah, right. Except the drivers are kids. Teenagers. Don't look old enough to have a license. And the cars they drive? More dents than you can find in a demolition derby."

"But the pizza is good? Hot?"

"Best in town. And certainly as good as what you brought over the other night. So . . . You still like an all-meat combo?" She was already sliding her cell phone from a pocket in her purse and saw him nod. "Then we'll split a medium. I'll get the veggie special on my half."

"Broccoli should never be anywhere near a pizza pie."

"Glad you feel that way. Then I don't have to worry about you stealing any of mine, do I?" Grateful that the atmosphere had lightened a bit, she offered him a smile as she hit a number on the keypad and Dino's number flashed on the screen as it connected.

"You have the pizza parlor on speed dial?" he asked, apparently surprised.

"Of course, O'Keefe!" She actually laughed. "Doesn't everyone?"

CHAPTER 16

"I wondered if you'd show," Santana said as he closed the door to his cabin behind Pescoli. Inside, the smell of wood smoke mingled with the tangy scent of roasting pork.

"Been a little busy. New Christmas whacko on the loose. Just in case you hadn't heard."

"I did. It's all anyone in town is talking about. The ice mummy."

"She's a little more than that to me," Pescoli admitted and couldn't help wondering about the other missing women, Lissa Parsons and Brenda Sutherland. She felt the clock ticking, each second a reminder that those women, too, could be in the hands of the nut job with the affinity for ice chisels and saws. She'd already run down the rap sheets on the two violent ice sculptors for the winter festival in Missoula and discovered they had each already arrived and had picked up their entrance information from the registrar.

The first, Hank Yardley, had brought his latest wife and kids along and checked into a Missoula motel not far from the event. Hank had, according to records and his parole officer, kept his nose clean since the domestic abuse charge stemming from a bitter divorce. He'd been in no trouble in the past six years.

However, the second guy, George Flanders, lived around here, just outside of town on a farm. His first offense had been getting into a squabble with his neighbors that had escalated over the years and had turned violent, the neighbor ending up in ICU for three weeks, compliments of George and his ice pick. George pled to a lesser charge and spent a few years in the slammer. Now he was married, attended church irregularly, and was a member of a local lodge. He seemed to now be able to keep his legendary temper in check. Since he'd been out of prison, his only offense was rear-ending a woman with his pickup at a stop light. The woman had claimed it was intentional, the result of road rage as George had thought she'd cut him off while merging into traffic. She'd said he turned "nasty" and looked as if he might "kill her" when he'd gotten out of his car and approached her at the stop sign. It had "freaked her out." As he'd stepped closer to her open window, she'd thought better of talking to him and punched it, "afraid for her life." Later, she'd filed a complaint and an insurance claim, insisting she was suffering from neck injuries and psychological trauma. The case had been settled out of court.

"Hey?" Santana said, bringing Pescoli to the present. "Need a drink?"

"At least one. Maybe six."

He chuckled and Pescoli felt her tense muscles begin to relax a bit. At least she had a few hours to unwind. Both kids were out with friends for the entire night, and though that still made her a little nervous, she let it go. She'd keep her cell phone on . . . just in case they needed her.

Oh, yeah, if they're in trouble, you're the first one they'd call, their mother, the cop.

Nonetheless, she threw her keys and wallet onto a scratched table near the front door and wondered why this drafty three-room cabin with a sleeping loft tucked under the roof felt more like home— a haven—than her own house did. Over a hundred years old, the place had been the original home-stead of the Long family, Santana's employer. Santana already had plans to build a larger home on the property he'd inherited, but so far, the construction crew hadn't broken ground on the home he'd invited her, and her children and dog, to share.

Pescoli started walking toward the warmth of the woodstove when he caught the crook of her elbow. "Hey, you forgot something."

"What?" She looked up just as he grabbed her, dragged her body against his and kissed her hard. As if of their own accord, her bones felt as if they could melt and she wrapped her arms around his neck and opened her mouth willingly. He just felt so damned good. One of his hands grabbed hold of her rump, and that old, familiar heat, the one that got her into trouble, began to sing through her veins.

Even through her jeans, his fingertips brushing the split between her buttocks, and erotic images filled her mind.

"You're bad," she whispered. "The worst."

"And you love it."

"Mmm. That I do." As he pressed her up against the wall, the back of her leg hit the small table where her keys had been tossed. They slid off the surface and, jangling, landed on the floor. From his position near the fire, Nakita, Santana's Husky, let out a soft woof.

"Guard dog," Santana joked, lifting his head for a second and looking into her eyes. His hand found the zipper of her jeans while she pushed the flannel shirt off his shoulders and pulled the hem of his T-shirt from his battered jeans.

He moaned softly as her fingers found his skin.

"Jesus, woman!" he said and picked her up off her feet.

"Hey!" Startled, she started to protest. "What're you doing?"

"You'll see."

She wasn't a petite woman, had played college basketball, but he carried her as if she weighed little and hauled her up the stairs to the room under the eaves and tumbled with her onto the big bed with the creaking mattress. "I, uh, I thought you promised me a drink."

"You want me to stop?" he teased as he lifted her sweater over her head. He tossed it, along with both his shirts, to a darkened corner of the room.

Lying on her back, a pillow that smelled of his aftershave supporting her head, she felt her throat catch. "Never."

"That's what I thought." Straddling her, he unclasped the front opening of her bra, letting her breasts spill out. Cold air caressed her skin, causing her nipples to pucker. Even in the half-light, she saw his smile, a crooked slash of white. "You *are* beautiful," he whispered, then began to suckle at one breast while he skimmed the jeans down her legs, his fingers scraping the skin of her thighs and calves.

Pescoli lost herself in the feel of him, in the pure animal sensations of his body against hers. Closing her eyes, her fingers tangled in his hair, she tingled at the feel of his calloused hands and his wet, hot tongue. They would pleasure each other for hours, bringing each other to the brink over and over again, and she couldn't think of anywhere she'd rather be than in this cowboy's bed.

They'd made little progress, O'Keefe thought as he scraped his chair away from the table, then carried his three empties into the kitchen, where Alvarez was tidying up.

The clock mounted near the stove indicated it was ten past midnight.

After going through all the information each of them had on Gabriel Reeve, they weren't any closer to finding him than they had been before the damned pizza had arrived. Alvarez had used all of her connections, including some contacts with the state guys. O'Keefe had touched base with Trey Williams, conference calling with Alvarez included, but the kid was a ghost.

The trouble was there were lots of places to get lost in this part of Montana—forest, streams, caves, hills—and worse yet, there were lots of areas where, if a person wasn't equipped to battle the elements, he could die of exposure, his remains going undiscovered until the spring thaw, if then.

"He must've left town," Alvarez said as she rinsed their two plates under the tap, then set the wet dishes onto a tray in the dishwasher.

"Maybe, but he seemed dead set on coming here. To your place."

"So we're back to that?" Wiping her hands on a towel, she shoved the dishwasher shut with a foot just as her cat hopped onto the counter from a bar stool. "Hey, you . . . down!" Alvarez admonished and the cat proceeded to sit, black tail curling over her white toes, before she began to wash her face. "Great. That's it! You're outta here." She lifted Jane from the counter, only to set her on the floor. Miffed, with a dark glare cast over one sleek shoulder to Alvarez, Jane slunk out of the kitchen, padding quickly to the living room.

"I never figured you for a cat person."

"Or a dog person, whatever that is?"

"Neither," he admitted. "You just didn't seem the type."

"And why's that?" She swiped at a bit of dirt on the counter, glared at it, then swiped again.

"Animals are messy. You know, litter boxes and nose and paw prints on windows, torn-up cushions."

"I do know and you're right. I never really thought I needed . . . or wanted an animal. But . . ." She glanced over her shoulder at him as she folded her towel neatly and placed it over the handle of the stove. ". . . people change."

"Do they?" He wasn't convinced, but he let it slide. Damn, she looked good. A few hours ago, while sitting at her laptop, studying the birth records Selena had surrendered, she'd taken the rubber band from her hair and shaken it free. So black it nearly shined blue in the lamplight, it had fallen to the middle of her back. Unconsciously, she'd tossed a wayward hank over her shoulders, showing off the long column of her throat as she'd worked.

So engrossed in her computer screen, she'd adjusted the rubber band and snapped it back into place, lifting her hands behind her head, and again, without realizing it, stretching her sweater across her breasts.

He'd caught the motion and looked away quickly, suddenly uncomfortable as he'd remembered how her coppery skin had looked against the white sheets of the bed, and the perfectly round disks of her dark nipples.

Now he said, "I'd better go. If you hear anything more or find out anything, give me a call."

"You, too." Her dark gaze met his for an instant, before she walked him to the door, where he found himself wanting to kiss her good night.

Idiot.

Selena Alvarez is the last woman you need to think about kissing—the very last!

After grabbing his jacket, he walked outside and he noticed the snow hadn't started falling yet; the night was bitter cold, but clouds were gathering, blocking the moon and stars. Once inside his Ford, he fired up the engine and blew on his hands.

The heater would take a while, so he grudgingly pulled on a pair of gloves as she turned out the porch light. What was it about her that had such a hold on him? From the minute he'd first laid eyes on her years ago in San Bernardino, he'd found her fascinating; a combination of fire and ice, she could be coldly calculating one minute and passionately volatile the next. Of course she was beautiful, but he'd met lots of beautiful women in his life. None, unfortunately, had touched him the way Alvarez had.

As he did a quick U-turn, avoiding other cars parked on the snowy streets, he wondered about the son she'd borne. What kind of coincidence was it that a fugitive sixteen-year-old had led him straight to Alvarez's home? Not one to believe in kismet or fate or any of that other idealistic crap, he couldn't help but believe that Gabe had run here thinking his birth mother could shelter him when his adoptive parents wouldn't. But how would he have found her?

He slowed for a traffic light, watching the red glow reflect on the snow and ice in the road.

So who was the mystery man who had fathered her child? When he'd asked about Gabe's father, he'd been met with a frosty rebuff. She'd insinuated it wasn't any of O'Keefe's business, which, considering the circumstances, was a flat-out lie and they'd both known it, but he hadn't pressed the issue tonight, preferring to let her come around to telling him the truth. If he had to, he'd find out himself. He knew she grew up in Woodburn, Oregon, and that her family was still there. *Some*one knew the full story and it wouldn't take too much talking to pry it out of the local gossips. Families resided for generations in a small town the size of Woodburn, or Grizzly Falls, for that matter. And people had long memories when it came to gossip.

She'd acted as if the father didn't even know that he'd sired a kid. Maybe that was true. Maybe it wasn't. Either way, he thought as the light turned green and he noticed headlights behind him, identifying Gabe's biological father could stir up a whole new hornet's nest.

Alvarez ignored the tugs on her heart.

A tug because she was so close to meeting her son and now was worried about the boy she'd never met.

A tug because she missed the rambunctious puppy.

A tug because Dylan O'Keefe brought back memories of a happiness that was almost within her reach and yet she'd let it slip between her fingers.

Disgusted at the turn of her thoughts, she snapped off the lights and reminded herself that even though tomorrow was Saturday, she had to go into the office.

But tonight her town house seemed empty. "Well, come on," she said to the cat as she mounted the stairs.

O'Keefe was still good-looking, sexy in a rough-and-tumble kind of way. He was also the man to whom she'd nearly bared her soul and given her body, the one to whom she'd gotten way too close and had definitely gotten burned. Her irresponsibility in San Bernardino had nearly gotten herself and O'Keefe killed. He had the visible scars to prove it and she the night terrors. Her rashness had cost him his job.

Now, as she stripped out of her street clothes and slipped into a huge T-shirt, guilt crept through her mind like a cold, dark snake. She should have known better. She'd been foolish and reckless. If she hadn't been involved with O'Keefe, if she hadn't crossed that sometimes blurry line that separated business from pleasure, she wouldn't have been so emotionally wrung out and wouldn't have made the crucial mistake of getting into a madman's line of fire. In so doing, she'd forced O'Keefe into shooting the suspect before he could be questioned.

O'Keefe had quit before he'd been fired, but the truth of the matter was that Alvarez had been young, dumb, green and stubborn, convinced of her own brilliance and infallibility. Though

O'Keefe had been older, and theoretically wiser, he'd been sexy as all get out and determined to get her into his bed. Theirs had been a fiery relationship and she'd gone as far with him as she'd dared, as far as her freaked-out mind had let her.

On the night of the shooting at De Maestro's cottage, Alvarez had made a bad decision that had nearly cost lives and certainly gave De Maestro room to point his crooked finger at the department and its employees.

All in all it had ended as a lose-lose-lose situation, and after O'Keefe quit, Alvarez had eventually made the move to Grizzly Falls. Having learned her painful lesson, she'd never allowed herself to get close to anyone again, the lone exception being Pescoli, and even that relationship was primarily professional.

She clicked off the overhead light and walked to the window, where darkness was held at bay by the snow on the ground, a blue-white mantel reflecting the watery illumination of a few street lamps. It was quiet outside, snow beginning to fall again, a peaceful setting, but she sensed an evil in shadows, all the more frightening because of the serenity of the night.

Outside a killer loomed large, hiding in the shadows, ducking through the alleyways, but ever vigilant. It was almost as if he could see her here, standing on the inside of the glass.

Goose bumps rose on the back of her neck as she searched the shadows. Though she usually had no faith in "feelings" or "sensations," tonight she experienced a soul-numbing coldness that reminded her that malevolence existed in the very actions of man.

She squinted, saw a movement, a shadow sliding across the white snow, but just out of focus, the edges of whatever dark form muted by a thin veil.

I'm coming for you, she heard, ricocheting through the recesses of her mind. *I'm coming for you and there is no escape.*

"Hogwash," she muttered, "*Adoquin!*" It was her grandmother's favorite admonition whenever she thought one of her many grandchildren were being foolish.

Refusing to freak herself out, Alvarez snapped the blinds shut and slid into the cold sheets as Jane jumped onto the bed. The cat, already purring, made a big production of finding the right spot on the pillow where Alvarez had once thought a man might rest his head.

That fantasy seemed impossible now, though the reappearance of Dylan O'Keefe into her life had softened her perspective a little. She couldn't help remembering how much in love with him she'd once believed herself to be.

"*Adoquin,*" she repeated in a whisper. Closing her eyes, she refused to think of O'Keefe and how, after all the years and heartache, she was still attracted to his slow, sensual smile and the glint of bad-boy humor in his eyes, and the way his jeans hugged his butt. He would only break her heart. Again. And he might just want a bit of revenge for what had happened in the past.

It didn't matter anyway, she told herself as she plumped her pillow and turned over. She had a major intimacy problem. Major. Courtesy of her cousin Emilio half a lifetime ago.

Damn that darned paperboy!

He never showed up on time, at least not early enough for Mabel Enstad, who rose well before dawn, around four o'clock in the morning, and wanted to read her newspaper with her morning tea and biscotti before her husband woke up. It was going on six now and Ollie, as always this early, was still sawing logs, his snoring rippling down the hallway and sounding like a flock of agitated geese.

She peered through the curtains and noticed that it was snowing heavily again, yet there were no tracks near the mail/newspaper box indicating that the daily had been delivered.

"Lazy whelp," she'd muttered, knowing full well that the delivery "boy" was really Arvin North, a thirty-six-year-old deadbeat father of four who fought his ex-wife for every nickel of child support she wanted. It galled Mabel to think that any of her hard-earned money went to the lazy loser, and at this time of year, when people gave a special gift to their mail and paper delivery people, Mabel sent a Christmas card and forty dollars in crisp ten-dollar bills, anonymously of course, to Roberta, the ex–Mrs. North, a lovely woman who sang in the church choir. Mabel always included a note with the money, instructing that each of Roberta's deserving children receive one of the bills for Christmas. As she let the drapery fall, Mabel made a mental note to go to the bank later this week and pick up the new bills so she could make her donation. However, as the curtain closed, she noticed something in the side yard between her house and the Swansons'.

A snowman . . . make that a large snowman, or maybe even a woman nearly anatomically correct, sat directly in front of the snowman her grandchildren had made two days ago. The "woman's" rump was pushed right up against what would have been the groin of Frosty.

"Oh, for the love of Saint Pete," she grumbled, knowing who the culprits were. They lived next door. Rented the old Brandt place and had been trouble ever since. Those neighbor kids, the Swanson boys, were trouble. Though she couldn't prove it, of course, Mabel was certain the teenagers had been behind the rearrangement of her Christmas yard ornaments just last year. The lighted, grapevine deer were her pride and joy and she placed them, along with a plastic Santa and his wife, strategically in her yard. The lights she'd strung in the fir trees only added to the charm of her display.

Buck, the larger of the deer, even moved its head slowly side to side.

Last year, that randy, mind-in-the-gutter Jeb Swanson had moved the perfectly innocent deer into the most unflattering and positively disgusting position, mounting it upon its more serene and unmoving mate as if they were fornicating! In the yard. A few feet from Santa and Mrs. Claus!

Now, it seemed, they'd come up with a new, perverse prank. Nasty little hellions! Destined to become criminals if the parents didn't take charge and quick!

And now look!

In her slippers, Mabel, muttering to herself, hurried to the back door, where she plucked her jacket off a hook and stepped into her waiting boots. She threw her knit cap onto her head and pulled on a pair of gloves before grabbing the big flashlight that Ollie kept by the back door.

Trudging toward the front of the house where four new inches had added to what was already half a foot of old snow, she made her way to the front yard, past her still intact Christmas display. So far, Santa, his wife and the deer hadn't been touched, but in the space separating her house from that of the Swansons', the snowman had definitely been messed with.

She had half a mind to bang on the Swansons' door and wake up the whole darned family, dragging them out of their snug beds to take a gander at what the sons had done. "Should be enrolled in art class," she muttered under her breath and noticed that the coal eyes of the snow woman had both fallen onto the ground . . . or weren't anywhere to be seen . . . No, actually, as she shined her light over the abomination, she realized that there were no finishing touches, no top hat or stick arms or carrot nose, as there were on Frosty directly behind her.

Nor was there a satisfied smile or a dangling cigarette on the snow woman's face, the kind of thing that would be just up those little brats' alley. To her horror, she even wondered if they'd taken Frosty's carrot nose and placed it lower . . . but, no! His nose was where it should be, thank the good Lord!

"Weird," she said aloud and heard the sound of a car behind her. She glanced over her shoulder and noticed the twin beams of headlights cutting through the veil of snow as a car came over the rise. Finally! That miserable paper delivery man decided to make his appearance, after six A.M., no less! Mabel told herself she needed to call the distributor of the paper and complain.

Too bad Arvin would get a view of this snow woman, a creation who definitely had curves in all the right places, even if she had no face, no scarf, no . . . What the heck was that?

Mabel squinted at the foul snow sculpture.

As the headlights from the approaching car flashed over the snow woman, something glinted beneath the dusting of powder, something bright and sparkling, high on the middle "ball" of the woman's body. Leaning over, Mabel shined her flashlight more directly on that area, a few inches below where the neck would be and, yes, there was something brilliant buried in the packed snow, something reflective.

"What the devil?"

As the beams from Arvin's little Mazda's headlights washed over the snowman, Mabel scowled and brushed away some of the snow that had collected as she tried to get to the glinting bit of metal . . . A ring, maybe? She had to work at it, scraping away the packed snow, her fingers, deep in her gloves, feeling a hardness that was surprising until she realized that it wasn't snow beneath the night's dusting, but ice. Thick, solid ice.

She felt the first niggle of anxiety.

The hairs on the back of her neck raised.

Jumping Jehoshaphat! Was the ring . . . was it . . . oh, my God, inserted through a nipple? A real breast?

Revulsion rippled through her and a new fear clutched at her heart. Was this "snow woman" a real woman, dead and trapped in ice? "No . . . oh . . . no . . ."

Jumping, startled as she heard the sound of her paper being slammed into its box, she brushed aside more snow, higher up, on the head of this sick creation.

Her heart was beating wildly now, panic settling in, and she wondered why she hadn't picked up Ollie's shotgun propped by the back door. She could have loaded that sucker before venturing out . . . Oh, dear God in heaven, she remembered what she'd seen in the news about a woman frozen and left in one of the town's church's nativity scenes.

Surely that was an isolated incident.

This couldn't be . . .

But as she brushed away the fresh powder, her heart thundering in her ears, the sound of the delivery car's engine revving as Arvin started to turn around and head back toward town, Mabel caught sight of something blue and . . . "Holy crap . . . Oh, dear God!" she cried, stepping back, her flashlight falling into the snow as the dead woman's eye, wide open and fixed, stared unseeing through a slab of ice.

CHAPTER 17

"It's Lissa Parsons," Alvarez whispered, sick at the thought of the once-lively woman she'd seen working out at the gym. Now, as she shined her flashlight's beam at the block of ice, light piercing the heavy clear layer to illuminate the face of the naked woman inside, Alvarez felt a fresh rush of anger sluicing through her veins. Who the hell would do this thing? What kind of creep—

"Damn it all to hell! I knew it!" Pescoli glared at the victim. Snow was collecting on her hat and shoulders, the wind starting to pick up. "That son of a bitch is a serial! God damn, son of a bitch! I was hoping—"

"That Lara Sue Gilfry was an isolated incident and the other women weren't in his clutches?" Alvarez finished for her. "Yeah, I know." She glanced at the still-dark sky, felt snowflakes catch on her cheeks. "Could be a copycat."

Pescoli snorted. "Yeah, right. Looks like we'll be letting the FBI know we've got ourselves another one."

This crime scene, a patch of lawn stretched between two houses on the outskirts of Grizzly Falls was about as remote as the first, and just as chilling. No, there were no religious overtones to the crime as there seemed to have been in the display of the first victim's body, but once again the killer showed some macabre sense of humor as Lissa's sculpted ice coffin had been set up against a snowman in the yard, a snowman, Mabel had raved, that had been created by her grand-children a couple of days earlier.

What the hell was that all about?

Who was this sicko who wanted to kill women, then display them in some kind of intricately macabre ice sculpture? They'd already talked briefly to the Enstads and their neighbors and now deputies were taking more complete statements.

Alvarez, after a rotten night's sleep, was already awake when the call had come through from dispatch. She'd phoned Pescoli's cell, roused her groggy partner, and they'd met here, arriving within minutes of each other.

Now the snow continued to fall and the arctic blast that raged caused the beams of their flashlights to cast weird shadows over the strange ice sculpture. The area had already been roped off with crime scene tape and the owners of the property, bundled in winter jackets, hats, gloves and scarves, were huddled together on the wraparound porch. A deputy was questioning the Enstads, and though she couldn't hear what was being said, Alvarez noticed that the woman— Mabel—was doing most of the talking. She was gesturing wildly, not only at the victim, but also to the neighboring house where a group of four had gathered on the cement steps.

A second deputy was talking to the Swansons, who were huddled together, mom, dad and two sons. The mother, Mandy, was nervously smoking a cigarette and the father had one arm around her shoulders as if to hold her upright.

Alvarez's stomach dropped as she stared at Lissa Parsons. Though she hadn't known her very well, they'd come across each other at the gym often enough to smile and say, "Hi." No more. Her short dark hair was spiked, somehow caught standing straight up in the ice, her eyes wide open as if she were staring straight ahead and she was naked except for a glistening object in the flashlight's glare, a slim gold ring hanging from the nipple of her right breast. "It's mine," Alvarez said disbelieving, her stomach knotting as she stared at the gold hoop with its winking bloodred stone.

"What's yours?" Pescoli asked. "Wait a second. The nipple ring?" Pescoli's eyebrows lifted skeptically, as if she didn't believe her partner for a second. "Are you kidding?"

"No, not a *nipple* ring . . . Oh, hell, it's the earring that went missing after the break in. I recognize it because of the stone, it's red glass, supposed to look like a ruby. A gift from my grandmother."

"The earring that disappeared with the kid?" Pescoli clarified, her own beam now centered on the victim's breast.

"Yes!" Alvarez nodded, her mind racing with the possibilities. How could Gabriel Reeve be mixed up with the whack job who had killed two women? Or, had he dropped the earring and the killer found it? Was it possible that Gabe had pawned it or sold it on the street? Or had he been with the killer when he'd broken into the house, or . . . had the killer come alone and taken the earring himself?

"Jesus H. Christ. You're sure it's yours?"

"Of course!" she snapped, suddenly frantic, her thoughts tearing through her brain. Dear God, where the hell was Gabe? *With the psycho? Held captive? Oh, God, not in league with the maniac! No, no, no . . . pull it together! Think, Selena, think. Rationally. Don't panic. Do NOT panic!* She had to focus. To take her emotions out of the case. To find the sadistic madman who was killing local women and enshrouding them in ice. Somehow this lunatic was connected to her boy.

Anxiety surged through her. "We have to locate this maniac," she said, attempting to sound calm despite the panic that was erupting inside of her. "Soon."

"I know." Pescoli was looking at her as if she'd lost her mind. "Calm down."

"I am calm!"

"Whoa!" Pescoli grabbed her by the crook of her arm. "Take yourself out of this, Alvarez. Right now! Or I'll get someone else to help me with this one." She was dead serious.

"No! Wait . . . no, I'm . . . I'll be . . . fine," Alvarez insisted, letting out her breath in a cloud as the crime scene team arrived and took over the area. Within two minutes, not one but two news vans arrived, parking on the street, technicians and cameramen adjusting the satellites and cameras while the reporters set up shop.

Alvarez didn't want to think for a second that the media might learn about her earring and learn that it was lost in a break-in by a runaway teenaged boy wanted for armed robbery at a judge's house in Helena. However, the news was sure to leak.

She would become besieged. More questions would be asked . . . *Dios!*

"Great. I think I'm going to find out what Hank Yardley and George Flanders were up to last night. Wonder if they have alibis?"

Eyeing the huge vehicles from the news stations, Alvarez let out her breath slowly. Why the media bothered her, she couldn't say. Really, the press had helped notify the community of impending danger and had spread the word in looking for lost kids or finding suspects. She decided it wasn't the press so much as a few reporters who really got under her skin. One of the worst of the lot was Manny Douglas of the *Mountain Reporter*. No doubt he would soon appear. She said, "Get ready. The media circus has already begun."

Pescoli slashed a look at her partner. "You okay?"

"Fine," Alvarez lied. "Let's get to it." She turned her attention back to the victim. *Get a grip, Selena. You can do this. You have to. For Gabe.* But the gold earring, with its winking, if fake, stone, seemed to mock her, and the panic that she fought so determinedly welled deep, questions echoing through her brain, plaguing her as they had no answers.

Who is this psycho?

What the hell has he done with my son?

This had just gotten personal. Extremely personal. As if she thought the freak could hear her, she whispered under her breath, "Get ready, you bastard, because I'm going to nail your ass and I'm going to nail it good."

". . . and that's all you know?" Pescoli asked hours later as she stared across the small table in the interrogation room at Ezzie Zwolski. Ezzie's small hands were folded in her lap as she sat in a chair next to an attorney who looked as if he'd just graduated from law school. Shaved head, nervous smile, pressed suit with a shiny tie, the lawyer said little during the questioning. To Pescoli, he seemed useless.

As for Ezzie, she was a mere mouse of a woman if one believed first impressions. Ezzie's graying hair was pinned tightly onto her head, a ruffled blouse was buttoned primly at her neck and a brown cardigan sweater was cinched around her waist. In her late fifties, she was still petite, wore little makeup and appeared more like a fussy Sunday school teacher out of the forties than the femme fatale Len Bradshaw's family painted her to be.

Except for her eye glasses. The frames were stylishly sleek, thin lavender plastic that was at odds with the rest of her aging, farm-wife ensemble. And she wore a pretty good-sized diamond ring on her left hand, a little flashier than the rest of her attire. Then there were her near-perfect teeth. Again, just a little out of sync with the rest of her.

"I'm telling you that Martin swore to me, on the family Bible no less," she insisted now, "that poor Len's death was an accident."

"Even though he'd embezzled money from the farm equipment business and had an affair with you?"

Ezzie's spine stiffened and her pale lips pursed ever so slightly. "Water under the bridge, Detective."

"It was over between you and Len?"

"Long ago."

"And your husband forgave you?"

"He's a good man."

"That didn't answer my question."

"Yes, Martin forgave me." She stared up at Pescoli with wide eyes behind the thick lenses of her glasses. "As I said, he's a good God-fearing man."

"Not a murderer."

"Of course not! It was a hunting accident! Why don't you people just believe him? There's no proof otherwise and . . . from what I understand, you have a real killer on the loose." Her little chin jutted in indignation, but still, Pescoli wasn't buying her sudden defense of a man she'd betrayed.

"Why didn't you come forward before?"

"Because, as you so aptly pointed out, I had nothing more to add. I wasn't with Martin and Len when the accident happened. I was home canning applesauce, but I can tell you this, when Martin got home that day, he was distraught. Horribly so. He couldn't believe that the gun had gone off and that Len had died. It tore him up inside. Still is." She let out a long sigh and looked away, as if gathering herself.

For what?

"What about the money that Bradshaw embezzled?" Pescoli asked. "Did Len ever offer to pay it back?"

"No . . . I don't think so. Martin was going to take it as a write off somehow." She waved her hand rapidly as if she didn't understand all of the details and was shooing the question aside. "You can do that, I guess, over time. Like a bad debt."

Maybe. If you truly were a "good, God-fearing man." Then again . . .

Pescoli asked a few more questions, didn't learn much more and decided Ezzie was right; she did have a more pressing case. But as the petite woman left the interrogation room, her attorney on her heels, Pescoli was left with a bad taste in her mouth.

Maybe it was the chic lavender glasses.

Or the fact that she'd been in a bad mood since roused from Santana's bed this morning. She'd called Jeremy and left a message that he go and let the dog out, then driven straight to the crime scene where Alvarez definitely was *not* her usually cool, level-headed self. Ever since spying the nipple ring, she'd flipped out. Well, maybe before that. Who wouldn't? Pescoli would have been a basket case if a child she'd given up for adoption had suddenly come knocking on her door, then ripped her off. Weird, all that. Disturbing. But then, so was Esmeralda Zwolski.

Bad mood aside, Pescoli sensed she couldn't trust Esmeralda "Ezzie" Zwolski any farther than she could throw the prim little woman, sensible shoes and all.

Still bothered by the interview, she collected her notes and recorder, then made a quick stop in the lunch room to survey whatever of Joelle's Christmas goodies might have been left on the tables. Nothing of interest had been left for the "weekend warriors," as Joelle had called those who pulled Saturday and Sunday duty. Seeing nothing that appealed to her, Pescoli grabbed a cup of coffee and walked to Alvarez's work area.

"How'd it go?" Alvarez asked, glancing up from her desk and computer monitor. While Pescoli had been interviewing Ezzie Zwolski, Alvarez had been trying to pinpoint any connection between Lara Sue Gilfry and Lissa Parsons.

"It went. I don't like the wife. Ezzie. And her Caspar Milquetoast of a lawyer."

"Who?"

"You never heard of someone being a 'milquetoast'?" At the blank stare she received, Pescoli shook her head. "Old expression. Some comic strip character, I think, from a kabillion years ago or something." She waved the idea away. "Doesn't matter. Anyway, the guy was meek or weak as hell . . . and Ezzie's lawyer, sheesh. He didn't look old enough to shave, let alone have graduated from law school. If you ask me, she's involved with either Bradshaw's death or at least the embezzling accusations."

"The autopsy report finally came in on him," Alvarez said, clicking her mouse to a new screen on her computer and printing out the document. Handing the pages to Pescoli, she said, "If he was killed on purpose it was a big waste of time. A couple of his arteries were ninety percent blocked and his liver was about shot. Cirrhosis taking hold."

"Wouldn't he know that?"

"Probably ignored the symptoms. He was a bit of an alpha-male type. You know, hunter, fisherman, farmer—"

"Tinker, tailor, soldier . . . Oh, wait!" Pescoli held up a finger. "Embezzler. And murder victim."

"Funny." She rolled her chair back.

"Not too."

Alvarez said, "The gunshot wound, the one where the bullet blew out Len's liver and nicked his heart? It was consistent with an accident. They recreated it in the lab and the bullet hit the dummy in just about the same spot as Zwolski's did in Bradshaw." She glanced up. "Even if it wasn't an accident, it would be hard to prove otherwise. So no first degree. Murder one is out unless we find more evidence to support it."

Pescoli's bad mood just got worse. "Great."

"Hey, it is what it is!"

"You think? I don't know. There's just something about Zwolski's wife. She's smug. Sanctimonious."

"Doesn't mean she and her husband plotted a murder."

"I know, but. There's just something about it that doesn't sit well." She took a sip of her cooling coffee. "Not well at all." Pointing the index finger of her cup-holding hand at Alvarez, she asked, "What about you? Find anything to tie the victims of our latest psycho together?"

"Nothing that jumps out between these two, but it turns out that Lissa Parsons did attend the same church as Brenda Sutherland."

"So does Cort Brewster, our illustrious under-sheriff."

"And boss," Alvarez pointed out.

"Whatever." Thinking hard, Pescoli chewed on the rim of her paper coffee cup. "You think there's a link?"

"Don't know. Brenda Sutherland was very active in the church and fund-raisers and Bible study. Volunteered all over the place and never missed a service."

"What about Lissa Parsons?"

"Not so much. Even though she was a parishioner at one time, she'd quit attending eighteen months ago. Before that, she'd show up once or twice a month. Or maybe there would be a gap, maybe when she was out of town, I'm working on that. Then, she was back again. Until eighteen months ago. She quit going altogether."

"Why?"

"Don't know. I thought I'd talk with her family and friends. Next of kin; her father—the mother is dead—was notified an hour ago."

"The press know this?" Pescoli asked, glancing

out the window where the same two news vans that had shown up at the crime scene had parked in the visitor's lot.

"They will in an hour. Darla's going to make a statement."

Darla Vale was the public information officer. She'd been with the department for a few years. Once a reporter for the *Seattle Times*, she'd come to Grizzly Falls when her husband, Herb, had decided to retire in Montana. She'd always joked that because of her ties to the press, she'd come from "the dark side."

"Good." Alvarez said, "We're still checking with any video cams going out of town, toward Sheldon Road, and deputies are checking with neighbors, see if they saw anything last night. Had to have happened sometime between ten, when Oliver Enstad shut off the porch light and looked outside before going to bed around eleven, and when the missus looked out the window the next morning around six. Probably around one A.M., judging from the snowfall over the tracks where the slab of ice was dragged and the amount of snow covering the statue, though it was already disturbed by the time that Mabel got her eyeful."

"Not much to go on."

"Did you get a chance to find out what the two ice sculptors with rap sheets were doing?"

"Both sleeping cozily in their beds with their wives."

"You believe the wives?"

Pescoli, irritated, lifted a shoulder. "Don't know what to believe." The case was going sideways and fast.

"What about the video taken of the crowd that collected at the Enstads' place this morning?"

"Nothing to write home about. Sage is looking it over, then enlarging pictures of the people who came gawking." Sage Zoller was a junior deputy and smart as a whip. But she had her work cut out for her. Pescoli had already viewed the tapes and, on first glance, was unable to find anyone suspicious who was at both scenes.

It had still been dark, but they'd taken pictures from hidden cameras of anyone who had slowed or stopped to rubberneck at the crime scene. Now Sage was comparing the people caught by the camera to the group of people who had shown up when Lara Sue Gilfry's body had been discovered, see if there were any duplicates. They could get lucky.

"Preliminary autopsy report's in on Gilfry," Alvarez said and printed out another document. As Pescoli plucked the warm papers from the printer, Alvarez added, "There's no tox screen yet, of course, but it looks like she died of hypothermia."

"That bastard froze her to death?"

"Appears so."

"Son of a bitch! Maybe he took some lessons

from our other friend," Pescoli said with more than a touch of rancor. That "friend" was another homicidal maniac who had terrorized Grizzly Falls two years earlier. He'd nearly taken Pescoli's life as well, and she couldn't think of the psycho without a frigid blackness clawing at her soul. She skimmed the report. "No tox screen, but I guess it's our girl, tattooed ankle, pierced tongue and all." She glanced up. "Anything else?"

"I talked to Slatkin earlier," Alvarez said, mentioning one of the forensic scientists on the crime scene team. "They took impressions of the sculpture before it melted, so there are saw, chisel, pick, tong and brush and sanding marks that they're analyzing, trying to find out where the products might have come from. We're checking local hardware stores, art supply stores, any-where they could have bought the items."

"Could be online. Or maybe he's had them for a long time; maybe they were great-granddaddy's."

"Even so . . ."

"I know. Long shot. I'm still hoping someone will get back to me from the hotels, catering companies, local artists, whoever, about anyone locally with a talent for shaving ice into something creative."

"What about Gordon Dobbs?" Pescoli asked. "He's always carving something and selling it off of his front porch."

"He works with wood."

"But a crack shot," Pescoli pointed out, knowing she was grasping at straws.

"No one's been shot yet. Well, besides Len Bradshaw, and he doesn't count on this one."

"Guess you're right. But I wouldn't tell his family that." She finished her cup and crushed it in her fingers. "They'll go bananas."

Alvarez sighed. "Well, then they can join the club."

"Around here that's not a big deal," Pescoli said. "The club's not all that damned exclusive!"

CHAPTER 18

So cold . . . so very, very cold.

Brenda couldn't move, couldn't so much as shiver as the water froze around her and she tried desperately to think of her children, her two boys who needed her. She couldn't give up and let go and yet the seduction of death was oh so real in this dark, hopeless cave where the monster had stripped her naked, then subdued her with a drug he'd slipped into her vein.

She'd called for help, she'd prayed, she'd endured the maniac's weird ministrations, even, God help her, begging him to let her go, promising to not tell a soul, to do anything he wanted. Now as she thought of her desperation, her humiliation, she wondered if it would be best if God would take her home. The boys, they would be all right. Ray would take care of them, wouldn't he? Maybe he'd get married again and they could have a stepmother . . .

Her mind went blank for a while as she dozed, the blackness a void for which she was grateful. Now, in that twilight between wakefulness and slumber, she didn't understand what was happening and knew in her heart she would never. He'd not hurt her, not made a mark upon her body aside for the tiny prick of his needle.

He'd washed her, over and over again, sluicing her with warm water that turned colder by the minute, until she'd been shivering wildly, her teeth chattering out of control, and then the beauty of nothingness when she'd lost consciousness. Oh, the serenity of blackness. As she roused, feeling the bitter cold deep in the marrow of her bones, she hoped she didn't have to look up into his cruel eyes, didn't want to watch him as he worked over her, didn't want to feel his lips upon her. Nor did she have the least desire to see the various drills and picks and saws hanging on the walls of this vast cavern that was complete with a workbench, running water and electricity. The tools terrorized her, and deep in her heart, she suspected that he would use them upon her.

Why, she didn't understand.

Who could?

He thought himself some kind of artist, he'd mentioned it as well as telling her how beautiful she was, how "perfect." Her stomach had twisted as he'd licked her navel and caressed her breast with the tip of his tongue. He'd wanted to do more to her, she'd read it in his eyes. He wanted to do all kinds of vile things to her, cruel, sadistic acts that she didn't want to imagine.

She'd been horrified, and had lain motionless, her muscles unable to move, her voice mute though inside she was screaming. How had she not suspected how deeply evil he was, this man she'd seen around Grizzly Falls? This *married* man had seemed somewhat normal, a person to whom she would cast a friendly smile when he'd come to her table at Wild Will's, but who was, beneath his normal facade, a madman, a demon sent straight from Satan himself. She'd seen a glimpse of his dark side once when he'd thought she'd ignored him on a day that was crazy-wild at work; it hadn't helped that the chef had messed up his order, but other than that one time . . .

She forced herself not to think of him or how helpless she was at his hand. Her mind began to wander again in the darkness, and for a second Brenda thought she heard another voice, one as frightened as her own. But of course, when she croaked out a response and waited, she heard nothing other than the beating of her own heart. What she'd heard was an audio hallucination;

there was no other person near enough to hear her or rescue her.

She was doomed.

Only Jesus could save her now.

Brenda was sure of it.

Her faith prevailed and so she began to pray. Silently. The familiar words coming to mind. *Our Father, who art in heaven; hallowed be Thy name . . .*

Though it was the weekend, the sheriff's department was buzzing. Not only were there the usual accidents, fights and altercations brought on by too much celebrating on Friday night, and the regular amount of thefts, but with these latest murders, the offices were busier than ever. Phones jangled, conversation hummed and, aside from Joelle's added Christmas enthusiasm, the station was filled with weekend officers or others, like Alvarez herself, pulling overtime.

While the press camped outside, the sheriff and undersheriff were both in their offices and, of course, Sturgis had taken up his usual spot near Grayson's desk. Seeing the dog had reminded Alvarez of her own missing pup, not to mention the son she'd given up half a lifetime previously.

She'd been too busy to think much about Gabriel Reeve or Roscoe.

Now, her back beginning to ache a little from hours at her desk, Alvarez read through Lissa

Parsons's phone log one more time. A computer had compared it to the numbers in Lara Sue Gilfry's and come up with only three matches: a clinic where Dr. Acacia Lambert practiced; Joltz, a local coffee shop; and a garage over on Seventh Street. It was all a dead end. Comparing personal computers was next on the agenda, but that was tough, as Lissa Parsons's car, laptop, and smartphone were still missing. They'd received records regarding her account from her server, that information requested weeks ago when she'd gone missing. Since then, there had been no activity on either her phone or computer. As for Lara Sue Gilfry, she'd used the common computer supplied by the Bull and Bear bed-and-breakfast, where she worked. Many times she hadn't bothered to log in personally, but just checked Web sites through the inn's account, so sorting what she'd done, as opposed to the rest of the staff or customers, had been tedious, nearly impossible. And that didn't count the library where she was known to hang out.

Fortunately, now that the FBI was involved, they and their hyped-up technology would take over. Alvarez had gone over the records of the inn before November sixth, when Lara Sue had last been seen, but those records were still being compared to those on Lissa Parsons's account with a national Internet server.

"Keep at it," she told herself.

Alvarez's cell phone rang and she noticed O'Keefe's name on the screen. Her stomach tightened a bit as she answered. "Tell me you have good news."

"Wish I could," he said and she wanted to close her eyes and envision his face. Instead she glanced at the clock on her computer and saw that it was nearing six. She'd been at this for twelve hours. "Rough day?"

"To put it mildly." She considered telling him about the nipple ring but held back, didn't want to compromise the case. Agents Halden and Chandler from the FBI field office in Salt Lake City were due to arrive within the next couple of hours. Had the weather been better, they would have been here earlier, but as it was, their plane was delayed in Missoula and they were driving the short distance to Grizzly Falls, but only after looking into the ice sculpture competition in the area along with the artists involved and anyone close to them.

Meanwhile a task force room, complete with dedicated phone lines, was being created in the very same area the sheriff's department had used in the past.

"How about I meet you after work? We can get something to eat and discuss the case."

"Is there anything to discuss?"

"Always."

That much was true, she supposed, but she

didn't think spending more time with him was such a good idea and she was still bothered that her earring was found on the victim. It just didn't seem like a random act. No, it was pointed. At her. At least she felt as if it was, but she couldn't make heads nor tails of it now and the night stretched out long before her. The thought of spending the hours alone, absently stroking Jane's head while worrying about her missing dog, her son, an old earring or the madman stalking the county held little appeal. She needed a break. Besides, any information he could give her was something.

"Come on, Selena. Live a little."

Her throat tightened at the familiar phrase, one he'd used often enough when they were both working in San Bernardino. "Okay, as long as it's not pizza."

"Deal," he said, unable to hide the bit of amusement in his voice.

"And this is *not* a date?"

"Of course not. Why would you think anything like that?"

"Oh, you know the old saying, if it walks like a duck and talks like a duck, then it's a date."

He laughed outright. "Call it what you want, Alvarez. I'll meet you at your place at what . . . six?"

"Six thirty. Good?"

"That'll work."

She glanced at the clock again. "Good. I still have some loose ends to wrap up."

"You've got yourself a deal, Lady. It's a . . . duck!"

Idiots!
 Morons!
 Cretins!
His hands tightened into fists and he felt the rage crawl up his neck, knew his face was heating as he stood and stared at the television screen in his den. His wife was out, thankfully, doing some shopping for dinner or something, so he could watch the news reports of the latest ice-mummy case over and over again, all without having to explain why he recorded all of the news stations and searched for the segments dedicated to the one story.

Aside from the sound coming from the television, the house was quiet. Empty. Snow was falling past the window, and a few cars traveled along the road that wound past the old family homestead. He heard the sound of their engines rumbling as they passed.

Inside his den, he hit the rewind button on the remote for his television recorder. Once more he watched that empty-headed Nia Del Ray, who had recently transferred from Helena to Missoula and now seemed to be KMJC's local crime reporter. There she was, standing in front of the

Enstads' yard, snow collecting in her hair as she stared into the camera and tried to sound intelligent, which, in her case, was impossible.

The press, like the stupid cops, just didn't get his art, didn't understand him. He'd watched the reports of the ice-mummy case online and on the television and, as usual, the cops were at a loss. No one who was reporting or investigating seemed to notice the beauty of his work, the intricacies involved, how much he labored over each tiny detail.

He wanted to toy with them, show them how pathetic they were.

Once again Nia was saying something inane, and behind her, half obliterated by the snowfall, were the two detectives involved in the case. He knew them both. Did Selena Alvarez remember him? Of course she did. They knew each other and he'd introduced himself in the most innocuous of places, the grocery store, a few years ago. He'd come up behind her with his cart and she'd jumped a mile, turned and sent him a look that could kill. She'd dropped a container of yogurt, which had cracked, squirting creamy whey over the shiny linoleum. As she'd bent down to retrieve it, he'd beat her to it, was just that much quicker. "Sorry," he said. "Didn't mean to scare you." Their gazes locked for just an instant, long enough for him to realize what a sexy bitch she really was. He'd caught a glimpse of her shoulder harness and weapon along with the way her slacks stretched tight over her perfect little rump. "I'll get someone to clean this up," he'd said and she'd let it go, walking away after muttering a quick, automatic "thanks" that held no meaning.

He'd seen her since, of course. Not only in person, but also on the television. During the investigation of the other cases, the ones that had fascinated him. He'd paid such close attention and seen how much more intelligent and sophisticated he was than any of the investigators.

So how had his perfection come to be referred to as the ice mummy? That galled him to no end. His head pounded and spit collected in his mouth as if he might actually vomit. He thought of the ice picks laid out so carefully on his workbench and he felt the urge to grab one and ram it over and over again into a block of ice, into the wooden surface of the table, into the frozen flesh of the woman. Faster and faster and harder and harder, sending ice chips flying, splintering wood, causing the blood to show, a few icy drops flying against . . .

Stop it!

The voice in his head roared to life.

Control yourself!

He sucked the spittle that had dampened his lips back into his mouth.

You cannot ruin everything you worked for! You! Cannot! Do not be an imbecile! Do not sink to their moronic levels. You are far superior to any of them. Remember that and hold your mission in reverence!

He was shaking. Violently. It was all he could do to suck in a deep breath through his bared teeth. Slowly, the rage receded, his heartbeat became normal and his clenched fists relaxed.

That's better. Calmly. With purpose. You have much to do.

He blinked. Heard Nia Del Ray refer to his masterpieces as "the work of the Ice Mummy Killer."

He held back a string of curses and told himself this was how he had to suffer at the hands of fools. Always at the hands of fools. Had he ever been recognized for his talent and intelligence, he wouldn't have to prove to them how inferior they were. Though he'd tried, he'd been met with resistance, but wasn't that the way it was so often.

If only they could see his files, the meticulous histories of those he'd chosen and honored to be a part of his art, then they would see his intelligence. They could then witness how dedicated he was, how thorough. He knew each woman's life story, her wants, her needs, those whom she trusted, those whom she considered enemies. He understood the fine details of their lives, including their shoe size and choice of perfume. All that information was carefully locked away on a separate hard drive no one could ever access.

His abductions were not random acts.

He'd waited years for the right moment to start this phase of his project, to start the sculpting and displaying his work. His inspirations, the women involved, were all perfect and, as a virile man, he wanted each one of them, had imagined what he would do to them in his bed.

He'd had to restrain himself from fucking the hell out of them, and, to his credit, he had not so much as mounted one, never driven his hard dick deep into their tight little . . .

Not now! Don't go there . . .

He sucked deep breaths into his lungs, then let the air out slowly, forcing his mind to go blank, concentrating on bringing his pulse rate down.

He could control himself.

He could!

Calmer, he pointed his remote at the television as if it were a gun, then hit the button so that the screen would go blank. There was work to do. It was definitely time to shake things up a bit.

"I've got to run," Pescoli said, pausing to stick her head into Alvarez's office as she zipped her jacket. "I haven't seen my kids for a couple of days, unless you can count Jeremy stumbling into his room and flopping on his bed yesterday morning as seeing him."

"It's Saturday night. They'll be home?"

"Briefly, I think." Pescoli shifted her bag on

her shoulder and flashed a tired grin. "Just long enough to ask for money. Let's just hope they took care of the dog."

She headed out and Alvarez glanced at the clock. Tomorrow was another day, even if it was Sunday. However, she couldn't help but feel time ticking away. Each minute that passed was another sixty seconds that the killer had to plot out his next move. In her job, Alvarez was forever racing against time.

Once more, she compared photos of the victims, before and after death, and felt a pang when she noticed the tattoo of the butterfly on Lara Sue's ankle. Absently she wondered what was the significance of the inking, if anything. Freedom? Beauty? Or just a whim for a poor kid who, as Taj had commented, "fell through the cracks" and had been on her own since she was a teenager. Lara was very different from victim number two, Lissa Parsons, who had an education, good job, a sometimes boyfriend, a father and a much younger sister in Pocatello, Idaho, who were all completely devastated.

So who was the common person they knew, the thread that so fatefully had linked them together? And Brenda Sutherland, where was she? Already in the clutches of the killer, or had she been kidnapped by someone else, or just taken off, a single mother who had just cracked under the pressure? No way. In her gut, Alvarez knew Brenda had somehow come upon the same maniac as had the other victims.

God help her.

After slipping on her shoulder holster, she threw on her jacket and gloves, then grabbed her laptop and purse and walked down the decorated hallway to the back door. A couple of the road deputies, Rule Kayan and Pete Watershed, were searching for any leftovers that Joelle might have put in the refrigerator or cupboards and bemoaning the fact that there wasn't a scrap of a cookie to be found. Rule was a tall African American who looked more like a power forward for the NBA than a cop, a guy Alvarez trusted. Watershed—not so much. He was handsome, knew it and thought crude jokes were the end-all, be-all. He was an okay cop, but Alvarez could do without him. Today, though, they were like two teenage boys, scavengers for anything edible.

"Good night," Alvarez said.

Rule flashed her a grin. "See ya." Watershed was still grumbling about the lack of cookies.

It seemed, Alvarez thought as she let herself out, that Pescoli was the only person in the entire department who didn't appreciate all of Joelle's efforts to bring a little Christmas spirit into the sheriff's offices.

And, Alvarez thought, even Pescoli had to admit that she liked a good cookie.

Outside, the temperature had definitely dropped

as the storm the weather people had been predicting for the better part of a week seemed to roar over this part of Montana. Snow, in the form of tiny crystals of ice, poured from the heavens only to be whipped by the wind. Not a great night for a non-date, Alvarez thought as she turned away from the wind and unlocked her car, but she and O'Keefe had to go out; they couldn't be alone in her apartment again.

She piled into her Outback and switched on the engine before backing out of her parking space and wheeling out of the parking lot, her tires crunching in the piling snow. Easing into traffic, she turned toward her town house. Traffic was a little slower than usual but hadn't slowed to a crawl, as people in this part of the country were used to snowy conditions on the roads in winter. However, the guy behind her in some jacked-up SUV had his headlights on bright and the glare was nearly blinding. Adjusting her mirror, she tried to ignore the reflection, but it still bothered her.

Down the hill and over the railroad tracks, she drove through the older part of the town that had been built upon the banks of the Grizzly River. Through the curtain of snow, she saw the light of the courthouse, and farther down the street, barely, she saw the sign for Wild Will's, where she'd first been accosted by Grace Perchant about her son, and where Sandi, the owner, had pointed her finger at Ray Sutherland. Was it possible? Had he somehow gotten rid of his ex-wife? Was the sheriff's department so focused on the Ice Mummy Killer that they were ignoring the obvious in the Brenda Sutherland disappearance?

Nah; she didn't think so.

She turned onto her own street and was grateful the guy with the blinding headlights drove past. Thank God.

She pulled into her drive, waited for the garage door to go up, then guided the car inside just as her cell phone rang. Thinking it was O'Keefe, she picked up and answered as she was getting out of the car. "Hello?"

Nothing.

"Hello?" she said, irritated, then saw that there was no number on the cell as she hit the switch for the garage door with the palm of her hand and started inside. "Hello?" The opener responded and the garage door began to grind into place.

"Hello, bitch," a deep voice said and she froze. The male voice was nearly an echo in the phone pressed against her ear and also through the garage.

She spun, dropping the phone and her purse as she reached for her service weapon.

"Too late," the voice said, the door continuing rolling down, a man standing just inside. Junior Green, older and fatter than she remembered, his thinning hair disheveled, his beard shadow patchy, was standing inside the slowly descending door. Bloodless lips twisted in satisfaction, he aimed a pistol straight at Alvarez. "I told you I was coming back for you, cunt, and you fuckin' didn't believe me. Well, here I am!"

He grinned soullessly. "And I brought my fuckin' gun!"

CHAPTER 19

Blam!

He fired.

Glass shattered!

Hundreds of dull-edged shards of tempered glass sprayed.

The back window of the Outback was blown apart.

Alvarez ducked behind the front of the car. She felt no searing pain. No blood dripped from her body. How in God's name had she not been hit?

He doesn't want to hit you.

He's toying with you.

The sick creep is enjoying this.

Yanking her weapon from its holster, she clicked off the safety, ready to fire. Protected by the tire, she leaned down to look under the car and gauge Green's position just as someone rolled quickly beneath the lowering garage door.

The door jerked to a stop!

O'Keefe!

Oh, God, no!

His body still spinning, O'Keefe knocked Green's legs out from under him.

"What the fuck?" the big man roared, toppling to the cement floor.

Thud! He hit hard. Cracked his skull. He cried out. "Shit! You goddamned cocksucker!"

Blam! Blam! Blam!

Gunshots echoed through the small space! Bullets ricocheted wildly, pinging against the car, splintering the wood walls, skittering against the cement.

Oh, God, no! Dylan!

Frantic, fear galvanizing her, Alvarez crouched and swiftly rounded the front end of the car as the shots went wild, a bullet zinging over her head and splintering the exposed studs of the front wall of the garage.

Blam!

Another bullet scraped across the side of the Outback before flying off in another direction as the men wrestled, fighting for the gun.

"Stop! Police!" she yelled automatically.

"Fuck off!" Green threw back at her. "Oh, ooowww! You bastard!"

Grunting and swearing, straining, the two men struggled, wrestling across the dirty concrete between the back of the car and the nearly shut garage door.

"Give it up, Green!" she ordered again, her heart in her throat, her pulse pounding in her ears as she inched past the back panel.

Bam!

"Goddamn it!" Green swore, breathing hard.

Thud! Their sweating bodies hit the side wall of the garage. A rake that had been propped in the corner fell down, clattering loudly.

"That's enough! Green, drop your weapon!" With her pistol in her hand, Alvarez came around the rear end of her Outback. Green, red-faced, cords standing out in his fleshy neck, was still holding fast to his gun, but O'Keefe, smaller but tougher, moved quickly, wrangling the ex-football player down to the ground.

"Get away!" he yelled at Alvarez because Green, face mashed into the floor, was still attempting to fire his weapon. "Call for backup. Oh, for Christ's sake!" His hand clamped over Green's wrist, forcing the gun onto the floor. He pressed his weight down hard as the bigger man was trying like hell to flip O'Keefe off his back. O'Keefe's nose was bleeding and he was sweating, breathing hard, as he straddled a wriggling, furious Green.

"Get the fuck off me," Green ground out, his voice muffled against the concrete where a series of oil leaks had stained the floor.

"Give it up!" she ordered. "Junior Green, drop your weapon!"

"Get out of here, Selena! Run!" O'Keefe yelled, trying to hold Green down. With his one hand rendering the big man's hand useless, he managed to grab hold of Green's free, flailing left hand with his own. Grimacing, he forced Green's meaty fist backward, twisting with all his strength.

"Yeooow," Green cried into the concrete.

"For God's sake, Selena," O'Keefe spat. "Call for backup!"

Alvarez shouted, "I said, give it up, Green!" Adrenaline pulsed through her. "Drop your weapon."

Green rolled an eye in her direction. "Shut up, bitch!"

With one quick motion, O'Keefe yanked hard on Green's left arm, forcing it farther up his back.

The big man shrieked in pain. He bucked, trying to throw O'Keefe off him. They slammed against the back of the car.

O'Keefe, straining, his own face red, the veins extended in his neck, applied pressure, twisting hard enough that Green screamed again.

Still he held on to the damned gun. Still he was a threat. Still he could, at any moment, toss O'Keefe off his back and turn his weapon on them both.

"*Bastardo*!" Weapon pointed directly at the big man, Alvarez hauled back and kicked. The toe of her boot connected with a sickening sound into the side of Junior Green's head. He let out another squeal of pain, but his fingers loosened on his gun and Alvarez kicked it away from him, the weapon skittering across the concrete and under her car. She was sweating, breathing hard, pumped. Her pistol was sighted on the jerk's head. With just one pull of the trigger . . .

The sound of sirens screaming in the distance snapped her out of it.

She prayed that someone had called 911 and backup was on its way to her home, that the sirens weren't for another call.

"Don't move!" she ordered Green, who lay panting on the floor of the garage. "Or I swear, I'll blow your head off."

Green forced an eye in her direction, but the fight was out of him. Blood smeared his face; bruises were already starting to appear.

O'Keefe, breathing hard, finally released the big man.

No one doubted for a second that Alvarez would use her weapon, so Green lay on her garage floor, a thick lump of useless human flesh.

Standing, O'Keefe backed away from the prisoner and allowed Alvarez a clear shot, should she need it.

Breathing hard, a bruise developing under his eye, he lifted a sleeve to his nose to stanch the flow of blood that stained his shirt as the siren's screams echoed through the night.

With her free hand, she found her phone in her pocket, hit a speed dial button and was connected to the station where she identified herself and gave her address and the situation, just to ensure that backup was indeed headed in her direction.

"I've got cuffs in the car. Glove box," she said to O'Keefe and he retrieved them, doing the honors of handcuffing Green as the ex-football player lay, swearing in pain but surprisingly docile, on her garage floor. Only when he was fully cuffed did some of his old acrimony return.

"I'm suing your ass," Green said to O'Keefe. "My fuckin' arm's broke."

"You'll live," O'Keefe said, his eyes bright. "And that's the bad news."

Tires crunched on the snow outside. Red and blue light flashed through the window. "Police," she yelled toward the partially open door as she identified herself. "Situation under control! Suspect in custody!" To Green, she said, "Get up, you bastard. Get onto your feet and don't do anything stupid, or I swear, I will shoot you dead and feel real good about it!"

Pescoli got the call about the shooting at Alvarez's address just as the timer went off on the tuna casserole she'd thrown together. The sheriff himself had decided to fill her in and she turned off the stove as well as the timer, then listened hard, giving the sheriff her full attention. It seemed that J. R., Junior Green, a pedophile and genuinely sick son of a bitch, had come back to make good on his promise. According to Grayson, he was in custody and Alvarez was fine, or as fine as one could be after being the victim of a near-death shooting. She and Dylan O'Keefe, who had been with her at the time, had been checked out by a nurse and refused to go to the hospital. Green, however, was banged up pretty bad, and Alvarez's Outback had sustained damage from stray bullets.

"I'm on my way," she said and Grayson didn't try to discourage her.

"Good. I'm thinkin' your partner could use a friend."

"Sounds like she's got one."

"I'm talkin' female friend. You know, so you can talk it to death."

"Yeah, I do know." And it was more than Grayson guessed, as Pescoli didn't think he, or anyone else at the station for that matter, knew that the runaway who had broken into her house could be her kid, though that was likely to come up. The sheriff understood that Alvarez would need some moral support. Though a private person, this kind of trauma needed discussion, with either a shrink or family. In Alvarez's case, Pescoli was the closest she had to either, at least within a hundred-mile or so radius.

She hung up and opened the oven door. Cisco,

thinking there might be a treat for him some-where, hurried into the kitchen and stared into the oven as well. Inside, the casserole bubbled, melting cheese beginning to brown on the top.

Shaking her head, Pescoli told the ever-hopeful mutt, "I don't think so."

The kitchen was already warm from the heat of the stove, the smell of melting cheese filling the air. Using kitchen mittens that showed burn marks from earlier mistakes, she retrieved the glass casserole dish and set it on the stove. It, too, had a chip or two from around twenty years of abuse. Idly, she remembered that her aunt had given her the damned thing at a shower thrown for her, just before she'd married Joe, when she'd been pregnant with Jeremy.

She glanced down the hallway leading to the back stairs. Her son was holed up in his bedroom, where he'd been for the better part of the last thirty-six hours. Though he'd claimed to have taken his final later in the day yesterday, she wasn't certain she believed him.

She didn't want to think about how her life had come to this, from the promise of a new life and showers where baking pans were given to the expectant bride to a boy who couldn't quite make the necessary steps to be a man nearly twenty years later. Down the stairs she went and tapped on the door.

No response. However, she knew he was inside.

Pushing open the door, she found him seated on the side of his bed, game controller in hand, earphones over his head, gaze trained on the television screen where some kind of bloody army game was being played. Currently, mazelike rooms of some kind of concrete bunker flashed and snipers appeared around corners before Jeremy deftly vaporized each one in a blood spray that turned the set a fiery red.

"Hey," she yelled and he, as if mesmerized, didn't so much as look up at her. "Rambo!" She touched him on the shoulder and he jumped ten feet.

"Mom!" he cried, his concentration blown. "Oh, shit! Look." He flung an arm at the screen. "I'm dead!"

Cisco, sensing the excitement, yapped and hopped onto the unmade bed.

Scowling hard, as if he wanted to rage at his mother but thought better of it, Jeremy asked, "What?"

"I have to run out." She was dead serious and he, calming a bit, caught on.

"Why?"

"There was a shooting over at Alvarez's place."

"What? Is she okay?" For the first time in weeks, she saw a glimpse of the caring boy he once was, a glimmer of the man he could become.

"Oh, sorry. I said that wrong. Guns were fired, but no one was hit. Everyone, including Selena, is okay, the suspect in custody, but, still, I need to see her, talk to her."

"Oh, uh, yeah." He was nodding his head, the earphones sliding to one side. "I get it. Sure."

"That means family dinner will have to be postponed."

"That's okay." He righted the headset.

"Tuna noodles are done. So go ahead and eat it when you want. I've even got salad in a bag in the refrigerator. It comes with its own dressing."

"Okay." Absently, in the illumination of the television screen and oddly shifting glow of his lava lamp, he petted the dog, who put his chin on Jeremy's jean-clad thigh.

Pescoli doubted her son would even open the bag. Greens just weren't his thing. "Don't know when I'll be home."

"I'm going out later, anyway."

"How much later?"

"Unknown."

"Jer?" she chided and thought she caught a whiff of marijuana. Quick as it came, it disappeared, as his window was cracked just an inch. For now she ignored the scent. "It's snowing."

He actually grinned, looking so much like Joe that her heart melted. "Yeah, I know. Mom, this is Montana. In the winter. It's always snowing."

"Guess you're right." She left him with the dog and his game, then made her way up the stairs, where she saw the hole in the wall that had been there since Jeremy had put his fist through it a few years back. She'd left it, hoping that the gaping opening would be a reminder for him to control his temper, but he never seemed to notice it. Sooner or later, she'd have to patch it . . . or find the right-sized picture to cover it.

On the main level, she tapped on Bianca's door and pushed it open. Her daughter was seated at her makeup table, applying another layer of mascara while simultaneously texting God only knew how many friends. Her hair was braided, the red highlights visible in her thick strands. She'd dyed her hair every color under the sun, but now, gratefully, it was back to what was near her natural color.

In the reflection, Bianca's gaze found her mother's. "Yeah?"

"I've got to go out for a while."

Bianca rolled her eyes, concentrated on making her lashes longer and stronger and all gunked up. "What else is new?"

"We'll have family dinner tomorrow. I promise."

Bianca lifted a shoulder. "Whatever."

"Look, Alvarez was nearly shot tonight. Attacked in her garage."

Bianca's mascara wand stopped in midair. She didn't so much as look at her phone for the next text. "Is she okay?"

"I think so. But I'm going to make sure."

"Oh, God, Mom." Bianca blinked, then spun on her tufted stool to look directly at Pescoli. "This is awful."

"I know, but she'll be fine."

"You should give up being a cop!" Her perfectly plucked eyebrows drew together over her large eyes. "It's too dangerous. Dad and Michelle, they think so, too!"

"All part of the job."

"But you could retire and . . . and work in a bookstore . . . Or if you don't like that . . . somewhere else."

"I'm a little young to be retiring. It's okay, Bianca." She walked into the pink room, where Christmas lights were wound year-round on the posts that supported the canopy of her bed. "But I think I'd better make sure she's okay."

Bianca nodded, and just like she had with her son, Pescoli caught a hint of the woman this girl would become and it wasn't all braids and pink ribbons and boys and nail polish. "Dinner's on the stove," she said, giving her the same rundown as she'd said to Jeremy five minutes earlier. "I should be back in a couple of hours." And again, as she had with her son, Pescoli heard that Bianca had plans to be out with her friends at a movie and that Candi's mom was driving them, as none of them yet had their licenses. "Just be back before midnight," Pescoli had instructed as Bianca had swiveled back to the mirror and picked up her cell phone, her fingers dancing over the keys.

Spoiled, Pescoli thought. *You've spoiled them.*

"But they'll be all right." She said it under her breath as much to convince herself as anything.

"I'm fine. Seriously." Alvarez glanced from her partner to Grayson and back again. "Other than tired and hungry, that is." They were standing in Grayson's office with O'Keefe, his face discolored from his emerging bruises, scrapes visible on his cheeks and nose. His lip was split, and soon, he'd have a shiner, as the area around his left eye was darkening. Still, he'd refused to go to the hospital or receive any serious medical attention. "I've filled out a report," Alvarez insisted. "Green is in custody, and there's nothing more to do once the crime guys are done with my garage and car."

"Shouldn't take long. We'll process everything and get your wagon to a shop at the beginning of the week," Grayson said, though the sheriff was clearly troubled. He looked tired, the result no doubt of the emergence of yet another serial murderer in Grizzly Falls. "I just don't like how this all went down."

"Neither do I." O'Keefe folded his arms over his chest. "How the hell did that son of a bitch find you?"

"Matter of public record," Alvarez said. The

problem was that records were so much more accessible now with computers, smartphones and all the data on the Internet. "It's not rocket science."

"That's the problem," Grayson said, shaking his head. He'd allowed O'Keefe to be a part of this conversation at Alvarez's insistence, but it was obvious he wasn't comfortable with the fourth person in the room. O'Keefe wasn't a working cop and he'd made no bones about the fact that he'd been spending time with Alvarez. Though, Alvarez thought, O'Keefe had insisted that his relationship with her was strictly professional, everyone in the room knew that wasn't quite true. Grayson hadn't become sheriff because he looked the part of a roguish cowboy-type lawman. He had the degrees and work experience to back him up and a natural cunning that saw through BS when he encountered it. That quality, along with his easygoing cowboy allure, had all but captured Alvarez's heart. He looked at her now. "I don't like you going home alone."

"I'll be fine." She was serious. "Green's behind bars."

Unconvinced of her mental state, Grayson stroked his moustache. "There's always the next nutcase."

"Part of the job." Alvarez voiced the obvious, but everyone in the room knew the risks, had lived them by being members of a law enforcement agency. "Green's the one who was the most vocal about getting to me."

"There are others. Silent ones," Grayson said. "They could be the most deadly." His eyes darkened, his crow's feet seeming more prominent. "Your home was already broken into, some of your things stolen. Less than a week ago. I don't think that was Green."

"It wasn't," Alvarez said.

"And an earring that was taken from your place ended up at a major crime scene," he prompted. His hips were balanced against the edge of his desk, hands holding him in place, dog at his feet.

"That's right." Alvarez realized she had to come clean. "The kid that broke into my place, that O'Keefe followed to Grizzly Falls, there's a chance . . . make that a very good chance . . . that Gabriel Reeve is my son."

CHAPTER 20

By the time O'Keefe pulled into Alvarez's driveway, it was after ten. Enough snow had fallen to cover up a lot of the tracks that had been made by the police vehicles and tow truck, but Alvarez couldn't shake the image of Junior Green and his gun pointed straight at her as the garage door had slowly closed behind him. If O'Keefe hadn't shown up when he had, the outcome of the standoff could have been much different. If Junior Green had been successful in his mission, she would undoubtedly be dead.

Once she'd admitted her possible connection to Gabriel Reeve and the ice-mummy case, both she and O'Keefe had been questioned by the FBI agents. Stephanie Chandler, a model-beautiful blonde whose personality was often described as "icy," had been all business, as usual. Her partner, Craig Halden, a self-proclaimed "cracker" originally from Georgia, too, had been intense, his good-old-boy smile sadly missing in the two hours they'd sat in one of the interview rooms, going over the case. Like Alvarez, Halden thought Junior Green's assault had nothing to do with the latest serial-killer case.

Chandler hadn't been so sure.

As snow piled on the windshield of O'Keefe's Explorer, Alvarez wondered why her world had turned upside down now. Ever since leaving San Bernardino, she'd attempted to keep her life in a neat, if sterile, order. That had begun to change when she'd adopted her cat, or, more precisely, Jane had adopted her. Since that time, Alvarez had softened a little and now . . . now disaster had struck. All of her neatly constructed walls had cracked and tumbled down around her.

"Come on, let's get you inside," O'Keefe said

as if he could read her thoughts. He cut the engine and grabbed the sack of food they'd ordered from Wild Will's and picked up on their way home.

Alvarez had called the restaurant from the station, and Sandi, the owner of the restaurant where Brenda Sutherland had worked, had answered. "Oh, tell me you have news about Brenda," she'd demanded, the minute Alvarez had identified herself.

"I don't." Alvarez had almost felt the woman's despair through the phone lines. "I wish I did, and the minute we locate her, I'm sure she'll want you to know."

"You've checked into that louse of an ex-husband of hers, though, right? I saw him on the television making a plea for her to be returned safely to him and the boys. Oh, yeah, right, like he gives a flying you know what. He knocked her around, I'm telling you, has a temper that's hotter'n hell. He's behind this." She drew a breath, then let it out slowly. "I know you know all this."

"I was just going to order dinner to go," Alvarez had said.

"Oh. Sorry. I'm just worried, that's all, and I hate seeing that loser go around as if he cares. Really chafes my hide, y'know what I mean? Okay, okay, I've said my piece. So . . . what can I get you? Oh, let's see, just checked with the kitchen and we're out of clam chowder and the bison chili. Got some of the special, trout almondine, left though . . ."

They'd ended up ordering sandwiches that they would eat in her kitchen, and O'Keefe had also stopped at a minimart for a six pack and a bottle of halfway decent wine. "It is Saturday night," he'd said in explanation.

"Good to have for a non-date," she'd said.

"Exactly."

Now, Alvarez walked past the garage and onto the front porch, where she unlocked the door and, once again, let Dylan O'Keefe into her house.

It was beginning to become a habit, she decided, and found the thought surprisingly comforting. Which it shouldn't be. She found plates and flatware while O'Keefe turned on the fireplace and the gas logs began to hiss softly. Jane threaded her way between Alvarez's legs. "Yeah, I know. I love you, too," she said, taking the time to pick up the cat and stroke her before Jane hopped from her hands and went into the living room by the fire.

O'Keefe cracked open a beer, held a second up for her but she shook her head. "Maybe a glass of wine." Why not? He was right. It was Saturday night and it had been one helluva day . . . make that one helluva week. She needed to relax and kick back.

"You got it."

After parceling out the sandwiches and small

side salads, he retrieved a plastic container from the sack. "Looks like we got a bonus." She couldn't help but smile at the slice of chocolate mousse pie, a specialty of Sandi's.

As they dove into their meal, O'Keefe said, "I talked to Aggie again today. She's been in contact with the lawyer who set up Gabe's adoption."

Alvarez's stomach tightened. "And?"

"He's going before a judge, or something. The bottom line is he's going through the motions of opening up the adoption."

"That could take months."

"The Helena PD is adding pressure."

"Does it matter?" she finally asked. "I mean, of course it matters to *me* and maybe to your cousin and her husband as well as Gabe. But for his alleged crime, it's pretty irrelevant."

"Just another lead. And I think it's more than alleged."

"We haven't heard his side of the story yet," she pointed out and he looked up at her sharply, not saying what they were both thinking, that she was defensive, acting like a mother.

She glanced out the sliding door, where the snow was piling against the glass, and wondered about the boy out in the elements. Was he shivering in the freezing cold? Had he found a place to hide? He could be long gone by now. It had been days since there had been any sign of him.

Except for the earring.

She picked at her sandwich and sipped the chardonnay, didn't argue when O'Keefe refilled it. Earlier, she'd been ravenous, but now, she wasn't hungry and the melted cheese on whole wheat had lost its appeal.

Not so for O'Keefe, he'd polished off his ham on rye and was eyeing her leftovers. "Be my guest," she offered, shoving her plate across the glass top of the table.

"Really?"

"Absolutely. Just leave room for the pie, it's really to die for." As he bit into her sandwich, she said, "So have you talked to the Helena PD?"

Nodding, he said, "Of course they've got their own people trying to track Gabe down." She nodded; she'd heard as much from Trey Williams. "But, unless they're lying, they don't have any more than I do; his trail's gone cold."

She knew this as well and suspected the reason that the cops in Helena and the state had worked with O'Keefe at all was because he was dogged, determined and savvy from his own years on the force. Besides, their departments, like the Pinewood Sheriff's Department, were stretched thin, more crime than cops.

"I was hoping he might show up here again," he said, then washed his last bite down by almost finishing his beer.

"So that's why you've been hanging out."

"One reason." His gaze found hers and she

saw something in his eyes she'd rather ignore, something that reminded her of a time when the sun shined and she had hope of love.

How stupid she'd been then. Still a little idealistic and naive. Ever hopeful. Even after what she'd endured. She cleared her throat, pushed aside the memories of palm trees, and warm winds and O'Keefe's touch. She noticed his split lip and that one of the deeper scratches beneath his eye had decided to bleed again, tiny drops of blood forming along the line of his cheekbone. "You know . . . you might need stitches."

"That bad?"

"You've looked better," she said and felt one of her eyebrows arch, as if she were baiting him, or worse yet, flirting.

"Thanks." Despite his scrapes and bruising, she thought him too good-looking for his own good. Or maybe hers. He grinned, that crooked, irreverent slash of white she'd found so beguiling years before. "What do they say, 'it's not the years, but the miles'?"

"Is that what 'they' say?"

"Something like that." He laughed, then winced a little before draining his beer.

"Well, *I'm* saying you should have had a doctor look at your injuries."

"Now you're the expert."

"Yeah, I think so."

He grinned again, testing her, then shrugged.

"Oh, for the love of God, I'd forgotten just how mule headed you could be. Look, I've got some antiseptic cream and a butterfly Band-Aid . . . upstairs." Before he could protest, she kicked back her chair and headed upstairs to the bathroom off her bedroom where she kept all of her first-aid supplies. In the drawer, she located a box of Band-Aids that she'd had for years and a small tube of Neosporin. She grabbed them, shut the drawer, then looked in the mirror, where she saw her reflection, her eyes shining a little, her cheeks pinker than usual. From the wine? Or some emotional reaction she just couldn't control? *That's ridiculous. You're in charge of yourself. You know that. You've proved it time and time again . . . Uh-oh.*

She heard his footsteps on the stairs seconds before he appeared behind her, his image filling the mirror.

"Oh, good," she said, nervous as a school girl and trying to control her suddenly wildly beating heart. "Take a seat"—she pointed to the toilet—"and Nurse Alvarez will fix you right up."

Hesitating a second, catching her gaze in the reflection, he grinned. "So are we going to play doctor and nurse?"

Swallowing back a smile, she said, "How about ER? Just be thankful you don't have serious head trauma, because I don't think the staff could take care of it. Okay?"

He'd settled onto the commode and looked up at her expectantly.

"Let's see . . ." She scrounged in the drawer again and came up with a package of antiseptic wipes, then washed his face with warm water and a soft cloth. "Close your eyes," she ordered, not because it was necessary for her ministrations, but so that she could look directly at him without him staring at her as she gently cleaned his face. She noticed the way a few wrinkles fanned from his eyes and the bits of gray showing in the hair at his temples. He smelled all male, but she disguised that all too enticing odor with the smell of the antiseptic as she gently cleaned his wounds, running the cloth over his skin, then allowing it to dry and finally applying a touch of Neosporin to the area.

Working this closely to him, leaning down to tend to him, was a little unsettling, but she ignored the fact that he was so damned near. "This shouldn't hurt," she said. "The cream claims it's got a pain reliever in it."

"And here I was believing the 'no pain, no gain' theory." His eyes opened and she found herself nose-to-nose with him, her hand on his cheek, her body leaning forward so that, should he look down, he could see the tops of her breasts and bra past the neckline of her sweater. "God, you're beautiful," he whispered and the phrase was like a caress, warm and welcome.

"Well, you're . . . you're not," she forced out. "Ugly bruises and cuts and—"

"And sexy as hell."

"I was going to say 'easily distracted.' "

His grin turned devilish as his eyes strayed to her neckline. "You know what, Selena, you've got that right."

Before she could respond, he wrapped his arms around her, pulled her so close she almost fell over and kissed her, hard, on the lips. She nearly fell directly on him, but somehow he stood, pulling her up against him, his mouth warm and encouraging, the hands upon her back making warm impressions through her sweater.

Don't do this, her mind warned and she, involuntarily, molded her lips against his and opened her mouth when his tongue pressed against her teeth.

Desire, pulled from the deepest part of her, curled through her veins, heating her blood, causing her pulse to pound. She didn't protest when he walked her backward, through the doorway, along a short hall to her bedroom, where the room was dark, the smell of her own perfume lingering. She felt his hardness, the thickening against the fly of his jeans, pressed deep into her abdomen as her own body responded, warmth invading the deepest part of her.

Selena, what are you thinking?

One of her grandmother's favorite phrases

sang through her mind: *Astrasado mental*!

Yes, she was being a moron, but she couldn't help herself. It seemed so right to be in his arms again, to fall onto the bed and sink into the mattress with him, to know that as the snow fell outside, here, with O'Keefe, she would be warm, would be safe.

Closing her mind to all the insecurities, to all of the pain, to all of her doubts, she wrapped her arms around his neck and drank in the sweet, male scent of him.

His hands moved to the hem of her sweater and she didn't resist, didn't stop him, just let the feel of his fingers climb up her skin.

Her breasts filled, her blood pounded in her veins, her lungs had trouble drawing a breath as he kissed her and moved over her.

Don't stop. Don't ever stop!

The sounds of his breathing and her own heart beating shut out noises from the rest of the world. For now, it was only the two of them, locked away. She pulled his shirt from his jeans and closed her eyes, allowing sensation after sensation to roll through her.

His hands were calloused, a little rough as they rubbed against her. Her own were softer but anxious, her fingers tracing the lines in the muscles of his back. He moaned in the back of his throat and an answering sound came from her own lips. He skimmed her jeans down her hips and lower, past her ankles, while her fingers found the button at his waistband. She hesitated, and he placed a hand over hers, encouraging her.

She tugged.

A string of pops accompanied the opening of his fly and again he groaned into her ear, his tongue wet and hot, his breath fanning fires already burning bright within.

All doubts fled as he stripped her of her bra and panties, mere scraps that he tossed aside before touching her body in ways she'd never experienced, hadn't allowed. Her mind wanted to wander down that dim corridor for a second but then he whispered her name and she was back, in her room, with the one man she'd almost loved.

His fingers touched her nipples, gently stroking, and she gasped. When he kissed her again, his lips lingering against her throat, she felt it, the palpitating, liquid heat fired by need. His lips grazed her nipple and she arched, her hips starting to move, a bloom of heat rising within, her skin suddenly damp with perspiration.

Her entire existence fell away and all that mattered was the pulsing need that pounded through her body. "Yes," she whispered, though there had been no question, and when he took her breast in his mouth, his tongue laving her nipple, his teeth scraping against her skin, she only wanted more.

Lust, long at bay and wanton, thundered through

her brain as he moved upon her, kneeing her legs apart, his body a strong, sinuous wedge. Her heart was thudding, her mind spinning in erotic images as he pressed against her.

"Selena?" he asked, his voice a rough whisper. "Are you—"

"Please!" she cried and he complied, thrusting into her in one swift stroke that stopped the breath in her lungs. Her fingernails dug deep into his shoulders as he began to move, achingly slowly at first and then with more and more momentum. Faster and faster, his shallow, short breaths an echo of her own.

Heat built at the base of her neck, radiating as he kissed her, touched her, loved her until, in a soul-shattering moment, she let go, the room melting away, the ceiling seeming to fall away and bright night stars bursting in the heavens. A scream erupted from her throat and she held tight to him as rush after rush of pleasure caused her body to convulse.

"Oh, God," she whispered fervently, her hair damp, the images in the room muted. "*Dios* . . ."

He held her as if he'd never let go, her head cradled to his chest. She heard the wild rampage of his heart beating frantically in his chest, felt the sheen of perspiration on his skin and the strength of his arms around her.

As she finally caught her breath, she realized what had happened. Unbidden, tears filled her eyes. She bit her lip, not wanting him to know, but he felt the track of one salty drop as it drizzled down her cheek.

"Jesus, Selena, I didn't mean to—"

"Shh. It's all right." She sniffed then, blinking back tears and managing a smile. "I'm not sad. Just emotional."

"Why?"

"You don't want to know."

"Yeah. I do."

"No . . ." Oh, God, could she tell him? He waited, brushing a damp curl from her forehead in such a tender gesture she thought her heart might crack.

"Selena?"

Slowly, she let out a long, shuddering sigh. She supposed he deserved the truth. "It's personal."

"I think what just happened here is pretty personal."

He wouldn't let it drop. She knew that, so she rolled to the side of the bed, walked naked to the closet and dragged her robe from its hook on the back of the door. Quickly she shoved her arms down its sleeves and cinched the belt around her waist, as if she could find strength in the everyday routine. Then, barefoot, she stood at the side of the bed and said, "Okay. So . . . you asked about Gabriel's father? If he was a high school boyfriend or something . . . It . . . He . . ." She cleared her throat and squared her shoulders, then glanced at the window, where snow was still falling past the panes. Gathering her strength, she said for the first time in half of her life, "My cousin Emilio, he's the father. Gabriel's father."

"Your cousin?"

She was shivering, cold despite the thick robe. "He raped me, O'Keefe," she finally admitted. "On the night of my sixteenth birthday."

CHAPTER 21

How had he missed all the signs? O'Keefe wondered and mentally kicked himself to hell and back for not understanding. "Come here," he said and reached out a hand. When she took his, he pulled her back onto the bed, flipped the thick coverlet over her and held her tight. "I'm sorry."

"Don't be. It's not your fault."

"I know, but—"

"It's over."

"Is it?" He didn't believe her and he felt her shudder against him.

"It's a long time ago." Still fighting tears, she admitted, "I've had trouble with intimacy ever since."

He remembered.

Now, her fleeing his home in San Bernardino made more sense, though he had to have been ignoring all the signs not to have realized what was wrong.

"I've . . . I've never told anyone," she admitted.

"Except your parents."

She hesitated and a slow-burning rage stole through his blood.

"They don't know," he guessed.

"No one does. But you."

"But they must've asked questions." He couldn't believe what she was telling him, that she alone had borne this burden, that her parents had allowed it.

"No, no. I mean, yes, they did and they knew I was raped, yes, but . . . but I said it was someone I didn't recognize, a random thing."

"Why?" Horrified, he wanted to shake her. It didn't seem that she would ever have backed down, that she, ever meticulous, determined to right every wrong and punish any criminal in her path, would have let this go.

"Emilio threatened me. Said he would come after me again and he would bring his brothers . . . I shouldn't have been afraid, but I was, and he swore that if I breathed a word of it, he'd see the same thing happened to my younger sister. So . . ."

"So you buried it?"

"I was only sixteen. And scared. And . . . and broken. My mother wanted me to be checked out by a doctor but my father, he sent me to the church, not to ask for forgiveness; he didn't blame me," she was quick to explain, as that was sometimes the case, "but for some kind of counseling, but the priest . . . No, it wasn't a good idea. Didn't work." She shook her head. "And then I turned up pregnant and my father was really upset. He and my mother thought it would be best to send me away, but I pleaded to stay close, because of my sister, so we reached a compromise and I stayed with my great-aunt in Portland, about thirty miles away. There, I did the home schooling thing and was counseled, again through the church, by a nun who . . . Sister Maria was . . . kind. Forgiving."

"Forgiving? What was to forgive?"

"Nothing, I know, but, that's . . . that's how it felt. I wasn't even seventeen, and I don't know, I thought maybe it was my fault, that I'd flirted with Emilio . . . I know now that I was the victim. And, yes, I . . . I saw a counselor for a while before I moved here, after you and I . . . After I realized how deep my problem with intimacy was."

"And the baby?" he asked softly.

"When the time came, I agreed to the private adoption. It was all handled between the church and attorneys. Everyone tried to make it as if it all had never happened, everything got swept under the rug: I poured myself into my school-work, got a scholarship and left."

A few seconds ticked by before he asked, "What happened to Emilio?"

"*Bastardo*!" she spat, her Spanish coming to the fore whenever she was angry. "He's in prison, last I heard."

"Good place for him."

She added, "For assault. And attempted rape. The victim was seventeen."

"Jesus."

He sensed that she was fighting the urge to break down altogether. "But she was stronger than I was. Her father was a cop, insisted she tell the truth, and they busted Emilio. He wouldn't take a deal, probably because he thought he got away with it once and he could do it again. He's nothing if not smug." For a second her cousin's face, dark eyes, straight nose, thin lips came to mind and she pushed it down, didn't want to be reminded of him or the fact that as children they had been playmates. The attack had been fueled by alcohol, yes, but was still such a horrendous, soul-numbing betrayal. "He's serving a long sentence."

"Parole?"

"Not if I have anything to say about it." She was determined. "His next victim, the one who filed charges, she did the right thing. Stood up for herself. I didn't. So I'm going to make certain he does every second of his time." He felt her guilt as if it were palpable. "If I'd had her guts, maybe she never would have had to go through what she did."

"You don't know that."

"Sure I do."

"You were a scared kid."

"So was she!"

He held her close. "It's all right."

"Of course, it's not all right! Never has been; never will be." Of that she sounded certain. "And, and now it's all there again. You show up here and this boy . . . this boy that I saw only briefly, my son, has returned, in trouble with the law, only to disappear again."

"Shh," he whispered against her hair, wishing there was some way to ease her pain, to let her know that he cared, but he had to tread lightly. She'd already opened up to him far more than he ever would have expected. "We'll find him."

"Will we?" She levered up on one elbow and stared down at him, her face illuminated by a bit of light through the window, her black hair falling like a curtain to one side of her face.

"If it's the last thing I do. Swear it," he said and she let out a bitter laugh.

"Now you're placating me; making promises you can't possibly guarantee."

"Okay, you're right." He pulled her down again, close to him so that her head rested in the crook of his shoulder. "But I will tell you this much, I'm going to give it my best damned shot."

"That," she said, relaxing a bit, her breath ruffling the hair of his chest, "I believe."

• • •

Johnna Phillips poured herself one last glass of alcohol-free punch from the bowl near the huge shimmering Christmas tree and told herself it was her last. She'd had it. The tree itself was a monstrosity, a fourteen-foot fir tree flocked white, then decorated with hanging red and blue logos of First Union, the bank she worked for.

Ug-ly. And probably had cost a fortune and was oh, so corporate, just like this lame party with its weak DJ, who seemed to favor *any*thing from the eighties. Really? Wasn't that, like, eons ago?

She sipped her punch and noticed it was going flat, not that it mattered. This was the first social event Johnna had attended alone since her breakup with Carl, which had now been all of thirty hours. She probably shouldn't have come, considering her state of mind, but if she hadn't shown, it would have been noticed by her boss, the overly friendly Monty. And besides, she wasn't going to let the fact that she wasn't hooked up with Carl anymore change her social life. Not one iota!

Damn Carl all to hell.

She set her glass on a tray that held other half-empty stemware. It was almost midnight and the party was winding down. Lots of people had already left and the music was scheduled to end at twelve, which was just fine. Johnna didn't think she could stand another "hit" by Madonna or

Michael Jackson or Duran Duran. Her head was pounding as it was, her feet ached from heels that were too high and her lower back was paining her. She was in a bad mood all around.

Just the beginning, she reminded herself and absently touched her flat abdomen. She was pregnant, though no one but she and Stephanie in New Accounts knew the happy news. She hadn't even told Carl yet, and wondered when she would, and how he would react, as they were suddenly no longer living together. Talk about bad timing.

It had to happen, though. Carl "the loser" Anderson was handsome as hell, a sexy ex-jock who'd never quite grown up. He was really good in bed; however, his prowess in the sack didn't translate to ability at a desk, or behind the wheel of a long-haul truck, or as a waiter at the café just outside of town. Nope, Carl had never, to her knowledge, held a job for more than six or eight months, or however long it was until he could collect unemployment.

Yeah, loser with a capital L.

She eyed the remaining canapés on a silver platter left on a table near the kitchen but passed on yet another bite of stuffed mushroom cap. Her stomach was a little queasy and she attributed it to the pregnancy, though it could have been attending the party and having to explain why Carl wasn't at her side. She'd witnessed the raised eyebrows and saw a spark of interest in the eyes of that slut, Chessa, from Home Loans, the department next to hers, as she was in charge of personal loans.

Why do you even care?

Carl would rather play freakin' video games than hold a job. At thirty-goddamned-five!

Really? *Grand Theft Auto*? *Dead Rising*? Stupid *Mario Galaxy* or whatever it was called? When he had a baby on the way? Well, of course, he didn't know that little news flash. Yet. She'd already had to give up alcohol and cigarettes and most of her breakfasts lately, and the loser hadn't even noticed because he was too wrapped up in himself. Yeah, he'd make a fine dad, she thought disgustedly.

The least he could do was put down the controllers for his Xbox or Wii or anything else that kept his hands from grabbing an actual paycheck! The few dollars a week from unemployment wasn't cutting it as it was, and now, with a baby on the way . . .

"Screw it," she muttered and plucked another one of the canapés from the tray before plopping it into her mouth. No reason to worry about calories, right? In a few months she'd be big as a barn but not before she ballooned on all this party food or had to fend off any more advances from Monty, the groping, drunk operations officer. He was always trying to cop a feel at work and she had half a mind to sue his randy ass. It would serve him, and his ice queen of a wife, right. As it was, the wife had shot Johnna dirty looks all night, as if it were *her* fault that Monty was such a lech. Maybe she'd let the bitch think the baby was Monty's, that would serve her right.

Yeah, right.

No frickin' way.

And she couldn't risk losing her job.

Not with a little one on the way.

Mad at the world, Johnna walked out of the main ballroom and into the lobby of the hotel, where she picked up her coat and slipped into it. She left the coat-check girl a buck as a tip and cringed a little. Suddenly each dollar was so much more important.

What the hell was she going to do? Already she worked a full-time job at the bank during the week and picked up shifts waitressing on the weekends and even some nights. On top of that, she took a couple of online classes, as she really wanted to get an associate's degree in accounting. But now . . . how would she be able to do all that, and care for a newborn?

This wasn't how it was supposed to be. She had planned on being married, owning a fabulous home, having a great part-time job before she got pregnant. And then she'd met Carl and the rest was history, including the part about throwing him out of the apartment last night when, once again, he hadn't even stepped outside and at least pretended to be looking for a job!

She swore under her breath and walked through the door of the old Mason's lodge that had been converted into a hotel. Planted along the shore of the river, overlooking the falls for which the town had been named, the brick and mortar building was one of the oldest and tallest in this, the lower section, of town. Crouched in the shadow of Boxer Bluff, Old Town was an eclectic collection of shops and connected to the newer part of town by a series of steep roads. For pedestrians, there was not only a series of stairs that climbed the cliffs, but also an elevator with a car that had, as it ascended, an incredible view of the river and falls.

From the front of the hotel, looking along the street, she saw the courthouse, its huge outdoor tree already glowing with lights for the holidays. The damned snow was still falling and a wind as bitter as her own feelings about Carl blew down the street, causing the tiny, icy flakes to swirl and spin over a few cars still parked at the curb. Everything was covered in snow and ice—the shrubbery around the hotel, the parked cars, the sidewalk and parking meters, all flocked with white.

"Merry Christmas," she said under her breath, then smiled at the thought that next year there would be a baby to share the holidays.

Her car was parked three blocks over, on the other side of the Black Horse Saloon, a pub where locals hung out and a couple of guys bundled in thick jackets and stocking caps were smoking beneath the awning of the tavern. They barely looked up as she passed.

Picking her way carefully, she nearly slipped twice and cursed the damned high heels, harsh wind and slick sidewalks.

For a split second she thought of returning to Albuquerque, sucking it up and telling her parents what was up. Unfortunately, they had more than enough on their plates already. Nana, already suffering from Alzheimer's disease, had recently broken her hip and was recuperating at their two-bedroom condo. No, they didn't need their adult daughter showing up with a brand-new set of problems, not when their other daughter was talking about a divorce from that jerk-wad De Lane Pettygrove. Talk about a prick! He made Carl look good, and right now, that was pretty damned tough.

She turned the corner and saw that her car was the only one parked on this street that ran parallel to the railroad tracks, a few blocks from the river and within two hundred yards of the lower level of the city's elevator. Covered in four inches of powder, it was nearly impossible to recognize her dented, fifteen-year-old Honda.

She'd have to scrape the windows and turn on the car, letting it idle to clear the windshield. Great.

After brushing aside some of the snow, she

managed to unlock the car and settle inside. God, it was cold. Shivering, she jabbed the key into the ignition and turned.

Nothing.

"Oh, no, not now." She tried again.

Still not so much as a click.

"Come on, come on!" she said and kept trying but the car was dead. "Great!" What else could go wrong? She reached for her phone, but she didn't have AAA or any other car service. The last time this had happened and her car had left her stranded, she'd called Carl and he'd shown up with jumper cables and his jacked-up Dodge pickup within ten minutes. Her car had been running like a top ever since.

Until tonight.

Well, she couldn't very well call her ex for help tonight.

Angry at the world, she climbed out of the car, slammed the door, locked the damned thing and, for good measure, gave it a kick. Why now? *Calm down. Just get home and pour yourself a glass of . . . apple juice. Crap!* Freezing, she decided she'd hike back to the party, where maybe one of the stragglers would give her a ride and she could deal with the dead Honda tomorrow in daylight. *Wearing boots,* she reminded herself, *and tights and a ski jacket and a scarf and warm gloves!*

Her bad mood worsening, she hoped that Allen, who worked as a teller, was still around. He was a little nerdy, but at least she wouldn't have to depend on that creep Monty and his uptight wife. Though, as desperate as she was, she'd even put up with them to get home. She passed the tavern again and noted the two guys who'd been smoking outside the door had vanished, then started for the bank.

"Johnna?"

Hearing her name, she turned, nearly toppling over on the damned heels as a dark figure emerged from the area of the tavern.

"What're you doing out here? God, it's freezing!"

Relaxing a little, recognizing him, she said, "Bank party. You know, the annual Christmas bash." Rolling her eyes, she offered him a smile. He was a customer, after all, a good customer, even if his credit score lacked what the bank had required for the personal loan he'd wanted the year before, the loan his wife refused to cosign.

"What about you?"

"Just had a couple of drinks down at the Black Horse." He hooked a gloved thumb behind him, in the direction of the pub. That made sense.

"You parked around here?" He eyed the near-empty street. She hesitated, then thought, *Why not see if he can help?* "I, uh, I'm going back to the party, hoping to catch a ride. It's my car." She motioned vaguely toward the area where she'd parked.

"Something wrong with it?" He seemed concerned.

"Other than it's got over two hundred thousand miles and a dead battery, it's fine," she said, her breath clouding. "It picked a great night to decide not to start."

"You're sure it's the battery and it's dead?"

"No."

"Has it happened before?"

"Once, maybe." It was waaay too cold to be outside discussing this.

"You know, sometimes that's an easy fix. Maybe I should look at it."

"It's pretty dead." She glanced at the hotel, where the lights of the lobby splashed through the glass doors. It was warm inside and she was starting to have the urge to pee. "Like, really dead."

"Doesn't hurt to have a look." Again, the smile. "I know engines. Have to. Equipment for the farm."

"Well . . ." She imagined dealing with Monty and his slobbering advances and the daggered stare from his wife again, then shuddered inside. "Uh . . . okay. Sure."

"Where is it?"

"Parked near the railroad tracks, not far from the elevator."

"Okay, let's have a look, shall we?" He was already heading toward the street where she'd left the damned Civic, so she thought, *Why the hell not?* She hurried and caught up with him, and as they rounded the corner of the street near the railroad tracks, he saw her car, the only one.

"Honda?" he asked, though how he could tell with all the snow was surprising. Must be a gearhead.

"Yeah."

"Usually reliable." He reached the car, shoved all of the snow off the hood, then, with his gloved hand, brushed the windshield and driver's side down to the glass. "Why don't you get in?" he said. "Then open the hood latch and, when I tell you to, try to start the engine."

"Okay." She knew already it was a waste of time, but Johnna did as she was bid and climbed into the frigid interior. She clicked open the latch and saw, beneath the crack separating the raised hood from the windshield that he had a small flashlight and was shining it over the engine. Obviously he came prepared. A little weird, but okay, guys always had way more stuff in their pockets than one would ever expect. Giving the key a turn, she heard nothing. "I told you," she muttered under her breath.

He fiddled around. She heard him messing with something—wires maybe—attached to the engine, which, she knew, was a major waste of time. He said something to her and she had to roll down the window. "What?"

"Try it again," he called and she did, and this time, wonder of wonders, the little engine sparked to life. She pressed on the accelerator and heard the familiar and comforting sound of the engine racing, pistons doing their thing.

"Wow!" she said through the open window as he slammed the hood down, locking it in place. "Thank you!"

A confident self-satisfied grin in place, he walked to her side of the car. "No problem." Then he leaned down as if to say something more. The smug smile on his face fixed. A little off. In that millisecond, she felt a premonition of fear, that something wasn't right. As if a ghost had breathed against the back of her neck. She reached for the gearshift and looked up to see him staring at her. His expression had turned blank, but his eyes . . . oh, God, his eyes looked like pure evil. Ridiculous, right?

"I'd better get going," she said and before she could ram the car into reverse, he'd pulled his hand from his pocket. In a heartbeat, he jammed the cold electrodes of a stun gun against her neck.

What? No!

Suddenly desperate, she tried to jerk away, to hit the gas hard and back the hell over him, to get out of there fast!

Too late!

He pulled the trigger.

CHAPTER 22

Alvarez was awake most of the night.

She lay in her bed with O'Keefe at her side, Jane curled on the pillow at her head. While O'Keefe slept as if nearly dead, his soft snores and warm body the only indication he was alive, she had been too wired to sleep. She would have thought sheer exhaustion would have overcome her, but it didn't. Though her body was tired, her mind was spinning. With her son. With Junior Green's attack. With the fact that she'd broken through the intimacy barriers that had surrounded her for half her life. She lay on the bed, nestled next to a man she'd once loved, and wondered where it would all lead. She knew that it was a major breakthrough to be able to make love, and for that she was grateful, but to complicate her life by being sexually involved with O'Keefe: That might not be so smart.

Turning her head, she stared out the window. Sometime in the early morning hours, the snow had stopped falling and the moon had cast a silvery glimmer that reflected on the snow and shone through the window.

Was this what it was supposed to feel like? A warm male body, one arm thrust protectively across her breasts, the world serene, the house noiseless aside from the gentle sound of his breathing and the quiet hum of the furnace. Did couples wake up feeling totally isolated from the rest of the world, the union between them strong enough to fight whatever external forces were outside the walls and ready to try to rend them apart?

Could she rouse slowly, maybe kiss him on the forehead, then roll out of bed and throw on her robe before padding barefoot downstairs to start the coffee, read the newspaper or turn on her laptop with one ear cocked as she listened for him to awaken?

It was strange and new.

And the man beside her, now her lover, how would he feel this morning? How would he react?

How do you *feel?*

How are you *reacting?*

She couldn't dissect this, was going to just let things happen and unfold naturally as she had the night before.

O'Keefe shifted, his hand moving across her body, and her breasts reacted, nipples puckering expectantly. He made a noise deep in his throat and she smiled. *Don't fight this. Just let things happen as they happen. It's not your nature, but for once, just . . .*

From the nightstand, her cell phone shrilled.

O'Keefe groaned as she picked up. "Yeah?" she

said, seeing that Pescoli was on the other end of the call.

"Rise and shine. Guess what was found up on Sawtell Road, near Keegan's corner."

"I couldn't," Alvarez said, tossing off the covers, her legs already swinging over the edge of the mattress.

"Lissa Parsons's car."

"Anyone in it?"

"First report, no, but the kids who were up there messing around with their four-wheel-drive trucks nearly hit it, looked inside and called it in. Had the presence of mind to give the make and model and plates. Looks like it's the missing Chevy Impala. First deputy on the scene was Rule and he's confirmed."

"I'll meet you at the station. I'm on my way," Alvarez said and finally noticed that O'Keefe was fully awake, sitting up, eavesdropping on the conversation. "We think we found the missing car of one of the victims," she said as a way of explaining, and found her jeans left, as they never were, in a pile at the foot of the bed. She grabbed a fresh pair of underwear from her drawer, then pulled on the jeans. O'Keefe was watching her and she was suddenly aware of her bare breasts. "This isn't a reverse strip show, you know."

"No?" His smile was an engaging bit of white against the beard that was starting to form on his face. "Depends upon your viewpoint."

Finding her bra, she slid her arms through the straps and hooked it behind her deftly. "You're such a pain."

"And you love it."

"Hardly." She was already locating socks and boots.

"I'm coming with you."

"No way. Police business."

"Mine, too."

"How so?" She zipped up a boot and looked up at him.

"I'm looking for a kid who stole an earring from you, darlin', and then it shows up on a victim, right? The victim whose car has just been located."

"Convoluted thinking."

"Straight thinking."

"Police business. FBI's sure to be there."

"Bring 'em on. Besides, you remember, don't you, that you don't have a car? I'm your ride."

"Crap!"

He was already yanking on his jeans.

"You're a real pain in the ass, you know that, don't you?"

"It's been pointed out a time or two."

She didn't have time for arguments, just pulled on her sweater, shook her hair free, then scraped it back in a ponytail. "Okay. Fine," she finally acquiesced. Unless she wanted to call Pescoli back, he did have a point. She strapped on her shoulder holster, retrieved her sidearm from the

332

locker in her closet, then checked the clip before pressing her weapon into place. "Just don't get in the way."

The scene was a mess. Frozen car, piled snow, FBI, deputies from the sheriff's department, crime scene techs and a snow-covered pile of brush that had hidden the car from the seldom-used logging road.

"So he parked it here, behind a thicket, and no one noticed in all this time," Halden said, eyeing the area.

"Private property borders this area. Owned by Long Logging, but no one's logging now," Pescoli said. "Brady Long died a while back—you remember the case—and he left nothing to any of his wives, didn't have children, at least none that have come forward, and the major heir, his sister, Padgett, spent years in a mental hospital, got out and disappeared. Hasn't been seen in almost two years."

"I do remember," Halden said.

"You tell me. Isn't the FBI supposed to be expert on that kind of thing? How come you haven't found Padgett?"

He ignored the jab. "Long Logging? Same as in Long Copper?"

"Uh-huh."

"But Long didn't live here all the time as I recall. That right?"

"He spent most of his time in Denver. His lodge was just for vacation use." She didn't add that Nate Santana was the foreman and, as such, had inherited a nice bit of the Long estate. If Halden wanted to know, he could figure it out easily enough, and once he made that connection, he'd realize that Pescoli and Santana were in a relationship. There would be a lot of questions thrown her way at that point and she wasn't ready to deal with them, just like she wasn't ready to take that relationship to another level.

At least she didn't think she was.

"Here we go," Halden said, and motioned toward the private road where a tow truck was chugging up the hill.

She and Alvarez had already double-checked the car, but it was clean, nothing inside, of course. The area around the vehicle had been roped off and was now being searched. Snow was carefully cleared and sifted through as the techs searched for any piece of evidence, any sign of a struggle, anything that might help them nail the bastard.

Alvarez had shown up with Dylan O'Keefe, the PI, lawyer, ex-cop and hunk that Pescoli didn't trust. Obviously her partner had needed a ride, as her own car was still at the department's garage, but why the hell had she dragged O'Keefe up here? Why not have Pescoli pick her up, even if it was out of her way? Whatever the reason,

Pescoli couldn't worry about it at this moment in time when, at least for the moment, the snow had stopped falling, dawn had broken and the sky above the pine and hemlock branches was a brilliant shade of blue that could be found only, she thought, in Montana.

Maybe now, they could catch a break. Maybe.

From the looks on everyone's face at the scene, it was evident they needed one.

"You and O'Keefe?" Pescoli asked hours later at the office as they walked out of the task force room. O'Keefe was being questioned by the FBI agents again, as Chandler and Halden were trying to determine if Gabriel Reeve's disappearance was connected to the recent murders, the link, of course, being the damned ear/nipple ring. They'd already spoken with Alvarez and now wanted to find out what, if anything, O'Keefe knew.

"What do you mean?"

"Oh, come on, Alvarez. You show up with him before dawn. I don't think you called him to pick you up. He stayed over."

They had made their way to Alvarez's work area. "And this is your business . . . how?"

"Oooh. Touchy."

She wanted to say that she hadn't had much sleep, but that, of course, would only fuel the fires of Pescoli's curiosity, so she didn't reply. "How're your kids?"

"Ghosts." Pescoli rubbed the knots from the back of her neck. "But then, I am, too." Closing one eye, she twisted her neck. "It's not a great situation, but there it is; nothing more to do."

"Until we nail this guy."

"Right."

But they were getting nowhere, spinning their wheels, finding little evidence to trace back to him. There was hope, though, the tiniest drop of blood in the ice of the first victim was being analyzed, and in the vacuuming of Brenda Sutherland's car, a hair had been found, one that was being compared to strands from her brush as well as samples from her kids and ex-husband, which he'd grudgingly given, after a considerable amount of grumbling about harassment. The hair hadn't been a match to anyone in the family.

"I have the feeling we're going to get another call, another body found somewhere," Pescoli said.

"Brenda Sutherland."

"She's on deck in the ice-queen batting order," Pescoli said, then said, "Sorry. That didn't come out right. I just wish we'd find her before Jack Frost does his thing with her."

"Probably too late." Her cell phone rang and Alvarez, seeing it was someone calling from the department's garage, answered. She'd called in all her markers, reminding Andy, the manager, of all the favors she'd done for him over the years, and asked that the techs go over her vehicle quickly, so that she could have it back. She figured they didn't need to do much. Junior Green was behind bars, the evidence pretty clear, pictures taken, slugs removed, the case, in her mind, a slam dunk. The bottom line was: She wanted her wheels back.

However Andy, on the other end of the line, reminded her that it was Sunday, and though he was working "round the clock these days, even God took a day of rest, you know." The upshot was that the earliest she would be able to pick up her Subaru was the next day, around five.

"Thanks." She hung up and said, "Great." She had access to the department's vehicles, of course, and like it or not, she'd have to drive one of the county's Jeeps until Andy and "the crew" were finished with her car. She reminded herself it was for a good cause, a very good cause, if that creep Green could be put away forever.

"Let me guess, your car's not ready," Pescoli said, as she'd eavesdropped Alvarez's side of the conversation and pieced together the rest.

"Your powers of detection are astounding."

"Pissed, are we?"

"Don't know about you, but I am."

"I'm pissed all the time, isn't that what you said? So when can you get it?"

"Tomorrow. At the earliest. 'Five-ish.' " Frowning, Alvarez shook her head.

"Any news on your dog?"

337

She made a face, having checked her cell, knowing that anyone who found Roscoe would have called the number on his collar, or if he were brought into a shelter and his tag was missing, someone would check the missing-dog notices. And then there was his ID microchip she'd had inserted with his first shots. If someone found him as a stray, a vet could ID him. "Nothing yet."

"Hang in. He'll show up." But there wasn't a lot of conviction in Pescoli's voice and all Alvarez had to do was look out the window and let the weather depress her. If Roscoe hadn't been taken in, if he hadn't found shelter . . . "Maybe you should contact Grace Perchant. She knew your son was in danger; maybe she can tell you where the dog is."

"Is that supposed to be a joke? Because if it is, it's not funny."

"Yeah, I know." Pescoli sighed. "You never told me what the deal is with you and O'Keefe. He's kind of a hunk."

"There's no deal." She glanced up at her partner. "Sorry to disappoint. Don't you have something better to do?"

Pescoli's grin grew from one side of her face to the other. "Yeah, unfortunately, I do. Always." As if to prove the point, one of the road deputies who was hauling a scruffy, cuffed man passed Alvarez's open door.

"Hey! Take it easy! Keep your fuckin' hands off me!" the suspect, skinny as a rail, his jeans about to slip off his butt, grumbled. His sweat-shirt was wet from melting snow, the hood falling off to expose a shaved head covered with tattoos.

"Come on, Reggie," the deputy ordered, leading the offender, a perpetual car thief with a particular interest in imports, down the hall just as Pescoli's phone rang. She answered, waved at Alvarez, and with the phone pressed to her ear, took off toward her own office.

Good. Grateful not to have to answer any more questions about O'Keefe, Alvarez turned back to her desk. How could she possibly respond to her partner's insinuations and speculation and flat-out curiosity when she couldn't answer her own?

Once she was alone in her office again and the noise of the station seemed to retreat a bit, Alvarez glanced at her computer screen. Lissa Parsons's autopsy report had come in and she compared it to that of Lara Sue Gilfry. Nothing out of the ordinary, no bruises or marks, cause of death hypothermia.

Her jaw clenched and she thought about how many others there could possibly be. God, they had to find this guy and fast.

She was about to go home when she caught a notation on the first victim's report. That she'd had a tongue stud and the area around the piercing was a little raw, as if it had been recent. Pulling up the file, she flipped through to the missing persons report and scanned the page. In the area where there was mention of identifying marks, her scar and tattoo were listed.

No mention of a tongue stud.

Maybe whoever filed the report didn't know.

Maybe it was too new.

"And maybe it's nothing," she said as she flipped through the images on the computer of Lara, her identifying marks and eventually the tongue stud. As she stared at the image, she realized it didn't look like any of the studs she'd seen before and yet, it was familiar.

No.

It couldn't be.

Her stomach dropped and she told herself that she was leaping to all the wrong conclusions. But a sick sensation took hold of her as she remembered her hoop earring used as a nipple ring on Lissa Parsons.

Was it possible? A whisper of dread skittered along the base of her skull.

Had the lunatic stolen the silver stud in the picture from her own home and then used it to make a statement on Lara Sue Gilfry?

"No way," she whispered, but even as the words left her mouth, she was out of her chair, on her way to the evidence room, and knew in her heart the piece of jewelry was hers, stolen from her home, then stuck into the naked victim and left for her to find.

Somehow, some way, the sick son of a bitch had broken into her place and now was mocking her.

And he wanted her to know about it.

CHAPTER 23

"Look, I really don't have time for this," O'Keefe insisted. Sitting on one of the molded plastic chairs in an interview room, he was slowly going out of his mind. With concrete walls painted a nondescript green and a tiled floor circa 1962 that showed wear near the door, the room had a mirror on one wall that was, undoubtedly, a window to a darkened room on the other side, where interviews could be observed in private, not that the glass fooled anyone.

O'Keefe had been interviewed by Agents Chandler and Halden for the past two hours and they were getting nowhere fast. "I've told you all I know about Gabriel Reeve and how I tracked him here." They'd gone over it several times, as if they thought his story would change if he told it often enough. He'd explained how he'd tracked down every lead, looked into any acquaintances

Reeve might have in the area, checked cell phone and computer records, talked with people on the street, searched all the areas he thought a kid might go if he was hiding and scared.

"Don't you think it was odd that he ended up in Detective Alvarez's home and later she discovers jewelry missing that ended up on one of the victims?"

"Of course." He'd answered that one before, too. The agents finally seemed satisfied that he was telling it to them straight, then Chandler brought up the past.

"You and Detective Alvarez, you worked together in San Bernardino, right?"

Here we go, he thought. "That's right, and we were involved. Romantically. Look, I'm telling you this so we can cut to the chase, okay? You have a killer to catch and I have a suspect to run down."

"We're working on that, too. Confirmed with the Helena Police Department. Detective Trey Williams. He said you were a deputy of the department, but just for this case." She waved her fingers as if that information was insignificant. "I'm not exactly sure how that works. It's a little loosey-goosey for me. Not exactly by the book."

"Not exactly," O'Keefe allowed.

"And there is that problem in San Bernardino."

"No problem. My record's clean."

"Mmm." She didn't seemed convinced.

"Detective Williams has been advised to keep us in the loop, but he insists you've been important to the case, he wants you to work with him," Chandler said, perusing a file.

"Good."

"We're all on the same side here," Halden pointed out. Slouching just a bit in his uncomfortable chair, Craig Halden was the friendlier of the two, almost seemed like the kind of guy you'd like to have a beer with. However, that could be all an act, a way to get O'Keefe to open up. Halden didn't have that cold exterior that Agent Chandler worked so hard to exude. From her blue eyes to her platinum hair to the set of her jaw and unsmiling lips, everything about her was about as warm as New Year's Eve in Alaska. Never displaying any emotion, Stephanie Chandler was as much an automaton as O'Keefe had ever seen in a woman, as much as he'd ever want to see. Halden said, "We're all part of a team. You, us—" Flipping his hand back and forth to indicate both himself and Chandler, he added, "Grayson and his deputies, including Detective Alvarez, we're all just trying to nail some bad dude's ass to the wall."

"I agree," O'Keefe said, reassessing his opinion of the agents. So they weren't idiots. Nor morons. But they were didactic, it seemed, in their quest to be thorough. And time was ticking by; O'Keefe felt each second as it passed. "So let's work together. I need to find Gabriel Reeve."

"And we need to find ourselves a killer," Halden said, even offering his good-old-boy smile that seemed genuine enough, though it didn't quite touch his eyes.

"Let me get this straight," Pescoli said to the caller on the other end of the line. She had one arm through her jacket and had been on her way home when her cell phone had jangled and she'd caught it on the fly. "You got my number from Luke Pescoli?"

"Yeah, uh, he said you were his ex and that you were a detective with the sheriff's department."

Terrific!

"And he gave you my *personal* cell phone number?" she clarified, ready to kill her ex-husband, not for the first time. Resting her hips against the edge of her desk, she shrugged out of her jacket and watched as it fell to the floor of her office.

"Yeah. Look, I'm worried. Because of my girlfriend, Johnna, uh, Johnna Phillips, she didn't come home last night. And, you know, with everything that's happening around here, I got worried, so I called up Lucky and he said I should call you."

Pescoli sighed and grabbed a piece of paper she kept near her computer monitor.

"What's your name again?"

"Carl. Anderson. I worked with your husband when I drove a truck."

"I got that and he's my *ex*-husband."

"Oh, yeah. He said that."

Amen for small blessings.

"Your girlfriend's name is Johnna Phillips?"

"Yeah, but, oh, technically, she's kinda my ex, too."

"How kinda?"

"We broke up the night before last."

That explained a lot. "And now she won't take your calls?" This was beginning to sound like a wild goose chase. She caught the neckline of her jacket with the edge of her boot, kicked it upward and caught it in her free hand.

"It's not like that. And I went to the house and she hasn't been back since last night when she went to that bank party. She works for First Union. In the loan department. And her car isn't at the apartment and she hasn't been back. I still have a key and I went in, you know, to try and work things out, and she wasn't there."

"Maybe she went home with . . . a friend?" Pescoli suggested, thinking the guy on the other end of the connection was dumb as a stone. The girlfriend had probably just moved on, hopefully to someone with a higher IQ and a better set of acquaintances than a group that included Lucky Pescoli.

You married him. You chose him to be the father

of your daughter. People in glass houses . . .

"I don't think so. She hadn't been feeling all that sharp and she was just going to the party because it was kind of, you know, expected. What did she call it? A royal something or other?"

"Command performance?"

"Yeah, that was it!" he said, amazed.

"Have you called all her friends?"

"Oh, yeah. And her sister and . . . and that Stephanie chick from the bank. No one's seen her and Stephanie said they had plans to meet up today and walk in the park. Johnna didn't show; but she thought maybe she just slept in. But she didn't."

"At least not at home."

"No. She . . . no."

Uh-oh. Now the *ex* was catching on.

Pescoli dropped the jacket over the back of her desk chair.

"What's her address?"

"Number two-one-five at the Park West Apartments." He gave her the address and she wrote it down. "Like I said, I probably wouldn't have called, but there's all this crazy shit goin' down and I'm worried. I've texted her and called and she's not picking up or returning my calls. I checked online at Facebook and, like . . . nothing for over twenty-four hours. And she's on there *all* the time. I even sent IMs to her friends and no one's sayin' they, like, heard from her. It's weird, man, I'm tellin' ya. Somethin's not right."

"Why don't you come in and file a report?" Pescoli suggested. Unconvinced that the ex-girlfriend wasn't just not responding to him, Pescoli was hesitant to follow up. However, he seemed so convinced that Johnna Phillips was really missing and had actually called searching for her, which gave Pescoli pause. She didn't want to take any chances, not with a lunatic terrorizing the area. "Check with Missing Persons. That's the department where you need to file the report."

"Cool!"

Not really, but she wasn't going to tell him.

Driving home in a department-issued vehicle, Alvarez decided she probably should have told Pescoli her theory about the earring but hadn't wanted to go off half-cocked. Just because she was missing an earring didn't mean the one found in Lara Sue Gilfry's tongue belonged to her. She wouldn't even have thought of it, as the silver stud wasn't all that unique, except for the hoop earring found pierced through Lissa Parsons's nipple.

That one was definitely hers.

So, she wondered, was it that much of a leap to think that the killer would use another one . . . no, make that the stud, the first piece of jewelry, if he'd killed the women in the order in which they'd been discovered? Because their bodies had been frozen, determining time or day of death was tricky, if not impossible.

She flipped on the Jeep's wipers, as snow was falling again, dusk slipping away, the police band crackling as she nosed down Boxer Bluff. This year, colored spotlights had been trained on the falls, and the river, not yet frozen, tumbled wildly, a rushing froth in green and red as it flowed past the courthouse and shops lining the street that flanked its deep banks.

She wasn't the only one who'd seen the new display. Sunday evening traffic was worse than usual as drivers slowed to take in the sight.

By the time she turned down her street, she was nervous and a little agitated. If the silver stud did prove to be hers, her life was going to be a lot more complicated. The FBI would be all over her and some connection made between the killer and her.

What the hell is that all about? Why has he targeted you? This is NOT random, Selena, you know that!

Troubled, she pulled into her drive and reached for the nonexistent garage-door opener. Of course it was still in her Subaru.

"Lovely," she said, ramming the gear shift into park. As soon as she made the determination that her stud earring was really and truly missing and that the remaining one was the twin of the bit of metal yanked out of Lissa Parsons's mouth, she'd call Pescoli as well as O'Keefe, whom she left at the station without so much as a goodbye.

Dylan O'Keefe was another issue, one she'd prefer to keep private. That being the case, she didn't want anyone from the department searching her place for her earring or evidence from a week-old break-in and coming up with any personal item from O'Keefe. She just wasn't ready to start answering questions about their relationship or lack of relationship; it was all too complicated and would certainly bring up the mess in San Bernardino and Alberto De Maestro again.

That, she would definitely like to avoid.

Grabbing her things, she stepped into the cold of winter again and walked swiftly through a fresh dusting of snow to her front door. On the porch, she inserted her key into the lock, and as she did, the door swung open, as if it hadn't been locked or latched.

Again?

Someone had broken in?

Her heart kicked into overtime as she tried to remember leaving early this morning, but she was certain the door had been shut and locked . . . or had it?

From habit she reached for her gun and pushed the door open farther.

No sound.

But there was a flickering light emanating from within . . . the gas fire? She *knew* she hadn't left it burning.

The hairs on the back of her neck rose.

Someone was in the house.

Heart hammering, every nerve stretched tight, her fingers wrapped tightly over the butt of her pistol, she stepped quietly inside.

Still no noise, no shuffling of frantic feet, but if she listened hard, she could hear the hiss of the fire as it burned.

This is nuts! Go outside. Call for backup!

Her heart thundered in her ears.

Holding her breath, she took one more step.

"Don't shoot!" a voice yelled frantically as she reached the living room. "Please, don't shoot!"

She froze.

The lights snapped on.

Looking haggard and scared out of his mind was a teenaged boy with shaggy black hair, a coppery complexion and fear in his dark, suspicious eyes. He was huddled in the corner of the couch, closest to the fire; a blanket was tucked around him and Jane Doe had curled herself into his lap.

"Please," he said, his hands raising to the side of his head, the cat, startled, leaping off the blanket to dive under a nearby table. "You're Selena Alvarez, right?" Before she could answer, he said, "Please, you have to help me!" His voice cracked with desperation and she felt something inside of her break as well. Still, she trained the muzzle of her gun straight into the face of Gabriel Reeve, the son she'd given up half a lifetime before.

CHAPTER 24

"You're Selena Alvarez," the kid said. His hands shook a little as he held them over his head. "My mother, right?"

Oh, God. She was thrown back in time to the austere hospital and the feeling of sheer terror that held her, the pain of the birth, the bright lights, the doctor's voice and the fear of the unknown of what would happen to her as she delivered the perfect little baby. She remembered his red face, the shock of black hair and his first squall, a sound that nearly broke her heart. Tears had flowed from her eyes and she had gasped for breath, torn between wanting to hold him and not wanting to see him at all.

What she caught was just a glimpse of a tiny face that seemed to stare straight into her soul before he was whisked away forever.

Now she stood, frozen, the weapon still pointed at him. "I don't know," she admitted, lowering her pistol, then putting it into its holster again and all the while feeling as if she'd been kicked in the gut, as if this surreal situation couldn't possibly be happening. Not to her. "I think . . . yes, maybe." Oh, Lord, was she beginning to cry? Were hot tears filling her eyes? That would never do! She sniffed them back. "Gabriel Reeve, right?" But she knew it was he, had from the second her gaze found him; she was reminded of her cousin at that age, handsome in that gawky way of a boy becoming a man. Yes, this teenager more than resembled her cousin; Gabriel Reeve was the spitting image of the prick who had spawned him.

Before she knew what to say to him, he shot to his feet. "You have to help me," he said again. "I'm in really big trouble."

"I know that."

"I'm innocent!" He seemed suddenly frantic. "That gun, the one my dad found, it was planted in my backpack. I swear."

If he didn't believe what he was saying, he was a damned good liar. She'd seen more than her share.

"I didn't know how to get rid of it, or even what to do with it. So I didn't do anything . . . and then . . . then I . . ."

"Ran," she supplied.

"Yeah. No one was gonna believe me. They never do."

"So you came here because you thought I could help you?"

"Yeah. I came once before, but some guy was following me so I left."

"Where have you been ever since?"

"By the falls. There's some shacks down there.

Empty. Cold. And the restaurant. Wild Bill's."

"Will's."

"Yeah, that's it. There's always scraps."

She told herself not to be taken in by him; he could well be a con man or even a hardened criminal.

Or he could be telling the truth and is a boy on the run, falsely accused, having nowhere to turn . . .

"Where's my dog?"

"What?"

"Roscoe." She pointed to the empty crate. "He was gone."

"There was no dog."

"Of course there was."

Shaking his head violently, Gabe insisted, "There was no dog here, I swear. I saw the cat, yeah, but no dog."

"Maybe you let him out by mistake—"

"I'm telling you! I did *not* see any damned dog. Okay? I know what a dog looks like! That pen thing," he said, hitching his chin at the crate, "that was open, I think, but I didn't take time to look around. The guy was chasing me. He's . . . he's my mom's cousin, I think. I met him a couple of times, but now he's like . . . like a Dog the Bounty Hunter–type of guy on TV!"

"Not quite," she said, and despite the raw emotion pulsing through the house, she almost laughed aloud to think of O'Keefe compared to

Duane "Dog" Chapman, the TV bounty hunter.

"Anyway, I finally lost him so I came back. Here. For you to help me."

"And you thought I would do that, why?"

"Because you're my mom. You owe me."

"Whoa . . . I don't think . . . I mean I'm not sure either of us owes anyone anything," she said, trying to get a grip while her own emotions were stretched thin. She wanted to reach out to him but didn't dare and then kicked herself for being afraid. Of what? Losing him again. "And the jewelry, you took that?"

"You think I stole your jewelry? Why would I do that?"

"To pawn."

"No, I just wanted out."

"There was some money."

"Twenty bucks! That's all!"

"And you took it."

He hesitated.

"With the jewelry."

"No! Damn it! I did *not* take any of your fuc— your jewelry. But, yeah—" His jaw set, again reminding her of Emilio, and he said, almost inaudibly, "I might have picked up the money."

There was no "might have" about it. "I don't care about it."

"You don't?" His eyes narrowed, as if he didn't believe a word that she said.

"Well, yes, of course, but, no. Not right now."

She was sounding as confused as he looked. Holding up a hand, as if she expected him to interrupt, she said, "Okay! Don't worry about the money. At least for now. Why don't you go into the bathroom and clean up and I'll get you something to eat? You must be starved. I've got some leftover pizza in the refrigerator."

"I ate it. The good kind. Not that kind with the squash on it!"

"The zucchini?"

"Whatever! It was nasty." He shuddered for effect as she walked into the kitchen and saw the evidence, the empty pizza boxes, a few wrinkled vegetables scraped onto the oil-soaked ridges of the cardboard that lined the boxes. He said from the other room, "I'm . . . I'm okay. Don't need a shower or nothing. Look, you just gotta help me."

"I'm a cop."

"I *know* that. That's one of the reasons I came here!" He was getting agitated, a little frantic. "Look, I've got nowhere else to go and . . . and I figure you might want to help me."

"What?" she asked. "How do you figure that?"

"You gave me away!"

That much was true, and she wanted to help him, but not more than she did any other teenager in trouble.

Are you kidding? Trying to balm your own sense of guilt? He's right. You have a responsibility to him, one that goes beyond just being a cop trying to help a troubled kid and bring him to justice. He could be your son, damn it, Selena!

"So . . . what *exactly* do you expect me to do?" she asked, trying to stay calm when she felt as if her entire world was turned inside out.

"Find out who planted the gun on me."

"One of your friends?"

"No!" he said quickly. Too quickly. His gaze skittered away and around the room, as if he were searching for the right answer. Or a place to hide. "Not my friend. No way. But, maybe one of his friends . . . those guys . . . I, uh, don't know . . . We were hanging with some people Joey knew that night."

"Joey?"

"Lizard."

"That's his nickname?"

"No!" She saw it, he nearly rolled his eyes but held back, probably was too scared. Or too smart. Was he playing her? How would she know? Gabe cleared things up a little, at least in his mind, by adding, "Joey's last name is Lizard. But, yeah, sometimes we, like, call him Lizard."

She knew that fact, of course, was just checking, trying to figure out how much of the truth she was getting and how much of what he said was just plain BS. Gabe had come to her, so she expected he wouldn't lie, at least not too much. If he had any brains at all, which he obviously did, then he'd know she'd already have some of the information on him. He just didn't know how much.

Joseph Peter Lizard's name had been all over the information O'Keefe had accumulated as well as on the original police report, which, of course, Alvarez had read. Lizard's "friends," Donovan Vale and Lincoln "Line" Holmes, had been listed along with Joseph Lizard and Gabriel Reeve, who were both underage and whose names had not been given to the press.

Not that they weren't guilty. Just young.

She said, "Tell me about Lizard's friends."

"Like, they're older."

"How much?"

"I dunno, around twenty or so, I think." He appeared to be thinking, hard, trying to come up with the right answer, or maybe just a plausible one.

So far, though, so good.

"What was the plan?"

"There wasn't really a plan. They just wanted to break into the judge's house and mess it up, I guess."

"Vandalize it?"

He shrugged, then stopped, as if sensing he might be digging himself in too deep.

"Why?" she asked. "Why mess it up?"

Another lift of the shoulders, but he did say, "I think, like, cuz the judge, he sent one of them's girlfriend to jail or something."

"Ramsey, he was the sentencing judge for the girlfriend? Is that what you're saying? Judge Victor Ramsey."

"Yeah, he was the guy." Worrying his lip, he added, "I guess."

"Not 'the guy.' Judge Ramsey, in this case, was the victim," she repeated, to clarify. "And his daughter, she's in your class at St. Francis's Academy in Helena?"

"You know this already, don't you?" he charged. "Crap! Then why are you asking me?"

Because that's what I do. This is my job. And you might be my son as well as a suspect. Oh, God, she wasn't handling this right. She wasn't arresting him, wasn't reading him his rights, wasn't even treating him as she would another juvenile offender, but she couldn't stop. "Clara, right? Clara Ramsey goes to your school?"

"Yeah . . ." He was wary, still edging toward the door that she'd left ajar. Any second he could bolt! She had to keep him here. Had to work this out. To connect with him.

And arrest him.

"I dunno. Yeah. I guess. I just didn't know that they were gonna rob the guy, and we, Joey and me, we were supposed to be the lookouts. But I didn't even know there was a gun until I heard the shots and then . . . we ran . . . and then it ends up in my backpack." He shook his head and glanced at the ceiling as if he couldn't believe his bad luck.

"With your fingerprints on it?"

"I picked it up when I found it in the pocket of the backpack! Wouldn't you? I mean, I didn't know how it got there. But I never shot it. I swear! You have to believe me!"

"So who put it there?"

He was still shaking his head. "Dunno."

"Joey?"

"What? I don't think so. Nah, he wouldn't." He looked at her through the fringe of the hair falling over his forehead and she recognized the fear in those eyes that reminded her so much of Emilio. He was pleading with her, and she believed he was scared out of his mind.

Good.

So was she.

Usually she was calm, a level-headed cop, aside from the one mistake in San Bernardino, but this, dealing with her own flesh and blood, her son, was new and had her second-guessing herself.

"You have to turn yourself in, you know."

"What?" He freaked. His expression turned to panic. "No!"

"Of course you do, but I'll be there. With you. And your mother, Aggie, she and your dad will be there, too. She's worried sick about you."

"You don't even know her."

"True. But I know she wants you to do the right thing."

"Which is turn myself in? No way!" He wasn't buying it.

As a cop, Alvarez believed in the system, trusted that truth and justice would win out, but he, of course, did not.

"Uh-uh. They'll put this all on me. No one will believe me!"

"I believe you, Gabe."

"You have to!"

"No, I don't." *Stay calm. Don't lose him.*

Angry now, Gabe looked as if he was about to turn and run, flee out the door and into the cold dark night.

"Don't leave!" she said.

"Why?" he said and kept backing toward the front door.

"Because we have to work this out. That's the only way."

"What's the only way? Going to jail. No way!" He turned.

"Gabriel! Stop!"

"Or what? You'll shoot?" he yelled over his shoulder. "Go ahead. You gave me up before, you may as well shoot me and get it over with! It won't be that big of a deal to you."

"What?" She'd barely met him and this was the way he was going to play her. "No, wait . . . We can make this work!" She was chasing him down, desperate for him to stay. "I'll be by your side. Promise!"

"Oh, yeah, right! Look, forget it. Just forget it!"

"I'm serious. You have to turn yourself in! I know the best defense attorneys, and if you're innocent, we'll prove it."

"If?" he threw back at her, spinning, his angry, dark gaze drilling into hers. "No, thanks, *Mom*. I'm outta here!"

"I don't think so." She was ready to tackle him if need be, and as tall and lanky and angry as he was, she figured she had the moves; thanks to police training and tae kwon do, she could drop him, force him to stay, even cuff him if she had to.

She just didn't want to go there.

Yet.

"Gabe, seriously. You need to listen to me."

"That's what I thought. But I was wrong." He spun and ran toward the door just as it flew open to bang against the wall.

Gabe jumped, then stopped dead in his tracks.

Alvarez caught up with him just as Dylan O'Keefe, weapon drawn, filled the doorway.

CHAPTER 25

"Don't shoot! For the love of God, don't shoot!" Alvarez ordered. "Stand down!"

Gabe, upon recognizing O'Keefe, froze. "Why the fuc—Hell, are you following me, man?" he

361

yelled, agitated. "I didn't do it! Whatever they're saying I did, I didn't freakin' do it! You tell him," he said, turning to Alvarez.

"He claims he's innocent," she agreed, grateful that he'd been blocked from disappearing into the night. "Didn't try to rob Judge Ramsey, that was all a mistake, and he didn't take any of my jewelry when you chased him here."

"Or the dog either!" Gabe insisted.

"So," Alvarez said calmly, meeting O'Keefe's gaze, "why don't we all come inside and talk this out?"

The boy shot her a look. "I'm done talkin'."

"But we need to sort things through."

"You just want me to turn myself in. You're gonna try to talk me into it and I'm not doing it. I know how this works. Uh-huh. Once I'm in jail, I won't get out. They'll send me to juvie!"

"Gabe, just listen," O'Keefe said. "No one wants you in jail, but we do have to take you into the station so you can explain your side of things. I'll call your mom, we'll get an attorney and we'll go from there." O'Keefe's voice was calm. Steady. But he didn't move from the front entry hall, where he stood between the boy and the base of the stairs as well as the front door. Alvarez, where she was positioned, blocked Gabe's path to the slider door and patio.

Trapped, sensing he had no escape, the kid looked at the ground and swore under his breath.

"I shouldn't have come here. All you want to do is get rid of me again!"

"I said I'm on your side. I meant it."

O'Keefe's lips folded in on themselves and he appeared to be waging some mental battle, probably the same one that raged within her, but there was no way to let him go.

"I think it would be best if I took Gabe, here, back to Helena."

"What, no!" Gabe's face drained of color.

"I agree. Let's take him down to the sheriff's department here," she said, thinking aloud. "I'm sure the Feds are going to want to talk to him."

"Feds? What do you mean?" Gabe said, glaring at her.

"It's just a formality."

"With who? The CIA or FBI, *what* Feds? Oh, Jesus—"

O'Keefe said, "A couple of agents with the FBI. It's no big deal. Both Detective Alvarez and I had to talk to them. Just tell them what you know and that'll be the end of it."

"About what? Tell them what I know about what?" His skin had blanched and he looked as if he'd seen a ghost. "Why are they here?" he asked Alvarez, then his eyes narrowed. "Wait . . . I heard about this from some kids on the street. It's that ice-mummy guy, right?" Gabe's eyes rounded and he looked as if he might wet himself. "They don't think I'm that guy! Oh, Christ!

I had nothing to do with any of that shit!"

"I know," Alvarez said. "Again, a formality."

"No! I'm not doing it! I want a lawyer. I want a phone call, don't I get one?" he demanded, then turned to O'Keefe. "Call my mom. My *real* mom!"

Before O'Keefe could reach for his phone, the sound of sirens split the air, louder and louder.

"Oh, God!" the kid said, turning on Alvarez, hate burning in his gaze. "You turned me in!"

"So the elusive Gabriel Reeve was *waiting* for you?" Pescoli asked an hour later as she and Alvarez were seated at a small table in a corner of the task force room. Computers and phones stood ready, and though it was Sunday, the room was filled with tension, officers coming and going, telephones jangling.

Currently Sage Zoller, a junior detective with the department, and Agent Craig Halden were manning the phones. A map of the area, complete with pins indicating where the bodies were found and where the victims lived and were last seen covered one wall. While on another, biographies and pictures of the victim had been placed, along with a timeline of their whereabouts. Pescoli glanced at the missing Brenda Sutherland's picture; it was included with a big question mark, indicating that she wasn't considered a victim yet as her body hadn't been discovered. Would the question mark be erased? Would Johnna Phillips's picture be the next one posted? God, she hoped not, but who knew?

Earlier, Pescoli had been about to leave the station when all hell had broken out, the kid had been run in, Alvarez and O'Keefe showing up with half a dozen cops who escorted Gabriel Reeve to the juvenile detention center as if he were Billy the Kid reincarnated. Not only was the sheriff's department involved, but the Helena PD had sent over a detective and the FBI agents were itching to talk to the boy about the missing jewelry from Alvarez's apartment and how it all tied in with the latest lunatic freezing women and putting them on public display.

Pescoli didn't think the boy knew anything.

Alvarez was nodding, as if agreeing with herself. "Gabe was sitting on my couch, had a blanket wrapped around him, my cat on his lap."

"All very domestic."

"All very weirdly domestic," Alvarez admitted.

"But at least he's in custody."

"Yeah," Alvarez said without enthusiasm. Usually, Selena Alvarez was one of the most rock-steady cops Pescoli had ever met. *That's what being a mother could do to a person. Throw in an ex or two and things only got worse.*

"He's your son?"

"I think so . . ." She let out a long sigh and shook her head. "He looks like his father." Pescoli was about to ask about the man who'd fathered

365

Gabriel Reeve, but Alvarez held up a hand. "I don't want to go there, not right now." Pescoli didn't blame her. Right now, Dave and Aggie Reeve, the only parents Gabriel had ever known, were on their way to Grizzly Falls from Helena. They were already trying to work through O'Keefe and making noise about getting their son a lawyer. Yep, it was getting sticky.

Alvarez, as exhausted as everyone, said, "He thinks I turned him in, though technically it was O'Keefe."

"But you think this is *your* earring?" Pescoli pushed the small bag across the table. Visible through the clear plastic, labeled as evidence, a tiny piece of jewelry glinted under the harsh fluorescent illumination of the task room.

Snapped back to the present, she studied the stud. "It's an earring. The size is all wrong for a regular tongue stud and it was obviously just jammed through the victim's tongue, there was no healing around the wound and the hole itself was too small. Abnormal. I checked with an expert. Anyway, I think this"—she pointed to the silver stud in the bag—"was stolen from my place. But not by Gabe," she was quick to add. "I think it was missing before the hoop and locket were taken. It's as if the killer, or his accomplice or someone, broke into my house before."

"You mean before the night that Gabriel Reeve broke in?"

"Yeah."

"What're the chances of that?"

"I know, I know, it's a stretch."

"A damned long one."

"I know, but I might be missing a ring, too."

"Might be?" Pescoli asked.

"It's been gone a while, and I thought I lost it in the move . . . Now I'm not so sure." She was twisting the cup of tea in her hands, a cup from which she hadn't taken so much as a sip. "But then, I'm not sure about anything anymore."

Deep in his cavern, he worked. Diligently. With dedication, ignoring the signs that he was beginning to become sleep deprived. So what? One had to suffer for his art, and so he would keep at it, finding deep reserves of strength when other, lesser men would succumb to the demands of the body.

Mind over matter, he told himself, working feverishly, already sweating though the temperature in his underground studio was below freezing, of course.

To calm himself, he listened to one of his favorite carols and hummed along with the strains, the words playing through his head as he worked.

Silent night, holy night.
All is calm, all is—
Bark! Bark! Bark!

The damned dog was at it again, destroying his concentration as he chiseled the most intricate part of his sculpture. It might have been a mistake stealing the beast, but the opportunity had arisen when he'd been searching for something valuable, something personal from that bitch of a cop when he'd broken into her home. The first time had been easy, nothing had gone wrong, even the dog just watching from his damned crate as he, the intruder, had climbed the stairs to her bedroom, where the smell of her had teased his nostrils, that same faint scent of perfume he'd noticed when she'd ignored him, years before, dismissed him as if he were nothing.

Nothing!

She'd find out differently.

As soon as she got his little present in the mail. He smiled at himself as he'd thought how clever he'd been. A few days earlier, before pouring the water over his current work of art, he'd carefully, lovingly hooked a chain around her neck and let the tiny locket fall delicately between her naked breasts. It had been painstaking to prop up the half-dead woman, posing her just so, then adjust the limited lighting in the best way to show off the jewelry. He'd waited until just the right moment, until she'd rolled her uncomprehending eyes to look at him, and he'd snapped the digital shot.

It wasn't as satisfying as the actual sculpting, of course. Oh, no. But it would give the cop something to think about when she picked up her mail at the station, an early Christmas card, sent anonymously.

Oh, what he would do to see her reaction!

It would almost be worth it to be at the station about the time the mail was delivered . . . He could come up with a plausible excuse, a complaint about a neighbor or the traffic or . . .

No! Don't indulge yourself! It's far too dangerous and you have too much important work to do! Stay focused.

He pulled himself out of that particular fantasy. He would get his chance with the cop; he'd just have to wait for it. Thankfully that lunatic Junior Green hadn't killed her and destroyed his plan. That's all it took, one psycho with a gun, and all the best-laid plans were destroyed. But she'd outwitted the sicko, she and that new man she was seeing.

Oh, yeah, he'd met that one, checked him out.

Dylan O'Keefe better not get in the way.

Not after all this work.

Again the dog began to howl and the killer swore under his breath. He'd nabbed the mutt during his last mission, to confuse Alvarez, but then that kid had shown up, running into the house, and he'd been forced to flee out an upstairs window, the boy following not far behind him.

It had been a disaster, but, of course, he'd managed to escape. And now he had the dog, a scruffy shepherd of some sort, not clean lines. He glanced at the beast and it had the naiveté to wag its damned tail at him.

Half grown, the animal seemed brainless . . . but would serve his purpose.

Ignoring the dog, he went back to work. Humming again, trying to find that peace of mind that came with sculpting. Sweating, willing his hands to be steady, for this, his most incredible piece of art yet, he softly tapped his chisel, right over the nose.

The dog whined.

"Hush!" he said under his breath, working carefully . . . gently shaving the ice away, making the sculpture perfect. Just one more tweak and—

Bark!

The damned mutt let out an anxious cry, and he hit the chisel a little too hard.

Craaack! The ice began to split, one fine line splintering into a dozen and filtering all over her face and neck.

"No! No!" In horror, he watched his work destroyed. Days of labor, weeks and months of planning, all ruined as the cracks, like an irregular spiderweb, marred the beauty of his creation.

His fingers tightened over his chisel and he glared at the mutt. "Shut up, you stupid mongrel!" he snarled, wanting to strangle the beast. The animal was more irritating than his Bible-thumping wife! "Just shut the hell up!"

Now, he would have to start over. Melt down the remaining ice and begin again, with fresh water, sluicing and freezing before the actual sculpting could begin again.

All because of the damned dog.

Closing his eyes, he slowly counted to ten and reminded himself that he could do this, the animal was just one more distraction. He could deal with it, even if he'd thought at one time that one of his favorite Christmas carols should have been renamed to "Bark! The Herald Angels Sing."

With effort, he calmed himself once more.

"Silent Night" was playing again . . . and as he stared down at the woman beneath the fractured ice, seeing her dead eyes looking up at him, he began to hum again, the lyrics rolling through his brain.

Sleep in heavenly peace . . .

CHAPTER 26

They made love that night.

Desperately, as if they knew they might not get a chance again. Alvarez had been already home, in her pajamas, when she'd heard the knock on the door and O'Keefe had been on her doorstep, looking as bone weary as she'd felt. She'd nearly broken down at the sight of him, and when he'd held his arms open, she'd flung herself into them, seeking solace and comfort for her battered heart.

She'd known of her son all of her life, of course, but tucked away in that locked corner of her mind, she'd kept the loneliness and despair at bay. Balmed by the fact that she'd "done the right thing," that "he was better off with a stable family who loved him," she'd gone about her life without looking too closely at her own feelings, just bottled them up and turned her attention first to school and then to her work.

Until now.

Until she'd met the boy and found out that he wasn't all right; that he was in trouble.

There was no need for explanations, no time for more conversation; she'd locked the door behind O'Keefe and walked up the stairs holding his hand, him one step behind her, even giving her rump a playful pat. When they'd reached the bedroom, they'd stripped each other of clothing and fallen into bed. There, Alvarez had taken out all of her frustration and pain, throwing herself into the lovemaking, closing her mind to what might have been and losing herself in the feel, smell and touch of this man.

Did she love him?

Who knew?

That thought had flitted through her mind as his mouth found hers, then trailed a hot path down the column of her throat, but all she really knew was that, with O'Keefe, she felt safe.

From the outside world.

From the inside demons.

She'd fallen asleep nestled in his arms and had awoken with a start and a crook in her neck. As her nightmare had receded and she was brought back to reality, she realized a night of lovemaking hadn't changed the world. No, the earth was still spinning as it had been when she'd fallen asleep and the evil that had pervaded this part of Montana hadn't disappeared in the night. In fact, it had followed her into the night.

Her dreams had been peppered with a faceless killer, a huge, swift monster, chasing her, his breath so cold it formed icicles on the back of her neck, his fingernails long, sharp talons dripping blood. She'd run and run and run, gasping for breath, her legs feeling leaden, her fear palpable. Gabe had been in the dreams, as well, and he'd always been in harm's way, yelling at her that she wasn't his real mother and catching the killer's attention. "No!" she'd cried as the monster had turned his sights on her boy.

She'd woken up with a start and O'Keefe had muttered something from deep in slumberland before turning over, his hair dark against her pillow, his long body stretching the length of the bed.

She climbed out of bed, threw on a robe and slid

into a pair of slippers before heading downstairs.

O'Keefe, dead to the world, didn't move, nor did Jane, the turncoat who had curled into a tight ball near his head.

Downstairs she didn't bother with lights but walked to the sliding doors and looked out at the snowy morning. Daylight hadn't broken and the night was thick, clouds hiding the stars, only the white landscape giving any illumination.

She thought about the victims that they'd located, and those still missing. In her mind's eye, she saw the earring through Lissa Parsons's nipple and the silver stud forced through Lara Sue's tongue. Obviously, the killer was sending a message to her.

What, if anything, did it have to do with her son?

"Who are you, you bastard?" she whispered, her breath fogging on the inside of the glass door. Uneasily, she wondered if, even now, he was standing just outside of her line of vision, hiding in the shadows, watching her. There was some reason he was attached to her, and she thought of those suspects she'd arrested, the most violent of them sent to prison for a very long time.

Or was it someone more personal?

A man she'd spurned?

Someone she'd slighted?

Junior Green was behind bars once more, thankfully, but there were others, perhaps not as vocal with their threats but certainly as deadly.

The skin on the back of her arms pimpled at the thought of the sadistic killers she'd arrested, not just here in Grizzly Falls, but in San Bernardino as well. Alberto De Maestro's face came to mind, the way his thin lips could twist into a superior sneer or the unholy light that would appear in his eyes when he was being questioned and he let his eyes stray a little too long on her neckline.

He was only one.

And there was nothing in his file to suggest he had an artistic bent, a need to express himself by letting his victims die a slow death and encasing them in ice. Alberto was more likely to slit your throat and enjoy your warm blood spilling over his hand as he held the knife.

No, this killer, hiding out there in the frozen night, he was different than De Maestro but just as inherently evil. Probably more so.

And somehow he was linked to her.

She heard a creak in the floorboards overhead and heavy footsteps on the stairs. Before she could turn to greet him, O'Keefe came up behind her and wrapped his arms around her waist. She saw his ghostly reflection in the glass, dark hair poking at odd angles, a smile crawling across the scruff covering his jaw. "Mornin'," he drawled against her ear.

"Back atcha."

"Coffee ready?"

"It is, if you make it."

He chuckled deep in his throat and she felt a little tingle of anticipation as one of his hands slipped inside her robe to find her breast and the nipple that was already puckering in interest.

"Come back to bed," he whispered as she leaned her head backward and felt his warm breath against her skin.

"Got a lot to do."

"It'll wait."

She was melting inside, and damn it, he could sense her resistance ebbing and she felt his hardness through her robe, pressed insistently against her backside. Erotic images began flitting through her mind. "Look, if you want coffee—"

"We can pick it up on the way into the office."

"Seriously?" she whispered as her knees gave way and, together, they tumbled to the floor.

"Damned straight."

What was that old expression? "Once burned, twice shy"? Or "once bitten, twice shy"? Didn't matter. Either one applied to him, because O'Keefe had it bad.

For Selena Alvarez.

The woman he'd sworn to avoid, the one who had cost him his job and nearly his life.

Water under the bridge, he thought now as he met with Aggie and her husband at a coffee shop not far from the sheriff's office. The place was crowded, crawling with Christmas shoppers from the mall just across the parking lot. Most of the tables were filled, women seated with packages at their feet, a group of men gathered at a large table, all talking sports, and other tables occupied by people of various ages, all with computers open. They seemed oblivious to the screech of grinding beans, the shouts of baristas when orders were ready or the general noise of a cacophony of battling conversations.

They were seated at a small bistro table in one corner of the coffee shop, near the windows. Outside, snow was beginning to fall again, collecting on the sidewalk, where pedestrians, bundled against the cold, hurried past.

"The FBI?" Aggie whispered across the table, her triple mocha untouched, the whipped cream beginning to run down the sides of her cup. "Why in the world would the FBI want to question Gabe?"

"I can't really say."

"Off the record," Dave insisted. A tall man with graying hair, Dave was an ex-college basketball player who'd developed a bit of a paunch after giving up the game, and his dream. His usually animated expression was missing, his glasses sliding down his nose so he could tip his head and stare at O'Keefe over the rims. His coffee was black and simple, and, usually, Dave was a no-nonsense accountant with a quick wit and easy laugh. Today he was dead serious, his expression a reflection of his wife's worried demeanor. Aggie was pale, her makeup already wearing thin, her eyes red from crying.

O'Keefe eyed his cousin. "It's not about the robbery in Helena."

"He's involved in something else?" Aggie said, her whisper louder than she'd intended as she half stood until her husband clasped his hand over her forearm, and she, realizing she was on the verge of making a scene, fell into her chair again.

"They're just checking out every angle." O'Keefe hoped he sounded more reassuring than he felt.

"They're here because of the murdered women they found," Dave said quietly.

"You mean for that ice-mummy case." Shaking her head, her red hair brushing her chin with the movement, Aggie closed her eyes as if to gather herself. "He's got nothing to do with that. You know that, Dylan. Nothing." She blinked her eyes open and focused on her husband. "We have to get an attorney, Dave. *Pronto!* We *have* to!"

"You saw Gabe, right?" O'Keefe said.

"Yes. But that's about it. 'Saw' him. He won't talk to us. It's as if . . . as if . . ." she squeaked out, "*we're* the enemy. *Us?* When all we've ever tried to do is help him? Oh, my God, this is all so unbelievable and now, Gabe says he's contacted his biological mother."

"Looks that way."

"And you?" she accused. "*You're* involved with her?"

Bad news traveled fast. "I *know* her. We worked together in San Bernardino."

"I remember that," Dave said, his bushy eyebrows pulling together over the thin rims of his glasses. "Seems as if it didn't turn out well."

"You lost your job!" Aggie reminded him.

"I quit."

She waved a hand frantically in the air. "Doesn't matter. But I don't want her having any contact with *my* son, okay? That's the deal. It's always been the deal. I . . . We don't want or need another parent trying to mess with our kid's emotions."

"He searched her out."

"He's a kid! He obviously doesn't know what he wants or what's best for him. I do *not* want her involved in his life, you got that? As for you, if I were you, I'd watch my step; tread carefully." Aggie was on a roll now. "But . . . we have to think, put things in perspective. Gabe's in serious trouble and we have to help him. We have to hire an attorney and get Gabe out of jail!"

"Maybe detention is the best place for him," her husband offered up before taking a long swallow from his coffee. "At least he's safe there and we know where he is."

"Are you out of your mind?" Aggie demanded, her voice rising again. She stared at her husband as if he'd turned into an alien from outer space. "Come on, Dave! That's the most ridiculous thing I've heard yet."

"Shh!" he snapped and Aggie, rebuffed, glanced around as if realizing she might be overheard.

Fortunately no one was paying the least bit of attention to them.

"Do you know the press have been calling us?" she asked O'Keefe. "They know Gabe's identity even though they're supposed to not report it and so I've been getting calls. They know he was arrested at Detective Alvarez's home; well how could they not when a whole cavalry of cops showed up, huh? They'll start digging, tying Gabe to this new series of crimes by the Ice Mummy Killer, just you wait, and then his life will be a living hell. Ours, too. And even that Selena Alvarez when they figure out she's his birth mother!"

"That hasn't been established."

"Yet. But a reporter's already on the story. Some guy called my cell phone. My cell, for God's sake, and he started asking about the adoption. That was two days ago. By now it could be all over the Internet! God, this is a nightmare!" She finally picked up her drink and licked the whipped cream from the cup's sides as she stared at her cousin. "You just wait! Things are only going to get worse. A whole lot worse." She took a swallow of her drink, then said to her husband, "We're getting a lawyer ASAP. I don't care what it costs. And, Dylan, send us your bill. You found Gabe, we've got him . . . sort of, but your job is over."

Dave said, "Wait a second, Aggie—"

"Don't even think about arguing with me about it!" she said to her husband, then her gaze turned to Dylan. "You're involved with her. She's Gabriel's biological mother. So it's over, you see? Just send us the bill."

Pescoli tried not to let her home life ruin her day, but Jeremy's surprise announcement that he wanted to move out coupled with a request for her to sign a lease for him burned through her brain as she drove into the parking lot of the sheriff's department. Their argument, as always, had been about chores, his responsibilities and her work. They'd both agreed that living together under the same roof wasn't a perfect arrangement, but the fact he thought she should still support him while he lived on his own really burned her butt.

She cut the engine and reminded herself that he was still in school and still working part time to pay for his truck and the insurance on it. That was something, she supposed, but not enough. He'd moved out once before and it hadn't worked out; he was still paying off bills from that fiasco, but he didn't seem to realize that it wasn't her goal in life to support him indefinitely.

She figured he could move out again if he

wanted to, but she sure as hell wasn't going to finance any part of it. "Give me strength," she said, taking a swallow from her travel coffee cup and realizing it was from two days ago, the coffee cold and bitter.

Hopefully someone had already brewed a fresh pot in the station. She pushed Jeremy and his problems to that back I'll-deal-with-this-later area of her mind and concentrated on her job. Somehow, whether she liked it or not, Alvarez was on the Ice Mummy Killer's radar, though Pescoli didn't know why, but there was a connection between the runaway kid, the killer and her partner.

Hauling her computer with her, she stepped out of her Jeep and headed toward the back door of the station. The press, as ever, was in position, two vans parked, reporters and cameramen already filming, the sheriff's office forming a backdrop, snow falling softly. From the corner of her eye, she noticed Manny Douglas, that weasel of a reporter for the *Mountain Reporter*, fast approaching. In his usual flannel and khakis, he raised a hand, "Detective Pescoli! Just a few questions. I see the FBI has been called in."

Not "called in." They always showed up when kidnapping or serial killers were involved in a case.

"You know I'm not going to comment," she said, reaching the back door.

"Is it true that Selena Alvarez is the birth mother of the boy brought into custody yesterday, the one wanted in the shooting at Judge Victor Ramsey's home in Helena?" he asked, trudging through the snow, his recorder in his gloved hand, a red light glowing, indicating that he was taping their conversation.

How did he get his information so fast? "I said, 'No comment.'"

"Is the ice-mummy case somehow related to the break-in at Judge Ramsey's home?"

Calm down. He doesn't know what he's talking about. He's just trying to get you to say something, anything he can report.

"Look, Manny, I don't have anything to say. You'll have to ask your questions at the next press conference."

"But Alvarez is your partner. Is that kid hers? The kid involved in the shooting at the judge's house in Helena?"

She didn't answer. Just strode through the back door and thankfully heard the locks click behind her. The coffee had been brewed, but only a few drops were left in the pot, as the undersheriff had just poured himself a cup and was adding a packet or two of artificial sweetener to his "I Heart Jesus" mug.

"You making a new pot?" she asked and he looked up, spilling a bit of white powder onto the counter.

"What? Nah." With a smile as saccharine as his artificial sweetener, he added, "I've mine." To prove his point he lifted his cup and took a swallow.

The sentiment on his cup reminded her that he was an elder in the Presbyterian church where Calvin Mullins was the preacher.

"Didn't see you here yesterday," she observed.

"I was here. In the afternoon." He scowled. "Why?"

"Just wondering how things are going at the church, after the body was discovered in the crèche."

"Oh. Yeah. It's not good. Got a lot of questions yesterday, especially from the preacher. He, of course, wants us to find the killer and asked the congregation to pray that he's brought to justice, which I went along with, though he did ask for God to forgive him." Brewster snorted into his cup. "I'm having a little trouble with that."

"Me, too." Grudgingly, she found a packet of coffee and placed it in the coffeemaker's basket, then filled the reservoir with water and hit the start button.

Almost immediately the machine started to gurgle, and within less than a minute, a stream of hot java began to fill the glass pot. Brewster left the room. She didn't like the man much, and they'd had their problems in the past, largely because of the attraction between their children, but at least they were speaking, keeping things professional, which, Pescoli thought, was about as good as it was going to get.

Like the sound of rapid-fire gunshots, the click of Joelle's high heels announced her arrival. Per the season, she was carrying two of those environmental reusable grocery bags, a red purse to match her shoes and balancing a white box. Before she toppled over, she set the box onto a counter and opened the top.

"Voila!" she said proudly as she displayed the contents: carefully stacked cupcakes. Some were decorated with Santa faces, while others were poinsettias or Christmas trees.

"More?" Pescoli asked. Then, "You did this?"

"Oh, no, no, no!" Joelle actually giggled, obviously pleased that anyone thought her capable of such artwork. Apparently she'd forgiven Pescoli for her rant against the decorations in the hallway of the week before. "I have a friend who's a baker down at Cedar's Market. We play Bunco every month, you know, a girls'-night-out kind of thing. She did them for me." Sliding a sly look at Pescoli, she added, "At cost." Beginning to set the small cakes onto a platter she'd hauled from one of the cupboards, Joelle added, "I just couldn't resist!"

"Who could?"

"Oh, dear." Joelle's perfectly made-up face crumpled a little as she noticed one of the frosting petals on one of the cupcakes had been squished.

"I'll take that one," Pescoli offered and grabbed the less-than-perfect treat before pouring herself a fresh cup of coffee and heading to her desk. Once seated, she called First Union bank. It was early, long before the bank's doors would open, but the employees should have arrived.

She was connected with a receptionist and was told, when asked, that Johnna Phillips "wasn't in yet." Declining the offer of having Ms. Phillips return the call, Pescoli hung up and dialed Missing Persons, confirming that, yes, a report had been filed on the woman and deputies were checking at her home and work place.

"Let me know," she told Tawilda Conrad, who worked with Taj Nayak in Missing Persons.

"Will do." She ate the cupcake, finished her coffee, then made her way the short distance to Alvarez's office.

Her partner was already at her desk, her computer monitor showing her e-mail account. She was on the phone and, glancing up at Pescoli, held up a finger. ". . . Okay, then I can pick it up between four and five at the garage?" she said into her cell and waited. "Yeah, that'll work. Thanks, Andy." She clicked off. "Good news, I get my car back."

"You should sue Junior Green for the damage."

"I'll let my insurance agent know." She glanced down at her desk, where a stack of mail had been left. A red squatty envelope, the size that held a greeting card, was on the top of the stack. "What's up?" she asked, finding her letter opener and slitting the packet open.

"Bad news. I told you about Johnna Phillips?"

"Banker. Works at First Union. Her boyfriend was worried about her?"

"Recent ex-boyfriend. I checked with her work. So far she hasn't shown."

"It's early."

"I know, but I've got a bad feeling about this."

She withdrew a Christmas card from the red envelope. "You think we have another victim?"

"Could be." Pescoli eyed the envelope and grinned. In a singsong voice, she said, "Uh-oh. Looks like someone got a Secret Santa card."

Alvarez rolled her eyes. "Could be, I guess." Then she turned the conversation back to Johnna Phillips. "Let's hope she's just avoiding the ex."

"Seems like she's going to extreme measures."

"Maybe that's what you have to do with this guy." She opened the card. "Oh, damn," she whispered, her eyes rounding, her face losing all color. She dropped the card onto her desk as if it had burned her fingers. "Son of a bitch!"

Pescoli saw the flap of the card open. Tucked inside, covering the message, was a photograph of a naked woman. "Oh, no."

"It's Brenda Sutherland," Alvarez whispered,

seeming to pull herself together a bit, though she was still white as a sheet.

Leaning over the desk, closer to the open card, Pescoli got a better look at the image of a woman who was either dead or nearly so, naked except for a locket on a chain surrounding her neck. And, yes, she was either Brenda Sutherland or her twin. The chain around her neck had been looped twice, the links cutting into Brenda's flesh, leaving her skin bruised and broken.

"Sick bastard," Pescoli whispered.

Alvarez visibly swallowed hard. "That's mine," she admitted. "The locket, it was one I got when I was confirmed in the church. Oh, Lord . . ." Alvarez was staring at the open card as if it were the embodiment of evil just as one of those prerecorded greetings that could be tucked inside began playing the tinny notes of "All I Want for Christmas Is You."

CHAPTER 27

"I don't know why anyone would single me out," Alvarez said, answering the same question for what seemed like the seventy-fifth time that day. Sitting in the passenger seat of Pescoli's Jeep, she stared out the windshield, watching the taillights of the other vehicles and the wipers slap away the ever-falling snow. It had been a long day but finally they were on their way to pick up Alvarez's car.

She hazarded a glance out the window as they drove past a school, where a few kids, dressed in jackets, scarves and hats, were playing in the snow on the flocked playground.

After receiving the sick Christmas card this morning, she'd been escorted into one of the interview rooms to discuss, with Agents Halden and Chandler, any connection she might have to the killer or any of his victims, Brenda Sutherland now confirmed as his third.

Since his identity was still unknown, she had no idea how she'd ever run across him. As for the victims, she knew Brenda by name, as she worked at Wild Will's, and she'd seen Lissa Parsons at her exercise club, but she was pretty certain she'd never seen Lara Sue Gilfry in her life. Even when questioning Rod Larimer, the obnoxious innkeeper of the Bull and Bear bed-and-breakfast on a previous case, she'd never run across Lara Sue, who had worked there.

She'd answered Halden and Chandler's questions as well as she could, going over her entire life history, but in the end, she'd given them nothing that could connect her to the killer. "Trust me, I'd love to nail the son of a bitch's hide," she'd sworn to Halden, "but I have no idea who he is."

Nor did they.

Yet.

After the intense interview with the FBI agents, Dan Grayson had called her into his office, and while his dog snored from his dog bed in the corner near a potted plant, Grayson had informed her that he was relieving her of her responsibilities in the ice-mummy case. "Somehow, the killer's targeted you. I don't know why, nor do you, but I think it would be best if we let someone else handle the case. Pescoli can work with Gage on this one."

Brett Gage was the chief criminal detective in the department. As such, he oversaw all of the cases and spent most of his time behind a desk. At forty, he was whip thin, a runner, and this was the first time since she'd been with Pinewood County that Alvarez had seen him in an actual investigative role.

"You can't take me off the case."

"I can and I will." He'd stared at her long and hard, this man whom she'd fantasized she'd loved. His eyes looked haunted, as if the weight not only of the county's safety, but that of the whole damned state rested on his broad shoulders. "I'm the sheriff. Remember?"

"But—"

"Don't argue, Detective," he'd said, all business. "And I'll see to it that your place is watched."

"You don't have to do that." She knew the department was stretched thin, despite the help from the state police and the FBI on this particular case. With the freezing of creeks and snapping of electrical lines, and a major blizzard predicted, there just weren't enough deputies to go around. Having one assigned to watch her just wasn't in the budget.

He'd slid three pictures across his desk, one of each of the victims. Including the most recent of Brenda Sutherland, the picture that had been sent to her from the killer. "These women are wearing pieces of your jewelry. Taken from your place. Isn't that what you said?" His jaw, beneath a day's worth of whiskers, had been set in stone.

"Yes."

"Thought so. And the boy, Gabriel Reeve, he's most likely your son, isn't that so?"

She nodded.

"Reeve showed up at your place at the same time as the killer."

"It seems so," she'd admitted.

"Quite a coincidence."

"I thought you didn't believe in coincidences."

"I don't." When Grayson had looked at her again, Alvarez had thought she'd glimpsed more than just the concern of a man who happened to be her boss; she'd seen a flicker of some deeper emotion that he'd quickly masked. He'd cleared his throat, then said, "Change your locks.

Immediately. And don't argue with me about the surveillance of your place. This is your safety we're talking about. And take Sturgis with you. He'll raise a ruckus if anyone tries to break in."

She'd looked over at the sleeping lab. His tail thumped at the sound of his name, but Sturgis hadn't so much as lifted his head.

"Thanks, but I want *my* dog back."

"It's just until you get your dog."

"No . . . really . . . But I appreciate the offer." Alvarez knew how much the lab meant to Grayson, and she wasn't going to borrow the dog, not even for a night. Despite the freak who had the nerve to break into her house and steal her things. Who was the guy? How did he know her? And more importantly, how the hell was she going to run him in?

There had to be some way.

Grayson had scratched at his beard. "If you change your mind . . ."

"I'll let you know." She'd left his office feeling stripped bare for the world to see, that all of her carefully kept secrets were suddenly thrown open for public viewing, and public discussion. It made her more than uncomfortable. It made her mad. Worse than that, it frightened her, caused her nerves to tighten, made her jump at shadows. Damn it all to hell, it freaked her out. She knew the son of a bitch had wanted to scare the liver out of her, and he'd just about done it.

Just about.

Now, driving to pick up her Subaru, her partner was once again asking her about her connection to the killer.

"It's got to be someone from your past," Pescoli said as she drove along the road winding down Boxer Bluff to the lower part of the city.

"I don't know who. We've been through this over and over again."

"Someone who knew Lara Sue Gilfry, Lissa Parsons and Brenda Sutherland." Since Alvarez had received the horrifying Christmas card this morning and turned it in, everyone associated with the ice-mummy case knew that Brenda Sutherland was, indeed, in the clutches of one of the sickest serial killers in the history of the state. The speculation of her being a runaway mother or anything else had been positively squelched. "I gave Chandler and Halden a list of everyone I've ever helped incarcerate, all my known enemies, everyone I've ever dated, anyone who might have a problem with me and anyone else I could think of, but no one whom I think would actually do this."

Pescoli braked at the base of the hill at the train tracks where the barriers had descended to block the road, lights flashing a warning. A freight train barreled past, clacking loudly on the tracks, and oddly, Alvarez remembered a time, long ago, when, growing up, she and her siblings, all piled in the old station wagon would, at railroad crossings, count the cars as they raced past. Alvarez had always wondered what was hidden in the boxcars and had guessed where the train was headed. It has always been to some exotic destination, the big cities of Los Angeles or San Francisco or Denver or Seattle, anywhere far from the little town of Woodburn.

"He's targeting you." Pescoli was reaching into the console, her fingers scrabbling inside until she came up with a crumpled pack of cigarettes. "Empty. Damn. Check the glove box, would you?"

Alvarez opened the compartment but found only tissues, eyeglass cases and a raft of papers. "Nuh-uh."

"Crap!"

"You'll live," Alvarez predicted, though she knew her partner, in times of great stress, would sneak a smoke or two, never really taking up the habit again but never completely and cold-turkey quitting. "Probably lots longer."

"Easy for you to say."

The train sped past, the last car flying past and the barriers, lights still flashing, slowly lifting.

Pescoli tossed the empty pack on the floor. "Did you hear me? I said the son of a bitch is targeting you."

"Yeah, I know. I just don't know why."

"Or who," Pescoli thought aloud.

"The FBI is working on it," Alvarez said uncomfortably. She'd never been one to like the limelight and now she was squarely in the middle of it. Because of the Christmas card with Brenda Sutherland's photo inside, Alvarez's life was being torn apart and examined under a microscope. Like the victims and those close to each of the women who had gone missing, Alvarez, too, was dealing with having her life studied and dissected. When pressed about the possibility of Gabriel Reeve being her son, she'd been forced to bare her soul. Emilio's name had come up as the boy's father. As she'd told Pescoli, everyone she'd ever dealt with had all of a sudden become potential suspects, especially anyone she'd thwarted. All the people she'd known, the men she'd dated, those criminals she'd helped convict and their families, were being stored in computer banks, cross-referenced to the known victims.

She thought now, as Pescoli wheeled into the garage where her car was parked, that it was really weird to be the subject of an investigation rather than being the detective investigating an incident. And now, she was off the case.

"So no one has a key to your place?" Pescoli asked and Alvarez sent her an I-can't-believe-you-asked-me-that look. "You dated a couple of guys . . ."

"As I told Chandler and Halden, no. Not even

the handyman who comes around and, no, I don't keep a key hidden outside, so I don't know how the guy got in."

"Could one of the men you dated have . . . 'borrowed' a key and had another one made?"

"I don't know," she admitted, thinking back to the few times that a man had brought her home from a date or picked up her purse at a ball game . . . or . . . who knew? Could one of them have taken an impression or found the spare key in the side pocket of her purse and made a duplicate only to return it? She didn't think so, but then when she remembered the look in Grover Pankretz's eyes when she'd broken it off with him, she'd felt a chill that ran surprisingly deep. He, though, was married now, presumably happily.

"You changed the locks when you bought the place?"

"What do you think?"

"Okay, okay. Just asking." Pescoli drove over the tracks and pulled into a convenience store. "This'll just take a sec. Want anything?"

"No." She was still shaking her head as Pescoli unstrapped her seat belt and let herself out of the car. She left the engine running, the wipers still flicking away snow accumulation, the police band crackling while officers and dispatch communicated crimes in progress. Within minutes she was back, a fresh pack of cigarettes and two drinks in her hands. "Here ya go. Diet Coke," she said as she handed one drink to Alvarez and stashed hers in a cup holder near the console.

"I don't drink diet."

"Then put it in your holder and I'll take care of it." After stashing the Marlboro Lights into the console and a second in the glove box, she put the Jeep into gear and wheeled out of the parking lot.

They drove along the river, past the falls, to an industrial section of town, where the department's garage was located, a tall fence with razor wire surrounding the building and parking area. As they pulled into the lot, Pescoli said, "I don't like that this psycho's got you on his radar."

"Neither do I."

"Grayson will see that you're protected," Pescoli said, though she sounded concerned.

"I'll be fine."

Pescoli parked and let the Jeep idle. "For the record, I'm not crazy about working with Gage. When was the last time he actually worked a case? In the nineties?"

"Ouch! Careful. I think he's younger than you."

"Probably, it seems like everyone who's hired these days is about three years older than Jeremy, and let me tell you, that's a scary thought."

Alvarez chuckled as she stepped out of the Jeep. "See ya tomorrow." But it was weird to say the words knowing that Pescoli would be still knee deep in the case and she'd be relegated to something else, most likely Len Bradshaw's death, which was about to be ruled accidental.

That, of course, was all for show.

No way would she stop investigating the ice-mummy murders. She knew it, Pescoli knew it and, of course, Dan Grayson knew it as well.

Pescoli lit up the minute she was out of the parking lot. She rolled the window down, of course, allowing the smoke to curl out the window and the frigid breath of winter into the Jeep's interior. Who did she think she was kidding? Everyone in the department, her kids and even Santana knew in times of deep stress she had a cig or two. That was it. Then she was done until the next calamity hit, which, unfortunately at this rate, would push her back to her pack-a-day habit again.

She took a long drag, then stubbed the damned thing out. She just needed to clear her head and think, and sometimes, it seemed, nicotine helped that process along.

Okay, she knew she was kidding herself, but as she drove out of town toward her little cabin in the woods, she drove by rote, or on automatic pilot, as she referred to it to everyone *but* her children. To Jeremy and Bianca, she swore that she was always completely alert behind the wheel, that she never once spaced out.

Following a van from the senior center that was

so slow she wanted to scream, she turned off the main road and took surface streets through the heart of town and behind the courthouse. She caught a glimpse of the First Union bank sign and felt her heart sink.

Johnna Phillips had never shown up for work, and when the deputies had checked throughout the day, they discovered she'd apparently never returned home. Just like the ex-boyfriend, Carl Anderson, had said when he'd called Pescoli's cell.

She still was going to give Luke a very sharp piece of her mind about handing out her cell phone, but in this case, she almost understood, as Carl, the recently dumped ex, was scared out of his mind to think his girlfriend had been abducted by the sadistic killer who worked so hard to kill his victims without any marks, then display them publicly.

"Who are you, you bastard?" she asked as she passed out of the business section where the office fronts gave way to apartments and houses, some decorated with hundreds of glowing lights, a few with lawn decorations that served to remind her only of the extra wise man in Preacher Mullins's nativity scene and the snowman in Mabel Enstad's yard. Now, because of the sick Christmas card sent to Alvarez, the police knew that Brenda Sutherland, no doubt already dead, would probably be joining the others in someone's Christmas display.

"Where, you creep?" she asked as the police band crackled in the console and she left the streetlights of Grizzly Falls behind her. Snowflakes danced in the beams of her headlights, and the open fields, blanketed in white, stretched away from the road as she considered the case and the victims, all different ages, sizes and shapes. The FBI was checking everyone associated with the Enstads and the Presbyterian church, cross-referencing them with friends, enemies or acquaintances of the victims. Alvarez was right, her own life was about to be thrown open to public scrutiny and Pescoli wondered about the men she'd sent up the river, or dated, or somehow wronged. Gabriel Reeve's biological father would be questioned, and even Alberto De Maestro would be tracked down and grilled.

Pescoli even flirted with the idea that the killer might be a woman, but it just didn't seem right; there were too many sexual innuendos involved, the naked bodies, the snow woman positioned as if the snowman was "doing" her from behind. No . . . Pescoli couldn't see a woman going to those lengths.

Anything's possible. Maybe the killer is trying to throw you off . . . Keep an open mind.

Despite the arguments running through her mind, she'd bet her next five months' salary that the creep was a man. Again, she thought of the "artists" who sculpted ice, those that had been in

Missoula over the weekend, none of which could be detained, all who had rock-solid alibis. Hank Yardley and George Flanders had been her best guesses, especially that hot-head Flanders, who had wielded an ice pick before, sending his neighbor to ICU. As a farmer, he worked his own hours, but he was married and the current Mrs. Flanders was her husband's alibi.

And Pescoli was looking into everyone who'd ever come into contact with Alvarez on a personal level, just checking their backgrounds to find out if there was a history of violence in their earlier years.

You just never knew.

And now they had new evidence to work with: the Christmas card sent to Alvarez. There was a chance the killer had gotten sloppy with a fingerprint or left saliva as he'd licked the flap of the envelope, or the block letters in the address would remind someone of a person's hand-writing, or that the card was bought locally and the store where it was purchased would be able to come up with a credit card or debit card account number. They'd already figured out that the card had been posted downtown, possibly at one of the drop boxes outside the post office, and security tapes were already being viewed. Maybe, just maybe, they'd get lucky.

CHAPTER 28

As he drove through the falling snow, O'Keefe decided he was going to stick like glue to Alvarez and he didn't care what she had to say about it. Truth to tell, he was scared for her, worried sick, because the Ice Mummy Killer or whatever you wanted to call him had some kind of fascination with Selena.

As he turned onto Alvarez's street, he caught his reflection in the rearview mirror, saw the bruises on his face, compliments of Junior Green. There was also a glint of determination in his eyes. Now that Aggie had fired him from his job of locating Gabe, he had no excuse to hang around, but he was going to. Whether Selena Alvarez knew it or not, she needed protection from the psycho, and O'Keefe would do what it took, including pissing her off, if he had to.

He parked his Explorer on the street across from her apartment and, armed with his tool kit, duffel bag, laptop and bag from the hardware store, walked through the falling snow to her apartment. Ringing the bell, he felt suddenly awkward, like a kid waiting for the door to be opened by his prom date.

He heard her moving around inside, then

saw her eye darken the peephole.

A second later, she unlocked the door and swung it open. In oversized flannel PJs, her hair twisted into an unruly knot on the top of her head, she appeared smaller and more fragile than she was.

"You're moving in?" Alvarez asked suspiciously as she eyed his duffel.

"How could you tell?" He wanted to keep things light.

"All those years of detective work, I guess."

"Aaah. Well, you're right. I thought I'd camp out here for a few days."

"Really?" She wasn't budging from the doorway. "Without even asking me?" Leaning one slim shoulder on the door frame, she added, "That's kinda funny, because I don't remember inviting you."

"You didn't." He'd expected this reaction and ignored it as he swept past her into the foyer. "Lock the door behind me."

"Hey, wait a sec, you can't just bring all your gear and—"

"Of course I can." Dropping his duffel on the floor of the living room and his laptop on the table, he said, "The killer's making a statement. To you personally."

"You found out about the Christmas card."

"That's just part of it, but, yeah. There's a reason your things were left at the scene, your dog was stolen, your—"

"You think he has Roscoe?"

"I don't know, but probably. Since he hasn't turned up."

"That son of a bitch. I mean, I thought it was a possibility, but I'd hoped . . . Damn it all to hell." She slammed the dead bolt shut and walked into the living room, where she dropped onto the couch. She was barefoot, her hair pinned onto her head haphazardly, as if she were getting ready for bed. Closing her eyes, she leaned back on the cushions, and the cat, hiding on a window ledge, hopped across a bookcase to navigate the back of the couch and nose Alvarez's hair. "Grayson kicked me off the case." Absently she plucked Jane from the couch and dropped her into her lap.

"He had to."

"Yeah, I know, but I don't like it."

"And it won't stop you from investigating."

"No comment." Sighing, she gave the cat one last pet, then straightened, her dark eyes opening. "I keep trying to figure out who the hell he is . . . It has to be someone I've met . . . but . . ." She shrugged. "So far, I'm out of ideas."

"We'll work on it together."

"Because you're moving in." It wasn't a question.

"Temporarily. Until we get this nut job behind bars." He tried to keep the desperation out of his tone, didn't want to freak her out any more than she already was, but they both knew that she was

404

in danger. The killer was becoming frustrated, not getting the attention he craved, so he'd sent the card. Who knew what his next move might be?

"Do I get a say in this?" she asked.

"Not really."

"Just like everything else. So you . . . what? You think you're going to be my self-appointed bodyguard or something?"

"Or something." He opened the plastic bag he'd picked up at the hardware store and pulled out a new doorknob and dead bolt. "I supposed you heard that Gabe was going to be transferred tomorrow."

"No." She lifted a shoulder, but he could see in her eyes that she was bothered. "Just one more loop I'm clearly out of." He realized that it made her a little crazy to think that homicide cases were being solved without her and that her own son's situation was being withheld from her.

"Don't suppose I can see him first?"

"Aggie doesn't want you to have contact with him. Or me, for that matter, I'm off the case."

"So we both got fired."

"Essentially."

"You know, I think Aggie can go . . . jump in a lake!" Her cheeks turned a little red and her eyes snapped as anger obviously surged through her. O'Keefe figured it was the first time in a long while she'd been thwarted or felt so impotent.

"Anyone ask Gabe what he wanted?"

"I doubt it."

"Damn." She walked into the kitchen and found a bottle of sparkling water, opened it and took a long swallow.

"Hit the spot?" he asked.

"No, but it'll have to do. For now."

"I'll take you to dinner," he offered, turning to look at her in the kitchen.

"Now?"

"No, not now, as soon as I'm finished."

"Finished with what?"

"Changing all the locks. I thought we'd start fresh. Just in case someone has a key."

"Nervy," she said but didn't offer up any objection. Though she was trying to disguise it, she was anxious, forcing herself to appear calmer than she really felt.

"The slider has a lock, right?"

She was nodding. "It's a dead bolt screwed into the track and floor and can't be accessed from outside."

"Good." Nonetheless, he checked and tested the screw knob that fastened the slider into place. Satisfied that it was secure, he straightened. "So I'll put the new lock into place on the front door and then double-check the windows and make certain they all latch. You"—he motioned at her with a screwdriver—"might want to change into something a little less casual. Dinner. Remember?"

"Oh, right." She was already heading for the stairs but stopped on the second step. "I don't think the killer will come back here."

He opened his toolbox and said, "Maybe not. But let's just make sure if he does show up, he won't get in. Damn. I need a different screwdriver. You have a Phillips?"

"In the garage, in the workbench."

"Great. I'll be right back and finish up." He started for the garage but sent a smile in her direction. "That bastard's never getting in here again."

Who, who, who?

Pescoli couldn't get the case out of her head, even as she waited for Jeremy to come home and she heard Bianca in the bathroom, taking what had to be the world's longest shower. Whereas Pescoli could be in and out of the bathroom, teeth brushed, showered, her hair shampooed, and in her pajamas in less than ten minutes, her daughter took a minimum of an hour, sometimes an hour and a half, which could be a problem since the house had only one bathroom and, unlike her son, Pescoli didn't find off the deck a secondary toilet. No matter how often she admonished him, Jeremy didn't feel the least bit abashed at "taking a leak" into the surrounding woods.

So now, while Cisco was curled into a ball in

his dog bed near the Christmas tree and Bianca went through her major beauty routine on the other side of the locked bathroom door, Pescoli fired up her laptop and went over everything she knew about the ice-mummy case. There were photo-graphs of the crime scenes and lists of people who knew the victims, more photographs of people who had stopped and looked at the scenes. The department had gathered security tapes from surrounding businesses, interviewed neighbors, checked traffic cams for large vehicles driving near the crime scenes late at night, talked to relatives and friends, listed enemies and come up with people who would benefit from the victims' disappearances.

Nothing came together.

A question that had been bandied about was the operation itself. Where did the killer take his victims to kill them and freeze their bodies in blocks of ice? It would take days for the water to solidify and then be carved into the intricate patterns, all of which had been studied. Did he have a large, commercial freezer? Was a ware-house complete with refrigeration and freezers involved? Could he be doing his work at home, but where? Did he live alone, or did he have an accomplice?

There had been no physical evidence aside from what appeared to be the tiniest drop of blood in the ice surrounding Lara Sue Gilfry's body, so little it was almost overlooked, maybe missed by the perpetrator.

The lab had been working on it; the blood was rare, didn't match the victim and had come from a male, as had the single short hair found on the floor mat near the door of Brenda Sutherland's car.

The FBI was running comparisons with known criminals, but so far they'd ended up with a big fat goose egg. There had been no latent prints on the card, envelope or photo, the last of which was computer generated, nor had the envelope tested positive for saliva. The creep had obviously been watching too much *CSI*.

But he would trip up; they always did.

Eventually.

How in the world did Alvarez connect with the killer and the known victims? There had to be a thread. The killer hadn't robbed her house and left his mark, in the way of her jewelry, on the victims for no reason.

Uh-uh.

Like a dog marking his territory, or Jeremy peeing off the deck, this maniac had taken Alvarez's jewelry for a reason, to make himself known to her.

She had a smaller version of the map in the task force room on her computer and she studied it again. There had to be a connection between where these women worked, where they were abducted, and where they lived . . . right? This guy was nothing if not organized. No one plots to break in to a homicide detective's home, steal her jewelry and display it without a plan.

He *had* to be someone Alvarez knew.

Possibly someone she knew, too.

So who the hell was he?

A child? Selena Alvarez had borne a child? And now his identity could be discovered?

As he, alone in the house, watched the television in his office, he wondered why he hadn't put two and two together before. His mind raced and he mentally went over all the information he had on the woman.

Of course there were holes in what he knew about her, but not many. He'd been meticulous but had never understood why she'd moved away from her parents in her high school years, transferred schools. He'd thought it was because she was in some kind of accelerated program or that her parents had moved her out to get her away from running with the wrong crowd, but he'd never really considered that she'd been pregnant. Not these days, because even fifteen years ago, it was acceptable to have a child as a teenager; if not the norm, certainly not something to be ashamed of.

It wasn't as if he hadn't considered the possibility.

He'd suspected she might have had a baby, of course, by tracking down her school records and addresses. She'd been moved away from her family when she was still in her teens, for just a year, but he'd never come back to the idea that she'd had a secret baby.

A mistake on his part.

An omission and one he didn't like.

But now, he knew.

His blood sang with that special little sizzle of adrenaline he always felt when he sensed everything coming seamlessly together. He'd thought he would lure her with her stupid dog . . . but this, *a child,* was so much more certain to force her to do what he wanted, what he needed.

The thrill he felt brought his cock to attention and caused his mind to start planning how to coerce her to do his bidding.

As he sat in his office, his eyes trained on the television screen, he imagined her in front of him. On her knees. Naked. Maybe a dog collar around her neck, but that was just sexual need and insignificant.

No, rather than watch her submission, he would lay her in her bath and pour the frigid water over her, preserving her perfection while destroying her spirit.

Oh, yes . . .

The door was closed, and his wife, all atwitter about next weekend's church Christmas bazaar, was out. He was alone, thankfully, the melody of "Angels We Have Heard on High," running through his brain. Transfixed, watching the news as he tried to put the pieces that he'd been missing together. According to the news, the person who had broken into Selena Alvarez's home was a teenager now in custody. That boy had "personal ties to the victim," though, of course, the newscaster didn't state the exact nature of the connection, only that an "anonymous source" had given the reporter her information, meaning there was a leak in the sheriff's department.

Nia Del Ray might be playing coy.

But he knew.

He'd done his research.

With a click, he opened his private files and found the one dedicated to Alvarez. He'd realized there was a hole in her upbringing, the year she'd been gone, but he hadn't realized until this moment that the detective had borne a son who was now . . . what? Fifteen, no, sixteen, still young enough to be underage to protect his identity.

Well, that had been blown. All he had to do was reach for his keyboard, and while music played softly and the television continued to run the story, search through the recent reports of crimes on the Internet, check news stories and local blogs and . . . Bingo! The name Gabriel Reeve came to light. A few more searches of "protected" high school databases and unprotected social network sites, and several pictures appeared on his screen.

"How about that?" he whispered under his breath. One of the suspects who was allegedly involved in an attempted robbery at the home of Judge Victor Ramsey was Detective Alvarez's son? How had he not known this?

He turned his attention back to the television, rewound the newscast and listened again. What had that idiot Nia said, something about "transferring the suspect."

He listened to that air-head Nia Del Ray, who was all puffed up as if she'd personally broken the story.

He watched, transfixed, then backed up the newscast and watched it again. Then again.

Quickly, on his computer, he began searching for more stories, more information and it seemed that the reporter for KMJC in Helena had her facts straight and this kid, who'd been adopted out at birth, had come snooping around Alvarez— good old Mommie Dearest—when he landed himself in some legal hot water.

This was good news.

Very good news.

Another way to get at that bitch of a detective who thought she was better than he. The song in the speakers changed to "Santa Claus Is Comin' to Town" and he grinned to himself as he thought about smart, sassy and oh-so-sexy Selena Alvarez.

"You better watch out, you'd better not cry, you'd better not pout, I'm tellin' you why . . ." he sang softly, then chuckled to himself. *Oh, yes, Detective Alvarez, you surely better watch out,* he thought, as the final, most important part of his plan, was coming together.

Compliments of Gabriel Reeve.

Johnna was freezing.

Stripped naked, locked in some kind of underground cell, she watched the sicko as he sluiced the dead woman with water, then, as the ice froze over her body, spent hours with an ice pick, brushes and chisels, even an electric saw.

It was creepy as hell and she was freaked out, but he'd given her something to calm her, so that she wouldn't scream and curse at him as she had when he'd first brought her here.

She'd pled with him, begged for her life, promised to do anything he wanted, swore she'd never tell a soul, but it was all for naught. He'd gone about his twisted business and seemed only irritated by the dog, a puppy of some sort, locked in a cell like the one she was in, poor thing. He yapped and cried incessantly, giving Johnna a headache that the drugs slipped into her veins couldn't quite relieve.

She had no idea of what time of day it was—morning, noon or night—nor did she know how long he'd held her captive, or how long he planned to keep her alive. She held no illusions that she would escape with her life; not after what she'd seen.

Now, she heard his footsteps on the stairs, the creak of his heavy tread, and she was wary. She'd looked for a weapon, something to use against him, and hadn't found anything.

At first she'd argued and screamed, but now she became silent, waiting, hoping to lull him into believing that she was scared out of her mind to the point of being petrified and unable to defend herself. That part wasn't true.

She thought about the baby growing inside her and wondered what the effects of this abject cold, the electric shock from the stun gun and the drugs he'd given her had on her unborn child.

Mentally kicking herself a dozen times over, she wondered how she could have trusted him, how she could have missed the obvious signs that he was a maniac . . . no, wait a minute, make that a homicidal maniac.

Well, she wasn't going down without one helluva fight.

But he ignored her, turning on the damned Christmas music and going to work on the horrendous ice sculpture he'd created, a clear, frozen block, chiseled and scraped to his satisfaction. Instead of doing any more sculpting, if that's what you'd call it, he set huge tongs on one end, near the feet of the thing, and elevated it onto a dolly.

Then, as she watched in horror, while the strains of "White Christmas" played from speakers mounted high on the cave's walls, he moved the macabre ice sculpture, wheeling it out of the cavern, past her cell and along a natural hallway into the darkness beyond.

CHAPTER 29

At seventy-five, Harry Barlow hated snow.

He also hated small, loud children.

And tiny, yappy dogs.

And now he was outside, in the middle of winter, with the storm those idiots on the weather channel had been predicting for days bearing down on him.

The wind was raw as it howled down the river's canyon, the snow in tiny, icy pellets and flying all over the place, smashing against his glasses, stinging his cheeks as he walked his wife's damned dog.

If he had his way, he'd be back living in Florida on a golf course and drinking mai tais or gimlets. He'd go back to one of those adult-only communities, like The Palms, where, if there were small irritating dogs, the gators would take care of them.

But because three years ago, after his beloved Winnie had passed on, he'd fallen in love with another lady in the church, Phyllis, who had been Winnie's best friend, things had changed for Harry. He'd expected to settle in with Phyllis just as he had with Winnie, that essentially, he'd just gotten a new wife who would fill the four-hundred-dollar shoes of his first love.

Not so.

The trouble was that Phyllis, much more practical than his first wife, had decided that along with buying sensible, sturdy shoes, she and Harry needed to move from the warmth of the Sunshine State to here, in the middle of no-damned-where freezing Montana, what the locals referred to as the Treasure State. Oh, right. Such a treasure!

However, Harry was committed to Phyllis so he'd traded in his golf-cart lifestyle for an austere way of living in what he unaffectionately called The Sticks.

In Florida, people mounted marlin on the walls, here . . . moose heads or antlers off dead deer, or even cougar hides were considered interesting art. It was enough to give Harry the willies.

But Phyllis had insisted they come to this godforsaken wasteland and take care of her mother, so now, the three of them were living in Mom's apartment overlooking the falls. Somehow it had become Harry's job to walk Baby, Mom's nasty little toy poodle–Chihuahua mutt. Baby knew that Harry didn't like him, too. He'd growl and bark and snap his sharp little fangs at him to the point that one time Baby had Harry cornered behind the pocket door of the half bath. For some reason Phyllis had found that incident uproariously funny.

It was enough to make him blush.

He was grateful only that Ralph and Bubba and Wiley, his golf buddies at The Palms, couldn't see him bundling up twice a day, leash and plastic bag in hand, following after the foul-tempered Baby and cleaning up after him.

Enough was enough!

He'd warned Phyllis that, after the first of the year, he was flying south. She could come with him or stay here in this damned ice fortress.

Baby, whose real name was Baby Love Supreme —*dear God, help me*—after the '60s singing group that Phyllis still adored, was in a particularly reticent mood this morning. He didn't want to get on the elevator and had refused to lift his little leg on any of his usual bushes.

Worse yet, the second they got into the elevator car to the lower part of town, he decided to piss on the door.

Great.

January second, and not a day later! Harry was out of this frozen hellhole, without the stupid dog!

At least no one was in the elevator at this early hour, so Baby's defiling of a public landmark might go unnoticed . . . well, except for the camera mounted overhead.

Damn!

The car descended, and as it opened, another blast of winter wind rushed inside. Harry adjusted his gloves and watch cap, then walked the damned thing onto the sidewalk that had once been shoveled clear of snow, but now was piling up again.

Miserable weather!

Morning traffic had barely started threading through the empty streets, as it was still dark, too early for most people to be on their way to work. Streetlights offered thin blue illumination in the blustery snowfall, but the morning was cold as a Viking's bare ass. He tugged on the leash and thought about leaving Baby tied to a parking meter while he went into one of the coffee shops and got his first cup. But the mutt, even dressed in his ridiculous green sweater, could conceivably freeze.

Phyllis wouldn't be pleased if the thing died on him.

Spying the sign for Joltz, he crossed at the light and headed toward the small storefront. As he did, he passed Wild Will's, the restaurant with the macabre stuffed animals lining the walls, and a small music store that had a display near the front door. A set of three wooden carolers, dressed as if they were in the 1890s, were chained to a ring in the building, to ensure they wouldn't be stolen, he supposed.

Baby nosed around the two-dimensional man in his top hat and morning coat. He stood between two women, one in a shirtwaist and pinstriped skirt, the second in a red dress, all of whom were holding song books, their mouths rounded as if they were indeed caroling.

"Get on with it," he muttered to the dog, who poked around behind the wooden people and began to whine. "For God's sake, what's wrong now?" he said, just as he noticed the fourth figure, different from the others, hidden slightly behind the tall figure in the top hat, tucked in the shadows of the store's awning.

What the devil? he wondered, peering more closely. A half scream bubbled in his throat as he realized he was looking at a sculpted block of ice with a very dead and very naked woman inside!

"We found Brenda Sutherland," Pescoli said when Alvarez answered her cell. Standing at the sink where she was filling a teapot, she'd answered on the second ring. "Right downtown, get this, across from Wild Will's, same as the others, naked and entombed in ice, placed behind a set of plywood carolers that Woody's Music always puts out this time of year. I know you're officially off the case, but . . . oh, hell. The way I see it, we can use all the manpower, or make that womanpower, we've got."

Alvarez, realizing the teapot was overflowing, turned off the water.

"That son of a bitch set her up right in the heart of downtown, wearing nothing but your damned locket. Found by a man walking his dog about half an hour ago. Freaked the hell out of him."

"I'll bet. So . . . the body wasn't far from the courthouse?"

"Right. Finally, the guy fouled up," Pescoli was saying, and the roar of the wind could be heard as she half yelled into her phone.

Alvarez had already forgotten the tea and was starting up the stairs.

"There are store and traffic cameras all over the place. We'll get him this time. A vehicle the size of his, we'll find it, and Woody, the owner of the music store, he's got surveillance cameras all over his display windows. We'll get this bastard."

"I'll be right there," Alvarez said, flying up the rest of the stairs.

"Good girl."

Alvarez heard the smile in Pescoli's voice and knew she was about to hang up. "Hey, wait!"

"Yeah?"

"Have you heard anything about Gabriel Reeve?"

"Other than the fact that the mother insists you stay away from him?" Pescoli asked. "Well, yeah, I have. He's being transferred back to Helena."

"So, it's today?"

"Looks like it. But with all of this and the storm, it might be hard to find a driver. The Helena PD might have to come and get him and . . . don't even suggest that you could do it, okay? Grayson won't go for it, nor will the parents."

Alvarez wanted to argue, but before she could, Pescoli added, "I've got to go," and clicked off.

In the bedroom, she found Dylan lying cross-wise over the bed, sheets and duvet wrapped around his naked body, his form barely visible in the half-light from windows. "Rise and shine," she said as she flipped on a bedside lamp, and Jane, still dozing, raised her furry head. O'Keefe blinked and winced, turning away from the light while the cat stretched, arching her back, yawning widely to show off her pink tongue and wicked little teeth.

"What the hell?" he grumbled, his voice still sounding sleepy, his hair spiked up at weird angles.

"We've got ourselves another one." She was already stepping into thermal underwear and locating a pair of jeans. Her boots were right where she'd left them on the closet floor and she zipped them on quickly.

"What do you mean?"

"Brenda Sutherland." Stretching her arms through the insulated undershirt, she added, "Found downtown." She poked her head through the neck hole and unpinned her hair, running her fingers through it before winding it onto the top of her head a little more neatly.

"What time did you get up?" Running a hand over his stubbled jaw, he glanced at the clock on her side of the bed. The digital readout blinked a bright red six thirteen.

"Hours ago," she lied.

He stretched, arms over one side of the bed, bare feet out the other, the covers unfortunately hiding his bare buttocks. "And what the hell time did that guy walk his dog?"

"Who knows? Early."

A blast of wind howled past the town house, rattling the windows.

"Nasty out there," he observed, but he was already rolling off the bed, scooping up his boxers and jeans.

"You got any ski pants? It's crazy cold outside. Saw it on the news already; the storm they've been predicting for a week has hit."

As if to punctuate her observation, the lights went out.

"Crap," he said as, fumbling, she turned on the flashlight app on her iPhone, then found a flashlight in the drawer and tossed it to him.

"Get a move on, O'Keefe; I need to get my car out of the garage."

"You know how to disable the electricity to the garage door opener?"

"Yeah, but it would be nice if you'd help."

He flashed her a grin in the half-light, a sexy slash of white that touched her heart. "You got it, Detective," he said and, as she walked by, took a playful swipe at her rump.

Once again the crime scene appeared to be a madhouse, Pescoli thought, though the department had contained it, separating the area from the rest of town. This time, since Woody's was located in the heart of the old town on the lower level of Grizzly Falls, the roads around the block had been cordoned off, barriers put in place and county vehicles were parked around the perimeter, their flashing lights in competition with the holiday strands strung over the city, with harsh-faced deputies ensuring that the crowd that had gathered was held at bay.

Despite the frigid temperature and blizzard-force winds, dozens of bystanders had collected, people on their way to work, clients on their way to appointments, joggers whose daily run was interrupted, even suspects who were being hauled into court. The heart of town was at a standstill, compliments of the Ice Mummy Killer, whoever the hell he was.

But they would catch him, Pescoli was certain, this time the maniac had fouled up. It would be impossible for him not to have been seen or captured on camera. Hopefully he would be identified.

She checked out the body, saw that it, like the others, had been posed, set in a public place, a woman trapped in an ice sculpture behind plywood cutouts of carolers holding songbooks, their two-dimensional faces posed as if they were singing, their garb reminiscent of a rudimentary version of something seen in a Currier and Ives lithograph.

Brenda Sutherland was naked aside from the locket, just as she had been in the photograph sent to Alvarez in the twisted Christmas card.

Security tapes for the store were only kept a day, and the camera was motion activated, but certainly it would give some clues as to the creep who had been brazen enough to leave his latest victim on the sidewalk of the main street of town.

"There's someone who insists on talking with you," Pete Watershed said as he approached. "It's Sandi Aldridge from Wild Will's."

Pescoli's heart sank, but she walked to the barrier in front of the restaurant, where Sandi, wearing a thick ski jacket and matching pants, stood under the awning. There were other people gathered in the relative protection of the building, but Sandi stood a little apart from them. Her arms were wrapped around her middle and her jaw seemed to tremble a bit. Pescoli approached and saw that Sandi's glasses were a little fogged with the cold, but she stared through them with frantic eyes shaded in a brilliant purple. "It's

Brenda, isn't it? Oh, God, I was afraid of this."

She lifted a gloved hand to her mouth and bit into it, as if to stop herself from breaking down and sobbing.

"It's early. Next of kin hasn't—"

"Screw next of kin. Brenda was like a daughter to me! I knew it. I knew that whack job had her." She sniffed loudly. "You've checked on that louse of an ex-husband of hers, right? I swear—"

"I know, Sandi. We're looking at everyone."

"But Brenda . . ." Her voice broke. "It's just not fair!"

It never is.

Pescoli was called away and Sandi shuffled off, shoulders shaking as she made her way into the restaurant. "Crime scene team's here," Watershed told her. "And Detective Alvarez."

"Good." If anyone wanted to pick a fight with her about her partner being involved, well, bring them on. Pescoli didn't have time for protocol and now, as she saw Brett Gage approaching, she inwardly groaned. The guy was a good enough cop, just a little soft for her liking.

Fortunately Alvarez had shown. She was talking to the cop and signing in to the scene. She walked up to Pescoli and said, "Show me."

Gage looked about to say something, but Pescoli held up a gloved hand, warning him to tread lightly. "Over here," she said, leading the way to the front of the music store, where techs were taking pictures of the scene, complete with the plywood decorations and the ice sculpture. "Yours?" she asked, shining her flashlight directly onto the dead woman and the locket that hung from a tiny gold chain at her neck.

"Looks like."

Pescoli snapped off her light. "Figured." She gazed at the ice mummy. "This whack job, he's got a thing for you, Alvarez."

"So you said."

"No, I said he was targeting you. But I think it goes deeper than that. He was in your house, stole your things, displays them along with the women he kills. It's more than targeting," she thought aloud. "This is personal."

CHAPTER 30

Pescoli's warning, if that's what you'd call it, followed Alvarez as she drove to the station.

She thought of the frozen women, wearing nothing but pieces of her jewelry.

This is personal.

How? The men who had just cause to hate her, she supposed, Emilio Alvarez and Alberto De Maestro, were nowhere near the area, and the men she'd sent to prison were, for the most part, still incarcerated. Junior Green had tried his best to take her out but failed and was back in custody, and she didn't think she'd pissed off anyone else, at least not to the point of the guy becoming a homicidal maniac.

That's not how it works and you know it; this guy is a serial killer, he has a history. Somewhere. A bed wetter. Abused and neglected, probably molested as a child. Someone cruel to animals . . . And has crossed your path without you knowing it. Someone who also knew Lara Sue Gilfry, Lissa Parsons, Brenda Sutherland and probably Johnna Phillips. Someone in the community. So . . . who? Who?

Frustrated, she spent the day thinking about it in her office while the storm continued to rage, snapping trees, tearing down power lines, freezing pipes and shutting down roads. It was as bad as she'd ever seen it here.

People in this part of Montana were used to blizzardlike conditions in the depths of winter, but even the locals, the residents who had lived here for decades, were forced to batten down the hatches.

The sheriff's department called in everyone to help out, so the station was buzzing with deputies, half-frozen, returning from road duty to warm up with hot coffee and Joelle's rapidly disappearing cupcakes and candy, before heading out again to help elderly shut-ins who were freezing without power, or clearing accidents on the roads that had been plowed, or assisting with tree removal.

On top of the bad weather, the department, along with the FBI and state troopers, was dealing with the serial killer.

The joviality of the Christmas season was buried deep in the icy drifts surrounding Grizzly Falls and even Joelle seemed to have had her spirits dampened; her usual smile was a little forced and she, always in strappy, glittery heels this time of year, had donned knee-high red boots and a black skirt and sweater that were decorated in poinsettias that seemed to be falling from her left shoulder and tumbling to the hem of the skirt on the right side of her body.

"I suppose the church's bazaar will have to be postponed from this weekend," she said, tight-lipped as she brushed crumbs from one of the tables.

"Least of our problems, I'd say." Pescoli had spent a good part of the day in the task force room and had just stepped out to refill her coffee cup. Alvarez, too, was allowed in and had been working the case as well. Grayson had backed down on his edict that she couldn't be a part of the team and the FBI agents had agreed, thinking that she might offer some insight into the case.

There had been tips called in to the station that the task force had sorted, filed and, of course, verified. Though each tip had been checked out, nothing had panned out, including the call from

Sherwin Hahn, who insisted his neighbor was doing "weird things" with his watering trough outside. Sherwin was a farmer whose family had homesteaded around Grizzly Falls generations earlier. Because of a farming accident and crippling arthritis, Sherwin, pushing a hundred years, was relegated to a wheelchair while his son and grandson ran the farm. From his position near the window and with the aid of a telescope, he could look down the hill to his neighbor's farm, where Abe Nelson raised winter wheat and sheep. It was the sheep trough that had caught Sherwin's attention, and his imagination had run wild as he was certain Abe was freezing bodies in the trough. As it turned out Abe Nelson was just trying to keep the water from freezing and worked with the troughs every evening and morning. He'd talked to the FBI and Pescoli and Gage, throwing a disgusted glance up the hill to Sherwin Hahn's old farmhouse and saying, "The blind old fart should just mind his own business. For the record, I don't like him, nor his son and especially not his grandson!"

They'd looked around, Nelson had invited them to comb his property. "While you're at it, would you mind looking for a ewe I lost two days ago?" he'd asked, and his wife had even offered them coffee. The tip had been a bust. Like the others. Pescoli had confided to Alvarez later while seated at her desk, "The Nelson farm?"

She'd rolled her eyes and shaken her head. "It was just one more wrong tree we managed to bark up."

His job was officially over, O'Keefe acknowledged as he drove toward the hotel where Aggie and Dave were staying. They were checking out later in the day. As soon as the storm broke and the roads were passable, they intended to head back to Helena to await their son's arrival at the juvenile center there and meet with an attorney. Gabe was being transported to Helena later in the day, if and when the roads were passable, though no one knew the exact time of his release; it all depended, O'Keefe had heard from Alvarez, upon when a driver was available and the center in Helena could accept him inside their locked gates.

Officially, it was time for him to leave, too, O'Keefe thought, squinting a little, as the snow was really coming down, making visibility almost impossible. Traffic was light but crawling, snow piling only to pack down to ice before piling onto the slick surface all over again.

He'd cleared out of his motel room the day before and his stuff was either in his SUV or Alvarez's town house. His life, though, was back in Helena. He couldn't hang out here in Grizzly Falls forever. He had a duplex and an office downtown in Helena, both of which he'd ignored for the past week and a half.

Because of Gabe.

Check that. Originally it was because of Gabe, but now, he was hanging around because of Alvarez. He told himself it was to protect her, that because she was in the killer's sights, he couldn't leave now.

But it was more than that, and now, as he drove along the road that rimmed the river, he had to acknowledge the simple fact that he was falling in love with her. Which was just plain stupid. He had mixed feelings about her, of course, and once he'd found out that she'd been raped as a teenager, that her problems with intimacy had sprung from that horrific crime, he should have backed off, per-haps, and gave her space. But he hadn't and, it seemed, she didn't want him to leave. She cer-tainly hadn't had a snit fit when he'd practically moved in the night before.

A twinge of guilt needled his mind, because he hadn't been completely honest with her. So, he'd pushed the sex thing, unknowingly, of course, but forced her to admit to what had happened to her, how Gabe had been conceived, and now every-one knew; he felt a little guilt for being a party to that, but not too much. It was a good thing, right? He glanced in his rearview mirror and caught his own reflection as if for confirmation.

But he also hadn't been completely truthful to her either about his reasons for staying.

This time, as he slowed for a red light and

looked into the mirror again, he caught recriminations in his bruised countenance. So, he'd lied. So, she'd be pissed as hell when and if she found out. So what?

He remembered the fear that had jolted through him when he realized that Junior Green had her cornered in her garage, that the big man was intent on killing her, that he'd come within inches of taking her life.

O'Keefe had panicked, rolled under the garage door, sweeping the bigger man's legs out from him and eventually winning that brutal wrestling match, but it had haunted him ever since. What if he hadn't arrived at just that moment?

True, Selena Alvarez was a trained policewoman, knew how to use a firearm and had taken classes in self-defense and martial arts, but still, would that have been enough when the madman with a loaded .45 had confronted her?

It was a chance he didn't want to take, not ever again.

Face it, O'Keefe. You've got it bad for her. You never really fell out of love with Selena Alvarez.

And that was the sorry truth.

"The next of kin for Brenda Sutherland has been notified," Pescoli announced as she walked into Alvarez's office a little later in the day.

"I heard." Alvarez had been at the computer all morning and through lunch, catching up on other work while going over all of the evidence for the ice-mummy murders one more time. The autopsy report on Brenda Sutherland wouldn't be in for a few days, but she expected it would be about the same as the two other victims.

So far. Three victims so far. There was still Johnna Phillips who hadn't been accounted for and there could be others as well, women who hadn't yet been reported missing. Somehow they had to stop him. She rotated the kinks from her neck and couldn't help but notice the faint strains of some familiar Christmas song just audible over the noise and clatter of the station. Phones rang, the printers chunked out information, the old heating system rumbled, conversation floated down the hallways and every so often there was a bark of laughter over the click of keystrokes. Still, above it all, a Christmas carol could be heard, if you listened hard enough.

"Darla's going to give another press conference, right? With the FBI?"

"Later. Yeah. The FBI is planning to ask the public for help." Pescoli was smiling a little.

"What?" Alvarez asked. "You know something . . ." She felt a little trickle of excitement in her blood. "What?"

"We finally have the tape from a security camera mounted over the alley behind the music store. The film's pretty grainy, but the computer geeks have cleaned it up. Nigel Timmons might be a pain in the ass, but he knows what he's doing. They've got it in the task force room. I thought you'd want to take a look."

"Is he on it?" Alvarez asked, shoving back her chair.

"Yep."

"Who is he?"

"Don't know. Thought you might want to take a look."

"Hell, yeah, I do." Already on her feet, Alvarez hurried down the hallway. Was it possible? Could they have the creep? Had he finally fouled up enough that they could ID him and arrest the maniac?

Adrenaline fired her blood as she walked into the task force room. On the largest television screen, a tape had been stopped, but Nigel Timmons, self-important as ever, was explaining how they'd improved the quality of the film.

"Just play it," Pescoli said to the tech. His faux hawk was a little messy today, his eyes a tad blood-shot from his contacts, but he did as he was bid.

"We've actually spliced the tape of the alley with that from the traffic cams," he said and Alvarez watched as, in grainy black and white, a pickup with a canopy came into view, its license plate obscured, and a big man climbed out of the driver's side, then opened the back end of the truck, where he pulled out a dolly and placed a huge trash can upon it.

"Dear God," Alvarez said as she realized she was watching the killer. He was dressed all in a dark color, black or navy blue, probably, wearing a ski coat and ski pants, gloves, ski mask and hat, nothing distinctive about any of the apparel. He was even wearing ski goggles, as if he knew that he might be filmed and, even in darkness, was disguising his eyes.

Jerkily, he rolled the trash can on the dolly out of the camera's field of vision but was picked up again, on another camera, this one placed under the awning in the front of the store. Quickly, he moved the plywood carolers as far as the security chain would allow, deposited the ice statue, replaced the singers into their original position and hurried back down the alley pushing the dolly.

"He accomplishes this in less than four minutes," Nigel said as the truck, obviously left idling, drove away from the screen.

"Just like that," Pescoli said.

"Here are shots from the traffic cams." Alvarez watched as a series of pictures that had been spliced together showed up.

"You got those plates, right?"

"Stolen," Halden said. "Off an '86 Chevy Nova hatchback and put on this truck, a Dodge. Already checked; the report was made six weeks ago. The guy noticed them after a night of drinking at a bar in Missoula. We know the date, he's got a receipt for his drinks, so we're checking there, but he was parked on a side street, no camera."

The image on the television went back to the perpetrator pushing his trash can on the dolly.

"Didn't anyone see him?"

"Three fifty-seven in the morning. In the middle of a blizzard. And get this, it was garbage pickup morning."

"Not quite that early."

"Right. The trucks don't reach that part of town until between six and six thirty, so that was probably just random. Anyway, we'll ask the public today, see if anyone was up looking out their window at that time, but it's a long shot," Chandler said, and Halden, holding a cup of coffee and staring at the screen, nodded.

"There is nothing identifying about this guy, aside from the fact that he's probably about six foot one, maybe two."

"Or he's got lifts in his boots."

"Looks like he weighs anywhere from two hundred to two thirty, depending upon how many layers he's got on." Halden scowled. "We think his hair is brown, if the one we found in Brenda Sutherland's car is his. And his blood type is O positive, if the drop we found in the ice belongs to him." He nodded to Nigel, who hit another switch. A new picture leapt to the screen and Alvarez noticed it was the crowd that had gathered at the first crime scene at the church. "Take a look here. We've got some stills, and put 'em together. See the guy, there?" He was pointing with the index finger of the hand surrounding his coffee cup. "That guy's about the right size. He's with a group of people, but not really. Standing a little to the side, under that hemlock."

"And the truck?" Alvarez asked.

"Several white ones that passed by. One a Dodge."

"Plates?"

Halden shook his head. "Obscured. But it's possible the guy drove by, then parked and hiked back to the scene to have a look."

Alvarez studied the pictures and she felt as if a ghost were walking on her spine. *This* was the madman? *This* was the killer who spent time working tediously on the sculptures so that it was as if you were seeing the woman's features caught in ice before you actually saw her flesh below the surface? *This* was the pervert who had sent her the twisted card with the picture of Brenda Sutherland, the creep who had been in her house and taken her dog, stolen her jewelry and had done no telling what else to her place?

She shuddered as she stared at his pictures, because they were pictures of any man; there was nothing that identified him from any of the men she knew.

And that, more than anything else, terrified her.

CHAPTER 31

Pescoli's headache had started out small in the morning, but by seven thirty was a rager. She'd worked all day and heard that the road to her house was closed. Both kids were okay, though, Luke, bless his itty-bitty dark heart, had picked up Bianca when school was closed early in the morning, so she was safely with her father and stepmother.

Jeremy had called and informed her he was at a friend's house and, before hanging up, had wheedled that he just needed her signature and three hundred dollars for his part of the lease.

Pescoli had told him to "join the club" and refused. She bought a sandwich and a Diet Coke out of the vending machine, and while she ate the sandwich, stared at her computer screen, where she studied the footage of the suspect with his dolly and garbage can for what had to be the fortieth time.

Biting into the tuna on rye, she also looked through the names she'd gotten from the DMV of Dodge trucks registered in Pinewood and the surrounding three counties. Though all the victims lived, worked and had been abducted in Pinewood, it didn't mean the killer didn't live somewhere else, somewhere nearby and just used the area around Grizzly Falls as his personal hunting ground.

"Prick," she muttered as she saw him on the screen one more time and set her sandwich aside. There was something about him that seemed familiar.

Of course there is; you've been studying him all day.

No, she thought, taking another look. She knew this guy; she was sure of it, but she couldn't put her finger on what it was.

It's his eyes. Why the hell does he keep covering them up?

It was true, as she flipped through all of the shots of the suspect, his eyes were covered. Ski goggles at the music store, and at the scene with the church, when he stood under the tree, it seemed as if he, again, was wearing some protective covering though it wasn't quite light.

What was that all about?

She searched the pictures of the crowd that had collected near the Enstad place where the second victim, Lissa Parsons, was found. No white truck showed in any of the pictures and she couldn't pinpoint the guy, but she knew he was there, hiding in the shadows, like the sick coward he was.

"We're gonna get you," she said, her gaze returning to her computer screen, where his likeness as he wheeled the dolly by the music store had been enlarged. She took a long swallow of her Diet Coke. "And when we do, you loser, I'm going to make it my personal mission to make sure you never see the light of day again."

Trilby Van Droz drew the short straw.

Because every other road deputy and officer in the department was out helping with emergencies, she got the duty of driving the juvenile back to Helena.

Go figure.

Already bone weary, she chewed gum and sipped coffee as she drove toward Helena. The storm was really gathering force, dumping snow at an incredible rate, and yet, here she was. For some reason she didn't understand, probably due to Judge Victor Ramsey himself, it was imperative that Gabriel Reeve return to Helena tonight.

This road, usually fairly busy, was already nearly impassable, traffic extremely light as people hunkered down to wait out what the newscasters were calling "the storm of the century." Yeah, well, wasn't that what they'd called last year's blizzard?

As it was, her Jeep was sliding a bit, but she was used to driving in bad weather. A native Montanan, she wasn't scared by a little snow . . . well, make that a lot of snow.

Glancing in the rearview mirror, she saw her charge staring back at her. Reeve's dark eyes were filled with hate . . . or was it fear? How bad could he be? Geez, he was only sixteen, just a year older than her daughter. It wasn't as if he was a hardened criminal, for God's sake, just a kid who'd taken a wrong turn, one his family was trying to straighten out.

Weird that. The gossip running through the department was that the kid was Detective Alvarez's biological son, but other than the fact that he was obviously Latino, there wasn't a lot of resemblance, at least none that Trilby could see.

That, at least, wasn't her problem, she reminded herself as she cranked up the heat in the Jeep. All she had to do was haul him to Helena, let the local boys deal with him and return to Grizzly Falls, if the roads allowed.

She yawned and sipped some hot coffee from her travel mug. She had her own problems with her own kid. Her teenaged daughter was giving her fits, sneaking out, and it was all Trilby could do to keep an eye on her at night while working overtime as a deputy with the sheriff's department. It was times like these that she hated being a single mother, though the thought of remarriage was enough to make her shudder. Her ex had cured her of ever trusting in the idea of marital bliss, and whenever she thought being alone and raising a kid was tough, she remembered being married and feeling as if she was mother to her husband, too.

No, she'd deal with her kid by herself, and aside from the fact that finances were tight, she could handle it. She knew people who married, divorced, got along and shared parental responsibilities. Her friend Callie's husband was involved with his kids, even paid more than what the court ordered and his new wife was incredible with Callie's sons.

Trilby hadn't gotten so lucky, and on days like this, when she hadn't gotten much sleep the night before and a damned blizzard was sweeping across the country, she felt stretched to the max.

It was only the thought of overtime that kept her going.

She turned the wipers up a notch, noticed that ice was starting to form on the windshield and that the police band was going nuts with calls about traffic accidents, power outages and a possible drowning in September Creek where someone had fallen through the ice.

"Damn," she said under her breath and realized it was going to be another long day. She'd get this kid to Helena and . . .

She saw something in her headlights. Something in the road. "What in God's name?" A large van had slid halfway into the ditch on the side of the road. Its emergency lights were flashing, the front end still sideways in the road, its engine rumbling as it idled.

"Great." Slowing, she flipped on her own lights, radioed her position and, when the Jeep came to a stop, climbed out of the car.

"Hey," she said as she saw a guy in front of the van, caught in the twin beams of his headlights, snow falling all around, collecting on his jacket and cap. He was bending down, on one knee, and there was an animal in front of him, an animal that wasn't moving. "Sir, is there a problem?"

"It's the dog. He just came out of nowhere. Shot across the road and . . . I hit the brakes, but . . ." His voice cracked as he looked over his shoulder at her. "I skidded, but I couldn't avoid him . . . I think it's still alive. Oh, God."

"Let's see," she said, moving for a better look at the motionless dog. Was it even breathing? And where was the blood? Wait—

She knew her mistake the minute she leaned forward.

He swung around quickly, a stun gun in the hand that had been hidden from her. *Damn!* Before she could draw her weapon, or fight back, he pressed the electrodes to her neck and squeezed the trigger.

A hundred thousand volts shot through her system.

In a heartbeat, she lost all control and flopped into the snow beside the dog only to watch helplessly as he packed her and the animal into the back of his van. He cuffed her to the sides of his rig and left the dog on the floor, then he took her keys off her ring, her phone from her pocket, her walkie microphone off her uniform and slammed the door shut.

Trilby could do nothing but twitch.

"How about I meet you somewhere for dinner, say in half an hour or so?" O'Keefe suggested from his end of the wireless connection. "I was just at the town house; still no electricity."

Alvarez glanced at the clock on her computer. It was late, close to seven thirty; she'd been working most of the day. "If we wanted to start a fire," she said, stretching, "we could start the fire in the fireplace, it's gas. There must be a way to do it without the electric starter and somehow not cause an explosion."

"You'd think."

"And I have candles for light."

"But no food in the house, last I checked."

"Good point."

"After dinner we can decide what we're going to do. Why don't we meet at the Grizzly Hotel; they're open and they're serving dinner. I know because Dave and Aggie stayed there earlier."

"They left?" she asked, thinking of Gabe and feeling a stupid new tug on her heart.

"Tried to beat the storm. They want to see their

other kids, then meet Gabe when he gets to Helena. According to Aggie, Leo's been taking care of Josie while they've been here and that makes them nervous. He's eighteen and a good kid, but that can change without supervision. When they call, Josie makes a lot of noise about seeing Gabe. She misses him and wants to see him."

So do I, Alvarez thought, but didn't say it. Legally, she wasn't Gabe's mother, she had no rights and she understood that she'd given them up long ago, but she couldn't stop the pain in her heart at the thought of the son she would probably never see again.

A little saddened, she leaned back in her desk chair. It had been a long, frustrating day in so many ways, from the moment she'd heard about Brenda Sutherland to now, even with all the new footage and pictures pointing out the killer, this man she felt like she should be able to ID and couldn't.

Her muscles ached, she was tired, the kid she'd reconnected with was leaving and the madman intent on terrorizing the area was taunting her, sending her cards, laughing at her, begging her to find him.

She should just stay here and work through the dinner hour, but she did need a break and the thought of spending a little time with O'Keefe was oh so appealing. Maybe just what she needed.

She glanced at her computer screen again, at a

still picture, a moment caught on the tape of him rolling the garbage can holding Brenda Sutherland. He'd looked up. Directly into the camera, his dark goggles nearly reflective. It was the cleanest shot they had of him, the one that had been given to the press and the public, but it could be any man in a ski mask, goggles and cap.

She was tired of staring at the image, of being taunted by the bastard.

Yeah, she needed a break. And she wanted to see O'Keefe. More than she admitted to herself. "So," she said into the phone as she turned away from the computer monitor. "You're sticking around for a while?" she asked.

"At least tonight."

"And after that?"

"Depends on the storm."

"Oh." It was strange how disappointed she felt at the thought of his leaving.

"And it also depends upon a woman."

Her breath caught in her throat. "Really?"

"Yeah, you see, I like her. A lot; but I'm not sure where I stand with her."

Alvarez felt the room shrink, and all at once she remembered how it felt to touch him and kiss him and wake up to him in the morning. How they laughed, how he'd come to her rescue when Junior Green wanted her dead, how he'd accepted what she'd told him about Emilio and Gabe . . . how right it felt to be with him. Suddenly, her throat grew thick and she felt heat steal up the back of her neck. "Maybe you should just tell her how you feel," she suggested.

"She might run the other way."

"And she might not." Dear God, she couldn't believe they were having this conversation while she was still at the station, the door to her office open. "Maybe you should have a little faith. She might be a strong woman and it could be she feels the same way about you."

"She's run away before."

"But she's older now, right? More mature. Dealt with some of her demons?" Alvarez found herself smiling while blinking back tears. This was ridiculous . . . She was overly tired, that was it. Right?

Or, was it possible to fall in love this fast?

Take it slow. There's so much going on. You're on the edge. Frazzled. Another serial killer's on the loose and you just met your son that you gave up for adoption years ago. You're fragile. Don't rush this. Despite the voice of reason arguing in her head, she said into her phone, "I really think you should give her a chance, O'Keefe. She just might surprise you."

"Okay, *one* more," he said. "See you in forty-five."

"You got it."

She hung up and told herself everyone was right; she did need more of a life than working eighty hours a week. Yes, her pets had helped, but she was finally open to the thought of a family, and that, she knew, started with O'Keefe.

She spent the next half hour finishing a few loose ends, then actually spent a few minutes in the restroom, combing her hair and adding lip gloss. Her reflection appeared tired, worn out; no amount of makeup could hide the dark smudges under her eyes or mask the lines of strain at the edge of her mouth.

"Too bad," she told herself and wound her scarf tight around her neck before she told Pescoli—her non-partner on this case—that she'd be back in a couple of hours.

"You don't have to work round the clock," Pescoli said from her station, where a half-eaten tuna salad sandwich sat on a napkin and stunk up her work area.

"Neither do you, but you're still here."

"I just want to nail this sucker's ass."

"You and me both. I'll see ya later." She walked outside to a night that was brutally cold, then dashed to her Subaru, which ran despite a bullet hole or two.

Inside she switched on the engine, turned the heater on high and pulled out of the lot. God, it was cold. As the heater finally started blowing warm air, she drove to the road that wound down Boxer Bluff. Once she was down the hill and across the railroad tracks, she followed a slow-moving van to the road overlooking the river, only a few blocks from the courthouse and less than five from where Brenda Sutherland's body had been found early this morning.

The roads were no longer blocked, but traffic was light, thankfully, since the storm was still blowing snow through the rustic streets of this, the old section of town.

She pulled into the hotel's small parking lot and noted that several cars were buried in snow, nearly a foot covering their roofs and hoods. The space she chose had been shoveled and it was close to the front door. Erected at the turn of the last century, the clapboard building was four stories and built with a western facade and wide, wraparound porch. Clear lights had been strung along the roofline and a huge Christmas tree guarded the front door. Through each window, chandeliers were giving off a warm, inviting light.

As she cut the engine, her cell phone buzzed, indicating she was receiving a text, and though she thought about ignoring it as this was her personal time, she couldn't. O'Keefe might be sending her a message, or there could be a break in the case, or . . .

She touched the screen and froze as a picture appeared. A picture of Gabriel Reeve. But, no . . . it wasn't just a picture, it was a small recording. She pressed the play button and he became animated.

"You have to help me," he said as her heart nearly stopped. "You have to do what he says . . ." He glanced to the side and there was a whisper, a man's chilling lowered voice. "Tell her to drive to Cougar Pass. No cops. Just show up. If she doesn't, you'll be dead."

Gabriel, ashen-faced, eyes round and scared to death, repeated the message. "You have to come to Cougar Pass. Please. He says he'll kill me." His voice broke and again the man said, "Tell her 'no cops.' If she has any kind of backup, you're dead. You got that?"

"D-Don't tell . . ." Gabe repeated, looking panicked, and Alvarez saw a movement behind him, a shadow. Her heart froze as she recognized the sharp blade of a knife poised right above her son's left ear. And . . . oh, God, it had blood on it. The sharp blade glinted silver and dripped red. Oh, sweet Jesus.

Was he going to slit Gabe's throat right now? *No! Don't!*

Panicked, fear gripping her heart in its deadly talons, she cried out, "Stop! Don't hurt him! For the love of God!" But, of course, neither Gabe nor his abductor could hear her desperate pleas. Gabe, too, was frantic, scared out of his mind. "No cops!" he ordered, repeating what he'd been told. "Mom, he says, 'no cops,' or . . . or . . . he's gonna kill me!"

CHAPTER 32

"Thanks," O'Keefe said, accepting his glass of Scotch from a waitress whose name tag read Tiffany and who looked too young to be serving alcohol. The room was crowded, conversation humming around him, a fire in an ancient grate burning, the interior of the hotel warm and glowing with lights in the cold, winter night. "Just leave the wine there." He pointed to a spot across the small table from him. "She'll be here any minute."

"Sure." Deftly Tiffany placed the glass of merlot where he'd indicated and then hurried off through the crowded restaurant of the hotel. Everyone, it seemed, who could get out had come up with the same idea that O'Keefe had, and he'd been lucky to get a reservation for a window table. He'd hoped for a view of the river and the falls, which were starting to freeze, but he'd taken the spot overlooking the parking lot and was just glad that she'd be showing up soon. Ever since she'd told him about the pointed card she'd received from the killer, he'd been more nervous than ever, didn't want to think of her as the target she surely was.

So the hours spent apart from her had been

difficult and all of his platitudes to himself about how she could take care of herself, trust her cop instincts, or handle any perp just didn't cut it, not when he considered the sadistic determination of this psycho.

Swirling his drink, causing the ice cubes to dance, he told himself that he was going to quit fighting his feelings. He loved the woman—be that bad or good, smart or stupid. He couldn't imagine living his life apart from her and he sure as hell wasn't going to let some sick son of a bitch mess with her life.

He took a sip from his glass, tasted the smoky flavor of Scotch on his tongue and told himself to relax when he saw her car wheel into the lot to cruise into the last parking spot.

Good.

He could relax now. His heart filled a bit at the sight of her and he waited, watching her fiddle with something . . . Her phone? She didn't make a call or take one before he realized she'd received a text message. Taking another sip, he watched her through the curtain of snow. She tossed down the phone, started the engine and, as quickly as she'd cruised into the lot, she backed up and took off, snow spraying from her tires as she barely paused as she entered the street.

The case!

There had to be a break in the ice-mummy case.

He found his phone and dialed, hoping she'd

pick up. She had a hands-free device, so he expected that she would answer and give him a short explanation.

Nothing.

Four rings and then voice mail.

Not good.

Rather than wait, he found his wallet, tossed several bills onto the table and strode out of the restaurant, nearly knocking over a busboy with a load of dishes, and cutting around an elderly woman with a walker. "Excuse me," he said, though he didn't mean it as he shouldered through the doors and around a middle-aged couple who were just entering.

Down the steps he flew, and onto the street where his Explorer was parked. After jumping inside, he started the engine and threw the Ford into gear. Within seconds he was following the road Alvarez had taken, flipping on his wipers and cranking up the defrost as well as calling her again on her cell.

No response.

It's all right. She's a cop. They have emergencies.

He didn't believe it for a second. Not when the creep had called her out on that freaky Christmas card. The message, "All I Want for Christmas," was crystal clear.

Again his call went straight to voice mail. "Hell!" He flipped on his wipers, searching, looking for her car and not seeing it. "Come on, come on."

Relax. She'll call you . . . It's the case . . .

But he couldn't stop the tightening in his chest and the feeling of dread stealing over him as he paused at a red light, searching the snowy streets, looking for any trace of her car.

But she was gone.

Not a trace of her little Outback anywhere.

A snow plow was scraping the street near the railroad tracks and a small SUV was climbing the hill, heading toward the newer section of town, but Alvarez's vehicle had disappeared.

Damn it all to hell!

He tried to calm himself.

It's going to be all right. She's fine.

But he didn't believe it for an instant.

"Desperate times call for desperate measures," he told himself and pulled out his phone once more.

Alvarez's heart was beating faster than that of a frightened hummingbird. She knew she was making a mistake and walking full on into a trap. She would have advised anyone in the same situation to call the police or the FBI, any agency equipped to handle a situation like this, but she couldn't make the call. This was Gabe, her son, and she didn't doubt for a second that if she screwed up, the monster who held him would take his life. Probably on camera and send it not only to Alvarez, but the media as well.

"Sick freak." Driving faster than she should have, she weighed the options. What were the chances of saving Gabe on her own? With the help of all the police resources?

She slid around a corner and tried to get a grip, forcing her racing heart to slow.

It all came down to Preacher Mullins's Presbyterian church, Pescoli decided as she stared at the legal pad on which she'd made notes. There were printouts spread all over her desk area, and her computer was still cross-referencing every bit of information they had on the victims. But she liked to write. To doodle. To think rather than allow a machine to do all the work for her.

So, she'd come back to the church. Again. She'd thought it might be the key before, as the Presbyterian church was the one connecting link to most of the victims. Lara Sue Gilfry had been to that particular church a couple of times and, in death, encased in ice, had been placed in the nativity scene at the Presbyterian church. Though there were other crèches in the area, six in all, five at different churches and the sixth in the front of the parochial school, for some reason, the freak had chosen Preacher Mullins's private crèche to display his first victim.

Why?

Originally, Pescoli had thought it was because of the location or the size of the figures, but now she wasn't so certain. The killer had pinpointed that crèche for a reason.

Then there was victim number two. Lissa Parsons. She, too, had been a parishioner at Mullins's church, though her attendance had been spotty of late.

Brenda Sutherland, also, had been active in the parish, had even been there for a meeting on the night she was abducted.

Yep, all three connected directly in one way or another to Mullins's parish.

The fourth woman who had gone missing, Johnna Phillips, had never been a member at Mullins's church, but her ex-boyfriend Carl's aunt attended . . . That was a stretch, but at least some connection, and so far, they weren't certain Johnna was a victim or potential victim of the killer.

So how does Alvarez fit into this? "There's the rub," Pescoli said aloud.

Alvarez, by her own admission, had been raised Catholic in some tiny spot in Oregon and hadn't, to Pescoli's knowledge, attended any church since leaving home. Her baby had been adopted out through the help of the Catholic church and then, sixteen years ago, as far as Pescoli could tell, Selena Alvarez's relationship with God had either ended or become personal to the level that she never attended church, not even on Christmas or Easter.

She was the one piece of this particular puzzle that didn't fit. Closing her eyes, she leaned back in her chair. "How does she know you?" she whispered, as if the lunatic were standing in the room with her rather than holed up in his damned lair somewhere not far from Grizzly Falls.

As she walked into the task force room, she called Alvarez, wanted her to think about any connection she might have to the church or someone within the church. It was a long shot, but . . .

As soon as the call connected, it went straight to voice mail, so Pescoli left a voice message and then wrote a quick text, which, because of her children, she'd learn to do rapidly, without really thinking. Then she hit send and stood in front of the large map of the county, eyeing the different-colored pins representing different areas of this part of the state. Though terrain wasn't included on the political map, she knew where the mountains rose, the cliffs fell and the forests covered the ground.

So many places to hide.

But the victims had all been found within two miles from the heart of the city. He had to be close by. Someone who knew Alvarez . . . She'd checked out the people Alvarez had dated. Kevin Miller, Grover Pankretz, Terry Longstrom and now Dylan O'Keefe. Aside from O'Keefe, there was no history of violence and Alvarez didn't know any of the ice sculptors who'd shown up for that festival . . .

She looked at the pictures of the suspect, blown up and pinned to the same wall where the victims were pictured, their personal information noted. How were they connected?

Johnna Phillips's photograph had been included, though the question mark beside her name hadn't been erased.

In a dark moment, she imagined she saw Alvarez's name on the wall, a picture of her posted as one of the Ice Mummy Killer's victims, and in that briefest of seconds, Regan Pescoli's blood ran cold as ice.

This was nuts!

Gabe couldn't believe what was going on.

Freezing in the back of the dark pickup, handcuffed to the sides, he and the cop lady were captive of some sick prick. He knew who the freak was. The jerk who had tricked them was the frickin' Ice Mummy Killer and he was going to kill them both. And the dog, too. It was alive, drugged maybe, and the deputy, she was alive, too, but bound and gagged, and when she'd tried to go for her gun, he'd stabbed her; the freakin' madman had plunged the knife deep into her side and then taunted both of them with it. She was losing a lot of blood, moaning and out of it. The dog, too, just lay in the cold back of the pickup's bed, a canopy over them.

The bastard had made Gabe record the video sent to Alvarez and he'd wangled the knife he'd used to slice the deputy at him to keep him in line.

Scared to death, huddled in the back of the damned pickup, Gabe wished he'd never left home, never gotten involved with Lizard and his stupid friends. Jesus, God, this was a mess. All those times he'd been mad at his mom, or his little sister had bugged him, or he'd been pissed at Leo for being so damned perfect taunted him now, rolled around in his head, and he wished he could take every one of them back. Even finding his "real" mom because he was mad at Aggie and Dave. How dumb was that?

His wrists were chafed raw from him pulling and straining against the handcuffs and his fingers and toes felt numb from the cold. While the prick had kept the truck idling here in the woods, keeping himself warm in the cab, the rest of them were freezing. Gabe's nose was numb, his teeth chattering uncontrollably, though he thought that might be more from fear than the elements.

This freak was going to kill them. All of them. Gabe had seen it in his dead eyes how he wanted to dispose of them all. The deputy and dog, half dead already, and Gabe, yeah, the guy would love to slice his throat. As for Selena Alvarez, the cop, Gabe wanted to believe in her, to trust that she was smarter and stronger and would be able to kick the bastard's ass, but the truth of it was that she, too, was going to die.

And the prick who held them, he was going to love killing her.

With Alvarez at the wheel, her little car sped up the road that cut through this section of forest where huge spruce and pine trees towered over the mountain sides, reaching upward to the darkened evening sky. Far below, hidden by the night, Cougar Creek, a jagged rush of spring-fed water, had, no doubt, frozen over and was silenced for the winter. Aside from the grind of the Outback's engine, the forest was silent, deafeningly so. Here the snow was thick, recent tracks from one other vehicle cutting through the powder.

She wasn't alone.

He was here.

The maniac who had kidnapped Gabe, no doubt the psycho the press had dubbed the Ice Mummy Killer, he was hiding in these thick woods. Did he have Gabe with him? And what about Trilby Van Droz, the deputy who had been charged with driving Gabe to Helena? The killer wouldn't have let her go . . . No, there had to have been some kind of confrontation.

Trilby's dead. He wouldn't have let her survive. He couldn't. No, he would dispose of her.

A bit of bile rose up her throat, but she kept driving and held on to the fact that someone in the department would be missing Trilby. When she didn't show up with Gabe, someone would start looking for her . . . a lot of someones in the department and with the FBI and—

Too late. Yes, they will realize that something's gone terribly wrong, but it will be too late.

The same with O'Keefe. He would be wondering what had happened to her when she didn't show up for dinner. Had been calling her. But he wouldn't know how to find her.

No, she was on her own.

Alvarez felt the weight of the pistol in her shoulder holster. Her sidearm had always given her comfort, even strength, but tonight it seemed a dead weight. She didn't doubt that she'd be stripped of it immediately.

She had a backup weapon though and she felt the pressure of a knife she'd slipped into the side of her boot. It was awkward, and probably anticipated, but it was more than nothing; she might be able to use it to gain time or some kind of an edge.

Other than those two weapons, she had nothing but her brains and instinct to save herself and her son.

God help me, she thought, though long ago she'd lost her faith in a higher being. Today, though, she second-guessed herself as she hit the gas, speeding through the forest, her tires spinning at times, not gaining traction, the engine of her Outback straining.

This old mining road hadn't been plowed, but because of the canopy of trees overhead, cutting the density of the snowfall, and her car's ability to drive in all conditions, she was able to reach the summit.

Jaw tight, she stared through the windshield, her heart pounding, the wipers slapping at the snow as she finally crested the hill at Cougar Pass.

You should call. Now, for backup. Let the department know your latest position. You can't take him on alone.

She reached for the phone, then let it drop. She couldn't take a chance on Gabe's life.

And what chance does he have with just you?

"Van Droz didn't make it to Helena." Dan Grayson walked into Pescoli's office with the bad news.

"What?"

"She's missing. Along with the kid. Her vehicle was discovered on the highway about halfway there, lights flashing, still idling, but she's MIA."

"I don't understand."

"Neither do I, but I'm heading out there. Got the place cordoned off. Kayan and Watershed are already on the scene."

"She's an experienced driver," Pescoli said,

thinking aloud. "Even if she slid off the road, why wouldn't she call in?"

"Exactly." His gaze collided with hers and she saw the worry in his eyes, the muscle working near his temple.

"You think there's foul play?"

"Don't know." His lips became thin as razors. "But I aim to find out."

"I'll drive up there."

"Somebody better call Alvarez, since she's involved in this. Helena PD is already hunting down the parents."

"I've already left her a message and a text, neither of which she answered," Pescoli said, "but I'll get hold of her."

"I'm on my way to the scene now," he said, whistling to his dog. "I don't like this. At all."

"Neither do I." She grabbed her sidearm and was reaching for her jacket when her phone jangled. She didn't recognize the number on caller ID and it didn't identify who was on the other end of the phone. She nearly didn't answer because there was a chance that her ex had passed out her private cell number again.

"Pescoli," she answered, reminding herself that it had turned out to be a good thing that Carl Anderson had called and alerted the department to the fact that Johnna Phillips had gone missing.

"Dylan O'Keefe. I'm looking for Detective Alvarez."

"I thought she was with you. She left the station, what?" Pescoli glanced at the clock. "Twenty, maybe thirty minutes ago."

"That fits," he said, then told her about spying Alvarez drive into the lot and out. "I thought maybe she got called away, but I can't get hold of her. She's not answering her phone."

"I know," Pescoli said and the worry that had been with her intensified. "Did you try the house?"

"There's no electricity there; at least, there wasn't earlier and I can't get hold of the maintenance guy that Alvarez uses, don't know his number, not that it would help. The complex is out."

Something clicked in Pescoli's brain. "Her maintenance guy? You remember his name?"

"Jon something . . . I think."

That was right. She'd mentioned him to Pescoli before. "Jon Oestergard?"

"I don't think I ever heard his last name."

But Pescoli had.

"I'll call you if I hear from her," she said, then hung up.

She fell into her desk chair and clicked through some pages until she found the file of parishioners for the Presbyterian church. There, right in the middle of the telephone and prayer directory, were Jon and Dorie Oestergard.

And there was a note that Jon was the builder

of the new church . . . This couldn't be . . . Or could it? She pulled up Oestergard's driver's license and searched for other pictures of him, all of which showed him wearing shaded glasses.

Could it be?

She did a quick history, looking for priors, and in recent years he'd kept his nose clean, but there was an incident, years ago, a woman who'd been caring for him, an aunt, who had died from knife wounds, the result of an attack by "a group of men in ski masks," according to her young charge . . . Jon Oestergard, who had sustained his share of injuries at the time.

Could he have been so traumatized from the event to have turned into a killer?

Or could he have killed his aunt himself and no one believed a fourteen-year-old boy capable of such a hideous crime? A crime that had cost him part of the vision in his right eye. "God all mighty," she whispered. The man was married. No children. Had worked different jobs and inherited a farm, learned to build from his grandfather, or so she gleaned from a few articles about him that had been written as the builder for the new church was being decided upon.

Was it possible? Was Jon Oestergard the damned Ice Mummy Killer?

CHAPTER 33

The pickup was idling, its headlights beacons in the night.

A white Dodge with a camper, poised at the highest part of the road. The hills rose above this point, but here the road was a snow-covered S curve that wound down the back side of the mountain.

Standing in front of the truck, Gabriel Reeve, shackled and handcuffed, was visibly shaking, and at his feet was a lump of fur . . . oh, Jesus, her dog!

Bait!

This was worse than she thought.

She had the phone in her lap, and without looking down, texted Pescoli:

With killer @ Cougar Pass. Help!

It was too late, of course.

She hit the send button and mute button, then dialed Pescoli and slid the phone into her pocket and calmly said, hoping her mouth didn't move too much, just in case she was being watched through some kind of mega night scope, "I'm at Cougar Pass, on the old mining road. Trying to get Gabriel Reeve. Send backup. ASAP!"

Her car rolled to a stop.

"Throw your weapon out of the car," a voice boomed and she visibly started.

He was watching!

Gabriel, shackled in knee-deep snow, started to run toward her.

Craaack!

The report of a rifle echoed across the canyon.

Gabriel tumbled forward.

"Oh, God, no!" Alvarez yanked her gun from her holster, opened the door of her Outback and, weapon drawn, certain she would find blood blooming across her son's chest, did everything she shouldn't. With no idea where the assailant was, she flung herself through the falling snow and across the few feet to her boy.

"Come on," she said when she reached him. "Are you hit?"

"No!" He was already moving with her, awkwardly stumbling toward the Outback, when another shot was fired.

The back window of her car blew out and she threw them both to the ground again.

Where the hell was the sniper?

Higher on the hill, above the road, looking down on them. If so, they were sitting ducks.

"Crawl to the car," she whispered, frantically. She thought the sniper was above them on the hillside, but the back window had blown in, so she thought he might be behind them.

He's playing with you.

This is a game. Sport.

He probably has night vision goggles and God knows what else in his arsenal.

"Get under the car," she ordered. "Use it for cover!"

"Don't leave." Gabe was frantic with fear.

"Just get under the car!"

She was already moving around the Subaru, hoping to draw fire away from her son, at the very least, to split the sniper's attention.

"I will kill the boy!" the voice boomed. It sounded familiar. And determined. "Drop your weapon!"

"Show yourself, you coward," she said, holding tight to her pistol.

"I will kill the boy!" To prove his point, another round was fired, the rifle cracking so loudly it echoed. Another window in her car blew out, glass raining into the snow. The passenger-side window was demolished.

Gabe let out a frightened squeal.

She yelled, "Stay down, Gabe!"

If she could get him into her car, they had a chance, could outrun the guy down the hill. She'd throw the Subaru into reverse and back down the road to the wide spot she'd noticed on her way up, turn around and they might just make it.

Blam!

This time she pinpointed the shot. At least audibly.

The assailant was definitely up the hill, where

the ground crested above the road. He was probably hiding behind one of the huge trees for protection, then taking his time picking them off.

Blam!

Another shot.

Gabe covered his head.

A back tire of the Subaru deflated and Gabe, half under the vehicle, squirmed out from under it.

"No!"

Crap! Now her chances of the Outback being the getaway vehicle had plummeted. This was getting them nowhere fast. She had to do something. They were sitting ducks!

Pescoli got the message.

She'd just reached her Jeep and slid behind the wheel when the text came in.

"What?" she whispered and started to call Alvarez when a call came in.

"Hello?" she yelled into the phone. "What the hell's going on? I just got a text that—" Her voice faded as she heard Alvarez's voice.

"I'm at Cougar Pass, on the old mining road. Trying to get Gabriel Reeve. Send backup. ASAP!" And then the hollow, terrifying sound of a shot being fired.

"Shit!" She clicked over to another line, dialed 911, and when the operator picked up, identified herself, all the while wheeling out of the lot.

". . . I said, I'm Detective Regan Pescoli and

my partner's under fire. At Cougar Pass, off of Leland Road, I think. She's requesting backup. I'm on my way, but we need more units. Make sure the FBI knows. We might need a helicopter and I don't want to hear about the snow storm. Got it?"

"Yes, but—"

"Also," she barreled on, "I need someone to do a background check and try to locate Jonathan Oestergard. He lives out of town, the old Oestergard place on Eve's Road, that's right, E-V-E-S!"

She didn't wait for a response, just clicked back, and as she turned on her lights and siren, heard more shots being fired some fifteen miles away.

By the time she got there and backup arrived, it would be all over!

"God damn it, Alvarez," she muttered. "This isn't the time to go all superhero!" Why hadn't she informed Pescoli of her plans? How the hell had she ended up alone and under siege?

Because of the boy, her son.

That was it. Ever since she found out about Gabriel Reeve, all of Alvarez's cold, hard cop sense had eroded. The by-the-book cop was now dealing with emotion. And right now that emotion was pure, raw fear.

"Damn it all to hell!" Pescoli slammed a fist against the steering wheel and, siren screaming, ran a series of red lights as she headed for the foothills.

It would take her twenty minutes to get to Cougar Pass, and that was if she was lucky. Probably more like thirty, considering the snow.

This was all messed up.

All messed up.

And she was pretty damned sure she was too late to fix it.

"Stay down!" Alvarez ordered at her son.

Drawing fire on herself, she ran, hunched over, plowing through the snow, toward the idling truck. As she crouched, she fired her pistol, shooting wildly toward the area where she thought the guy was hiding, hoping to force him to take cover and pin him down for just a few precious seconds.

She was halfway to the truck when she spied her dog.

Lying motionless in the snow because the maniac had killed him.

You sick bastard, she thought, and as she ran past him, the poor animal let out a whimper.

Alive? Roscoe was alive?

Oh, hell. Without thinking, she scooped up the dog and threw herself across the remaining distance toward the idling truck.

The dog cried, and in that second, bullets rained around her.

As if he'd realized his mistake, the killer started firing in rapid succession.

Blam! Blam! Blam!

Rifle shots echoed down the canyon; snow shook from the trees. She could only hope that the damned fool would start an avalanche that would swallow him whole and crush him with the weight of thousands of tons of frozen white powder. Would serve the prick right.

No such luck.

The mountain remained stable.

Heart beating frantically, nerves stretched to the breaking point, she climbed into the truck on the driver's side, away from the upper hill. She got behind the wheel and threw it into gear.

Head ducked, she hit the gas. The big rig lurched forward, down the hill. All she had to do was reach the Subaru, get Gabe inside and then take off down the hill, leaving the creep with only her disabled Outback.

Craaack!

A bullet hit the driver's door.

She jumped but kept her foot on the gas, the truck moving. Her head barely above the dash, she angled the moving car next to her Subaru. What were the chances she could pull this off? How had he been so foolish as to leave the keys in the ignition, the car running?

Theirs not to reason why . . . theirs but to do or die . . . Something she'd learned long ago in school rolled through her brain.

Reaching the Subaru, she hit the brakes and

reached across the cab, opening the passenger side, and yelled, "Gabe, get in! Gabe!"

The boy, hiding behind the Outback, stood up and started running awkwardly toward the car.

"Stay down!" she screamed and the rifle fired again, closer this time.

Blam!

Gabe's body jerked.

He pitched forward.

As Alvarez watched in horror, he toppled face down into the snow and a red stain oozed through his thin jacket.

"No!" she screamed and flung herself from behind the wheel.

As she reached her boy, throwing herself on the frozen ground, she heard the resonant sound of a huge gun firing again.

So close!

Pain, blistering and hot tore down her side.

Blackness swept over her.

She swung around, her own gun firing wildly, seeing the dark figure from the corner of her eye. Trying to aim, she focused on him and squeezed the trigger again just as she felt the cold electrodes of the stun gun against her neck.

Panicked, she fired.

Die, you freak. Die! Die! Die!

O'Keefe punched it.

Snow flew from beneath his tires.

The engine of his Explorer ground but he managed to keep the wheels churning up the steep road in the foothills over Cougar Creek, his wipers working overtime against the snowstorm. "Come on, come on." He was sweating, fear driving him, his heart a drum. If that bastard had laid a finger on Alvarez, he'd personally slit the son of a bitch's throat.

Staring at the map on his smartphone, he followed the signal of the GPS device he'd stuck under the quarter panel of Alvarez's Outback. He saw that she'd driven to a remote area of the foothills, and decided he had to call Pescoli back.

When he'd first called Selena's partner, he hadn't admitted to placing the device on the Subaru, hadn't thought he had to activate it. He'd figured she was on police business or doing something privately, and wasn't about to rat her out. After all, the sheriff had taken her off the ice-mummy case.

But he'd made a mistake and now was mentally kicking himself.

The tracking system on his phone indicated that the car had stopped and he had the coordinates.

Pescoli answered curtly.

"It's O'Keefe. Alvarez is on Cougar Point Road, about fifteen miles out of town." He gave her the coordinates.

"So what makes you think so?" Pescoli asked, obviously irritated.

"I'm tracking her."

"You put a bug on her?"

"On her car. Yeah." He thought about explaining that he'd been worried she'd do something foolish and go off half-cocked, but held his tongue.

"So why didn't you tell me this earlier?" Pescoli demanded, practically seething. "Why did you call me earlier and ask me where she was?"

"I didn't want to overstep," he started to explain. "I wasn't sure." It sounded lame. It *was* lame.

"But you put an effin' bug in her Outback. I'd say that was overstepping. Wouldn't you? Damn!" She said something else he couldn't hear over the noise of his engine and the wind howling as it roared across this part of Montana. "Look, I'm on my way. I've called for backup."

"You *knew?*"

"Just figured it out."

"I'm almost there."

"What? NO! STAND DOWN, O'KEEFE! Jesus H. Christ, I've got the FBI and the whole damned department. We're already on this, so stand the hell down!"

He clicked off and muttered, "Yeah, right." He only hoped they were somehow on this, ahead of the game, but he didn't believe it, not for a second. And no one, not Regan Pescoli, Sheriff Dan Grayson or any agent from the freakin' FBI, was going to stop him.

Stepping on the gas, he drove ever upward,

following the ruts leading through this desolate part of the mountains and hoping beyond hope that he was wrong, that Alvarez was fine, that he'd find her safe and sound.

Even though he knew he was only lying to himself.

The beams of his headlights were weak against the ever-falling snow; his nerves were stretched to the breaking point, and he was filled with an overriding fear that he was already too late, that whatever danger Alvarez had placed herself in, it wasn't going well.

He figured whatever standoff he was about to face, it involved the damned Ice Mummy Killer.

But why would she track him down alone?

Why wouldn't she have the whole damned department with her? She'd driven off on her own; he'd seen that, watched her check her phone and then, after receiving a call or a text or something, she'd taken off like a shot.

Somehow she'd been lured away. Somehow . . .

His phone jangled and he picked up before it rang twice. "O'Keefe," he said, eyes trained on the snowy landscape, the quiet mountains.

"Oh, God, Dylan," a woman wailed. "He's gone again!"

"What?"

"There was an accident or something, they won't tell us much, but Gabe . . . he's missing." Finally he realized that his cousin was on the line. "He . . . he's gone and the woman cop, too."

Woman cop?

Alvarez!

His heart sank.

"Aggie? What the hell are you talking about?" O'Keefe demanded; he could hardly understand her as she dissolved into broken sobs and hiccups. "Aggie!"

A second later Dave's voice, sober but strong, explained. "There was some kind of an accident; we don't have all the details. But Gabe never made it to Helena. Both he and the driver of the car, a deputy with the department, are missing."

Not Alvarez? He felt a modicum of short-lived relief. Gabe was still missing. "Wait a second! Missing *how?* What the hell are you talking about? I thought he was back in Helena."

"That's what I'm trying to say. He never made it."

As Aggie sobbed in the background and Dave explained everything that they'd been told, O'Keefe listened, one hand holding the steering wheel in a death grip, his mind filling in the blanks in Dave's story. As the miles rolled under the wheels of his Ford, he got it, putting together the missing puzzle pieces.

"I'll do what I can," he promised Gabe's distraught father, and as he hung up, he understood what had happened. The reason Alvarez had torn out of the parking lot at the hotel an hour earlier was because she'd gotten word about her son.

O'Keefe's jaw tightened over the wheel. It didn't take a master detective to realize that the "accident" had been staged, why the people in the Jeep had gone missing. Because somehow the Ice Mummy Killer was involved. Had to be. No other explanation that he could come up with made any sense.

That's why Alvarez got the call, why she left without saying a word, because Gabriel was being used to lure her away.

The killer wasn't content with just teasing her with stupid little Christmas cards any longer.

All I want for Christmas is you . . .

And now the maniac had her.

CHAPTER 34

Pain pounded through her brain and she was cold . . . so damned cold . . . shivering, teeth chattering, the darkness threatening to drag her under again.

She had blacked out, remembered nothing but snow and blood and . . . Gabe!

Forcing one eye open, Alvarez found herself in a cave of sorts, lying in a trough, unable to move because of the icy water sluicing around her.

Oh, sweet Jesus!

Had she been out for hours? Or minutes? *Or days?*

She didn't know, but enough time had passed for him to drag her here, strip her and lay her in this water bath.

Her leg and arm spasmed.

The stun gun.

He'd subdued her with it and, as she was still reacting, it couldn't have been that long ago . . . right?

But she was groggy . . . She heard the sounds of soft sobbing from somewhere nearby and then the notes of a Christmas carol drifting through her brain as she tried to pass out again.

I heard the bells on Christmas day . . .

She blinked and suddenly everything changed, a shadow loomed over her and, as her eyes came into focus, she saw him, the Ice Mummy Killer.

"Hello, Selena," he said, his eyes glowing with a triumphant fire.

Jon Oestergard? Her handyman? The farmer? A married man who . . . ?

"And you thought you could outsmart me," he said, again in that monotone she found so irritating. "Tsk-tsk." He smiled that self-abashing smile she'd noticed before. What the hell had she ever done to him?

What did it matter?

She was drifting again, floating back to the

darkness, the comfort and safety of unconscious-ness, where she wouldn't feel the cold, wouldn't think about . . .

Gabe! Where was he?

Forcing her eyes open, she tried to look around, past the dark-coved, rock ceilings of this cave to the room . . . this huge room with a work-bench and hanging lights and . . . If she could only look around!

"So you are awake! Good." He wasn't smiling now; instead, he was looking down at her through his darkened glasses.

"Where's Gabe?" she forced out, trying to yell, though her voice was a whisper.

"The boy? Oh, don't worry about him." He was actually humming to the music now, almost in a dream world.

"Where is he?" she spat.

"I left him there, of course. With your stupid dog . . . Give them lots to think about." His smile turned nasty. "So we won't be disturbed."

"Why are you doing this? Why, Jon?"

"Oh, now I'm Jon. Do you know that you never called me by my name?"

"What?"

"And when I helped you in the grocery store, you acted as if I didn't exist."

"What grocery store . . . What are you talking about?" she said, though her words were breathy, in a rush, almost garbled.

He sluiced more water over her and her body twitched. So much for thinking he'd calmed his victims with a drug to keep them from feeling pain. This guy got off on pain, on being superior, on being in control.

Don't give him the power. Don't ask the questions he's anticipating. Don't show him any fear.

"What does your wife think about this?" she threw out and he visibly reacted. That's when she saw the blood. A trickle running down his arm, as if one of her bullets had found its mark. "Dorie? Isn't that her name? Is she part of this?"

"No!" he yelled, stung, his face pulling into an expression of revulsion.

"Oh, come on. She must have some idea."

"Leave her out of this." He drew in a deep breath. "It doesn't matter anyway. She's . . . gone."

"Gone?"

"He killed her!" a woman's voice yelled and the freak looked up quickly.

Someone else was down here? Oh, yes . . . she'd heard a woman crying . . . Slowly her brain was snapping to.

"Shut the fuck up!" Jon yelled, but the woman wouldn't obey him.

"He killed her. Bragged about it! Didn't you, you fucking abomination of nature!"

He turned then, distracted, and Alvarez knew, if she was ever going to get the drop on him, it was now!

• • •

O'Keefe rounded a final corner and saw the boy, face down in the snow, blood pooling around him. Alvarez's Outback, still idling, shot to hell, was parked at the crest of the hill, but it was empty. Weapon drawn, O'Keefe pulled up to the boy and carefully got out of his car.

Where was she?

No sign of her, nor the killer, nor another vehicle.

But a dog lay motionless in the snow and O'Keefe realized he'd finally found Alvarez's Roscoe.

Too little, too late.

His gaze searching the area, his hand tight over his weapon, he readied himself and crouched over the boy. *Please be alive, Gabe. Please . . .*

He expected a hail of bullets, but it was quiet in the surrounding forest, no sound but the thrum of the car's idling engine and his own thudding heart.

Too damned quiet.

And no Selena . . . He wouldn't let his mind wander to that forbidden territory, the dark corner of his brain that accused him of moving too slowly, of not chasing her down faster, of letting her end up here and, now, most likely dead.

His throat tightened and he focused on the here and now, what he could do rather than the cold, stark fact that he'd never see Alvarez alive again.

Reaching the kid, still keeping a wary eye out

for an ambush that could happen at any second, he felt the weakest of pulses and, as he checked for injuries, dialed 911. When the operator answered, he cut her off before she could ask about his emergency. "I need an ambulance stat." He gave his name and position and explained that Gabriel Reeve had been shot, was clinging to life. After assuring him that help was on the way, the operator insisted Gabe stay on the line as she patched him through to an EMT, who over the phone would help him stabilize the boy.

"Come on, Gabe, hang in there, buddy," O'Keefe said, opening the boy's jacket and shirt, seeing the bullet hole high in his chest.

The boy moaned, and over the sound, he heard the whine of another engine.

Backup?

Or the killer?

Positioning himself between the boy and the oncoming vehicle, O'Keefe aimed his gun at the rise. Twin beams appeared, and as the Jeep rounded the corner, O'Keefe saw Regan Pescoli at the wheel.

"It's a damned blood bath, one victim, a woman, naked and unrecognizable, on the bed, blood all over the walls and carpet and bed . . . Man, it's a friggin' nightmare. Right out of some horror movie," Peter Watershed was saying to Pescoli over the phone. He and Rule Kayan had been sent to the Oestergard farm and, after calling the station, Watershed had phoned her.

"No sign of the husband?"

"No, and the only vehicle in the garage is a Honda Civic registered to the wife. But we haven't checked all the outbuildings yet and it's obvious someone goes down to the barn and sheds; there's a pretty clear path in the snow. We're heading that way next."

"Be careful."

"Always."

"Hey, Pete," she said, before he hung up. "You think the victim is Dorie Oestergard?"

Watershed said, "Maybe. I'm telling you, Pescoli, I've never seen anything like it. Her eyes cut, her nose and mouth, too, as if he was disfiguring her on purpose. This guy's beyond psycho."

"Rage," she said, sick inside.

"I'll be there as soon as backup arrives."

Not only was the killer, whom she assumed was Oestergard, escalating, but it was as if he'd snapped. No more quiet deaths where the victim was covered in ice, even sedated; now he was in a state of full-on homicidal madness.

She drove around the final corner and her headlights caught Dylan O'Keefe, his weapon pointed straight at her. As he recognized her and lowered his pistol, she cut the engine and got out of the Jeep.

"What the hell went on here? Where's Alvarez?"

"Don't know. Not here. And it looks like another vehicle went down the other side of the mountain."

"To the Oestergard place."

In the distance, sirens cut through the night. "Ambulance," she said and, kneeling next to the boy, knew it couldn't come fast enough.

She, too, talked to the kid, tried to keep him awake and focused. The dog, it seemed, was a lost cause and there was no sign of Alvarez, Trilby Van Droz or the killer. "Gabe, can you hear me?" she asked. "Stay with me. Gabe?"

The sirens shrieked, closer and closer, engines cutting through the snowy night.

Gabe groaned, though it looked as if O'Keefe had managed to stanch the flow of blood for now. Maybe, just maybe, the kid would make it.

"You've been nothing but trouble!" Oestergard yelled to the woman, who, Alvarez saw now, was locked in a cage in this dungeon of a cavern. There were two other jail-like cells that had been constructed down here and Alvarez didn't have to be told that they'd held other captives. She imagined the other victims being trapped in here, awaiting their fate, probably watching the ones before them slowly being killed before this jerk took the time to sculpt their own visages over their frozen bodies.

She wondered about this man whom she'd known as an acquaintance for the past five years, but didn't dwell on it. As he approached the woman, whom Alvarez guessed was Johnna Phillips, Alvarez slowly moved, forcing her body to respond.

Now, if only Johnna would understand, not tip him off.

"You know what," he said to the caged woman, "I should fuck you. Huh? How about that?"

"With what?" she threw back at him. She actually smiled as she taunted him. "You probably can't even get it up." In the case next to her was another woman, naked and unmoving. Trilby Van Droz was lying on a bare mattress, her hair a mess, her skin blue, and if she was breathing, Alvarez couldn't see any sign of it.

"You think not? Well, how about I show you?" Oestergard yelled back at Johnna. As Alvarez raised her head a little higher, forcing her eyes to focus, she saw him at the gate, his key jangling in the lock. His face was red, his anger palpable as he was obviously off the rails completely. So intent at getting at the woman in his cage, he didn't notice Alvarez or hear the sound that was barely discernible over the Christmas music: the distinct sound of footsteps on the staircase. *Oh, God, please let it be help . . . not an accomplice.*

Johnna, naked, her lips blue, her skin covered in goose pimples, slid the barest of glances Alvarez's way, and then said, "You can't do it. I bet you haven't been hard in years. Maybe never. So that's why you're down here making your stupid ice statues, because you don't know how to satisfy a real woman. I've heard you talk about your wife. She's a twit, isn't that what you call her? Do you say that when you try to fuck her? Is that what you call her?"

"Just keep talking," Jon said through clenched teeth as he unlocked the gate. "I'll shut you up. For good."

"Oh, big man . . . sure . . . Let's see what you've got."

Alvarez pulled her torso up as quietly as possible, then, with all her effort, swung her numb legs over the edge of the trough. Pain sizzled up her side from her bullet wound and she had to bite down on her tongue to keep from shouting out.

The music changed, a new song filtering through the speakers:

I don't want a lot for Christmas . . .

The song he'd sent her in the card. Alvarez drew in a deep breath. She had to take care of the bastard. Now! She slid to the ground, but her bad leg gave on her and she had to grab the side of the tub to keep on her feet.

Her gun.

Somewhere he had her gun.

Or the knife she'd hidden in her boot . . . Where the hell were they?

Think, Selena, think. Get your bearings and take care of this prick!

There were weapons on the far wall over the workbench. Saws and chisels and . . .

"What the fuck!" As if suddenly alerted that he was being played, Oestergard spun quickly, his face a mask of horror. "You bitches!" Spying Alvarez, he forgot about the unlocked gate to Johnna's cage.

With a flying leap, he came at Alvarez and she tried to sidestep him, but her bad leg folded.

He was on her in an instant, wrestling her to the ground, his big, heaving body, atop her. "You're not getting away from me, you little bitch," he growled, his breath hot on her cold face, his nose inches from hers.

Oh, God, she was trapped, his heavy body pinning her to the floor, his pelvis crushing hers. "Maybe I should start with you." Roughly he mauled her breast and his teeth, yellowed and crooked, flashed in a new-felt power. "That's it."

She flashed back.

To another time. Another struggle. In Emilio's car.

Oestergard wrapped his fingers in her hair and she saw it then, just above his head, the end of an ice pick left near the tub where he bathed, then froze and sculpted his victims.

"Like this?" he snarled, then looked up to the

489

cage. "You can watch," he said to Johnna, then froze. "What the hell?"

Alvarez heard the creak of hinges as the gate swept open.

"Fuck," he yelled, moving a bit, giving her breathing room. It was now or never!

Throwing herself upward, her naked body crashing into him, she stretched her arm, reached up and knocked the ice pick to the ground. It rolled crazily away.

"No, you don't!" he screamed, straining for the weapon, intent on killing her; she saw it in the rage burning up his face.

"Stop!" Johnna yelled and the maniac's attention diverted for the merest of seconds.

Alvarez inched her body away, her fingers scraping along the dirty floor before wrapping around the hilt of the ice pick.

He turned his head just then, his gaze fastening on her hand.

She reacted.

Threw herself at him, the weapon curled in her fingers. With all of her weight, she swung upward, shoving the pick with her good hand, thrusting it hard into the soft underside of his throat.

With a sickening sound, the pick jabbed through soft tissue to his larynx.

Rolling backward, Oestergard clawed at the offensive spike, gasping and spraying bloody spittle over the floor and Alvarez. She scooted away from him as he jerked out the ice pick and more blood spurted from his neck.

Johnna Phillips wasn't done.

Not satisfied with letting him die a slow, painful death, she reached for a pair of ice tongs. Using all of her strength, she swung hard, sending him to his knees. Blood gushed from his abdomen as he fell onto the cold stone floor, his head hitting so hard his glasses sprang from his face, showing off the scars that he bore near his eye.

"That'll teach ya," Johnna said, breathing hard as she stood over the dying man. "Don't ever mess with a pregnant woman." Footsteps thundered down the stairway, and Alvarez, barely able to climb to her feet, felt tears roll down her cheeks as O'Keefe, with Pescoli one step behind, appeared.

"Selena," he whispered and ran to her, holding her close. "It's gonna be all right," he said as she clung to him, though she didn't know how it ever would be. "It's over. Darlin', hang on. It's over," he whispered as the room was suddenly filled with deputies and the notes of the Christmas carol were barely audible. Still, with O'Keefe holding her close, the lyrics whispered softly through Alvarez's brain and she mouthed the words, "All I want for Christmas . . . is you."

EPILOGUE

Alvarez stared out the window of the town house. It was early. Not quite five and the ground outside her sliding door was covered in white. Most of the snow from the blizzard of three weeks earlier had melted, but a thin layer remained and there was talk of a new snowfall yet to come.

So what else was new?

Montana and the winter usually meant snow.

She turned on the lights of the Christmas tree and then the gas fire, warming the place. She was lucky to be alive and she knew it. If she didn't believe it herself, all she had to do was listen to everyone she met or reporters on newscasts, who all reminded her how close she'd come to death.

As it was, the Ice Mummy Killer hadn't survived the ordeal. Johnna Phillips had become a local heroine, the officials at First Union bank taking every chance they could to gain some good, free press from her help in getting rid of the serial killer who had terrorized the town.

Trilby Van Droz had survived but tendered her resignation. The sheriff hadn't accepted it and put her on a leave of absence, asking that she reconsider her decision after the new year. Gabe had been returned to his parents and Helena, where the DA was trying to work a deal with him as an accessory to the crime, and hopefully only probation; that was yet to be seen, but he was walking the straight and narrow for the time being and Aggie was opening up to the idea that he might be able to see Alvarez and have "some kind" of relationship with her.

Now, Alvarez remembered her last visit with him in the hospital where he'd held her hand for a couple of seconds under Aggie's watchful eyes. "I'm glad I met you, Gabe," she said, her throat catching when he released his fingers.

"Me, too." His eyes glistened, but he didn't cry. Aggie, though, turned away. "I'll call you when I'm out of here," he promised.

"You do that." She was so incredibly grateful he was all right.

Aggie let out a little sob even though Alvarez had already assured her that she'd never intrude in Gabe's life.

It was amazing that they'd ever connected, but Gabe was smart, had searched the Internet, joined chat rooms, had found a way to hack his way into the court documents meant to protect his identity.

"Stay in school," she told him.

"I will. Maybe I'll become a cop."

Again a squeak from Aggie.

"Better walk the straight and narrow," Alvarez

advised and then, while Aggie's back was turned, she brushed a kiss over his forehead. "Be good, Gabe, cuz if you aren't, I'll hear about it."

A grin stretched across his face and she, after touching Gabe's mother on the shoulder, had left the room. But his image—those dark eyes, that incredible smile, the shaggy hair and irreverent attitude—all of it had stayed with her. Always would.

Also, she had another connection to him. Through O'Keefe.

But not everything had ended well in the case.

The victim in the Oestergard house had indeed been Jon's wife, Dorie. The prevailing theory, which originated with Johnna Phillips, was that the wife had started questioning Oestergard and hinted that she might want to come down to the barn.

The series of caves beneath the Oestergard property had become part of a folk legend, and once all the crime scene evidence had been secured, teenagers had snuck into the place as a form of initiation or as the ultimate risk in games akin to Truth or Dare.

She walked up the stairs now, her leg paining a bit. She'd taken time off from work, but Pescoli was clamoring for her to return, as she was getting tired of working with Brett Gage. She'd admitted that Santana was pressuring her to move in again and even Pescoli had admitted that it was "time to fish or cut bait," probably because of her ongoing problems with her kids.

Joelle had seen that Alvarez had gained five pounds on the goodies she'd dropped by, and O'Keefe had pretty much settled in, for now, or at least until she returned to work.

Now, she walked into the bedroom to find Dylan propped up by pillows, the cat beside him, the dog in his bed on the floor, curled into a ball. Roscoe raised his head when Alvarez walked into the room and thumped his tail.

"Traitor," she said, bending down and patting his head, her heart welling. "Both of you." But she wasn't angry, just thankful the dog had so miraculously survived when all of them had been sure he was dead.

"Hey, I wondered what happened to you?" O'Keefe said as she settled back into her side of the bed.

"Just counting."

"Silverware?"

"Yeah, that's it. I get up and count silverware."

"Well, not sheep or you'd still be in bed."

"Maybe all the ways you irritate me."

He laughed then and she was glad she hadn't said "blessings." Theirs was a relationship still developing. She was rethinking some aspects of her life, even planning to reconnect with her family in the coming year, but, for now, she was content to let things happen.

O'Keefe was talking about moving to Grizzly Falls, but so far it was just talk.

Was it time to take their relationship to the next level?

She didn't know, but for now, she thought, nestling into his arms, she wasn't going to overthink it. She heard the dog give off the soft yips of a puppy dream from his bed and O'Keefe chuckled, deep in his throat.

It was, she admitted to herself, a sound she could live with for a very long time.

Center Point Large Print
600 Brooks Road / PO Box 1
Thorndike ME 04986-0001 USA

(207) 568-3717

US & Canada:
1 800 929-9108
www.centerpointlargeprint.com